PUPPETS
OF THE
PAST

PUPPETS
OF THE
PAST

(Trilogy - Part 3)

G. P. Schumacher

DISCLAIMER

This novel is a work of fiction. Names, characters, and events are products of the author's imagination. Any resemblance to real people, living or dead, and actual events is purely coincidental. Certain long-standing institutions, agencies, public offices, and places are mentioned in this novel, but the events happening and the characters involved are entirely imaginary.

Interested in learning more about the author?

Follow me on Facebook: G. P. Schumacher

Follow me on Instagram: author.g.p.schumacher

Find me on Pinterest: G. P. Schumacher

Email me at author@gpschumacher.com

BEFORE YOU BEGIN

I would like to thank you for joining me on this author journey by offering a free eBook copy of *The Last Day*, a prequel to *Maria's Past Trilogy*. Click here to tell me where to send it.

To Inga—
A wonderful human being, strong woman, awesome mom,
and best sister in the world!

CHAPTER 1

*M*aria *was surrounded by water. Her heart was pounding, sweat forming on her forehead.*

Water? Water all around me? No, no, please, I don't want to drown again....

She closed her eyes, trying to calm her thoughts. Put a hand on her fast-beating heart and took a deep breath in.

I can breathe. Good.

She wiggled her legs, touched what felt like a sandy bank beneath the water. She found she could stand. The cold, clear water rose only to her chest.

Where am I? In a river?

Maria searched the tree line for any clue to where she was. She studied the growth that lined the riverbank. There were palm trees, pine trees, cypress trees, buttonwoods. All common to the Florida swamplands. A comfortingly familiar sight. Though not the long shadows they cast, which stretched across the calm waters, making it seem as though the trees might fall and crush her at any moment.

Without warning, it got dark. The darkness crept in quickly, and she could barely see anything now.

What's happening?

Maria took another deep breath in, seeking reassurance, but found the air had gone all sticky, as if the oxygen in it refused to flow into her lungs. Her beautiful, unique eyes grew wide. Goose bumps broke out all over her body. The hot, humid, sticky air brushed against them in the slight breeze.

Sweat ran down her face and dripped into the water, causing little ripples on the surface. Her upper body was drenched in sweat now.

I can't stand this heat any longer. Need to cool off.

She lowered herself into the cold, clear water, but as her lips touched the waterline, she tasted it. The freshwater river didn't taste fresh at all. It tasted metallic, like...

Blood?

Quickly, Maria spat out the bloody water, only to realize it was all around her now, sticky, bright-red blood. The whole creek ran red. She shot out of the water, tried to wade over to the dark, shallow riverbank as quickly as possible, needed to get out of there. An arm shot out of the red water, latched onto hers, and pulled her back. She turned around and saw him.

Clifford? Senator Clifford?

The senator's curly beach-blonde hair stuck to his tan forehead, his teeth pearly white, shining in the darkness. Blood was dripping out of his nose and mouth, blood gushed out of a round, gaping wound in his upper belly. He didn't seem to notice it, to feel any pain. Instead, he grinned an evil grin.

"Just wait, just you wait! Bullet's gonna getcha!"

She stared at him. The senator started laughing, a loud, evil laugh that echoed through the dark swampland. Then he unexpectedly raised both arms, as if holding an invisible gun, and aimed at her. Squeezed his trigger finger. "Boom," he said.

Maria felt a piercing pain in her chest, a terrible, mind-numbing pain, as if she'd really been shot by the gun that wasn't there, and splashed backward into the red water.

The senator came closer and pushed her down beneath the surface. Her unique hazel eyes now bright green as she saw the grin on his bloody tan face shining through the ripples on the water.

"Just you wait till Bullet gets ya!" she heard him say again, but his voice came to her muffled underwater, his hands still pushing her down, deeper and deeper into the water, the red water, now turning dark, black, muddy, murky.

Now I am drowning. Drowning for sure, this time.

Helpless, she sank deeper and deeper into the darkness, the senator's evil laughter still ringing in her ears.

😃 😃 😃

With a scream, Maria awoke and abruptly sat up in her bed. Her head was pounding; she rubbed her temples.

"Mija?" she heard. "¿Estás bien? ¿Qué pasa? Did you have bad dreams, Maria? A nightmare?"

Mamá? Oh good. Mamá is here. Maria nodded. "Bad dream, a strange nightmare."

"Poor mija," came her mamá's calming voice from across the room.

Her head still throbbing, her heart beating, sweat on her forehead with loose strands of hair stuck to it, Maria finally opened her eyes. As they adjusted to the darkness, she realized her mamá, Martina, was standing by her bedside. Martina took her hand, and Maria felt the warmth of her touch also warming her heart.

Where am I?

Maria looked around. Across from her, she made out two big armchairs standing in front of a blank white wall. One of them was empty, a blanket draped over the pulled-out footrest; the other was occupied by someone, someone sleeping.

Maria's eyes grew wide. *Who's there?*

Wide-awake now, she took in everything around her. There was another bed next to hers, and a constant beeping sound—no, *two* constant beeping sounds—filling the room. She clutched her mamá's hand tighter when she realized the beeping came from two vital signs monitors, one attached to her, one attached to…

"Aaron?" Maria yelled. "Oh my gosh, Aaron. Is he okay? Mamá, what happened?" Her throat was dry, her hand squishing Martina's so hard that the older woman shifted under the intense grip.

"Mija, you're alright. Aaron is alright. Everything's alright, está bien. Both you and Aaron, you're safe here at the hospital, both of you." Martina started stroking Maria's hand in hers, caressing it lovingly.

Maria's grip loosened a bit as she took in the situation, trying to remember what happened. *We were both hospitalized? My fiancé and me? Why?*

In an instant, her memories came rushing back into her brain, coupled with pain that flooded her mind and body. *Oh my gosh, I remember now. We were attacked. Last night. By Senator Clifford. It wasn't a dream, it was real.…*

Her breathing quickened and she tried to calm herself, tried not to think of it, but she couldn't help herself. She ripped her hand out of Martina's hold and formed two fists in her lap. "Mamá. I remember now. We met Senator Clifford, didn't we?"

In the faint light the monitors threw across her mamá's face, Maria saw her nod. Silent tears fell from Martina's big brown eyes.

"Sí, mija. You met the senator. At a press conference. With your parents, Brad and Elisabeth. And with an FBI and police escort. Even Dr. Davies was there to help. He's the expert, they told me. The expert in child trauma. He said it was safe. They all assured me it was safe. ¡Dios mío! It wasn't, it just wasn't. I should've never said okay to that stupid plan.…" Martina started crying.

Maria's mind was racing as the memories washed over her, her head pounding. She felt wetness on her fist closest to Martina. She looked down and realized Martina's tears were dripping onto her hand.

"I'm so sorry, mija. So sorry. I should've never said okay to that silly plan, that dangerous plan. ¡Perdóname!" Martina choked on her tears, big sobs rocking her small, round body, her beautiful brown curls jumping up and down with every sob.

Maria's heart ached seeing her mamá like this, and the feeling of sadness washed away the pain in her head. She sat up tall in her hospital bed. "It's okay, Mamá. It's okay. It wasn't your fault. It was the police's plan, wasn't it? They wanted me to identify my captor from twenty years ago. Thought I'd recognize him."

"Sí." Martina sobbed. "And you did. You *did* recognize him. The bad guy. Senator Clifford."

Maria nodded. "Now I remember. I was so confused. Shocked. I had to sit down... and then it's all a blur."

"Because he drugged you, my mija. He drugged you, then kidnapped you *again*. At gunpoint. With a gun he stole from Chief Parlot. It went so wrong, the plan. Went so wrong."

Maria nodded, then heard a slight snore coming from the other hospital bed. *Oh, Aaron, my brave Aaron. He found me and fought with Clifford. Together, we fought him off. Right there, in the river.*

"But luckily, the bad guy is dead now. Gone. Can't hurt you anymore." Martina wiped a tear away from her big brown eyes, a faint smile spreading over her face.

Dead? Clifford is dead? The color drained from Maria's face as she remembered the attack. Her breathing got faster; tears welled in her eyes. Her headache came back with such force that she had to lie back down, curled up in her bed like an infant, holding her throbbing head. She tried to squeeze the memories out of it, tried to focus on something else, on her mom, on Aaron's slight snore, but couldn't. Her memory was too strong, her thoughts held her prisoner.

I remember it all. Oh my gosh. It was horrible. And I killed him. I killed a person!

Maria burst into tears.

13

Martina sat down on Maria's bed and rubbed her back. "Don't cry, mija. Don't cry. Mamá está aquí. I'm here!"

"I know, I know, Mamá," Maria whispered, and tried to hold back her sobs. "It was just so horrible. Gosh, so terrible. You know, Aaron found me. On that creek in Niceville, just as Clifford was taking me away on a canoe."

"I know, mija, I know." Martina kept rubbing Maria's back.

Maria stared into the dark room, her eyes wide, her tears now dried up from the horror of that painful memory. "Aaron fought with Clifford. But he couldn't fight him off. I had to help him. Together, we had to fight him, and I... I... found the gun. In the water. Found it. I held it, wanted to stall him... wanted to stall Clifford until the police got to us. I... I... you know, already heard the dogs, the K-9 unit coming, but I... I don't know what happened. The gun just went off. I shot him!"

"Mija, it's okay. Don't worry, mija. It was self-defense. You *had* to shoot him. You hear me? Not your fault. You had to. To save you and Aaron."

Maria didn't react. She stared at the wall, the beeping vital signs monitor lights illuminating the armchair across from her bed. The chair threw a ghostly shadow on the otherwise blank wall, the white wall.

As she stared at it, trying to forget those awful memories, trying to rid herself of the unbearable pounding that occupied every slope of her brain, she saw the wall suddenly turn red. Blood-red. There was blood dripping down the wall.

What the heck is going on? She sat up abruptly and started screaming, closed her eyes.

She felt her mamá hug her, felt her mamá's heart beat against her, and started calming down, stopped screaming. Through her own heartbeat pounding in her ears, she detected footsteps nearing her bed, then a dark, male voice. "What's going on here? Maria, are you okay?"

14

She opened her eyes and recognized the tall, slender, middle-aged man with greyish-blonde hair kneeling before her. *Jack. It's just Jack. Aaron's dad.*

"Maria, hey… you're alright. A lot happened, but you're okay now. Just bad memories, bad dreams. You'll be alright," Jack said, his voice calm, soft, comforting.

"But I shot a man…" Maria whispered, her eyes wide.

Jack nodded. "Yes, you did. But please don't worry about that, Maria, or anything else that happened yesterday. You acted in self-defense. Obvious self-defense. That deranged senator posed an imminent danger to both you and Aaron, imminent danger of great bodily harm. You as the defendant exhausted every reasonable means to escape such danger, but Senator Clifford persisted in his threats, even though you clearly communicated the withdrawal and—"

"¿Qué?" Martina interrupted Jack. "I don't understand a word of that language you're using."

"Oh, I'm sorry." Jack cleared his throat. "I just go into lawyer-mode whenever I talk about legal things. All I'm saying is this was a clear-cut case of self-defense. Maria shouldn't worry about it at all. She had to shoot to save herself and Aaron."

"Sí. I agree." Martina rubbed Maria's back.

Maria slowly nodded. She still sat straight up in her bed, her face pale, the big Band-Aid on her forehead covering her stitches. Stitches from an earlier fight, another attack.

"Maria, I suggest you go back to sleep. You need more rest. You need to get healthy again. The fight last night didn't help your previous concussion, and the ketamine the senator used to drug you still needs to be flushed out. Get some rest. Aaron needs the same. He's pretty banged up from the fight, though luckily nothing serious. A broken collarbone is probably the worst injury, otherwise just cuts and bruises," Jack said.

Maria stared at Aaron's dad now. "Broken collarbone? Aaron broke his collarbone?"

"Yeah, he sure did." Jack sighed.

Martina took Jack's hand and squeezed it. "Your son was so brave, Jack, so brave. I'm very thankful he rushed to Turkey Creek to help my daughter. So thankful for our brave boy. Our mijo."

Jack nodded, and they all looked over to the other hospital bed where Aaron was sleeping—his left arm in a sling, his face bruised, a big Band-Aid that matched Maria's on his forehead.

"Oh, my Aaron. My poor Aaron. Is he okay? Does he need surgery?" Maria studied both Jack's and Martina's faces.

"Nope, no surgery necessary. The broken bone should heal on its own—but he needs to rest and take it easy. The doctors slightly sedated him so that he could sleep well after the eventful night," Jack explained, "and I suggest you, young lady, better get some rest yourself. We're all here; we're all watching over you. It's still nighttime—well, early morning now, but time enough yet to sleep."

"Sí, mija. Jack's right." Martina smiled. "We all need some rest. We're all okay. Estára bien."

Maria nodded and lay back down, but then she shot straight back up. "And my dad? My mom and dad?"

"Brad and Elisabeth are okay. They're in the room next door, dozing last I checked," Jack said. "Your dad's surgery went well. The bullet Clifford shot at him only grazed his arm but hit an artery. He needed surgery, but he's okay now."

Maria's eyes were wide. "He needed surgery? That's terrible. What about Elisabeth—my... you know... my mom?" She glanced at Martina, who smiled at her.

"It's okay, mija. Don't be embarrassed. Elisabeth is your mom. She gave birth to you. And we made up, you know that. It's all good. And she's good. She only had a couple of bruises, slight concussion from the fall, but she's okay. But the docs had to give her a pill to sleep. She was very upset and so worried. Worried about you—her daughter. Well, *our* daughter."

"Sí, Mamá, I'm both her daughter *and* yours. She gave birth to me; you raised me." Maria smiled now and squeezed Martina's hand. "I'm glad you both made up. Happy my mom forgave you. Well, she *had to* because we all know now *you* certainly didn't kidnap me twenty years ago. Clifford and his gang did."

Martina nodded. "Sí, he and his gang. For revenge on Brad. ¡Increíble!"

"Yeah, it's unbelievable." Jack sighed. "What a story. But best not to talk about that now. We're lucky everyone is fine. Both our families are okay and nobody else got injured. The police team certainly has lots of explaining to do. I bet we'll see them tomorrow: Chief Parlot, Officer Johnson, the two FBI agents. They'll surely want to discuss everything with us, and especially you, Maria. You need to be fit for it. So, please, get some rest."

"Agreed, let's get more rest," Martina said, and yawned, but remained by her daughter's bedside.

They both watched Jack walk over to his chair pushed against the wall opposite Aaron's bed, next to Martina's chair. "Yeah… if only *we* could get some good rest. These chairs are super uncomfortable."

Martina laughed softly. "Sí, but better than plain plastic chairs."

"Guess so," Jack mumbled, and tried to get snuggled up in his armchair that barely reclined backward.

Martina gave Maria one last squeeze and made sure she lay back down. "Buenas noches, mija. Your parents are okay. Luckily the bullet didn't seriously injure Brad. He's okay. Believe me. Everything's okay. Rest now. Sleep now." She gave Maria a quick kiss on the forehead, right next to the Band-Aid, then went to sit in her armchair.

Maria heard her fumbling with a blanket. Aaron's slight snores reached her ears, followed by a louder snore from across the room. She grinned. *Guess Jack falls asleep as quickly as his son, huh? How uncomfortable can those chairs be if he's already asleep?* With a smile still on her face, Maria concentrated on all of the calming noises in the room. She tried to soak up the happiness of having her loved ones all around her. *Not only are Mamá and Aaron here but also Jack, my future father-in-law, as well as my long-lost parents Brad and Elisabeth Collins. So glad I got them back. And we uncovered the mastermind behind my kidnapping twenty years ago. Senator Clifford.*

She sighed. *He did it just to take revenge on my dad. Revenge for getting kicked out of the Air Force Academy because my dad told his superiors about Clifford's unacceptable behavior.*

Maria grimaced. *Can't believe he held such a grudge that he would kidnap his friend's daughter when she was just a small little toddler. Kidnap me.* She shook her head in disbelief. *Unbelievable. And then he tried to shoot my dad last night? My gosh. Glad to hear the bullet only grazed him. Only hit his arm. The bullet…*

Suddenly, all her arm hairs stood on end. It felt like her head was spinning. *Bullet. Bullet… will get me? Did someone tell me that?*

She shook off the strange thought, tried not to think about it. But it preoccupied her mind, the same phrase looping over and over again. She felt like a puppet, as if someone was playing with her, pulling on her strings, meddling with her thoughts. She tried to get a hold of herself, tried to be the master of her thinking again, tried to assure herself. *I'm just being silly. I'm fine, completely fine. The danger's past, the bad guy is gone. Why should I fear a bullet will get me?*

CHAPTER 2

"Me?" Lu turned away from the small, round window and peered at the young passenger next to her. "Are you talking to me?"

"Yes, ma'am, I was. I'm sorry, I didn't mean to disturb you. Was just commenting on how beautiful the view is. The way the vast ocean meets the sky. Breathtaking, isn't it, ma'am?" the young man said, his British accent clearly audible.

Lu smiled. "Yes, it sure is. I love the view from a plane."

The man nodded, a smirk on his face. "Yes, ma'am. It's wonderful."

"It is—but not the way you talk to me." She stared straight into her seat-neighbor's eyes.

The young Englishman's grin suddenly disappeared. "Ma'am?"

Lu laughed. "Didn't I tell you a while ago, like eight hours ago, when we started this flight, that you don't need to call me *ma'am*? I'm Lu. Simply Lu."

He nodded. "Yes, you did say that. Terribly sorry, but I feel like it's not proper, you know? You're a person of respect, a woman in uniform. Says right there you're an officer in the U.S. military. Thus, at the very least I should call you 'ma'am' and probably 'General Thomas' if I'm being strict about it, shouldn't I?"

Lu laughed. "Are we in an official meeting at this moment, where you need to address me according to rank?" The young Englishman shook his head. "And what about me? Do I call you by your last name? Or address you as 'sir'?" He shook his head again. "You told me your name is Sam, so I will call you Sam. And you should call me Lu. We're just two passengers, two ordinary travelers who happen to find themselves sitting next to each other on a plane. No need to be so formal."

"Okay, ma'am. I mean, Lu! Yes, let's be… informal. Like all you Americans." He winked at her.

Lu grinned. "Exactly, like all us Americans."

"I'm excited to go to America." Sam smiled. "First time there, you know. I'm looking forward to vacationing in Florida."

"I bet you are. And I bet you'll love it," Lu said, then sighed. "Lucky you. Wish I could go on a vacation. But I gotta get back to work."

"To Texas, correct? You mentioned earlier you work in Texas, didn't you?"

Lu nodded. "Yeah. At Joint Base San Antonio-Lackland. Meaning once we land, I gotta catch another flight."

"I'm awfully sorry your travels take so long," Sam said. "How much longer will it be from Orlando?"

"Too long. I have quite the layover to wait out, then luckily a direct flight from Orlando to San Antonio. It's a three-hour flight— enough for a one-hour time difference between Central United States and the East Coast."

"Oh yeah, big country, this America, isn't it?" Sam winked at her again, his blue eyes shining.

Lu and Sam continued to talk and laugh together until the overhead speakers crackled on. "Ladies and gentlemen, we've begun our descent into Orlando, Florida. Please turn off all electronic devices and stow them until we have arrived at the gate. In preparation for landing, please be certain your seat back is straight up, your seat belt is fastened, and your tray table is put away."

Lu and Sam did as they were told, then she went back to look out the window while Sam yelled over to his four friends seated in the middle of the plane, "Oh boy, I'm just thrilled to be in Orlando soon. Disney World, here we come, right, my blokes?"

Lu smiled and sat back in her seat, more than ready to be back in her home country after a long work trip abroad.

😃 😃 😃

"Bye, Sam, was very nice to meet you," Lu said.

"Same here. Very nice to meet you. Thank you for tolerating me going on and on about how excited I am to be visiting America for the first time. And thanks for all the tips on what to look out for, what food to try, what—"

"My pleasure. You made for an entertaining overseas flight, my young *bloke*." She laughed. "See, you taught me a lot of good, *proper* English vocabulary."

The young Englishman grinned, then shook her hand. "Thank you, Lu. You were awfully nice to me. Appreciate it. But now it's goodbye to you and hello to the queue. Looks like mine is much longer than yours."

Lu nodded and winked at him. "That's because you're a tourist. Of course, customs and immigration take a bit longer for you non-Americans."

"I suppose." He let go of her hand and waved as Lu turned to the left and walked up to the end of the short line marked U.S. Citizens Only. She blew through customs and immigration in no time. *Guess the diplomat passport and military uniform doesn't hurt.*

She grimaced. *If I travel for fun, the immigration officers always look me up and down. All they see is the Hispanic in me, even though I've*

21

lived in the U.S. since I was two years old. They always triple check I'm a citizen—but not today. Of course. No questions asked. She rolled her eyes, then checked her watch. She had quite a few hours to burn before her next flight.

Even though she'd eaten not too long ago on the overseas flight, she was still hungry. There were plenty of fast food options in the airport, but she had time enough to sit down in a real restaurant for lunch. Lu researched all her options inside the airport on her phone and decided to try the Sunshine Diner.

Oh yeah, good ol' American food again. And coffee. Need that American coffee. That'll be refreshing after a week of biscuits, tea, beans on toast, and fish 'n' chips. She grinned. Well, not that I minded too much. I love trying local specialties when I'm abroad.

She made her way over to the diner and quickly sent a text to her husband. Made it through customs and immigration, getting lunch now. Love you. Can't wait to see you.

Her phone blinked with an immediate reply. Love you, too. Missed you so much! Glad you'll be home soon. Enjoy lunch. Keep me posted. XOX

She smiled. Daniel is such a good guy. I'm lucky to have him.

"Seat for one, ma'am?" asked the hostess, ripping Lu out of her thoughts.

"Yes, please." Lu nodded, then followed the hostess, who seated her at a table across from the bar, right by a window overlooking one of the runways.

"How's this table, ma'am?" The hostess smiled.

"It's wonderful, thank you." Lu sat down on the comfy bench by the window.

"Glad to hear. Only the best for our military. Thank you for your service, ma'am," the hostess said. "One of our waitresses will be right with you."

"Thank you." Lu laid her heavy carry-on bag next to her on the bench. When she looked up again, a waitress was already there. She took her drink order and handed her a menu. Lu started studying it.

Around her she heard the faint roar of planes landing and taking off outside, the chatter of people talking in all kinds of languages. She looked up and noticed a row of TVs running by the bar.

Aw, it's good to be home. And I already know what I'm going to order. She smiled and set down the menu in front of her, her eyes resting on the TV screen across from her. What she saw caused her smile to quickly fade away.

Oh my gosh! The color washed out of her beautiful face. *I can't believe this. How could this happen? What did I miss while I was gone?*

On the TV was the local Florida news. A scrolling banner read: COLLINS FAMILY HOSPITALIZED—SENATOR CLIFFORD DEAD AFTER LAST NIGHT'S ATTACK.

Lu swallowed hard. *Collins family?*

She didn't even notice when the waitress returned to her table. "Here you go, ma'am. A glass of water with lots of ice and an iced latte. Enjoy! Are you ready to order some food now?"

Lu didn't even acknowledge the waitress; she remained fixated on the TV. *The Collins?* Her hands started shaking, sweat started forming on the perfectly combed hairline of her shiny black hair pulled back into a perfect low bun. The shaking spread to the rest of her body.

"Ma'am, are you alright?"

Only then did Lu notice the waitress standing there peering at her, her eyebrows raised in concern. She managed to peel her eyes off the TV and met the waitress's gaze. She nodded. "Yeah, I'm okay."

The waitress eyed her. "You sure? You look like you just seen a ghost."

Lu took a quick sip of her iced latte and felt the cold liquid run down her dry throat. "No, I was just… shocked by what's on the news. I hadn't heard about any of that yet."

The waitress looked up to see what Lu was talking about and gasped. "Oh my, you haven't? It's been on a couple of days now. Crazy, crazy thing happened up there in the Panhandle. Oh my goodness, just horrible," she said, and kept talking. "You know that missing toddler from twenty years ago, Moana Collins? She's *alive*. She found her parents—they found each other again, reunited after twenty years, like a real-life fairy tale come true. Isn't that wonderful?"

All Lu could do was nod stiffly. *Yeah right, wonderful.* She took another sip of her latte, felt it give her strength again. She took another few gulps and the shakes calmed. She listened as the waitress went on.

"But then, a plumber *attacked* the girl. The guy on her birth certificate, can you believe it? He kidnapped her, *again*—it was the same guy who did it when she was two—then tried to drown her. Right outside a local restaurant, with the police and her parents inside. But she got away. He caught up to her and they fought. Both of them ended up in the hospital, and then this guy, he suddenly passed away. The bad guy died before he could spill the beans about the kidnapping cover-up. A cover-up—imagine that. Yeah, this girl didn't accidentally drown back then twenty years ago like the police had said—no, she was kidnapped off Eglin Air Force Base when she was a little girl. Isn't that something?"

Lu nodded and chugged her latte while the waitress kept talking.

"And then, they found out the former police chief was somehow involved. And a former FBI agent, too. The very people in charge of the missing toddler case back then. Unbelievable—they were a part of it! Who knew? Who knew?" The waitress shook her head. "But even more unbelievable: our senator, our dear Senator Clifford turned out to be the mastermind behind it all. My goodness, Florida's senator! Can you believe it? What's this world coming to?"

Lu shook her head. She tossed back a leftover ice cube from her latte and started chewing on it, making sure her dry throat stayed lubricated, her thoughts clear.

"The girl recognized the senator as her kidnapper at a press conference. Wanna guess what he did?"

Lu swallowed the crushed ice cube and noticed the waitress was waiting for a reaction from her, was staring keenly at her. "Umm... I don't know. What did he do, the senator?"

"He *drugged* the girl, then *stole* the police chief's gun and *kidnapped* her at gunpoint. Goodness gracious! Isn't that something?" The waitress shook her head again. "I would've never guessed Senator Clifford was pure evil. He was such a good-looking, likable guy. A good leader, you know? How could a guy like him turn out to be so evil, so cold-hearted, so brutal?"

Lu grimaced. *Yeah, how* could *a leader turn out like that? You have no idea, lady, how evil they can be.* She felt the waitress's stare again and looked up at her. "Oh, I don't know… it's terrible. Sounds just horrible."

"Yes, indeed. That poor girl, kidnapped again. The senator tried to flee with her by canoe, but her fiancé stopped them. And then, the girl *shot* him. She shot the senator! In self-defense, I suppose." The waitress's head hung low now, her eyes watery. "Poor thing, poor, poor thing. But at least she found her parents. Both of 'em, Brad and Elisabeth Collins. At least that's comforting, isn't it? A family made whole again. They got their happily-ever-after."

Lu crunched down on another ice cube and nodded. "Yeah, sure, good for them."

"Yes, real good. Really good." The waitress sighed. "Like the TV says, the Collinses are all recovering in the hospital right now. The girl's dad, Brad Collins, got hurt pretty bad. The senator shot him. I still just can't believe this whole story, I just can't." She shook her head again, then turned and saw Lu chewing up a third ice cube. "Oh goodness, dearie, I'm sorry. Here I am babbling away while you're all hungry and thirsty after a long trip. I'm sorry, dear. Sorry, ma'am, I mean."

She eyed Lu's camo uniform up and down. "Goodness, you sure are young for being such a high-ranking officer. My uncle was Air Force, but he got out after four years. Anyhow, I know a thing or two about ranks in the military. I recognize the star on your uniform. You sure are high up there, ma'am. Wow! You know, you don't see that often. Such a young and pretty girl like you, ranked so high. Incredible."

Lu glanced at her. *So unbelievable a woman could become a higher-up, huh? And why bring up my looks? As if that has something to do with my rank. Or does she think I only got where I am because I'm pretty?*

Before Lu could get worked up, the waitress interrupted her thoughts. "Enough talk, ma'am, what can I bring you to eat? I see your iced latte is gone already. Would you like another one?"

Lu nodded, then ordered her food. As soon as the waitress left, she glanced back at the TV. It showed dramatic scenes from last night, replayed the kidnapping at gunpoint. Lu saw the girl being dragged away by the senator, but she was fixated on something else. *Someone else.*

She stared at a middle-aged lady in a pixie cut lying underneath the police chief on the ground, crying, begging for her child.

Lu frowned. Her eyes hardened. *Elisabeth Collins. It is you. You've changed the past twenty years, but I still recognize you. And I didn't forget. Unlike you. And I don't feel sorry for you—no, I hate you, Elisabeth!*

CHAPTER 3

Elisabeth sat next to Brad and held his plate in place whenever it was in danger of sliding off the little tray-top table the hospital staff had positioned over his bed. "I'm sorry for being so needy," he said, and stuffed another forkful of mashed potatoes inside his mouth.

"Nonsense, I don't mind," she reassured him. "I wouldn't even mind feeding you."

"Goodness, no. I'm fully capable of feeding myself. I can already sit up, and luckily I'm right-handed." He wiggled the fork in his right hand at her clumsily.

Elisabeth laughed. "Yeah, good thing only your left arm got hurt. Lucky you." Her smile faded. "I still can't believe what happened last night. How could Mike do this to us?"

"'Cuz he just hated me. Hated me so much he kidnapped our child to take revenge. To get back at me, just to get back at me." Brad's head hung low; his good hand formed a fist around the fork it was still holding. "Damn it!" He slammed his fist onto the little tray table. The plastic plate on it with his lunch briefly jumped into the air and slid dangerously close to the edge of the tray.

Elisabeth pushed the plate back into the center of the tray once more, then got up and rubbed Brad's back. "I know, hun, I know. It's just crazy. But we have to look at the bright side. All is well now. We finally know who took our daughter away from us twenty years ago. We finally have closure."

Brad nodded. "I guess so."

"And she's here, with us. She's alive. A phenomenal young lady now. Smart, strong, and beautiful." A bright new smile came over Elisabeth's face while Brad relaxed as well.

"Yeah, I know. We should be grateful she's alive and here with us. You're right. We have a bright future ahead of us now. We'll recover, get well, get out of here—together. You and me and her. Our family, whole again."

"Yeah, along with Aaron and his family. And Martina—the other mom. Guess she will always be a part of our lives from now on. Must admit, she sure did a great job raising our daughter."

Brad nodded. "Yeah, she did. That's very true. I'm glad you two get along and are willing to share our wonderful daughter."

Elisabeth nodded, the tender smile still on her face. "Speaking of Martina, she told me she'd visit us in our room once they were all awake next door. It's already lunchtime but she hasn't been over yet. I wonder why." Her eyes widened. "You don't think something happened, do you?"

Brad shook his head and stuffed more food in his mouth, chewed it, swallowed. "I think they're fine. After everything that's happened lately, I'd say no news is good news. Maybe they're eating lunch right now also? Not everyone snarfs it down as fast as you do." He grinned and pointed at Elisabeth's empty plate on the table by her bed.

"Oh, come on. You know why that is. As a teacher, you just don't get much time to sit and eat. Always something to do—you can't even let down your hair at recess. So I learned to eat fast."

"No kidding," Brad said, and winked at her. "I suppose it wasn't so dissimilar for me. Basic training saw us chowing down our meals in only five minutes flat."

Elisabeth checked her watch. "Five minutes? Well, General, I regret to inform you that you've failed the 'chow-it-down-fast test.'" She grinned. "You've been eating your food for the past fifteen minutes."

"Oh, come on, you're being mean, ma'am. I'm injured."

"Aw, poor General Collins. *Injured.* Well, anything your private nurse can do to make you feel better?"

Brad laughed and put his fork down, then grabbed her arm and pulled her in for a kiss. "Yeah, that. I'm already feeling better now."

Elisabeth smiled at him, sat down on the bed, and leaned in to give him a more passionate kiss. She lifted her hand to touch his face and felt the roughness of his beard stubble. She smiled when their lips parted and kept stroking his face.

Just like twenty years ago. A stubble always meant we were on vacation. 'Cuz the military demanded their Airmen be clean-shaven on the job. Brad always enjoyed not shaving on the weekends or during vacation.

"What are you thinking about, Elisabeth?" Brad's whisper ripped her out of her thoughts.

"Oh, just how your beard coming in reminds me of old times when we would vacation." She smiled and kept caressing his face, but then stopped in an instant. Her hand seemingly frozen on his cheek, her eyes wide.

"But this isn't a vacation. We're in the hospital because our daughter, our grown-up daughter, got attacked last night. Held up at gunpoint. And you got shot. It was horrible, just horrible."

Brad took Elisabeth's hand off his face and cupped it in his. "I know, hun, I know. It was bad. The investigators' great plan really devolved into a real shitshow, didn't it?"

She nodded, tears forming in her eyes.

"But we're all okay. You said it yourself: gotta look on the bright side here. And look at you. You seem to be doing great despite those bruises and a mild concussion. And even our daughter is fine. Everyone's fine, including Maria."

Elisabeth nodded and squeezed his hand. "I know. It's just so hard. I can't stand the thought of losing her again—we just found her."

"You won't, Elisabeth. You won't ever lose her again. *We* won't."

A knock on the door.

"Come in," Brad shouted, and the door swung open.

"Martina! There you are. Is everything okay?" Elisabeth asked.

Martina waved and smiled, closed the door behind her. Stepped further toward the hospital bed. "Sí, everything okay. Late night. We all just woke up."

"Woke up? Now?" Elisabeth checked her watch again. "It's lunchtime!"

Martina laughed; her brown curls shook under her warm laughter. "Sí, we were told as much. Though it is strange, here at the hospital. So early lunch here. Who else eats lunch at ten thirty? They woke us up when they brought in the food."

"Wow, you all slept in then?" Brad asked.

Martina nodded, her curls bouncing up and down. "Sí, we were all so tired. Didn't sleep well before, but guess we all did sleep soundly after Maria's nightmare."

Elisabeth stood up. "Nightmare? Our daughter had a nightmare again?"

Martina nodded, the smile vanishing from her face. "I think she's in shock. From the attack. From… you know… from the shooting. She told me she didn't mean to shoot him."

Brad snorted. "Doesn't matter. It was self-defense."

"That's what Jack told her," Martina said.

"Exactly," Elisabeth blurted out. "She doesn't need to feel bad about it. He deserved it anyway. Bastard! Asshole! He took her from us, tried to kill her, drown her, and then held her captive on that boat when it didn't work out. My poor baby girl. She was just a toddler. And then he kidnaps her again, twenty years later? Idiot! Such a jerk! It's for the best he's dead."

"Elisabeth," Brad scolded, but she was on a roll.

"The world *is* better off without Mike Clifford," she insisted. "He was a mean guy, a guy who held a grudge for years, a kidnapper, a bad person. Nobody will miss him. He wasn't even in touch with his family—disowned by them, as far as I know. So nobody will miss him. It's good he's dead. It really is. Right, Martina?"

Martina shrugged. "Agreed. He was a bad guy, bad person. I guess it's better, no? Better that he's dead?"

CHAPTER 4

*H**e's dead. My son. He's dead!*
    The man sat on his king-sized bed with the Air-Force-blue satin sheets and watched the morning news on his big TV. He stared at the news anchor reporting live from Niceville, Florida.

I had no idea. I didn't catch the news last night. I was too busy entertaining. Too busy living my life. My old life. I've lived a nice, long life. But he didn't. He was young, still so young. And now he's dead. My son. He had his whole life in front of him.

A tear escaped the man's green eyes. *We had our differences, but I loved him. My God, I loved him. I didn't get to tell him that—at least not lately. Barely been in contact with him. And now he's gone?*

Tears openly streamed down his face now and ran over his reddish beard stubble, got caught in it. His shoulders drooped down, his hands shook as he continued to watch the developing story about the kidnapping at gunpoint.

Son. You got yourself killed. I can't believe it. It should've never come to this. Never. I didn't mean to place you in harm's way.

"The police recovered the gun from the bottom of Turkey Creek during the night," he heard the reporter say. "Forensics has already determined that this gun, the gun Maria Collins used to shoot Mike Clifford, is the same gun the senator used to shoot Maria's father, Brad

Collins. Luckily the bullet merely grazed Brad Collins's arm, and he's now being cared for in the hospital and expected to make a full recovery. The one bullet Maria shot at her attacker, however, proved deadly. We're still waiting for the full autopsy report but preliminary findings indicate the bullet passed through several major organs. Senator Mike Clifford quickly bled to death at the scene. A tragic ending to this captivating, twenty-year-old case."

His tears were dripping onto his bedsheet now. *No. My son. Shot. Killed.*

The reporter leaned forward with an intense expression. "How could this have happened? How did the senator get ahold of the police chief's gun? If there's one thing that's certain, it's that Chief Parlot sure has a lot of explaining to do. The gun was secured in his holster, yet Clifford managed to steal it away from Chief Parlot, allowing him to kidnap Maria at gunpoint and wound Brad Collins. Shouldn't the chief have fought off the senator? If he had, this story would've had a much better ending." The reporter nodded for his audience. "We will keep you all posted as we learn more. There's a press conference scheduled this early afternoon. Until then, back to the studio."

He fumbled with the remote and turned off the TV. *No, no, no! Mike was a good guy, he really was. Hot-headed, sure, sometimes impossible. But he was good.*

He now cried helplessly, the remote clutched loosely in his hands.

He was good. My son was a good guy. Good at politics. Cared for his people, represented them well in the Senate. He cared for his state, his country. Mike. I was always proud to call you my son. Happy to give you advice. You always took it and were thankful for it. Always grateful.

He closed his eyes, tears still streaming out of them, and a scene from a long-ago time played out in his mind.

His son stood before him. His son at his best. "Thanks, *you're* the best," Mike said, and smiled, his pearly white teeth shining, his bright-blue eyes sparkling, his blonde curls bouncing up and down as he laughed his warm laugh. "I really appreciate you. And your advice. Thanks for treating me so well."

He smiled back. "No problem, son, you deserve it."

"Well, don't know about that, but thank you." Mike winked at him. "Really, thank you, Father." Next thing he knew, Mike pulled him in for a hug. A warm hug.

He patted Mike on his strong shoulders. "You're welcome, son, very welcome. Appreciate your gratitude."

He felt Mike squeeze him tight, felt his blonde curls tickle his jawline, felt the warmth of that hug fill his heart with joy.

He opened his eyes and stared at the black TV screen. *And now he's dead? Shot dead? Gone forever? But I loved that kid. Loved him. My son… dead… damn it!*

With a lightning-quick jerk of his wrist, he threw the remote across the room.

Bam!

It hit the TV and left a small crack in the wide screen hanging on the wall across from his bed. The remote dropped to the floor and cracked open. The batteries popped out and rolled across the floor.

Damn it! He didn't deserve to die.

He pulled the sheets off him and jumped up.

But my son won't have died in vain. Someone will pay for this.

He started pacing in front of his bed, back and forth, back and forth.

Yes, someone has to pay for it. And I already know who. The Collinses. That fucking Collins daughter. Oh how I wish she'd died when she was supposed to twenty years ago. Then my son would still be alive. She's the reason he's dead.

He grimaced. *I'll make sure her luck runs out. She won't survive this time!*

CHAPTER 5

"This time, it's really the end of our ordeal, isn't it?" Elisabeth smiled and gave Maria a big hug. "Mein Engel, I'm so happy you're okay. So relieved."

Maria hugged her back, and they stood there for a while, right there in Maria's room, right next to Maria's hospital bed. She felt her mom's heart beating as they embraced each other, felt wetness on her neck. *She's crying. Out of relief. Yeah, we're gonna be okay.*

Maria had a hard time holding back her own tears. She glanced over her mom's shoulder and saw her mamá standing nearby, blinking back tears of her own from her big brown eyes.

"Come on over, Mamá. Come on, group hug time." Maria waved Martina over. She immediately joined them, and the three women embraced each other, all crying.

"Hey, what's… what is going on… here? Am I… missing out on something?" they heard from across the room.

"Aaron?" Maria quickly got out of the group hug and went over to Aaron. "You're finally awake." She sat down on his hospital bed and leaned over to give him a kiss on his forehead, careful not to bump his injured shoulder. "How are you feeling? How is your arm? Your head? And how is—"

He put a finger to her mouth. "Too many questions. Let me wake up first."

By now, the rest of the room had assembled by his hospital bed. Jack, Elisabeth, and Martina all smiled at him. "So glad you're finally awake, son. Guess that sleeping pill really knocked you out, huh?" Jack laughed. "You didn't even wake up for lunch."

"No, not even for lunch," Martina said. "But don't worry, mijo, you didn't miss anything. Wasn't very good."

"Agreed," Elisabeth said, and shivered a little remembering the taste of the hospital food.

Maria laughed. "Come on, what did you guys expect? It's hospital food. It's not going to be gourmet cooking. It wasn't *that* bad, was it?"

"I liked it," Jack said. "And we still have yours over there, Aaron." Jack pointed to the covered tray sitting on the little table by Aaron's bed. "Hungry, son?"

Aaron shook his head. "Not yet. I feel kinda dizzy."

"Of course you do. You have a moderate concussion." Maria sighed. "And a broken collarbone."

Aaron eyed his left arm all bandaged up in a sling. "Oh, really? Well, that explains the look of this." He tried to lift his shoulder but winced in pain. "Yeah, it's broken, alright."

"Take it easy, Aaron. You were very brave last night, very brave. I'm—well, we are *all* so very thankful for what you did last night, the way you tracked down Maria with... with... you know...." Elisabeth stopped talking and swallowed hard.

"With Clifford," Aaron finished her sentence. "Yeah, that was a crazy time swimming up Turkey Creek. Pure adrenaline kept me going."

"How did you even know Maria was there, mijo?" Martina asked.

"Well, I didn't. I just had a feeling...."

Maria burst out laughing. "You had *a feeling*? You, Mr. Show-Me-The-Evidence?" Maria saw Aaron blush. "Guess those pesky feelings are useful sometimes, huh?"

Aaron winked at Maria. "Yeah, yeah, you got me. I admit it. Sometimes you just have to go with your gut feeling."

"It sure came in handy last night, Aaron. I'm proud of you, son, very proud of you," Jack said, but his smile quickly vanished. "But I'm also mad. It was absolutely reckless of you to just run out and take matters into your own hands. We were worried sick about you. Both your mom and I. And your sister. Come on, Aaron, you know better. Leave it to the authorities, look to the facts and—"

"Aha, another Mr. Show-Me-The-Evidence?" Elisabeth interrupted Jack's scolding spree. Stunned, he stopped and looked at her. "Like father, like son, I guess?" Elisabeth grinned at him.

"Yeah, like father, like son," Jack admitted, and sighed. "Anyway, we were all so worried for you and Maria. Your mom, young man, is getting ready to fly out here. Not sure I can hold her back from the idea. And your sister wants to tag along."

"Fantástico," Martina said, a big smile on her face. "I love Grace and Emma. Would be so fun to see them again. Aw, Maria, so fun, no?"

But Maria didn't react at all. She just stared down at the bright-white bedsheets on Aaron's hospital bed, lost in thought.

Like father, like son. Like father… like son? Father. Son. These two words got stuck in her brain, echoed down every slope of it. *Father. Son. It seems important. Why? Where did I hear that? Who said that?*

Maria felt a warm hand on her bare leg below the hem of her hospital gown. Aaron's voice reached her ears. "Maria? Still with us?" Slowly, she turned her head to him.

Aaron saw it. Her now-green eyes. "What is it, Maria?"

Her brain was racing, thinking about these two simple words. *Father. Son. Why does it seem so important to me? There's something important about it. But what?*

Another warm hand touched her shoulder. Maria turned around and looked straight into Martina's face, her brown eyes peering suspiciously up at hers. "Mija, I know that look. You got your thinking cap on. What is it?"

"I don't know," Maria mumbled, her mind still preoccupied. "Somehow 'father' is important."

"Father? Did you just say 'father'?" Elisabeth said. "You mean *your father*? Brad is next door. You mean Brad, your father?"

Maria shook her head, her head that suddenly started hurting, a dull pain that spread from her temples all over her forehead, radiating down into the rest of her. She felt her stitches pulsing as the pain spread. *Father*. She pressed her eyes shut to bear the pain and found her mind transported back to last night.

She was back in the canoe with Mike Clifford, her kidnapper. "I eventually ran for representative, then governor, now senator. Impressive, huh?" Maria heard him say.

She heard herself whisper back, "Yeah, impressive."

"I know, I know. Father thinks so, too. Thinks highly of me still. And that trust, that impression of me, shouldn't be destroyed. Can't be. Not now or ever. So I'll do anything to keep that trust, that love, to not disappoint him. Yeah, I won't disappoint my father again," Clifford said, his face determined.

Father? Clifford's father? They made up? Maria thought to herself, her head spinning, the pain unbearable. *Father. Clifford's father. The mastermind.*

Then the pain swelled up and swept through her brain like a wave, getting stuck in her temples. Instinctively, she touched her head, rubbed at the pain, and abruptly opened her eyes. The memory of her lying captive in the canoe vanished.

All she saw was Aaron's blue eyes intensely studying her face.

Maria jumped up, Aaron's hand slid off her leg, Martina's off her shoulder. "Oh my gosh, I remember now. I remember what Clifford told me." Everyone stared at her. "He said his father thinks highly of him and he can't destroy his trust. He said he couldn't disappoint his father again, that he needed to finish this."

Silence in the room.

"Mija, no entiendo—"

"What?" Jack interrupted Martina. "Are you implying that Mike Clifford was *working for someone else*? That he wasn't the mastermind behind this madness? Is that what you're saying, Maria? Is that what he told you?"

Maria nodded, her throat dry. "I think so. He talked about his father."

"Clifford's… father?" Jack started pacing back and forth in front of Aaron's bed. "Clifford's father? The general?"

Maria nodded again.

Elisabeth's mouth hung open. Martina's eyes were wide. Aaron said aloud what they were all thinking. "You think Clifford's father was in on this, Maria?"

"I'm afraid so," she whispered. "He definitely talked about not wanting to disappoint his father again."

Elisabeth closed her mouth. "But… but… why? What interest does Mike Clifford's father have in any of this?"

"Well, we don't know," Jack mumbled, still pacing. "But it *does* make sense given all we know. The police talked about there being a possible fourth guy, another one of the Fearless Four, didn't they?"

Martina gaped at Jack, eyebrows raised. "So you're saying my ex, Jonathan Sullivan, *wasn't* the fourth member of the Fearless Four?"

Jack shook his head. "Probably not. He was just a middleman that got wrangled into all this. He did it for money. Didn't you say so yourself, Martina?"

Martina nodded, her eyes wide.

"What was that name again… the purported nickname for the fourth guy? The police mentioned it during one of their press conferences." Jack looked at each and every one of them.

Martina shrugged. Elisabeth spoke her thoughts aloud. "JB, Bill, Cliff, and… and…"

"Bullet!" Aaron blurted out. "Wasn't it Bullet?"

Maria had to hold onto the side of Aaron's hospital bed to not fall over. "That's right," she mumbled, "that's right. Bullet. Bullet will get me."

"What did you say?" Aaron looked at her, her pale skin sharply contrasting with her freckles. Maria's breaths came quick, her eyes were bright green. She held on to Aaron's bed so tightly that her knuckles turned white.

"Maria? Mija? Are you okay?" Martina gently touched her daughter's arm hanging by her side, the hand in a fist.

Maria jumped at the touch, ripped out of her thoughts. She inhaled deeply, then stood up tall, letting go of Aaron's bed. "Aaron is right. The police said there might be an unknown fourth guy at large. I think this guy we're talking about is the one they're looking for. And his name is Bullet. Not sure where this name came from—a code name, I'm guessing—but I remember everything so clearly now. Before Clifford died, he told me, 'Bullet will get me.' And he talked about his father. So yes, I think Mike Clifford's father was in on the kidnapping plot."

"But why?" Elisabeth said. "We didn't even know Mike's father. Why would he want to kidnap our child?"

"Maybe he also wanted revenge for his son getting kicked out of the Air Force Academy?" Aaron said.

"Possible," Jack mumbled.

"Either way, we need to let the police know," Maria said, her voice determined. "We have to call the chief. His team needs to look into this. They need to talk to General Clifford."

CHAPTER 6

General Clifford was pacing back and forth in his living room. His wife Dorothy watched him. She sat silently on the couch, her back against the big window-wall, heavy blinds drawn to block out the outside world. Despite closing her eyes, she could still make out the small little flickers illuminating their living room. She heard the click of camera shutters, the mumble of voices outside.

A silent tear ran down her wrinkled, tan face. "Stop it, Richard," she told her husband through closed eyes, then opened them to stare at him, her voice sharp. "Stop pacing. It's not helpful at all."

Right away, Richard stopped and just stood there in the middle of the living room. His shoulders drooped inward, his head hung low. He glanced at his wife. "I'm sorry, dear. I didn't mean to agitate you."

"I know, Richard, I know." Dorothy dabbed at her eyes with a tissue. "It's simply too much for me to bear at the moment. It's hard enough as it is."

Richard gave a slight nod, his head still hanging low. "It sure is," he whispered, and closed his eyes. A tear escaped and dropped onto the carpet. He slammed his right fist into his left hand. "Damn it. I can't believe he's dead. Our son. Oh no, our son. You know we had our differences, but I loved him. My God, I loved him."

Dorothy got up and walked over to Richard, who now cried helplessly, just standing there in the middle of the living room. She rubbed his back. "I know, dear, I know."

Richard's arms still hung by his side and jerked up with every sob. "I loved him. And I didn't get to tell him that, at least not lately. We've barely had any contact with him. And now he's gone? It's not fair. I wish this whole story with the Collinses would just go away. Would've never happened."

Dorothy stopped rubbing his shoulder and leaned into him. "I know. I wish that as well. Wish he'd never met the Collinses. Wish it had all gone differently." She joined him in crying. "It's all just so unbelievable. I can't believe he's gone. Our son. I'm proud of what he accomplished. He came so far. Wish we made a point of telling him that." Tears streamed down her face and dripped onto Richard's shirt.

Feeling the wetness on his back, Richard took a deep breath in, then stood up tall, turned around, and gave his wife a long hug. As they embraced, they heard the constant clicking of cameras and babbling of voices outside their house.

"Those damn reporters. They need to leave us alone, allow us to grieve. But no, they're camping right outside our front lawn? It's unfair, it's not right." A reddish color now flushed Richard's pale face.

He felt Dorothy nod. "I know, dear, I know. I miss seeing the sun. It's not right, having to keep the blinds drawn all day. We'll have to stay inside the house until the news cycle tires of the story and the reporters all leave."

"Good plan," Richard whispered, and pulled her in even closer. "We'll just hide out in here. Nobody can get to us in here. We certainly won't be talking to anyone."

Dorothy nodded, and the elderly couple continued to hold one another, comforting each other, blocking out not only the chaos outside their home but also the thoughts in their heads. A certain calmness engulfed them.

The shrill ringing of their landline cut through the stillness. Both Richard and Dorothy jumped at the sound of it. Richard pressed his lips together, then said, "Damn it, could that be more reporters? Calling again to harass us while standing outside our front door? What the heck?"

Dorothy felt the tension in his body. "It's okay, dear, it's okay. We don't need to answer. Let it go to voicemail."

He nodded, and they both ignored the ringing of the phone. A loud beep from the answering machine cut through the air, then a dark, determined voice leaving a voicemail.

"General Clifford and Mrs. Clifford. This is the Niceville Police Department, Chief Parlot speaking. My team and I are investigating last night's attack. We need to talk to you right away about your son, Mike Clifford. We have a few questions. Please come into the Niceville station before noon."

Dorothy jerked her head up and shook it sharply. "No, we most definitely will *not*. Go to the police station to be interrogated? Definitely not, I will not be questioned and—"

"Shhh…" Clifford hushed, and pointed to the answering machine. The police chief was still talking.

"You have an hour and a half to come in. If you fail to show by noon, we'll send a police car to your home to pick you up and bring you in. Thank you in advance for your understanding and cooperation. We'll see you soon."

The line clicked. The chief had delivered his message, not so much a request as an ultimatum. Silence in the room again, except for the clicking noises and muffled voices.

"A police car?" Dorothy said, her voice shrill. "They'll send a police car? Here? Oh no, Richard." She got out of his hug and threw her hands in front of her face, tears streaming through her fingers. "Mike messed up again, didn't he? Oh no. Richard, make it go away. Please. The police, the bad press… our name, our family name, getting dragged through the mud... I can't handle going through another ordeal again...."

Richard held her close. "It'll be okay, Dorothy, it'll be okay. Don't worry. We'll fix this. Like we always have. Whatever he's done, we'll fix Mike's mistakes. Trust me, I already have a plan. I know who's to blame. The Collinses won't get away with it again."

CHAPTER 7

"Again we were wrong?" Officer Sally Johnson gasped, her big blue eyes wide, jumping from face to face across the gathered investigative team. "We got it wrong again? Oh my…." She exhaled deeply, then the words just tumbled out of her. "At first, we thought Martina and Jonathan Sullivan were the kidnappers behind the twenty-year-old case. Then we became convinced Sullivan was part of a bigger scheme because we uncovered proof that Chief Billings, the former Niceville police chief, and James Borman, the FBI agent who worked with him on the case back then, were involved."

The others nodded.

Sally went on. "We clearly have proof that Senator Mike Clifford is 'Cliff,' the guy behind little Moana Collins's kidnapping, the mastermind behind it all. We know for sure he held little Moana captive on his personal yacht. That he created her new identity as Maria Gabriella Sullivan, put her up in a new home with Martina Sullivan. Had a birth certificate and social security number forged. Evidence supports the narrative every step of the way." She let out a deep breath. "But now you're saying Senator Mike Clifford *wasn't* the mastermind behind the twenty-year-old kidnapping? With all due respect, are you for real, Chief?"

Chief Parlot shrugged. "We can't be sure, Sally, not at this stage. You're right; we've had every reason to believe Mike Clifford *was* the mastermind behind the kidnapping—but when Maria called me, she spoke adamantly about Mike Clifford revealing to her his father is this so-called Bullet we've been looking for. She's convinced Clifford's father is the true mastermind behind it all."

FBI Agent Tonya Anderson paced back and forth in their workroom, her cornrow bun bobbing with every determined step she took. "She's not wrong to keep her guard up. Remember how Jonathan Sullivan, the middleman, told us this Bullet guy might be involved?"

Tom Cooper, the other FBI agent, laughed and shook his head. "Yeah, but silly Sullivan wasn't the brightest and unfortunately couldn't remember whether there really was a guy named Bullet, or if he himself had gotten inducted into the Fearless Four as the fourth guy, as Sully."

"Too bad Sullivan wasn't sure." Sally sighed. "He admitted he was too wasted the night he met them all to remember properly."

Tonya abruptly stopped pacing. "*Exactly.* Memories are always hard to use as proof. And we're dealing with two sets of memories here: Sullivan's, from twenty years prior, and Maria's, across a lifetime of trauma."

Chief Parlot sighed. *She's right. Memories are never reliable. Especially when recalling stressful or traumatic situations. We need proof. Real, hard proof.* His face lit up. *That's it. Proof!* "Tom," he said, and pointed to the young FBI agent, "before we get Mike Clifford's father and mother in here, I need you to find out if General Richard Clifford ever made up with his son."

"Everything in print, all the news articles say they were estranged, so why—" Sally began, but the chief spoke over her, continuing his thoughts.

"Even if they made up for only a short time. Namely, twenty years ago, when the kidnapping happened. Maybe they met somewhere? Can you find us something, Tom?" The chief was almost begging. "'Cuz we really do need some hard proof here…. *I* can't afford to mess this up again…." He swallowed hard.

Tonya came over to him and patted him on his back. "Aw, Isaac my man. Don't be too hard on yourself. It's not your fault Clifford got away with Maria at the press conference. Nobody saw that coming. And we were all there. All of us. And none of us were able to stop him."

The chief let out a sigh. His shoulders drooped down; his arms hung by his side. "Yeah, but he didn't steal *your* gun, now did he? He stole *mine*. Used it to shoot Brad Collins, then kidnap Maria. And then *she* used it to shoot *him*! Jeez. I messed up!"

"No, Chief, we all did," Sally said. "We're a team. And we won't rest until all this is solved. We'll find out if Mike's father, General Richard Clifford, is the mastermind behind the kidnapping, like Maria is claiming. If she's telling the truth, then General Clifford might just be this mysterious Bullet we've been looking for. We have a lead. We know what we need to do. So let's do it. Let's see if the senator and his dad made up, then interrogate General Richard Clifford and find out the truth once and for all."

"Yeah, girl, you rock! Passionate speech." Tonya gave Sally a fist bump while still rubbing Chief Parlot's shoulder with her other hand. She then turned to her FBI colleague. "Tom, get to hacking like my man Isaac said. Let's find out if General Richard Clifford was tight with his son at any point."

"Okay, sounds good. Time to do some deep research on the general." Tom's hands were already flying over his laptop keyboard. "There's some websites on the dark web you guys wouldn't know about that should help…. Go ahead and do your own research while I work. How about that?"

"Great idea, Tom," Tonya said. "I believe we have some time before General Richard Clifford shows up here. Doubt he'll jump into his car the moment he's done listening to your voicemail, Chief. So come on, everyone, get to researching." She gave the chief a slight bump on his shoulder that made him snap out of his thoughts.

"You're right," he said, "let's look at everything. Sally, you're responsible for creating a dossier covering his Air Force career."

Sally grinned and sat down in front of her computer. "On it, Chief."

"Tonya, how about you and I look into his private life, then?"

A wide smile spread over the agent's face. "Yeah, let's do it, my man Isaac. Let's find some dirt on General Clifford."

🎭 🎭 🎭

It was quiet in the workroom as the team worked on their assignments, until a loud whistle followed by an "Interesting!" cut through the air. Everyone stopped in their tracks and looked at Sally.

"What did you find out?" Tonya wanted to know.

"Well," Sally started, a big grin on her face, "you ever wonder why the press never covered Senator Mike Clifford being kicked out of the Air Force Academy decades ago? Why nobody seemed to even know about it?"

Chief Parlot nodded. "First time I heard about it was when Brad Collins told us. That revelation gave us a clear motive as to why Mike Clifford would kidnap the Collinses' child."

"I bet you weren't the only one surprised to hear about it, Chief," Sally said. "The voters wouldn't have known, thanks to the media blackout. The senator's short stint in the Air Force was often referenced but only in passing, with very few details. Just enough fluff to help him get some voters."

Tonya tilted her head. Her forehead wrinkled. "A cover-up?"

"Bingo." Sally grinned. "Wanna guess who pulled that off?"

Tonya, the chief, and Tom said in unison, "General Richard Clifford."

"I definitely think so," Sally said, and waved them over. She showed them an old newspaper article of an interview with General Richard Clifford. "Look what it says here." They all read quietly.

"Yes, of course I am very disappointed that my son decided to quit the Air Force. I always thought he'd follow in my footsteps. But he's chosen a different path," General Clifford explains.

"Well, Mike was adamant about leaving right then and there," General Clifford continues when pressed on why his son dropped out a month before graduation. "He says he needs to find himself. He's broken all contact with us. And that's okay. He needs to figure out what to do with his life, needs to chart a course without our influence. Being on his own, away from us, away from his support network and the life he knew—yes, even the Air Force—will be good for him."

They all looked at each other.

"This sure is interesting, Sally." Chief Parlot gave her a pat on the shoulder. "That was fast on your part. Good job researching."

"But does this interview really contribute anything? It hardly proves General Clifford covered up the incident," Tonya said, her forehead in wrinkles.

"You're right, it doesn't." Sally grinned, then clicked to another window on her screen. "But *this* does. General Richard Clifford was good friends with the Air Force Academy's dean. They went to school together, stationed together. And thanks to Tom's earlier research, we know Brad Collins's story is true, that Mike Clifford actually got kicked out—he didn't drop out voluntarily. Meaning we've caught the general lying in this interview."

"Nice job, Sally." Tom high-fived her, and they grinned at each other. Then he turned to Tonya and the chief. "I found something too, something I think all of you should look at." The team moved over to Tom's laptop. His screen showed a bunch of receipts from different years and for different things.

The chief raised his eyebrows. "What am I looking at here, Tom?"

Tonya shrugged. "Yeah, I'm with Isaac. Can't make sense of anything here. Tom, please enlighten us."

"Sure, my pleasure." Tom grinned and magnified one specific receipt until it filled the screen. "They might not have had much to do with each other and were perhaps 'estranged' as the newspaper articles put it, but rich daddy sure took care of his son on the down-low. Gave him this lovely white yacht to live on, for example."

Sally gasped. "The same one used to hold Maria captive when she was a toddler?"

"Yep, the very same. Was gifted to Mike Clifford from one Richard Clifford about a year before the kidnapping." Tom clicked on another image on his computer. "And these are bank statements. They all show Richard Clifford started wiring his son money again about two years before the kidnapping."

Chief Parlot started pacing. "So they resumed contact about three years after Mike Clifford got kicked out of the Academy?"

Tom nodded. "Indeed. They met up out in Utah, where Mike Clifford was hanging out at the time. That's where they went to a bank together to open up a new account for Mike." Before Tom could show them more of his findings, Sally jumped up.

"*Utah*? Isn't that where the corrupt FBI Agent James Borman, also known as our Fearless Four member 'JB,' was stationed at the time?"

Tonya stared at her, then started pacing. "Yes. And it's where our good old Chief Jim Billings, a.k.a. 'Bill' of the Fearless Four, went to visit his friend JB often."

"Yeah, and apparently Bill saw Mike Clifford, a.k.a. 'Cliff,' there as well," Chief Parlot mumbled. "And then Mike's dad flew out there to see him? Are you sure? You got proof for that?"

Tom clicked and another window popped up. "Yes, I'm positive. Before Sally interrupted me, I was going to show you this receipt to a hotel Richard Clifford stayed at in Utah, a credit card statement for a flight for *one* person—not two, meaning he traveled without his wife—but then dinner was often paid for two."

Sally stared at Tom. "You're thinking he paid for his son's and his own dinner?"

"We can safely assume so. Look here, like I said earlier, they went to the bank together during this trip to open a new bank account in Mike's name. His dad co-signed as Mike was still young and didn't have good enough credit to open an account with a debit and credit card by himself."

"Good research, Tom, good research. This proves that father and son *did* reestablish contact."

Tonya was still pacing back and forth. She abruptly stopped pacing, stared down at Tom. "It's good. But is it enough?"

Tom grinned and winked at Tonya. "I knew you'd ask, FBI Agent Anderson. Always one to seek out proof beyond a reasonable doubt. Yeah, it's enough. Because of this." With a quick click of a button, another large receipt showed up. They all studied it.

Sally's mouth dropped open. "Is that a receipt of a stay at the MGM Grand Casino in Las Vegas under Richard Clifford's name?"

"Ta-dah," Tom yelled, "that's right, Sally. That's our hard proof right there!" He jammed his finger at the receipt on the computer screen. "General Richard Clifford was at the casino the very night we know Jonathan Sullivan met the Fearless Four. So Richard Clifford *must* be Bullet. The mysterious fourth member of the Fearless Four that Sullivan told us about, surrounded by a cloud of cigarette smoke, watching JB, Bill, Cliff, and Sully play their poker game. The game where Sullivan fell into so much debt that those men were able to strong-arm him into assisting with the kidnapping a few months later."

"Wow," was all that the chief, Sally, and Tonya could say.

"And there you have it, ladies and gentlemen," Tom said. "We've found our Bullet!"

CHAPTER 8

*B*ullet. Lu shuddered at the thought. *I suppose I should call him?*
It was all she could think about as she made her way to her gate inside the Orlando airport. But just thinking of him, thinking of having to speak to him again, made her freeze up and she came to a halt in the concourse.

Maybe it's not important. Why should anything bad happen? Nobody will draw a connection to me or him or that stupid club. They're focused on Mike Clifford now. He's the one who kidnapped Elisabeth's daughter twice. He's all they'll focus on.

She resumed walking through the busy airport again and searched for the gate her next flight would depart from. Her flight to Texas, her flight back home.

Back to Daniel. My husband. I just love him so much. He's such a gentle, kind guy. And I'm so lucky he loves me.

A smile spread across her lips, and her steps became more determined. She felt more certain of herself now. Acting like the general she was, she strode toward the gate, her head high, a resolute look on her face. She made it to the gate, read the monitor, saw her flight was on time. She sat down in one of the black leather chairs nearby to wait for boarding.

Can't wait to see Daniel again. He's my everything. Well, him and my career. Love that he supports me with that. He's not jealous I've made it this far. He's proud of me and loves me unconditionally. The smile on her face vanished. *But would he still love me and be proud of me if he knew my secret?*

Lu sank deeper into her chair, her confidence shattered. *He can never find out. Nobody can ever find out. They'd think less of me. They'd pity me. And there's nothing worse than pity. They'll think I'm weak, think what I've built wasn't the result of hard work but just handed to me. And Daniel wouldn't be proud anymore.*

The color drained from Lu's beautiful face until her skin tone contrasted starkly with her dark, black hair.

But I need him. I need Daniel and his support. Like I needed Elisabeth, back then.

She sighed. *But Elisabeth let me down, just left me, forgot about me. Even though she promised she'd always be there for me. Told me I was like a daughter to her—as important as her own daughter.*

Lu couldn't help but chuckle. *Yeah right. As important as her own daughter? Definitely not. She never forgot about her daughter—only about me. And I needed her, desperately needed her. I was counting on her. On her promise. But she broke it. And I hate it when someone breaks a promise. I really needed her.*

A frown came across her face. *But not anymore. Don't need you anymore, Elisabeth. I'm strong now. I doubt you even remember me. Once forgotten, always forgotten. I don't have to worry. I'm in control now.*

Lu's phone vibrated against her leg and took her away from her thoughts. She fished her hand inside her large military pants pocket, found it, and pulled it out. She smiled when she saw who was calling and picked up.

"Hey, Daniel. How are you, my hubby?"

"Hey there, lovely wife," she heard Daniel say, his voice gentle and dark, "I'm worried about you."

"What? Why? You don't need to worry about me. You know I'm a big girl, a strong woman."

"Of course I know that, General," he teased and laughed. "I'm worried about you not making it home today."

Lu raised her eyebrows. "What? Why? What would keep me from making it home today? I'm already at my gate."

"I know, you texted me that."

"Exactly. So?"

"There's huge thunderstorms rolling over here in good ol' San Antonio at the moment. Forecasted to last all day."

Lu smiled. "Don't worry, you know the weather can clear up in the blink of an eye. Those storms will probably be over soon. Besides, the monitor still shows my flight running on time."

"Okay. That's good. Fingers crossed it stays that way. Keep me posted—even though I'm over here constantly checking the flight-tracker app as well."

"Aw, Daniel. You're such a worrier. Get off that app and get to work. That'll distract you. And I'll keep you posted. You know that. I always do."

"I know," he said. "You always do. And you always have a plan."

"Exactly. I'll figure something out if I have to. I'm good at coming up with a plan when needed."

"I know. Well, hope you don't get stuck. Keep me posted."

"I will. And you better get back to work now," she said, and checked her watch. "Coffee break is over, Retired Lieutenant Colonel Thomas."

She heard him sigh on the other end, then gulp down the last of his drink. "You know me all too well."

"I sure do, sir." Lu smiled. "And now I'm ordering you, Lieutenant Colonel Thomas, to return to whatever it was you were working on before you called."

"Yes, ma'am, my love," he said, amusement in his voice, "will do. I certainly don't want to make the general mad."

"That's right," Lu said. "*Nobody* wants to make the general mad."

CHAPTER 9

"**M**ake the general mad?" Brad looked at everyone standing around his hospital bed in his room. "I have no idea what I could've possibly done to make General Clifford mad. I only met him once—the day he and his wife dropped Mike off at the dorms in the Academy. It was a long time ago. Are you sure he's involved?"

"We're not *sure*," Maria said, "but I'm positive Mike Clifford mentioned his father. Right before he told me a bullet would get me."

"Mike *threatened* you?" Brad sat up taller in his hospital bed and stared at his daughter standing beside him, holding hands with Aaron. Brad's face flushed. "He spent his final moments saying someone else would take your life?"

Maria nodded.

Brad felt someone squeeze his hand. Elisabeth, sitting on his bed, trying to take the edge off his anger. "That's why we think Mike wasn't the only one behind the kidnapping." She frowned.

Brad turned to her. "You also think Mike's dad was involved?"

Elisabeth shrugged her shoulders.

"I sure think so," said Jack, who stood next to Martina at the end of Brad's bed. "It makes sense. Whether you knew him or not, Mike's dad might have developed a grudge because you were the one who got his son kicked out."

"Sí," Martina said. "Makes sense, no?"

Brad looked from one person to the next, deep in thought. *Mike's dad? Mike's dad had my child kidnapped? Seems a bit far-fetched. They weren't even close, Mike and his dad.* Brad rested his eyes on Aaron, whose arm was bound in a sling similar to his own. *Glad Aaron didn't need surgery. Guess his injury will heal on its own. Brave guy.*

Brad then noticed Aaron was staring intensely at him. *Why is he looking at me like that?* He returned the stare. "Aaron, you seem deep in thought. Coming up with a fresh new theory, I take it?"

For a split second Aaron flinched, then cleared his throat. "Well, you know... I was there. I fought with Clifford. He was determined to keep the truth a secret, as crazy as that sounds in light of his actions. But it seems to me, like more than anything, he wanted to protect his own hide rather than someone else's."

"What do you mean?" Maria let go of Aaron's hand and crossed her arms. "You think I'm wrong?"

Aaron turned to her. "No, not wrong. Just saying you'd only fight like he did for someone you really, really love. Like I did for you."

Maria uncrossed her arms and took Aaron's hand again, a big smile on her face. "Aw, thanks Aaron. You're the best."

"Sí, our brave Aaron," Martina said, tears in her eyes.

"We all have you to thank for Maria's safety. So grateful you were there to help." Elisabeth smiled.

"Indeed, thank you, Aaron. Thanks for helping our daughter," Brad said, and saw Aaron's face flush.

"You're welcome," he whispered.

Brad studied his face. *There's something more. I see it in his eyes.* "So, Aaron, what did you mean earlier when you said you'd only fight like that for someone you really love? Can you elaborate?"

"Well, if Mike was trying to protect someone else's hide, not just his own, it must be someone he highly respected and loved. Someone he was willing to die for rather than rat them out. Was he that close to his dad?"

Brad stared at him, then shook his head. "No, he wasn't. When I knew him he found his dad annoying. Got pushed into the Air Force by him but never really wanted a career in it. Mike complained about his dad the whole time we were at the Academy together."

"That's what I thought. He wouldn't protect his father, then," Aaron concluded.

Everyone stared at him and said nothing.

Maria let go of his hand, her lip quivering, her arms again crossed in front of her. "Wait a second, you *do* think I'm remembering it wrong! But I know Mike talked about his dad, I know it, I'm positive about it—"

"I know, Maria, I know you believe that, but—"

"You don't believe me?"

"No, Maria, I'm just saying that—"

"I'm crazy? Is that what you think?"

"Gosh, Maria, no, I'm—"

"Stop it," Brad said in a loud voice. Silence in the room. "No need to argue. We need to learn more. Need to find out more. Need to know if there was another person involved or not. Because if there was, they're still at large. And it sounds like the police are already working on it."

Jack nodded. "I got a text from Chief Parlot saying they're looking into General Richard Clifford at this very moment. Let the investigators do their work. They make a good team and are already working this new lead. No matter if General Clifford was involved or not, the police need to talk to him anyway after what his son did."

"Si," Martina said. "Jack's right. The police will handle it. Most important now is that Maria is safe. And that all of you get healthy."

They all nodded.

Brad found his daughter's gaze. "Maria, pumpkin, your mamá is right. We all need to focus on getting healthy and keeping safe. You're lucky you've found such a nice young man who loves you so much he's willing to die for you."

He felt Elisabeth squeeze his hand, then a tear dripped on it. He noticed Martina was crying, too. He studied Maria's face and saw a big smile flush away her anger.

"You're right, Dad," she said. "I'm a lucky girl to have Aaron love me so. He kept me safe. And I know you all love me. You've all fought for me." She uncrossed her arms and threw them around Aaron, making sure to mind his injured shoulder. "I love you, Aaron."

"Love you, too." He gave her a kiss.

"Aw, there's my happy couple." Martina smiled, tears dripping out of her big, brown eyes. "Your dad's right, Aaron is always there for you. All of us are there for you and fight for you. We all love you so much, mija. Your safety is most important."

"That's right, mein Engel," Elisabeth said. "We'll all take good care of you and keep you safe. No matter what. We promise."

Brad swallowed hard. *That's a big promise. Can we keep it? Look at us, all injured.* His throat was suddenly bone-dry as he looked at his beautiful daughter. *Can we keep Maria safe?*

CHAPTER 10

"Safe to say, the whole town is watching as Senator Mike Clifford's father, General Richard Clifford, and his wife, Dorothy, arrive at the police station," the reporter said. "We're intrigued to see what will happen next. Are the Cliffords being interrogated out of an abundance of caution because of their son's crimes, or is there more to the story? Stay tuned. We'll be back with the latest as the investigation unfolds."

Maria turned off the TV and sighed. She glanced over at Aaron, who was asleep in his hospital bed. *Guess he needs his rest to heal. But couldn't he do so in his fancy new apartment? I wish we could get out of here and get back to living our regular lives. Our normal lives. Forget about the last few crazy days.*

Sunrays shone through the half-open blinds and flooded the room, making her white bedsheet almost shine. One ray shone straight onto her thigh, and she felt its warmth flood through her. She pulled down the hem of her blue hospital gown and frowned. *These gowns are ridiculous. Hate the open back. I feel so exposed.*

She sighed again. *Exposed to the world. My whole life is exposed, not just my body in this gown.* She shifted in her bed and felt the strings holding the gown together loosen. Quickly, she reached her hands behind her back and attempted to retie them. *I sure hope Jack and*

Mamá bring me real clothes to wear soon. I wonder how long they'll be at the Air Force Inn before they come back with fresh clothes for all of us?

She successfully tied the strings into a bow, then got up to look out the window. The blue sky above, the palm trees beneath her... she closed her eyes and wished herself away from all of this. She could almost taste the salty air as if she were standing on a beach.

A knock at the hospital room door.

The beautiful, peaceful picture in mind vanished. She opened her eyes and turned around. *I bet it's the nurse checking on us again. Like she does every half hour.* She rolled her eyes, exhaled deeply.

"Come on in," she said.

The door opened and in came the nurse.

Knew it. Her again, of course.

"Oh, hi there, Maria. Seems like you were enjoying the view? Glad to see you're feeling strong, more back to normal. Seems like the ketamine is nearly flushed from your body."

"Yeah, I'm feeling better."

"Good, good. How's our other patient?"

"Asleep. It's hard, though, for him to stay that way when there's constant interruptions."

The nurse raised her eyebrows and remained where she was, in the doorway. "I see. Suppose you'd like to be left alone?"

Maria sighed. "Sorry. I didn't mean to be rude. I know you're just doing your job. So, what do you need to check this time? Blood pressure? Temperature?"

The nurse grinned. "Nothing, actually." Maria tilted her head and looked at her. "I just came in to see if you're up for visitors. But if Mr. Heikinnen is resting, I can tell them to come back later."

Maria stepped closer to her. "Visitors? Who?"

"Four people who are eager to talk to both of you."

"Four people... the police team?"

The nurse laughed. "No, no police here. Though I hear they're keeping busy at the station."

Maria now heard giggles from outside the half-closed door. *Who's there?* She stepped closer to the nurse. "I don't think Aaron will mind having visitors, depending on who it is."

"I think you'll both be surprised," the nurse said. She stepped into the room and swung the door fully open, giving Maria a view of the hallway.

A big smile spread across her face. "Keisha? Brandy? Jim and Nick?"

"Surprise," they all yelled.

Maria ran past the nurse and fell around Keisha's neck. "Yep, your good friends couldn't leave you alone up here in the Panhandle any longer," Keisha said. She squeezed Maria tight. "Jeez, girl, are you alright?"

Maria nodded, blinking back tears. She let go of Keisha and gave Brandy a big hug next. "How'd you guys get here?"

"Drove all night," Brandy said while swaying Maria back and forth in a hug. "Couldn't believe what happened to y'all, just had to come see you, darlin'."

"And we promised our fellow second lieutenant we'd always have his back. It sounds like he's had a rough start to his Air Force career," Jim said as he gave Maria a hug.

"Yeah, that's my fault." Maria let go of him and glanced at the floor.

"Always told Aaron you're trouble," Nick said. He winked at Maria and pulled her in for a hug. "But frankly, he needed more excitement to spice up his boring life."

Brandy flashed him an angry look. "C'mon, Nick, that's not funny."

"C'mon, Brandy, it kinda is. Maria chuckled, I felt it." Nick grinned and let go of Maria.

"I feel like slapping you, silly goose," Brandy said, and took Maria by the hand. "So, darlin', let's have a look at that fiancé of yours. We didn't drive all night to not see both of you. Where is he?"

Maria winked at Nick, then took Keisha's hand as well and walked her girlfriends into the hospital room. "Over there. Resting from all the excitement."

"Aw, he's actually sleeping," Keisha said, hushing her voice. "We can come back later."

Maria shook her head. "No, it's fine. He's just tired from walking around earlier. I'm sure he'll be up soon enough."

"Sure, darlin'. How about we all get some coffee then? Go down to the cafeteria, maybe?"

"I'm up for that," Jim whispered, and Nick nodded.

"I won't go down in this." Maria pointed to her outfit. "Not in this ugly hospital gown with the open back."

"As long as nothing's hanging out the back, you're fine." Nick grinned and got elbowed by Brandy. Everyone had a chuckle, including the nurse.

"I'm afraid Maria is not allowed to leave this floor of the hospital yet," the nurse said. "But you could always bring a coffee to her. Anyway, I'll leave you guys alone now. The doc and I will be back later to check on both our patients. Press the call button if you need anything before that."

Maria nodded, then she and her friends said goodbye to the nurse, who closed the door behind her as she left. They all turned back to Aaron.

"Holy cow, Aaron looks pretty banged up," Jim said.

"He has a broken collarbone and a concussion," Maria explained.

"From the fight with that guy?" Nick wanted to know.

Maria nodded.

"Boys, let him sleep. C'mon, bring those two plastic chairs over next to these… armchairs?" Keisha pointed at the pullout chairs shoved against the wall.

Maria laughed. "Not sure what they're called, but my mamá and Jack slept on them."

"Where are those two now?" Brandy asked.

"Getting some clothes for me and the others."

"Great, then nobody but Aaron is around to ogle your behind." Nick grinned, while bringing over one of the plastic chairs.

"Nick, please, behave." Brandy ripped the chair out of his hands and pushed him toward the door. "Go get coffee for us. And while you're down there, think about what you've said."

"Yes, ma'am," Nick said. He gave Brandy a kiss and headed out. "The coffee's on me. Consider it punishment for my loose tongue."

Keisha and Maria rolled their eyes.

"Wait for me, man," Jim said. "I'll help you out with carrying everything. That way the girls can have some alone time to catch up first."

Nick and Jim left while the girls set the two plastic chairs next to the armchairs to form a little circle where they could all hang out. Brandy plopped down in one of the plastic chairs while Maria and Keisha sat in the more comfortable ones.

"Girl, tell us all about what happened," Keisha said. "You've had quite the week so far."

Maria snorted. "Yeah, no kidding."

"Darlin', I'm so sorry for everything that's happened to you. Please, start at the beginning and help us understand. We listened to the story on the radio while driving up here, it's all over the news, but it's so confusing," Brandy said.

Maria nodded. "It is. I'm still a little confused myself. I have another mom now. And a dad. And I'm half German, not half Venezuelan. And I got kidnapped, almost drowned, and then I shot someone—"

Keisha held up her hands. "Whoa, girl! Hold on, hold on. You're making even less sense than what we heard on the TV and the radio. One thing at a time, girl. Okay? Unless you don't wanna talk about any of it. We understand if you don't."

Maria nodded, tears in her eyes. "Thanks, guys. I just don't know where to start."

"Oh, darlin', there, there. We're just happy to see you, happy to know you're alright." Brandy got out of her plastic chair to give Maria a hug. Keisha came over, too, and they all hugged for a while without saying a word.

"I'm glad you guys are here," Maria whispered, and squeezed them tight. "Thank you for driving all the way up here."

"Of course, girl. We couldn't just sit and hang out in Daytona without a care in the world, whiling away our time before the boys move to their duty stations, while you and Aaron were in danger here. We had to come."

"What about the graduation trip you guys had planned?" Maria asked.

"Don't you worry your pretty little head about that, darlin'." Brandy smiled. "That's not until the end of the month. We won't miss it. Besides, the trip here was more important."

Maria nodded in gratitude. Brandy and Keisha sat back in their chairs.

"So, girl, do you want to tell us about what happened so we can better understand? Or would you rather talk about something else?" Keisha glanced at Maria, her dark-brown eyes full of worry.

Maria shrugged her shoulders.

"Maybe focus on the good things first, darlin'?" Brandy batted her eyes playfully.

Maria gave her a look. "The… good things?"

"Yeah, like finding your real parents? Or having all those charges dropped against your mamá? Darlin', I'm so excited to see them all. Y'all one big, happy family now: the Collinses and your mamá's family. That's a nice outcome from all this, right?"

A slight smile lit Maria's face. *Brandy's right. There are good things that came out of this ordeal. And all of us are going to be okay.*

"Alright, yeah, let's start there. I'll start with how I met my parents." Maria smiled, and the words just tumbled out of her.

They were all sipping their coffees and listening to Maria finish her story when they heard a grunt followed by a bellow. Maria jumped out of her chair and ran over to Aaron's bed. His eyes were closed as he thrashed, throwing his head left to right, his uninjured arm swinging in the air. He yelled, "No, no, don't! No, no!"

Maria stared at him. *Oh my gosh. Aaron!*

Her friends joined her around Aaron's bed. Brandy raised her eyebrows. "What's going on, y'all?"

"Seems like he's having a horrible nightmare," Jim said. "I bet the last few days were tough on him."

The crinkling of bedsheets and Aaron's shouts were the only sounds in the room for a while. They all stared at him kicking the sheets, swinging his arm, moving his head. A big tear dripped down Maria's nose. *This is my fault. My crazy past finally caught up to him. It's playing with his mind. Playing with him like he's a puppet. Playing with all of us.*

"This has gone on long enough, we have to wake him up," Keisha said. "C'mon, guys." Keisha grabbed one of his feet to keep it from kicking. Brandy, standing on the opposite side of the bed, did the same with the other. Nick held his right arm, so that only Aaron's head was moving back and forth.

Then Aaron lunged with his right arm so quickly that Nick let go of it in surprise. Aaron's hand in a fist, it swung about and almost clobbered Nick by accident.

"No, let go!" Aaron screamed, his eyes still closed, his eyelids fluttering. "Let go of me!" He kicked his legs again with such power that neither Brandy nor Keisha could hold them still.

Maria threw her hands over her mouth. *Oh my gosh, Aaron. You're reliving the fight. It's forever burned into your brain. You have PTSD— just like me. Now we're both just puppets of the past. Unable to shake it off, forever tied to our pasts by an invisible string. I'm sorry I dragged you into this....*

"Wake up, man," Jim yelled, his voice loud and firm. He turned to Maria and elbowed her. "C'mon, Maria, you gotta wake him."

Maria snapped out of it and focused on Aaron now. She sat next to him on the bed, careful to avoid his kicking and arm-swinging, trying to avoid bumping his injured arm. She reached out and touched his face. "Aaron, wake up, you're dreaming. Wake up! You're okay. I'm here. We're both okay." She felt the sweat on his face as she stroked his cheek. "It's okay, my love. We're okay," she whispered, silent tears dripping down onto the bedsheet.

Aaron grew calmer, his legs stopped kicking, his right arm stopped swinging. Maria laid her head on his chest. The fast beating of his heart pounded in her ear, her tears left a wet spot on the bedsheets loosely covering his chest. His heavy breathing brushed against her hair and made a few strands jump back and forth.

"You're alright," she whispered. "I'm here, my love. We're safe." She closed her eyes and felt him relax. His heartbeat slowed down, his breathing came more evenly.

"Maria?" she heard him say.

She sat up, a smile on her face, silent tears still streaming down. "Yeah, I'm here," she whispered. Their eyes met. His ocean-blue eyes showed turmoil but took on a soft, concerned look as he gazed at her.

"Why are you crying? Are you alright?" he said, focused on her only.

She nodded. "Yeah, I am. Just sad to see you're having bad nightmares now as well."

"Me? I did?"

"Yeah, man. Pretty crazy nightmares, I'd say," Nick blurted out, and only then did Aaron notice his friends all standing beside his bed.

"Nick? Brandy? What are you guys doing here?" Aaron looked to his left. A big smile lit up his face. "Jim and Keisha? You're all here?"

Jim grinned. "Of course, man. Couldn't leave you to fight the bad guys all by yourself, Lieutenant. We're all in this together."

"Yeah, we've got your back, Lieutenant," Nick said.

Aaron gave Nick and Jim a fist bump with his good arm. "You guys are awesome."

Nick winked at him. "We know."

Brandy rolled her eyes. "Don't tell him that too often or it'll go to his big head."

They all had a laugh and the conversation started flowing. They brought the plastic chairs back over to sit around Aaron's bed, Brandy and Keisha on their boyfriends' laps. Maria still sat with Aaron on his bed. As the others talked and joked, Maria was quiet.

Jim finally pulled out his phone and studied it. "The news says the police are talking to General Clifford right now," he blurted out. "The media's speculating that General Clifford is Bullet, that mystery guy in the Fearless Four group who planned Maria's kidnapping way back when. Crazy!"

"No kidding." Nick nodded. "It's all crazy."

"Sure is." Keisha glanced at Maria, who just stared at the bedsheets.

"But they got him, y'all. It'll be fine. No more bad guys left. You can start your new life here now. Together." Brandy smiled.

Out of the corner of her eye, Maria saw her four friends and Aaron nod, but the little hairs on her arm stood up, alert. She felt dizzy. *New life? Start it, here and now? I guess. But I still don't feel free. Not free of my past. I feel like someone else is holding the strings to my life.*

"Maria, girl, you alright?" Keisha's voice made it to her ears.

Maria looked up. "Yeah, sure. I'm alright."

"Good, that's good," Jim said. "You're both alright. Both safe."

Maria looked at him. *Are we, really?*

CHAPTER 11

"**R**eally? You have nothing to say on the matter, General Clifford?" Chief Parlot eyed the elderly man sitting in front of him behind the metal desk in the interrogation room.

"No, not without my lawyer present," General Clifford said, his voice firm, his eyes fiery.

The chief now glanced at Dorothy Clifford, who sat beside her husband. A tear rolled down her cheek, but she avoided all eye contact and instead stared at the desk. The chief sighed. *They're lawyering up, I knew it.* He then nodded at his colleague, FBI Agent Anderson.

She returned his nod and took over. "What about you, ma'am? Do you have anything to say?"

"Not without my lawyer," Dorothy Clifford whispered, her voice almost breaking.

Agent Anderson and Chief Parlot exchanged a glance. Then the chief took out a paper and put it on the table. "Since you're both requesting a lawyer, here's a list of public defenders in the area, in the event you—"

General Clifford suppressed a sharp laugh. "That won't be necessary." He pushed the paper back toward the police chief. "We intend to consult our personal lawyer immediately. Shall I be the one to call him, or will you?"

His own lawyer, of course. Chief Parlot swallowed hard, then tried to smile. "Sure, General Clifford, my team will take care of it. Do you have his number?"

"No, I don't know it by heart," General Clifford barked. "We're not the sort of folks to have our lawyer on speed dial. Not the sort of folks that cause trouble. Ever. I do have our lawyer's business card in my wallet, but since you took everything away from us at the front desk, I can't give it to you."

"Oh, no worries, General, we'll find it," Agent Anderson said with a smile.

The general jumped up. "No you will not. You will not go through my wallet or any other of our personal belongings."

"Sir, we need to—" the chief started to say, but got interrupted again.

"You need *to do nothing*, Chief. You've done enough already, for Chrissake, and yet nowhere near enough. *You should've held on to your gun.* Then none of this would've happened."

Say what? The chief's jaw dropped, and he couldn't say anything for a second.

"General Clifford, it was *your son* who stole my colleague's gun," Agent Anderson said, her voice sharp. "And your son used that weapon to illegally kidnap an innocent woman at gunpoint and to shoot his former friend. Therefore—"

"It was the chief's fault," the general interrupted. "He failed to maintain peace and order. His gun killed our son. It was pure negligence on the chief's part."

I can't believe this! He's blaming me? Chief Parlot was about to say something when General Clifford suddenly jumped up.

"That girl shot our son and *we're* the ones being interrogated? How about you bring *her* in? How about you arrest *her* for manslaughter! She's a killer! And I intend to have my lawyers sue you into oblivion on behalf of my son."

Dorothy Clifford looked up and touched her husband's arm. "Richard, please…."

But he shook her off. "Your crazy plan went wrong, Chief Parlot, extremely wrong. You and your team should've just brought my son in for interrogation—yet you chose to herd along the crazy girl to entrap our son as her kidnapper. Ridiculous. Shameful. And so wrong, Chief! Blaming my son for something he didn't do."

Chief Parlot raised his eyebrows. *What? He's defending his son now? Guess they did make up then, didn't they? Interesting. Despite the audacity of blaming me and my team, his rambling might have proven the very thing we needed to know.* The chief grinned. "General Clifford, please sit back down and be careful what you say in here. Remember, everything you say can and will be—"

"I know that," General Clifford yelled, but sat down again. "Get us our lawyer."

"Sure, we'll have it taken care of, General and Mrs. Clifford," the chief said. "Until then, could I offer you a water?"

General Clifford snorted. "No thank you. I've heard the amenities you offer your accused here tend to turn out deadly."

Agent Anderson and the chief stared at him flatly. It took all of Chief Parlot's willpower to hold his tongue as his thoughts raced. *Unbelievable. Blaming us for that death as well? It was your son who sent poisonous chocolates to the former chief who aided him in getting away with the kidnapping twenty years ago.*

Chief Parlot cleared his throat and glanced at Agent Anderson. "Fine, then, General Clifford. We won't offer you anything else. You'll have to wait here until your lawyer arrives."

"Fine," General Clifford said, and crossed his arms in front of his chest. Dorothy Clifford stared down at the metal table again. Agent Anderson and the chief left the room.

Back inside their workroom, Tonya Anderson knocked elbows with the chief. "That was quite something, huh, my man Isaac?"

He just nodded. "Yeah…. He's very confrontational. Not sure how much we'll get out of him."

"We do have proof he was at the MGM Grand Casino, though," Tom Cooper said, while Sally Johnson nodded enthusiastically.

"I know, team. It's good we have all that," the chief agreed, and sighed. "But his lawyers will tear this evidence apart, no matter what. 'Too old,' they'll say. 'Too vague.' We all know he was there, but we still don't have hard proof General Richard Clifford met the rest of the Fearless Four that night, only a dead man's testimony. And it's such a big casino… easy to make the case they wouldn't have possibly seen each other, even if they were there at the same time." He sighed again.

Tonya gave him a pat on the shoulder. "Regardless, the way the general behaved in there suggests he's covering something up, that's for sure. And remember, we've got those receipts as hard proof, those count for something. Now all we need is for him to admit he's the guy the others all called Bullet."

"He won't ever admit to that." Sally sighed, then her face lit up. "But his wife might. She seems awfully quiet. Pensive, almost. Maybe we interrogate her separately? See if she says more on her own."

"Or perhaps she knows nothing about her husband's shady dealings?" Tom said.

Sally's smile faded. "Well, that's always a possibility…."

"All speculation," the chief interrupted. "We need to move forward. We have more work to do. Tom and Sally, I need you to dig deeper. Ferret out proof that General Richard Clifford was, in fact, part of his son's life and involved in his crazy gangster group."

"Okay, Chief, on it." Sally and Tom immediately sat down in front of their laptops and got to work.

"And Tonya, you and I unfortunately have a first press conference to get ready for. One of many to come, I assume." The chief frowned.

Tonya nodded. "No worries, my man Isaac. We can do this. Let's listen to the recording again of when Maria called to let us know about Mike Clifford's father and the threat he made. Important to recall exactly what our man Mike said before he died. Or do you want to bring Maria in for firsthand verification?"

Chief Parlot shook his head. "No, not right now. She's still in the hospital. We can go over and talk to her in a bit unless she gets released and wants to come in to talk to us here. Either way, for now, let's focus on what we've got and prepare a press conference that'll shake the community to its core. That way, if anyone out there knows more, they might be induced to come forward with additional information that could aid us."

"Absolutely right, Isaac," Tonya said. "We need all the info we can get. So, come on, let's do this. Let's make it a presser to remember."

CHAPTER 12

*R*emember to get something to eat, my love, read the text message on Lu's phone.

She smiled. *Oh, Daniel, you're such an awesome husband. Always worrying about my well-being. But I'm a big girl.*

Don't worry. I'll get a snack for lunch in a bit, she texted back, then looked up at the monitor above the gate again. "*FLIGHT DELAYED,*" it read. She sighed, let herself sink further into the leather chair, and focused on her phone again.

She opened the news app on her phone and scrolled through the headlines. She found what she was looking for: further breaking news streaming live out of Florida's Panhandle. Her arm hairs stood up as she pressed the button to watch the press conference as it aired.

🎭 🎭 🎭

Thirty minutes later, Lu shifted in her seat, sweat glistening on her forehead. She stared at her phone. *I can't believe the police already know so much. They've dug deep.* With shaky hands, she logged out of the news app and put the phone in her pocket. *They went back years. They know about the Academy incident Mike Clifford was involved in. Know*

General Clifford made that incident disappear off the books. Lu rolled her eyes. *Typical.*

She went over everything that had been brought up during the conference. *The police already know General Clifford met his son in Salt Lake City and Las Vegas. At the MGM Grand Casino. How did they even find all that out? How's it possible? That was decades ago, well before everyone started leaving a digital footprint on the internet.*

She felt sweat forming on her bottom and shifted again in her seat. The leather squeaked. *Oh dear. That's embarrassing.*

She jumped up and inhaled deeply. Picked up her bag and started walking, back and forth, in front of the gate. Using her lower lip she blew air up at her forehead to help herself stop sweating. But it didn't work.

She stopped walking. The color drained from her beautiful face. *What else will they find? Will they find other things from back then, things like... No! I can't let that happen.*

Her heart was beating fast underneath her uniform, pushing against the name tag on her chest. She started walking again, but with her mind occupied, she wasn't paying much attention to where she was going in the busy airport and accidentally bumped into a stranger.

"Oh my, are you okay, ma'am?" she heard a middle-aged man ask.

"I'm so sorry, sir, so sorry. I didn't mean to run into you, I was just..."

"...wondering what to do next?" the man said, a friendly smile on his lips.

Lu stared at him. *Who is this man? How does he know I'm trying to come up with a plan? Does he know my secret?*

"I figured you're upset about the cancelation." The man pointed at the monitor above the gate. "It's too bad they canceled the flight. You're affected as well, I assume?"

What? Lu now focused on the monitor. "*CANCELED*," it said in big red letters.

"Bad storms, I heard. Sounds like many flights into and out of Texas are grounded, but hey, you could always try your luck, ma'am." The man now pointed toward the line forming in front of the gate Lu was supposed to fly out of.

She snapped out of her thoughts. "Oh no." She sighed. "I need to get back to Texas today."

The man nodded. "Yeah, I bet many folks here feel the same. Well, get in line and maybe you'll have a shot at flying out later today." He smiled at her. "Good luck."

"Thank you, sir. And sorry again for not paying attention earlier."

"No worries at all." The stranger waved as he walked off. "Safe travels to you."

Lu returned the wave. "Thanks, you as well."

She took his advice and got in line. As she was waiting there, trying to figure out how she'd get back home to Texas, a sentence she'd heard the chief utter at the press conference haunted her. *And we promise you, the fine citizens of Florida, we will unearth all secrets surrounding this case. No matter how long ago schemes were hatched, no matter who was involved, we will bring the perpetrators to justice. Once and for all.*

Lu shifted from one leg to the other and felt sweat form on her forehead again. She shook her head. *They can't find out. Nobody can! I might have to make contact with Bullet somehow. I'm sure he doesn't want anyone to find out either.*

A shudder ran down her spine. *I despise that man. He's evil, pure evil. But he's kept his promise. He sure helped me. And I deserved that help, after everything I endured.* Her hands started shaking just thinking about it. *It was horrible... but nobody can find out.*

Elisabeth needs to stay silent. We'll silence her, if we have to.

CHAPTER 13

"If we have to, yeah, we'd prefer you talk to us here," Maria told the chief. "I think we'll be released this afternoon, but not sure when. So yes, if it's urgent, just come meet us here at the hospital."

Maria listened for a while, her phone pressed to her ear, and started pacing back and forth in front of the windows in their hospital room. "Sounds good," she finally said. "See you soon then." She hung up.

Martina studied her daughter's face. "¿Mija, qué pasa?"

Maria sighed and turned to her. Keisha, Brandy, Nick, Jim, and Jack were idling inside the room, all eyes on Maria.

"Yeah, what's going on, girl?" Keisha asked.

"The police have to talk to me and Aaron."

"Me too?" Aaron sat up in his hospital bed.

Maria nodded. "Yeah, I'm afraid so. It's about last night. The attack."

Aaron exhaled deeply. "That makes sense. I figured they'd need to question us at some point."

"Yes, it's standard procedure with this sort of thing," Jack said. "Nothing to worry about, Maria and Aaron. Just tell them exactly what happened. You acted in self-defense. That's very clear. No need to be nervous."

"You'll be fine, darlin'." Brandy walked over to Maria and gave her a hug. "And at least you're dressed now."

Keisha winked at her. "That's right, girl. No more open-back nightgown. Your mamá sure found you a nice outfit."

Maria nodded. "True. Gracias, Mamá."

"De nada." Martina smiled.

"Hey, man, you might want to get dressed as well." Nick winked at Aaron. "Unless you don't mind your butt hanging out of your hospital gown while you talk to the police."

A giggle went through the room.

Aaron rolled his eyes. "Very funny, guys. I might need help getting dressed, though. So, everyone out, except for Maria."

"Sure, sure." Jim smiled. "We'll give you two all the privacy you need."

Maria blushed. Everyone else grinned.

"Vamos, guys, let's get out." Martina hurried everyone along.

"But where are we supposed to go?" Jim pouted as he stepped out of the room.

"Go visit my parents," Maria yelled after them. "They'd love to get to know you guys better. Next room over."

"Good idea, Maria," Jack said, and closed the door behind him.

Maria picked up the backpack with Aaron's clothes his dad had brought and walked over to Aaron's bed. "Let's see what we have here." She went through the bag. "Shirt, shorts, underwear, flip-flops…" She laid the clothes out across the foot of the bed.

"Looks good, thanks." With his right arm, Aaron pulled her in for a kiss. "Now, nurse, please be gentle."

She grinned. "No worries, I will be, my poor patient." Then her grin faded. "I'm sorry you broke your collarbone. It'll take weeks to heal, but you're supposed to start work. I've been nothing but trouble."

"Oh, c'mon, Maria. You know none of this is your fault. Nobody could have seen it coming." He took her hand. "Besides, I'd rather have a broken collarbone than a dead fiancée."

Maria squeezed his hand and stroked his face, got lost in his ocean-blue eyes while tears filled hers. "You came close to getting killed yourself."

"Close, but Mike Clifford didn't succeed. And now we got his dad. He's in custody. It'll be fine, we're safe."

"I hope so."

"Trust me, Maria. We're safe now. I won't let anything happen to you. You're my everything."

She nodded, a tear escaping her eye. "I love you, too, Aaron. Thank you for helping me beat the bad guys."

Aaron pulled her chin in; they were eye to eye now. "Anytime, my love. You're worth dying for."

She snorted. "How very chivalrous of you. But please, don't actually do that. Because I need you."

"I know," he whispered, then gave her a long, warm kiss. They got lost in their love.

Some time later, the door opened and Keisha stepped in. "Hey, guys, I just forgot my phone on the chair somewhere and…" She noticed Aaron and Maria kissing, lowered her voice. "Oops, ahem, sorry. I just… oh, there it is. Found it." She picked it up from the chair, then turned around and walked out. "You can get back to making out now. But don't forget to actually get dressed. The police will be here soon."

The door closed and they were alone again.

Maria grinned at Aaron. "Guess she's right. Better get ready. Here, boxers first. Let me lift up the blanket… lift your feet, and I'll slide them on. Okay, now lift your butt and—"

"Alright, alright, nurse, not so fast." Aaron laughed. "And be careful, please."

"Yes, Lieutenant, I will be." Maria smirked and got to work helping her injured fiancé dress in preparation for the police's questioning.

Chief Parlot, Agent Tonya Anderson, Officer Sally Johnson, and Agent Tom Cooper were all standing in Aaron and Maria's hospital room, listening to them recount the events surrounding Mike Clifford's attack. Officer Johnson took notes while Agent Cooper recorded the conversation.

As Aaron told his side of the story, Maria stared out the window. Her hands in fists, her knuckles white, her face pale, she tried to focus on her breathing. *Inhale, exhale, inhale, exhale*, she told herself. *We're fine, we're safe.* Her mind threatened to wander off, but she forced herself to focus on the conversation.

"Aaron, would you also say the shooting was an accident, as Maria previously stated?" Chief Parlot asked him.

Aaron nodded. "Yes, definitely. She was in grave danger, we both were, but even then she didn't want to shoot Mike Clifford. She wanted to stall him, wait for the search and rescue team to come. But he attacked her again. They wrestled with the gun and it just went off."

"I see," the chief said. "Anything that Mike Clifford said before he died?"

"Yes. 'Bullet will get you. Just you wait, Bullet will get you,'" Maria blurted out, the green in her unique hazel eyes shining brightly.

"Yes, thank you for that, Maria, you've already told us," Agent Anderson said. "Right now we'd like to hear Aaron speak, please."

Maria nodded, and Aaron went on, "I didn't hear him say anything. I was further away. All I heard was some mumbling, then a moan... and then he splashed into the water."

"Okay, thank you, Aaron," the chief said. "What happened next?"

"I went over to Maria to see if she was okay. She had lost the gun, splashed into the water herself. She was in shock, hysterical. I hugged her and told her it would be okay. Then we heard the dogs and saw the search and rescue team. They took us in."

"Thank you, Aaron," Agent Anderson said, and turned to Chief Parlot. "Any other questions, Chief?"

The chief shook his head. "No, no further questions for Aaron." He turned to Maria. "But I'm wondering if you can tell us again, Maria, what Mike Clifford said about his father."

She nodded, her eyes as emerald green as the water outside of the hospital. She closed them and was transported back to that night at Turkey Creek. She heard Mike Clifford's words in her ears, as if it was happening that very moment. "He said my dad took everything away from him. Cut him off from his family. He wanted to hurt my dad. Said he knew losing his daughter would break him. Said he was totally drunk when they came up with the plan. Everyone was. Said he was chosen to plan the absurd kidnapping. He was eager to please his father because he built him up after he'd fallen and made him great again."

"Ha, now *that's* proof he made up with his father," Officer Johnson blurted out, and was immediately shushed by the chief.

"Anything else, Maria?"

"He said he couldn't kill me because my eyes reminded me of his friend... my dad. That my dad had once been the one and only real friend he ever had." Maria's knuckles turned even more white as she pressed her hands into a fist.

"Okay, thank you, Maria. Very helpful. We appreciate your cooperation," the chief said. "And yours, too, Aaron. Thank you."

"Yes, thanks to the both of you." Agent Anderson gave them a nod. "We assure you, we have General Richard Clifford and his wife under our thumb. We'll find out the truth. We'll prove he's the mastermind behind it all."

"Yeah, we'll prove he's our Bullet," Officer Johnson said, her voice determined. She got another look from her colleagues.

"But everyone's dead... killed...." Maria whispered.

"What?" Agent Anderson raised her eyebrows. "What's that, Maria?"

Suddenly, Maria jumped up. "Everyone who knew about the kidnapping back then is dead, right? They all got killed somehow. But not Bullet. He's still out there."

"Yes, Maria, but we have him in custody," the chief said.

"And not everyone was killed," Agent Cooper said. "Remember, JB, the former FBI agent, killed himself."

"Did he?" Maria's green eyes rested on Agent Cooper. He shifted from one leg to the next, then nodded. "Or was he murdered too and we just don't know how?" Maria started pacing.

"What do you mean?" Agent Anderson asked.

"What if there's more to it? What if JB got killed also? And if so, by whom? Mike Clifford? Or his father? Did General Clifford even know JB?"

"Well, we're pretty sure we've proved that—" Officer Johnson started but got interrupted by Maria.

"Or do we have the wrong Bullet?" Maria stopped pacing.

Silence in the room. Everyone stared at her.

"Maria, you just said yourself the senator talked about his father…." the chief finally said, breaking the silence, but Maria was on a roll.

"Clifford mentioned *meeting* them, the Fearless Four. If his father was one of them, why would he use the word 'meet'? You don't *meet* your father, do you?"

"Well, hold on." Aaron smirked. "You didn't know your father for the longest time and technically just 'met' him. Maybe Mike Clifford used such language because it was his first time seeing his father in years following their falling-out? Maybe you're reading too much into this."

Maria saw both the agents and the police officers nod. She sighed. *I guess. Maybe they're right?*

"Well, again, we thank you for your cooperation," Chief Parlot said. "You've given us fresh new insight on the matter. Maria, we're convinced you acted in self-defense. We're glad you're both safe and sound and doing alright. You're both free to go but will need to remain in the area. Just so you know, after everything that's happened, expect to have an officer around to escort you at all times."

Aaron nodded. "Okay. Understood, Chief."

The chief returned his nod. "To keep is simple, we'll talk to the base police force to see if they can assign Lieutenant Martinez with your group again—to keep an eye on you, and for your own protection."

Our protection? Maria stared out of the window, her eyes emerald green. *Can they protect us?* Her heart was pounding, her hands shaking. *Can they?*

"Got it, thanks, Chief," Aaron said. "And please keep us posted on everything. This crazy case needs to be solved once and for all."

Agent Anderson nodded. "Agreed. We assure you we'll get General Richard Clifford to talk. One way or another that should lead us to getting our guy. And he'll be punished to the full extent of the law. We're close to uncovering the truth. All evidence points to Richard Clifford being Bullet, the mastermind behind it all."

"That's right." Officer Johnson smiled at Maria. "And we'll bring him down. Don't you worry."

Maria glanced at the officer. A shudder ran down her spine. *Don't worry? But I* am *worried. I have a bad feeling something's not right here.*

CHAPTER 14

"Right here, hun." Elisabeth put Brad's cell phone on the nightstand next to his hospital bed. "Here's your phone. Please text me with any updates. I'll miss you. Are you sure you don't want me to stay?"

Brad smiled at her. "I'm sure. Go with the others. Go and get to know our daughter's friends. And stay close to her. Make sure she's alright."

Elisabeth gave him a kiss. "Yes, I'll keep an eye on her and make sure she's okay. I promise."

"Good. Now go."

She leaned her head against his. Felt his beard stubble on her cheek. *Oh, Brad. I've missed you so much. I don't want to lose another minute with you.* "Wish you could come with us," she whispered into his ear.

"I know, hun, I wish that, too. But you heard the doctor. I have to stay here until I'm in the clear." He sighed.

"I feel bad leaving you all alone." Elisabeth gave him another kiss on the cheek, the beard stubble rough against her soft lips.

"Hey, he's not alone," Drew said from across the room. "He has me, his best bud. No more meetings today, so I'm happy to hang with him here. No worries, I'll keep him entertained."

Elisabeth gave Brad one last kiss, then got up and walked over to Drew. She gave him a pat on the shoulder. "Thanks. Please make sure our patient gets his rest, okay? I need him to heal quickly so he can get out of here as soon as possible."

Drew saluted her. "Yes, ma'am."

Elisabeth smirked. "Thanks, Drew. You're a great friend."

"Oh, I know." He winked at her. "What about your friend? Where's Sarah at?"

Elisabeth pulled her cell phone out of her pocket and checked her messages. "She should be here any minute. She's already with the police escort."

"Quite the vacation for her, huh? Riding in an American police car—more than once! A holiday to remember."

Elisabeth let out a quick laugh. "No kidding. She brought me here to find closure. We opened up a can of worms instead."

Brad smiled. "Lucky for me she convinced you to come back here. We still wouldn't be talking if it wasn't for her."

Elisabeth winked at him. "True. I'm glad she made me come back. We found each other again, and our daughter. What more could I have asked for, right?"

"Exactly," both Brad and Drew agreed, and Elisabeth grinned.

Her grin faded. *Well, I guess there's a few more things. I want everyone to stay safe. And I want the press to leave us alone. Even poor Sarah was hounded by the paparazzi at our Destin resort and had to flee.* She sighed. "I better go catch up with the others. We're meeting Sarah at the back of the hospital. Hopefully we can sneak out without the press seeing us."

Drew walked over to the window and peeked through the blinds. "Seems you've got a good chance of that if you sneak out back. They're all gathered at the front entrance right now. All lined up like lemmings."

"Ugh, I bet." Elisabeth pressed her lips together. "Better get going then." She turned to Brad and waved goodbye. "Bye, hun. Rest up. I love you."

"Love you, too." Brad blew her an air-kiss with his good arm.

"Bye, Drew, thanks for hanging with Brad." Elisabeth walked over and gave him a quick hug.

He squeezed her tight. "Anytime, Elisabeth. I'll take good care of him."

With one last wave, she stepped out of the room and ran right into the big group assembled outside the door. Maria, Aaron, Martina, Jack, and all four of Maria's friends had been waiting for her.

Maria greeted her with a hug. "Hi, Mom."

The warmth of that hug flooded through Elisabeth and made her heart skip. She smelled the flowery shampoo Maria used and an immense happiness engulfed her. A big smile lit up her face. *My daughter. Mein Engel. She's here, she's back. I still can't believe it.*

"So, how's Dad?"

Maria's words brought Elisabeth back to reality. "He's fine. Sad he can't come, but his friend Drew will stay with him."

"That's good." Maria's smile faded. "Though I wish he could come with us."

Elisabeth squeezed her daughter again. "I know, mein Engel. I do, too. But he needs time to rest and heal."

Maria nodded, and Elisabeth recognized sadness in her unique hazel eyes. *Brad's eyes. She looks so much like her dad.*

"C'mon, everybody, I'm starving," Nick yelled. "Can we go already?"

"Not so fast," Maria said. "I have to say goodbye to my dad first."

"I'll come with you, Maria," Aaron said. They both walked into Brad's room.

"I'd like to say goodbye to General Collins." Keisha took Jim by the hand. "And you should, too, Jim. Let's go, boy."

Before long, the entire group had pushed their way back inside Brad's room to give him a hearty goodbye. Elisabeth stayed back and watched the scene. She saw them all talking, a bright smile on Brad's face. Maria next to him on his bed, leaning into him. They were laughing together, their mosaic eyes of golden-and-emerald-green flecks in the dark-brown centers sparkling, lighting up the whole room.

Elisabeth's heart almost burst with happiness at seeing them together. *My Brad. My daughter. We're whole again. A real family.*

The vibration of her phone in her back pocket took her away from the moment. She pulled it out and looked at the text message. *Wo bist du?* it read.

Oh, Sarah. She's here already and looking for me? We better go!

"Hey, guys, my friend Sarah arrived with the police escort. Time for us to go," she told the group.

Martina nodded. "Sí, Elisabeth is right. Can't let the police wait. ¡Vamos!"

It took a while to get the large group moving. Elisabeth's phone beeped again impatiently. She hopped from one leg to the other, felt her heart beat faster with anxiety. Even though Brad was across the room from her, he noticed. "Elisabeth, why don't you go ahead to meet Sarah and the police escort? You guys can figure out who will drive with whom. These guys will catch up with you soon."

She winked at him. *Gosh, he knows me well. He knows how I hate being late. My Brad.* "Sure. Sounds like a good idea. Okay, everyone, see you soon then."

🎭 🎭 🎭

They were all sitting at a big round table in the Officer's Club, a restaurant on Eglin Air Force Base, enjoying the lunch buffet. Elisabeth felt content, so happy, as if her heart might burst with joy. *I just love watching her. My daughter. Laughing with her friends, interacting with her fiancé. She looks so happy surrounded by her loved ones. So different from a few days ago when we sat in this restaurant and didn't know what to say to each other. A lot has happened since. But everything's fine now. She's happy, she's safe—and that's all I need.*

"Alles gut?" Sarah elbowed her.

"Oh, ja, ja," Elisabeth said. "Ich bin einfach glücklich, dass Maria glücklich ist."

"'Glücklich'?" Martina had overheard their back-and-forth. "What does that mean?"

"Oh, it means *happy*. I said in German, 'I'm happy that Maria is happy,'" Elisabeth explained to Martina.

"Sí, happy. Feliz!" Martina took Elisabeth's hand. "I'm happy, too. So happy to see her laugh with her friends and be with Aaron. They are a good couple."

"Yes, they are." Elisabeth gave Martina's hand a quick squeeze.

"Ja, they are," Sarah agreed. "Nice couple."

For a while, the three ladies just listened and watched the young friends joke around and talk. Jack was the only one truly focused on eating; he made regular trips between table and buffet to get more food.

"Hey, they laid out dessert," Jack announced on his latest return.

"Dessert? Fantastic, I love dessert. C'mon, darlings, let's go check it out." Brandy pulled Maria and Keisha up, and the three girls beelined for the buffet.

"Wanna go see what they have, Aaron?" Jim was already on his feet.

"You guys go ahead," Aaron told his friends. "I'm not feeling dessert. Not that hungry."

"But you barely ate, man," Nick protested.

"I'm just not hungry. Maybe it's the pain meds."

"Okay then. Bet your appetite comes back when we return with heaps of good stuff on our plates." Jim patted Aaron on his uninjured shoulder, then left with Nick to join the ladies at the buffet.

Martina raised her eyebrows. "You alright, Aaron, mijo?"

"Yeah, I'm fine. No worries, Martina. Besides, I already know none of the desserts will be able to compare to your homemade ones."

"Aw, charmer." Martina grinned and winked at him.

"I'd love to try some of your homemade stuff one day," Elisabeth said, and took Martina's hand.

"Sí, you will, I promise, Elisabeth. You'll try one day. You have to come visit me. See Miami. See where Maria grew up." Martina bit her lip then, pulled her hand away from Elisabeth, and glanced at her.

"Oh, it's okay, Martina. You know I've forgiven you. You didn't know who Maria really was. And I thank you for keeping her safe all those years," Elisabeth said, and took Martina's hand again. "And yes, I'd love to visit Miami and see where she grew up, the schools, just everything."

"Sí, it's a plan then." Martina smiled, and cupped Elisabeth's hands with both of hers. "And you *must* try my food. My sisters and I make good food. Everyone likes it—even my picky ex liked it."

"Your ex?" Sarah raised her eyebrows. "That... criminal who kidnapped Maria?"

Martina's hand slipped out of Elisabeth's. She sighed and nodded, then stared at her plate.

Elisabeth side-eyed her friend Sarah. "Let's not talk about Jonathan Sullivan now."

"Sullivan? The bad guy? What about him?" Nick said as he sat down at the table with his dessert. "Wasn't he the mean one who got killed in the hospital? Who attacked Maria first?"

Jack, Elisabeth, and Martina all nodded. The whole table was quiet when the girls returned from the buffet.

Maria noticed. "What's going on?"

Jack cleared his throat. "Jonathan Sullivan got brought up. Kinda dampened the mood."

Maria put her plate down roughly. The cake on it briefly jumped into the air and landed in the pudding beside it. "We shouldn't be talking about him right now. He did enough damage. To me and Mamá." She sat down, her face flushed red.

Everyone stayed quiet except for Brandy. "So, what did I miss? How exactly did Jonathan Sullivan damage y'all, Maria?" She turned to face Martina. "I thought you were married to him, Martina, darlin'? I don't understand what Maria means. Don't you marry the person you love?"

Keisha rolled her eyes. "Holy… jeez, girl. Get with the program, Brandy. He *wasn't* nice, and that's why they divorced."

Brandy was dumbfounded. "'Wasn't nice'? What do ya mean? Well, when he attacked Maria that sure wasn't nice but—"

"He was *abusive*," Martina blurted out. "He yelled at me, made me feel like a nothing. Threatened me, threw things at me, hit me. It was domestic abuse. I divorced him and got a restraining order against him."

"Oh my…." Brandy put a hand over her mouth, her eyes wide.

Everyone at the table was silent.

Elisabeth glanced over at Martina and noticed her hands were shaking in her lap. *Poor thing. Just thinking of the guy brings back bad memories.* She put her hands on top of Martina's and stroked them gently. "You're alright, Martina. He's dead now. Can't hurt you or Maria or anyone ever again."

Martina nodded and blinked back tears. Elisabeth kept stroking her hands. *She's a strong woman. She stood up to her abuser. More than once. Not everyone is able to do so.*

Martina took in a deep breath. "Well, everyone, let's eat. Enjoy your dessert—and *don't you dare* tell me it's better than mine." She winked at them.

"It won't be, I can assure you already." Maria smiled at her mamá.

Martina squeezed Elisabeth's hand. "So, should we ladies go get dessert, too, then?"

"Ja, ja, ja." Sarah was already up.

"Sure," Elisabeth agreed, and all three ladies set off for the buffet. While Sarah and Martina deliberated over which desserts to get, Elisabeth stared at Martina's back, lost in thought.

No, not everyone is as strong as Martina. That's why I formed the H.O.P.E. Club back in Utah. There were so many young girls who joined.

All needing help standing up to harassment or abuse. None of them as strong as Martina.

Like a robot, Elisabeth picked up a plate. Stared at its clean, shining white porcelain. *Especially the young Hispanic girl. I don't even remember her name; it was so long ago, but I remember I had to encourage her to stand up to her abuser. She didn't want to. He was a high-up guy. She never said who it was, but I almost got her to the point where she was willing to press charges—but then I left.*

The color drained from Elisabeth's face. *We were so close to holding the high-ranking person who hurt her accountable. She said she'd tell me everything once I came back. I promised her I would. But I never did. Because I lost my daughter....*

She took a step closer to the buffet and tried to focus on the delicious desserts laid out in rows. But her mind was racing. *I gave her hope, then crushed it. Took it all away again by leaving her hanging. By breaking my promise. And now, I can't even remember her name. I'm a terrible person.* The plate in her hand was shaking. *I just left her hanging. Didn't even call to tell her why I couldn't come help anymore. Oh my, what happened to that young woman? She must hate me for abandoning her.*

For a second, Elisabeth closed her eyes to choke back tears. The plate in her hand shook even more. *And her abuser? Did he know we were onto him? She told me this guy was scary, high-ranking, intimidating. Capable of doing anything.*

Suddenly, the plate slipped out of Elisabeth's hand and fell to the floor.

Bang!

Everyone around Elisabeth jumped at the loud noise, but she barely even noticed it. All she could think of was what the chief had told them a couple days ago: *Think of any enemies you might have made. Anyone. That'll help with solving your daughter's case.*

Taking quick breaths, she took out her phone, both hands shaking uncontrollably.

"Elisabeth, are you alright?" she heard Martina say.

"Alles okay, Elisabeth?" Sarah asked.

Her eyes wide, Elisabeth nodded. "I have to call the chief."

"The chief?" Both Sarah and Martina looked at each other.

"I have to tell him about the H.O.P.E. Club in Utah. We might have made more enemies. High-ranking enemies, afraid of being exposed," she whispered. "And others that hate me...."

Martina raised her eyebrows. "¿Qué? Exposed? Enemies? Hating you? Hope Club? I don't understand...."

"I, too, don't understand." Sarah shrugged. "Why would the club you founded in Utah for abuse survivors be interesting to the police? What does this have to do with your daughter's case?"

Elisabeth shrugged. "I don't know, I just have a feeling it's important." She started dialing Chief Parlot's number, her hands still shaking. "And if I'm wrong, we don't lose much by letting him know, right?"

"No, guess not." Martina started picking up pieces of the broken plate. "Go, Elisabeth, we'll take care of this. If you think it's important, go call the chief."

"Thank you." Elisabeth walked toward the big window overlooking the bay. Her legs wobbly, her hands still shaking, she dialed the chief's number. And while she wasn't sure why her emotions were in turmoil, just like the emerald-green water crashing ashore outside the window, something about remembering the H.O.P.E Club had brought on a terribly bad feeling.

CHAPTER 15

"Feeling tired?" Sally asked Tom, who was staring at his computer screen, no longer typing like crazy as he usually did.

He yawned and nodded.

"Lucky you, I just picked up two energy drinks for us." Sally handed one to Tom.

"Awesome, thanks." Tom grabbed it, then both he and Sally went back to their research while sipping at their beverages.

The door opened, Chief Parlot and Tonya Anderson walked in. "Listen up, team. We've got news," the chief said.

Sally turned her swivel chair around, her eyes wide and sparkling. "Are General Clifford and his wife ready to talk?"

Tom stopped typing. "That'd be great." He took another sip of his energy drink, then turned around as well, his eyes on the bosses.

Tonya winked at them. "Nah, you youngsters are too eager. The Cliffords are still with their lawyer, and will be for quite a while, we suspect." She pointed at Chief Parlot and herself. "Nope, we got a call from Elisabeth Collins."

Sally raised her eyebrows. "Elisabeth Collins? Why? What did she say?"

The chief cleared his throat. "It seems she's brainstormed more potential enemies."

"More… enemies? I don't understand. Don't we have the main suspect?" Tom looked from one person to the next.

"According to Elisabeth, there's something more to the Collins family story we didn't know about. Back when they were stationed at Hill Air Force Base in Utah, not long before Maria's kidnapping, Elisabeth founded the"—Chief Parlot looked at his notepad—"*H.O.P.E. Club*, a branch of the spouses' club on base. The first letters are an abbreviation for 'Hear Our Personal Experience.' It's a club for women—not just spouses of active-duty Airmen, but active-duty women working in the Air Force who didn't get the same opportunities as their male counterparts. It was originally supposed to be an outlet to talk about how to enhance those women's career opportunities, but discussion often turned to problems of misogyny. Work-related harassment, abuse of power, and so on."

"Yeah, Mrs. Collins apparently poked a hornet's nest," Tonya continued. "Turns out, the Air Force's male-dominated workspace not only denied these women the same rights and opportunities as their male counterparts, but made fun of them, harassed them, even forced them into doing things they didn't want to do."

Sally's eyes went wide. "You mean, like, sexual harassment?"

Chief Parlot sighed. "Apparently so."

Tonya exhaled deeply. "Nothing new, but still shocking."

Tom swallowed hard, then cleared his throat. "While I agree it's shocking and shouldn't happen anywhere, I do wonder what this has to do with Maria's kidnapping?"

Tonya winked at him. "That's the million-dollar question, my man."

"Apparently, these young women complained about some very high-up Air Force officers who were misusing their power to do some very shady, illegal things," Chief Parlot said. "Mrs. Collins doesn't have names, but some high-ranking officers—possibly even some generals— were included in the accused. And it was apparently going on for quite a while before Elisabeth Collins even founded that club."

Sally's mouth fell open. "Whoa."

"Wait, wait, let me get this straight." Tom spun around in his swivel chair as he sorted his thoughts. "We're now talking about combing through service members at Hill Air Force Base who possibly abused their power and harassed women? High-ranking Air Force personnel?"

Tonya nodded. "Yep. Let's see if some familiar faces pop up."

"You mean, like, General Clifford?" asked Sally.

"Maybe," the chief said. "Even though he was retired by that point, there might have been issues back when he served. Or maybe he knew someone who granted him post-retirement access to young, impressionable female Airmen? You never know…. Anyway, we have to make sure. Dig deep into his whole career. Find out if he was ever stationed in Utah."

"Come on, team, let's get to work," Tonya said. "We want to be ready to push our case at the next scheduled press conference."

Tom nodded and turned his swivel chair toward his laptop. Within seconds, his hands were flying across the keyboard. Except for the sounds of typing, the room fell silent, all of them focused on their research.

🎭 🎭 🎭

"Tom, you find anything?" the chief asked the young FBI agent, who just shook his head. "Then we know for a fact General Clifford was never stationed in Utah, nor was he close to anyone else who was."

Tom nodded while chewing on his lower lip. "I can't find anything at all placing him at Hill Air Force Base at any point."

"But we do have proof he was in Utah to meet his son there. In a hotel," Sally said. "So maybe he and his son Mike made up, then Mike took him on base to meet some—you know—young…" Her face drooped down, her eyes watering. She shook herself. "Ugh, disgusting. I can't even consider the possibility."

Chief Parlot gave her a pat on the shoulder. "It's alright, Sally, I understand. We witness a lot of horrifying stuff on the job, don't we? But we can only bring the general down if we find proof. Until then, he and his son meeting young ladies stationed at Hill AFB who ended up in Elisabeth's H.O.P.E. Club remains an assumption on our part, doesn't it?"

Sally nodded; Tom and Tonya agreed.

The chief sighed. *Well, Elisabeth Collins's club might not have anything to do with the case after all. We do have proof, though, that General Richard Clifford met his son both in Utah and Vegas. He must be our guy. Bullet.*

"Well, well, team, no new news then, right? Mrs. Collins was on the wrong track with her tip. Motive is still the general revenging his son, right?" Tonya said.

Everyone agreed. Chief Parlot started pacing and chewing on his pen. *I'm not so sure. Does that make sense? Sure points that direction. It's a plausible motive. But are we missing something? Something else?* He thought back to what Maria had said earlier. *Could it be possible we have the wrong Bullet?*

Tonya checked her watch. "Well, my man Isaac, guess the H.O.P.E. Club has nothing to do with this. Mrs. Collins herself said she had no idea if it would turn out important or not, and we've determined it's not. Right?"

Chief Parlot stopped in front of her and nodded, still chewing on his pen. Said nothing more.

"Well, my man, we better get going." Tonya pointed at her watch. "Almost time for the next presser. We got a little fresh meat to feed the hungry sharks out there. Can inform them what we've found out about General Richard Clifford so far. Let's go over our notes, *shall we?*"

Even though his mind was still racing, the chief smiled at her. "Yeah, sure, we shall." They sat down at the table and went over their notes until it was time to meet the press.

"Chief, you told us earlier you have proof General Richard Clifford met his son Mike Clifford on separate occasions in Utah and Las Vegas," one of the reporters said. "So now you're saying the general is definitely the mastermind behind Maria's kidnapping? You have proof he's the mysterious Bullet, the last unidentified member of the Fearless Four? And you know for a fact the general's motive was revenge for Brad Collins getting his son Mike Clifford dismissed from the Air Force Academy? That's why he masterminded the kidnapping of Brad Collins's daughter?"

Chief Parlot opened his mouth to answer, but somehow the words wouldn't come out. *I'm not so sure anymore.* That was all he could think of as he stared at the press sitting in front of him.

Tonya took a moment to notice the chief had frozen and finally answered for him. "Yes, so far, that's what we suspect. After all, General Richard Clifford was not only in Vegas at the same time as the Fearless Four, but he also helped bury the fact that his son Mike got kicked out of the Air Force Academy. Mike Clifford's current public record shows he decided to drop out, but we have proof that General Clifford, who knew the dean of the Air Force Academy very well, met with him a few years later and had his son's record cleaned up before Mike got started in politics."

Another reporter stood up. "But General Clifford never endorsed his son, not even when he became Florida's senator. They weren't close when Mike Clifford was in politics. We have several interviews with Senator Clifford saying he and his dad were estranged. Are you claiming he lied?"

The chief kept staring straight ahead, deep in thought. *No, the senator didn't lie. They weren't close. But maybe they forgave each other. Never really went to visit each other much, though, our records show.*

Tonya elbowed him, but he just stared at her, so she went ahead. "No, that's not a lie. Father and son were estranged when Mike became senator. But there was a small window of time where we think they

PUPPETS OF THE PAST

made up and mended their relationship. Which was right around the time of Moana Collins's disappearance."

One reporter after the other got up and they all started throwing out tons of questions.

"Do you have hard proof for that?"

"Isn't that claim too far-fetched?"

"Were they *that* close? So close they masterminded a crime together?"

"What he said. Unless they were very close, they wouldn't even take a chance to commit a crime together."

"Exactly. Seems strange."

"Chief, sounds like you're guessing here?"

Chief Parlot swallowed hard. *They're right. I share their doubt. We still don't have good proof for any of this. We're guessing. Missing something.*

"Please, ladies and gentlemen, sit back down and let's do this one question at a time. I can't hear all of you babbling at the same time," Tonya said.

After a collective sigh, the reporters took their seats again. One young man raised his hand, and Tonya pointed at him. He stood. "What did General Richard Clifford and Mrs. Clifford say to these accusations? Did they confirm with you they were close to their son again?"

"Well," Tonya said, then slightly elbowed Chief Parlot. He didn't react. She sighed and went on. "General and Mrs. Clifford are still with their lawyer."

Another reporter jumped up. "You haven't even interrogated them yet?"

Tonya shook her head. "Not yet."

"Chief! All this is speculation on your part? Wow, that's unprofessional," another reporter yelled out. "Just as much as letting your gun out of sight. What do you have to say to that, Chief?"

Turmoil broke out again.

"Yeah, Chief, what do you have to say to that?"

"Are you accusing an innocent couple of a crime they didn't commit?"

"Where's the hard proof?"

"Are you sure the senator wasn't the mastermind behind this after all?"

"Who the heck is Bullet anyway?"

"Chief, do you know *anything* anymore? Are you even mentally fit to lead this investigation?"

Tonya elbowed her colleague hard behind the podium and Chief Parlot finally reacted—all the reporters' questions made it to his ears. He snapped out of his thoughts and took the mic. "Ladies and gentlemen, please settle down. We understand how upsetting this all is. And believe me, we're upset, too. We hope to question both General and Mrs. Clifford as soon as we can to find out exactly why he met with his son around the time young Moana Collins disappeared. We *do* have proof that happened. Just as we *do* have proof he resumed financial support of his son at that time."

The press finally fell quiet, all of them scribbling notes on their notepads, phones, and iPads.

"There's still a lot of unknowns. While we are waiting for the Cliffords to make themselves available for interrogation, I need *your* help." Chief Parlot now pointed at the reporters. They all stared at him, as well as Tonya.

"We need your help with investigating a lead given to us just hours ago by Elisabeth Collins. Twenty years ago she formed a social club. My team is currently researching that club to see if the Collinses made any other enemies at the time, someone who desired to hurt them. Someone we don't expect. Someone who might have had a motive to help—possibly organize—the kidnapping of the Collinses' daughter."

"What club ya talking about, Chief?" one of the reporters yelled out, and all of them eagerly nodded.

"The H.O.P.E. Club at Hill Air Force Base, Utah. The first letters are an abbreviation for 'Hear Our Personal Experience.' Elisabeth

Collins is the one who founded this support club for women originally thought to be an outlet to talk about how to help active-duty women get the same opportunities as their male counterparts. However, seems like the club's focus evolved over time as work-related harassment and abuse of power came to light. It might have come close to exposing some sort of scandal on base." Chief Parlot looked directly into the camera now, pointed at his audience. "If anyone out there has any information on wrongdoing associated with the H.O.P.E. Club, no matter how long ago it happened, please contact us immediately. Thank you so much."

CHAPTER 16

Thank you so much? Lu felt as if the Niceville police chief had been speaking right to her. All color drained from her face. She couldn't believe what she had just heard on the news. *A scandal within the H.O.P.E. Club? Oh no. They can't. They just* cannot *find out about that.*

She closed down the live news report on her phone and stood up from her leather seat inside the Orlando airport. She checked the monitor by her new gate again. Saw it, too, said *DELAYED.* None of the airplane passenger service assistants were there; not even the plane was there yet.

She sighed. *I just want to go home. I just want to see my husband, Daniel. I need him. Now more than ever.*

Lu realized her hands were shaking. The phone in her hand was shaking. Before anyone could notice, she put it in one of the large pockets of her camo uniform, then briefly closed her eyes. *Nobody can ever find out about this. I promised him. If it gets out, it'll ruin my reputation. My career. Everything I've worked for.*

She opened her eyes again, took in a deep breath, and glanced around. Everyone was still scattered across the rows of chairs, waiting for the delayed plane to come, to take them to Texas. Then her eyes caught the blinking monitor above her gate that had just updated. She gasped. "Oh no."

PUPPETS OF THE PAST

Another passenger waiting in the rows of chairs looked up at her. "You alright, ma'am?"

Lu pointed at the monitor. "Yeah, I guess. But look."

The stranger followed her gaze. Stared at the words on the monitor. "*FLIGHT CANCELED*," it read.

The stranger jumped up. "What? Canceled *again*? This flight, too? But I have to get back to Texas today."

More and more people got up, some sighing, others mumbling, some yelling, some swearing.

Lu stopped staring at the monitor. *Guess I better look for yet another flight out of here before I get stuck in Orlando overnight.* She picked up her carry-on luggage and was about to hunt down an airline agent when she felt her phone buzzing in her pants pocket. She set her bag down again and pulled out the phone. A text message from Daniel.

Hey, hun, just saw online your new flight got canceled. Already checked other flights. Not looking good. Weather bad here. Bad storms. Sounds like no planes coming or going over San Antonio today anymore. Sucks. I miss you.

"Oh shoot," Lu mumbled, and texted her husband back, then made for the nearest airline agent to talk to. She made her way through the terminal and stumbled upon a long line that had formed in front of customer support. With another deep sigh, she took her place in line, her thoughts all over the place.

She barely noticed when a young woman in front of her turned around and started talking at her. "Do you have the airline's app? It's much faster rebooking on there. I just found a flight while waiting in line. Last one going out tonight, if the weather cooperates. Get on it quickly before it's all booked out."

Lu smiled at the woman. "Great idea. Thank you so much."

The stranger started gathering her belongings and left the line. "Good luck, ma'am."

"Thanks." Lu waved goodbye, then scooted up in line, taking the now-empty spot where the woman had been standing. There were still a lot of people in front of her. *I better try out that app.*

She took out her phone, and it started vibrating in her hand. She grinned. *Probably Daniel.* Without looking, she took the call. She froze when she heard his voice, a dark voice she hadn't heard in years.

"You better take care of this," the man barked in her ear. "If the police find out about the H.O.P.E. Club, you and me both go down. Your career will die a horrible death. You know that, don't you?"

Lu didn't know what to say, couldn't say anything. She wanted to scream at him, tell him the only one who'd be going down for what had happened was him, but the words refused to leave her mouth. They were stuck in her throat, practically strangling her.

Her head started spinning. *Or is he simply speaking the truth? Losing my career will be the least of my worries.*

"Keep your former friend in line. I know how close you were. I know you confided in her. So stop her, now, from saying anything further. You hear me?"

Stop her? How can I stop her? I haven't spoken to her in twenty years!

"Lulu-girl, you better do what I say. I don't care how you do it, but *do your damn job.* And I'm sure you know you don't want to piss *me* off, do you?"

Lu shook her head as if he could see her. *No, Lulu-girl doesn't want to piss you off.* A tear ran down her face.

"I know you play the tough general now, but we both know, deep down inside, you're still Lulu-girl, aren't you?"

Silent tears streamed down her cheeks now. She wished she could just hang up on him, hang up so she didn't have to hear his voice anymore, his dark, barking voice, his demands. Just hang up on him, stop the pain his voice brought back. But she couldn't. She was unable to do anything, unable to move, unable to hang up—the phone pressed to her ear as if an invisible hand was commanding her own hand, pushing the phone against her ear.

"Lulu-girl, I know you're listening. I hear you breathing. I like that. Always liked it. And I know you've always been a good girl. So now, be a good Lulu-girl again and *do as I say.*" His voice, now soft, singsongy, almost nice-sounding and comforting. But then he barked into her ear, "Stop the crazy Collins bitch now! Go now. Visit her, stop her, or else..."

Beep, beep, beep.

The dial tone. He'd hung up. Lu hadn't moved at all, was still pressing the phone to her ear, the beeping tone echoing down every slope of her brain. Her silent tears dried up in horror, leaving behind tiny salty trails on her face.

"Excuse me, ma'am," she heard, and felt a tap on her shoulder.

Without warning, she turned around, her face bright red now, her dark-brown eyes glowing in anger, her hands—one still holding the phone, the other raised in defense in front of her face—ready to hit. "Don't touch me," she growled.

Lu eyed her aggressor but only saw a mom holding a baby standing before her. The mom stared back at her, eyes wide with fear. The baby started crying.

Lu snapped out of it. "Oh my goodness, I'm so sorry, ma'am. I didn't know who was tapping my shoulder, and I..."

"Were you deployed, ma'am?" the mom asked as she comforted her baby.

"Err... yeah, but..."

"No worries, ma'am, I understand. Never surprise a soldier, I guess. I'm sorry," the mom said, the baby quietly sucking on a pacifier.

"Oh, yeah, I suppose." Lu blushed. "I didn't mean to scare you."

"I know. I understand. I was just trying to tell you, the line's moved up. You might want to step up to close the gap."

Lu saw there was a dozen feet of empty space in front of her now. "Oh, yes... thank you, ma'am. But please, go ahead." Lu gestured for the lady and her baby to cut in front of her.

"Oh no"—the mom shook her head—"you got in line before us. We don't want to skip."

Lu smiled at her now, then waved at the baby. She saw the baby's big blue eyes light up as it gave a little giggle. *Aw, sweet little thing. Wish I had kids. But I couldn't. Not after...*

"Aw, you made my little one laugh. You're very good with kids, ma'am."

"Yeah, I suppose." Lu smiled and stepped out of line. "Please, go ahead. Not just because I'm embarrassed about my behavior, but also because I just learned you can get a new flight using the airline's app." She held up her phone. "It's faster."

"Oh, I see. Well, I don't have the app and I'd like to speak to a real person. Hard to rebook myself and a lap child, you know."

"I bet. Well, good luck to you, ma'am. Bye, little one." Lu waved to the mom and her baby. The baby waved back at her. *Aw, cutest little thing.*

Lu had almost forgotten the nasty phone call, but it all came rushing back to her. Quickly, she found a seat at a gate to sit down and collect her thoughts. *What should I do now? Stop Elisabeth? Which means stopping her daughter as well, I suppose. But how? I don't have their contact info. I don't know how to reach either one of them.*

Then a smile crossed her face. *But I do know where they are currently. They're all over the news.* She opened the airline app on her phone and researched flights. Her grin broadened. *Yeah, Lulu-girl will listen. He's been good to me, and I need to listen to him.* With one click, she changed her ticket. Her new destination: Valparaiso's Destin-Fort Walton Beach Airport, right next to Eglin AFB.

CHAPTER 17

"**E**glin AFB? I? I stay on base?" Sarah's wide eyes peered at her friend Elisabeth questioningly.

Elisabeth smiled. "Natürlich, Sarah, warum nicht? Why not? We're already here on base anyway, you have your visitor's pass all set, and the press is swarming the old resort. To get away from those nasty paparazzi, just stay at the Air Force Inn with us."

Maria smiled at Sarah. "I think that's a great idea."

"Si, a great idea," Martina agreed. "Just stay with all of us. The whole group. All the young people are at the inn also."

"Yeah, Maria will have a whole support group just for her," Nick said. "That's what we all want, right? We're here to support Maria."

"*And* Aaron." Jim grinned, then gave his friend a pat on his uninjured shoulder.

"Sure, and Aaron. We're here to support the both of them." Nick winked at the young couple while Keisha and Brandy nodded, a smile on both their faces.

"Thanks, guys. Well, vamos, everyone. Let's head to the inn." Maria led the way out of the Officer's Club. Everyone piled into their cars and drove to the inn.

After they were all settled into their rooms, they met downstairs in the lounge. The friends started playing card games together while trying to teach Sarah and Elisabeth how to play. There was a lot of laughter at the two German ladies' expense given they had no idea how to play even the most basic American card games and constantly did things wrong.

"That's it, I give up." Elisabeth laughed, and threw down her cards.

Martina picked up the pile of cards and pushed them back into Elisabeth's hands. "No, no, you first learn to play. I had to learn, too." She winked at Elisabeth. "How about I sit this one out instead? Easier for you with less players. I'll just watch."

"Nein, you need to play too," Sarah said, but Martina shook her head.

"I'll just watch a bit and maybe catch up with my sisters." Martina wiggled her phone. "You know, they worry. Texting constantly."

Elisabeth winked at her. "Fine, Martina, you get a pass—but only once!"

"Ja, ja, just the one time." Sarah raised her thumb and waved it at Martina.

Everyone tilted their heads in curiosity as they watched Sarah's thumb. Martina raised an eyebrow. "Are you giving me a thumbs-up?"

Sarah looked at her raised thumb. "No, *one time*. I'm telling you with my finger—one time you cannot play. One. Eins."

Elisabeth started laughing. "I see the confusion now. In Germany, when we count with our hands, we start with our thumbs instead of our pointer fingers like you do here in America. Sarah isn't giving you a thumbs-up, Martina. She's telling you to only sit out once and counting it off with her thumb."

Everyone started laughing, while Sarah just stared at her still-raised thumb.

"Wow, y'all, talk about 'lost in translation,' huh?" Brandy grinned from ear to ear. "Still, what an interesting thing to learn."

"Very cool, I agree," Keisha said, and turned to Maria. "Do you remember learning to count thumbs-first when you were little?"

Martina saw sadness wash over Maria's face as she shook her head. Martina glanced at Elisabeth and saw her smile fade as well. *Oh dear, and we were having such a good time. I need to help out, help them get back to that. To happiness.*

"Well, fine then, I'll sit out only *eins*," Martina said, trying her best to pronounce the German word, which got Elisabeth smiling again.

"No, Martina, that's not quite right, you'd say: Ich spiele dieses eine Mal nicht mit."

"¿Qué?" Martina looked dumbfounded, which made Maria and everyone else laugh. "I will not even attempt to say that. No hablo alemana."

"What?" Elisabeth looked at Martina. "What did you say?"

Maria grinned. "Oh dear. My two moms... Guess we better stick to English, huh?"

"Yes, please, y'all," Brandy agreed. "I, for one, am totally lost."

"Okay," both Elisabeth and Martina said in unison, then winked at each other.

"So keep playing, everyone, and teach these German ladies some good American card games. I'll sit this one out and watch."

"Okay, Mamá, sounds good." Maria gave an approving nod.

Martina moved over to a chair further away from the whole group. *That went well. Crisis averted.* With a smile on her face, Martina watched the group socialize. *So good mija's friends are here. She needs a distraction. She needs fun. Needs to forget the terrible things that happened to her. Needs to forget Sullivan. And Clifford. And that she killed a man....*

Martina's face went pale. *¡Dios mío! She killed a man. In self-defense, yes, but... Poor mija.* She watched Maria's every move, enjoyed her laughter, her joking around. *I need you to be happy, mija. You've been through a lot. Too much.* She sighed. *And I'm part of the reason you were attacked. I should've called the police when Jonathan dropped you off at my doorstep. But then I would've never had you as my daughter....*

Loud, warm laughter drew Martina's attention. She watched as Elisabeth chortled over another game she'd lost in spectacular fashion. Martina saw her, her daughter's other mom, lay her head on Maria's shoulder, how Maria wrapped an arm around her. They turned to look at each other, their eyes sparkling, the little dimples on both their cheeks popping out in a big smile.

Tears dwelled in Martina's eyes. *Maria and her mom Elisabeth. They belong together. Finally, they are together again. A beautiful mother–daughter team. And me? Is there still room for me? Might be best if I wasn't here anymore. Let them have their time together… oh, but I love Maria so much….*

A touch on her shoulder made her jump. "Oh, I'm sorry, Martina, I didn't mean to startle you," came a soft, male voice.

She swiveled in her seat. It was Jack standing behind her, smiling at her. She quickly wiped away her somber thoughts and concentrated on Aaron's dad. "Oh, hi, Jack. You've come down to join the fun?"

He laughed. "No, I better not play. I get way too competitive with these games."

"I see. Well, join me then?"

Jack sat down next to her. "Sure. What are you up to?"

"Oh, just watching. And thinking, I guess." She blinked back tears from her big brown eyes.

Jack sighed. "Yeah, this week's been a lot, huh? I just watched the chief's press conference up in my room."

"You did? And?"

"Sounds like the chief's taking Elisabeth's idea seriously."

Martina raised her eyebrows. "'Idea'?"

"Well, *tip* is a better word, I suppose," Jack said. "The chief asked the press and those watching on TV to help his team. They want to investigate whether Elisabeth's H.O.P.E. Club resulted in the Collinses making some enemies we don't know about yet."

"Really? The chief said that?"

Jack nodded. "Yeah."

"So the chief doesn't think General Richard Clifford is the one behind Maria's kidnapping?" Martina's brown eyes were wide now.

"He said he's not sure," Jack admitted. "He expressed some doubt on the matter, made it sound like there might be another Bullet out there."

Martina jumped up. "So this isn't the end? Maria still is not safe?"

Jack shrugged. "I don't know. We'll just have to wait and see. Let the police do their research. And maybe encourage Elisabeth to think back on her time with the H.O.P.E Club. Maybe she can remember a specific event, a specific name? We should ask her."

Martina plopped back down in the chair and nodded. She looked over at the group, laughing, playing, without a care in the world other than to enjoy the card game they were playing. *They all seem so innocent. So careless. Just loving being together, as if on a fun vacation.* She said to Jack, "Let's not interrupt right now. Look, they're so happy, having so much fun. Forgetting the serious situation for once. Let's talk to Elisabeth later, okay?"

Jack nodded. "That's fine. Let's talk to her later to see if she has any idea who Bullet could possibly be, if it's not Mike Clifford's father."

CHAPTER 18

*F*ather. *He always called me Father. And I loved him for it. Oh, Mike. I still can't believe you're dead.* He let out a deep sigh and stared out the window. Outside the sun was shining bright, a big yellow ball in the clear, blue sky illuminating the many cacti growing outside his window. The big, solitary oak tree amidst them threw its shade onto the scraggy grass surrounding the building.

I swear I'll avenge you, Mike. I sure will. And Lulu-girl will help me. Well. She'll do my dirty work for me. He grinned from one ear to the next. *All we need to do is shut up the Collins girls. Both of them, if need be.*

His grin faded. *But can Lulu-girl do it? Can she do this on her own?* He started pacing back and forth along the window, from one end to the other, scratching his chin, which was as prickly as the cacti outside. He had his best ideas when he paced. He was always pacing, always had, especially while in the office. Sure drove people nuts sometimes, those working with him and sharing office space, but he just had to move to think.

I need them to stop digging into this stupid fucking H.O.P.E. Club. How did the police even get that name? We buried that business. It was taken care of. Mike's real dad would've made for such a fine scapegoat. And he deserves it. Never cared for his son. Not like I did. In the eyes of the public, General Clifford would've made the perfect Bullet.

He laughed. *But he's too weak. Not like me. I'm like my namesake. Always hit my target, always headed where I ought to be. And don't step into my way—otherwise, Bullet will get you. Just like a real bullet.*

He stopped to peer out the window at a cactus with a beautiful red flower on it. He smiled. *Wonderful, delicate flower. The girls always loved the flowers. It was consensual. Always. At least that's what I would say if someone ever found out.... But they never did—and they won't. It's enough they've already taken Mike away from me. The only person I ever gave a damn about.*

Damn it! He slammed his fist into the window. The whole window shook, blurring the image of the flower on the cactus.

Back and forth he paced again. A loud beep interrupted his thoughts, a vibration against his leg. *My phone.*

He took the phone out of his pocket and looked at it, then grinned. *Good girl, Lulu. Good girl. Glad you're about to meet your old friend and her long-lost daughter at Eglin. Have to admit, it was a great idea on your part.* He laughed out loud. *Who knew you could be so wicked, Lulu-girl? Beautiful and wicked. I like that combo.*

The thought of her made his heart beat faster. His hands got sweaty, his excitement grew. The phone almost slipped from his hands, but he caught it in time, reined himself in before he could get lost in his fantasies. Clearing his mind, he texted back, *Good. Keep me posted.*

He grinned. *She's always been my favorite. Sassy yet submissive. Strong yet weak. A girl of many faces. And so beautiful. Lulu-girl. Made a deal with the devil. With me.*

He laughed again. *A damn good deal. For the both of us. It worked out well all these years. Very well. Little does Lulu-girl know why it worked so well. How I hold her strings in my hand. Yeah, me, I'm the master. The master puppeteer. And I like to keep all my puppets in line. Lined up to my liking.*

He plopped down on the soft couch near the window, his green eyes fixated on the beautiful red cactus flower hanging in the dry air. Its beauty brought him a sense of calm. *Beautiful flower. Just as pretty as my Lulu-girl. She'll take care of it. I have faith in her. In my girl.*

CHAPTER 19

"**M**y girl, what's the plan?" Keisha's big, dark-brown eyes rested on Maria.

Maria shrugged. Empty pizza cartons lay in between the card games. Sarah, Elisabeth, Martina, Jack, Aaron, and the rest of their friends leaned back against the lounge chairs of the Air Force Inn's lobby. Nick rubbed his belly. "That pizza was good, wasn't it? I'm nice and full."

"Me, too." Jim started yawning. "And tired. Been a long day after that long drive."

Keisha laughed. "Goodness, boys, you're getting old. It's only eight."

"That's usually the time we're just getting started with our nighttime activities, right, y'all?" Brandy said. "But Jim's right, today was exceptional. I'm tired, too, darlin's."

"I guess we did drive all through the night last night. Maybe it'll be good to turn in soon? Rest and relax in our rooms?" Keisha turned to Maria. "What do you think, girl?"

"Yeah, sounds good," Maria whispered. *But I don't want to rest and relax. Being alone with my thoughts will only bring back bad memories. And nightmares will haunt me in my sleep.* She glanced at Aaron, who didn't say a word. *And him, too. My poor fiancé. Last night's attack was hard on both of us.*

Elisabeth interrupted her thoughts. "I want to go back to see Brad. I think I'll stay the night with him at the hospital. Sarah, you can have our room to yourself, okay?"

Sarah nodded. "Ja, das ist okay."

"Should we call it a night then and head up?" Jack looked at everyone. "There's plenty on the TV to watch."

Jim yawned again. "Sounds good to me. Besides, we need to be fit for tomorrow. Finally unloading that truck of yours and moving you into your new apartment, right, Aaron?"

Aaron nodded. "Way past due. I gotta return that truck, but first I need to move all those boxes into our new place."

Nick laughed. "You won't be moving anything with that injury of yours. We'll take care of it for you all by ourselves, right, guys?"

"Can't wait to see your new apartment, y'all." Brandy yawned. "But lifting heavy boxes sounds exhausting. Better head upstairs and get some rest."

Drew, who was still in his business suit after joining the group at the end of his workday, got up and stretched. "Sounds good to me. I'm ready to head up. It's been a long day between all the meetings and time with Brad." He turned to Elisabeth and paused. "Do you want me to drive you over to the hospital to see him?"

"No, *I* want to," Maria blurted out. "I want to say goodnight to my dad."

"If you're going, I'm going," Aaron said.

Martina patted him on his good shoulder. "But, Aaron, you need to rest your arm. And I don't think anyone with a concussion should drive. That means you, Maria. You need your rest, too."

"If you're worried about us, Mamá, just come along. You can drive us."

"Well, mija, don't know about that," Martina said.

She glanced at Elisabeth, then at the young base police officer Lieutenant Martinez, who was still on duty watching over the large group. He took the hint. "I can escort you all," the lieutenant said.

"So what do you say, Mom?" Maria turned to Elisabeth and saw she was thinking. "Please?"

A smile came over Elisabeth's face. "Sure, mein Engel, you and Aaron and Martina can all come."

Martina took a step forward. "Are you sure, Elisabeth? I can stay here. I just don't want Maria or Aaron to drive back home alone. I know they'll have an escort, but I'm always worried—"

Elisabeth's hug interrupted her. "I know, Martina, I know. You're always worrying about Maria. As do I. I think it'd be great if you drove with us and watched over Maria and Aaron on the way back to base. Come on then, let's go."

A wide smile lit up Martina's face. "¡Sí, vamos!"

They all said goodnight to each other. As the big group went upstairs to their rooms, Aaron, Maria, Martina, and Elisabeth walked outside to Maria's car. Martina got into the driver's seat, Aaron sat in the passenger seat, Elisabeth and Maria the backseat. Lieutenant Martinez followed in his official vehicle as their car rolled out of the parking lot.

Martina, Aaron, and Maria chitchatted while Elisabeth kept quiet, watching the palm trees fly past outside the window.

Finally, she whispered, "Not many reporters out tonight."

"What's that?" Maria took Elisabeth's hand. "What did you say?" Maria studied her birth mom's face. *She looks upset. Why? Because Dad's in the hospital? Or about me?*

"Oh, I just noticed there aren't as many reporters around anymore."

"I noticed that, too," Aaron said. "That's good. Though I do wonder where they all are."

Martina snorted. "Probably doing research. The chief sure keeps them busy."

All eyes were on Martina now.

"What?" Maria asked.

She cleared her throat. "Well, Aaron's dad told me that the chief had the press conference where he asked for help investigating Elisabeth's H.O.P.E. Club. Sounds like the chief believed you, Elisabeth. He wants to find out more. And asked the reporters to look into it. Into some kind of scandal."

Maria felt Elisabeth's hand get clammy in hers. With narrowed eyes, she glanced at her mom, who went back to staring out the window. *What isn't she telling us? Is she hiding something?*

"Scandal? H.O.P.E. Club? What did I miss?" Aaron turned around to look at Maria and Elisabeth in the backseat. Maria just shrugged; Elisabeth kept staring out of the window.

"Well, sounds like there might be more enemies, no?" Through the rearview mirror, Martina glanced at Elisabeth.

Maria felt her mom's hand stiffen in her hold. *What's going on here?* "Mom? Can you fill us in?" Maria squeezed her mom's damp, stiff hand. "Please?"

Elisabeth let out a sigh. "You already know I founded the H.O.P.E. Club as part of the spouses' club back in Utah."

"Yeah, I remember you talking about that," Aaron said. "The letters in H.O.P.E. stand for 'Hear Our Personal Experience.' It's a club for military women, not just spouses but active-duty women working in the Air Force. Women you wanted to help, right?"

Elisabeth nodded. "It was meant for women who didn't get the same work opportunities as their male counterparts. It was supposed to be an outlet to think up ideas on how to help those women better their career opportunities."

"So?" Aaron raised an eyebrow. "I mean, that sounds great… but what does it have to do with Maria's kidnapping?"

"Through my efforts with the H.O.P.E. Club, I discovered that the male-dominated Air Force workplace wasn't merely denying these women the same rights as their male counterparts—it was worse, much worse. Women were made fun of, harassed, some forced into doing things they didn't want to do. Some were sexually harassed. And… you know… I just…"

Maria felt her mom's hand shaking in hers. She held on tight. "What, Mom? What is it?"

"There was this one young girl who confided in me. She'd been raped by a high-ranking officer."

"Oh my gosh…" Maria squeezed hard, this time from her own distress.

Aaron turned around, his lips pressed together. "That's terrible. Unbelievable, actually. And disgusting. But still, my question is: what does that have to do with Maria?"

Suddenly, Elisabeth ripped her hand out of Maria's. Her voice sharp, she said, "I don't know, okay? I just told the chief there might be more enemies. I don't know if the guy who did this to the young lady was onto us. Or if *she* hates me because I… because I…" Tears were welling in Elisabeth's blue eyes.

Maria studied her mom's face. *She's about to cry? Why? What's up with this club?* "What, Mom? What's got you rattled? I can see how upset you are."

Elisabeth started sobbing. "I… I… You should've seen that young girl's face. She was so broken, so vulnerable. Thought it was her fault. But it wasn't…" Maria rubbed her mom's shoulder. "And she finally believed me. She finally wanted to face her abuser, bring him to justice. But then we had to move, Brad and I. Away from Utah. To Florida. I promised the girl I'd come back, go to the police with her. Be there to support her during the trial. But then… you know…" Elisabeth burst into tears.

Oh no, she's crying. I can't stand seeing her cry. My poor mom. What's happening? Maria had to blink back her own tears and took a deep breath in. "What then, Mom? What's making you so upset? You can tell us."

"I failed. I let her down. I never did any of those things I promised. Because we got to Florida and we… you…" Elisabeth buried her face in her hands.

"Then Maria got kidnapped." Aaron ended Elisabeth's sentence.

"I was so broken myself after I lost my daughter. Never made it back to Utah. I never helped the girl out. What happened to her? And what of her abuser? Did I make it all worse? I don't even remember her name." Elisabeth whispered, "I'm just a terrible person."

"No you're not," everyone else said in unison.

"Everyone here understands you couldn't go see her," Martina said, her voice firm. "You had just lost your baby girl. Your life was falling apart. Elisabeth, it's not your fault. Whatever happened to that young lady, she must have understood."

Silence for a bit, then Aaron asked, "Did she know?"

"What?" Elisabeth wiped her tears away.

"The young girl. Did she find out you lost your daughter? You told her?"

Elisabeth shook her head. "No. I never spoke to her again, just disappeared like a ghost into myself. But I assume she saw it on the news."

"Interesting," Aaron mumbled, then turned around to look outside the passenger side window.

Maria studied his side profile. *He's got his thinking cap on. I just know he's up to something.* "Aaron, what are you thinking?"

He turned to Martina. "What exactly did the chief say at the press conference?"

Martina shrugged. "Don't know. Your dad watched it, then told me about it. Said the chief had taken Elisabeth's tip seriously. You know, she called the chief at lunch today letting him know there might be enemies of that H.O.P.E. Club."

Maria was still rubbing her mom's back. "Ah, when you went outside to talk on the phone while we were having lunch?"

Elisabeth nodded.

Martina went on, "And I guess during the press conference, the chief asked the viewers to help find out if there was ever a scandal with the club. Maybe a hidden one."

"Mmm… interesting." Aaron rubbed his chin, his one eyebrow raised.

Maria knew something was up. "What are you thinking? You seem to have a theory."

"Maybe. But no proof."

Maria let out a quick laugh. "Don't worry, Mr. Show-Me-The-Evidence. Just fill us in on the basics."

Aaron turned around to glance at Maria and Elisabeth. "Well, this high-ranking officer who, you know, *abused* that young Airman girl… he was military?"

Elisabeth raised her eyebrows. "What? The girl told me the man who raped her was a high-ranking officer. She didn't give me a name, didn't even want to talk about it. But yeah, safe to assume a military officer. Who else would fit the description?"

Aaron's eyes lit up. Maria saw it. *I knew it, he has a theory. Personally, I'm feeling lost here.*

"Could it have been a *police* officer?" Aaron asked. "Or could she have meant an officer, a high-ranking person within an organization with a similar hierarchy as the military, such as the FBI? Like an FBI agent?"

"What?" All the ladies looked at Aaron.

"Didn't the police tell us the FBI agent who kidnapped Maria—this JB guy—was stationed at FBI headquarters in Utah for a while?"

Maria's eyes were wide. "What are you saying?"

"I'm looking for a connection here. A connection between this H.O.P.E. Club in Utah and your kidnapping."

"¡Dios mío! You think one of the Fearless Four was involved in the abuse scandal Elisabeth was about to uncover through her H.O.P.E. Club in Utah?"

"Maybe."

Maria shook her head. "But Aaron, I know for sure Mike Clifford mentioned his father and—"

"Bullet will get you, yes, I know," Aaron said, "but who exactly *is* this Bullet? Mike Clifford's father, or someone Mike *saw as a father*? Like a higher-up somewhere. Like a high-ranking person who helped get him into politics."

"So you're saying the police arrested *the wrong guy*?" Martina said, her voice almost shrill.

"Maybe. If the chief brought up the H.O.P.E. Club, it might be because he's not so sure General Richard Clifford is who we're looking for. The name 'Bullet' is a made-up name. A name to hide behind. A name to hide a scandal. A name to use when committing a crime."

"But there's no connection between the H.O.P.E Club and the kidnapping," Elisabeth said. "I've been thinking and thinking about it, but I see no connection."

"Jack was wondering the same after the press conference when he came downstairs and talked to me. He wondered about a possible connection," Martina said.

"Exactly. If Elisabeth made enemies, enemies with power, we need to find out who they are and how they're connected to Eglin Air Force Base."

"JB was at Eglin for sure. And Mike Clifford. And Bill," Maria whispered.

Aaron nodded. "Yes, exactly. Three of the Fearless Four were at Eglin around the time of your kidnapping. Why not also the fourth one? Bullet."

"General Richard Clifford lives close to Eglin," Martina said. "So he was there."

"True," Aaron mumbled. "Elisabeth, I need you to think back to what this young Airman girl told you. The one who was raped by this high-ranking official. What exactly did she say?"

Elisabeth's lip started quivering. "I don't really remember. It was so long ago. I do know she didn't name her rapist. I don't even recall her name anymore. I can't remember." Tears flowed down her cheeks again.

Maria gave Aaron a look and comforted her mom. *He needs to stop. This is painful for my poor mom.* Maria saw Aaron return the nod. *Good. Glad he understands without us having to exchange a word together.*

Martina flipped the car blinker and turned into the hospital's back parking lot, followed by the police escort, then found a parking space close to the rear entrance.

"Quickly unbuckle everyone and let's run inside. Before reporters can get to us. They're still camped out up front," Martina said. "¡Vamos!"

They did as they were told and hustled inside the hospital, Elisabeth first, then Martina, then Aaron and Maria, the lieutenant close on their heels. Once they were all safely inside, unnoticed by the press, Aaron took Maria's hand. The warmth of his skin flooded through her body and reached her heart. She intertwined her fingers in his. Holding his hand still made her heart skip and she couldn't help but smile.

Hand in hand, they walked behind Martina and Elisabeth. *My two moms. Yet we're still not quite sure who wanted to hurt my parents. Why did they take me from them?*

Even though she felt the warmth of Aaron's touch, an ice-cold shudder ran down her spine. *We need to find Bullet. Who is he, really? Richard Clifford? Or someone who felt threatened by the H.O.P.E. Club twenty years ago? The H.O.P.E. Club and my kidnapping... is there a connection?*

CHAPTER 20

"A connection?" General Richard Clifford laughed. "You're seriously asking me if I had a connection with my son Mike?"

Idiot! He knows what we're asking. The chief tried hard not to lose his temper. "Yes, General, we're asking if you reestablished a relationship with your son Mike after you had a fairly public falling-out."

General Richard Clifford exchanged a glance with his lawyer, then sighed and nodded.

"When and where did you see your son again?"

"Oh, here and there."

Seriously? This is going to be a long interview if he keeps acting like a child. Chief Parlot cleared his throat and nodded to Agent Anderson.

"Please define *here and there,*" Agent Anderson said firmly.

"We saw him on occasion."

A slight grin came over the chief's face. *We, huh? Well, fine, let's get your wife involved.* He turned to Dorothy Clifford, her head bowed, her eyes resting on the interrogation table. She had continued to avoid all eye contact. "Mrs. Clifford, how would you define *on occasion?* And how would you describe the relationship you had with your son Mike these past few decades?"

Dorothy Clifford briefly looked up. Tears in her eyes. "It wasn't good. Wish it would've been better. We tried to make up, you know, but just too much had happened. And as you already know, both my son and my husband are very stubborn individuals."

Chief Parlot tried hard not to smile. *She'll crack under pressure, unlike the general.* "'Stubborn'? In what sense, Mrs. Clifford?"

"You know, a mom forgives more easily, but a good wife wants to listen to her husband and—"

"*What she means to say* is that I went alone to visit our son Mike," the general said.

Agent Anderson gave General Clifford a stern look. "General, please, let your wife speak for herself."

"He's right in what he says," Dorothy Clifford whispered. "He went on his own to see Mike."

"When and where did your son and husband meet?" Dorothy Clifford stayed silent. Agent Anderson raised her eyebrows. "Mrs. Clifford, *when and where* did your husband meet your son Mike? When did they reestablish contact after the falling-out?"

But Dorothy Clifford just stayed silent and stared at the table again. Hands in her lap, folded as if in prayer. A silent tear ran down her nose and dripped onto the table. She quickly wiped it away.

Agent Anderson got up, walked around the table, and kneeled next to Dorothy. Said quietly, "Ma'am, are you afraid of your husband?"

General Clifford jumped up. "This is *unbelievable.* Are you nuts? How dare you accuse me of domestic violence. I'll sue your police station not only for negligence but defamation as well—"

His lawyer intervened, gestured for the general to sit back down. The general held his tongue as he took his seat, red-faced.

"My colleague has a right to ask this question. Obviously, you're not a patient man, General," Chief Parlot said, his voice clear and calm, his face betraying no emotion.

Unexpectedly, Dorothy jumped up. "Oh, he *is* a good husband, though! He's not mean to me, I'm not afraid of him. I just wish he'd been a little less harsh on our son growing up. Richard had big plans for Mike. He wanted him to serve his country, make a name for himself in the Air Force, be someone."

Agent Anderson returned to her spot on the other side of the table to put distance between herself and Dorothy. "Your son was a politician, ma'am. Wasn't that enough?"

"He came a long way. That's why we supported him. But the damage had been done. Mike knew his father wanted him to be in the Air Force, and he had failed. He'd shown promise, but I guess sometimes kids are good at things but their heart isn't in it. We pushed him too hard to live a life he didn't want. And Mike knew his father would never be able to overcome his disappointment."

"Dorothy, *please*." General Clifford gave his wife a stern look, and she sat back down again.

"Thank you, ma'am," Chief Parlot said. "So you met and made up. How did you support your son?"

"We helped him out financially. Gave him things he needed," she whispered.

"Like a bank account?" Chief Parlot saw her nod. "A car? A yacht?" She nodded again.

"And a clean slate to his name, to start something new?"

Dorothy looked up at Agent Anderson, a puzzled look on her face.

"I mean you made sure it looked like he 'dropped out' of the Air Force Academy instead of getting kicked out, which actually happened?"

"Well—"

"Yes, I met with the dean of the Air Force Academy. A buddy of mine," General Clifford interrupted. "He just did me a little favor, that's all."

"I see, General. A little favor. Wouldn't it be nice if we all had someone on high to wipe away our mistakes?" Chief Parlot said. He and the general stared each other down.

"Chief, Agent, please, can we get back on track here?" the lawyer finally said. "I believe we were discussing my clients' relationship with their son Mike?"

"Sure, sir, we can do that," Chief Parlot said, and gave his colleague a slight nod.

"General, we hope you're aware that nice yacht you gifted your son ultimately became a crime scene?" Tonya Anderson removed several faded pictures from a binder and slid them across the table. Several of the yacht, as well as receipts from Destin Marina at Destin Harbor where the yacht had been moored. "It's the same yacht Moana Marie Collins was held captive on for months, when she was a toddler. Did you know of this?"

Chief Parlot studied the Cliffords' faces. *He shows no emotion, but Dorothy Clifford is struggling to maintain her composure.*

"And here are receipts showing you wired your son money *on occasion*—all transactions taking place about two years before the kidnapping." Agent Anderson stared at the pair as they studied the printouts and pictures. "Why then, General? Why give him so much money at that time?"

Silence.

Time to press our luck. "Please, General, work with us here," the chief said. "We already know you met Mike out in Utah. We have a receipt for the hotel you stayed at there, a credit card statement for a flight for one person—not two, just one, you, General—but then we see here you paid for dinner for two for most of that trip."

The lawyer nodded at General Clifford, like they'd been expecting this. The general sighed, then started speaking. "Yes, I flew out there to see Mike. We hadn't spoken for three years following the Academy incident, and we'd decided he'd learned his lesson. He had suffered enough. We wanted to help him out. So yes, I met with him and offered to open a new bank account in his name. I had to co-sign because his credit was lousy."

"I see. And then what happened?"

"Dorothy and I thought giving Mike all these things, all these opportunities, was enough. We knew he loved boating. We kept his yacht in Pensacola—close to us but far enough away for him to be independent. We tried to help him get a job in Pensacola, or perhaps at Eglin AFB as a civilian, once he moved back to Florida, but he didn't want to hear about it. Even after he moved back to this area, he didn't want to work on base." General Clifford sighed. "He accused me of pressuring him just like before, wanting him to step into my shoes, wanting him to live my life. He thought by going back to base, he would get trapped in the Air Force life he'd obviously rejected."

"I see," the chief said. "How did that make you feel?"

"What?"

"What the chief means is, how did you feel getting rejected by your son? Even though you obviously meant well and tried to help him?" Agent Anderson explained.

The general looked at both chief and agent. "How are my feelings of importance?"

The chief smiled at him. "General, maybe you felt so angry, were so livid, that you decided to play by Mike's rules?"

"What?"

Agent Anderson slid another piece of paper across the table. "This, General, is a receipt of your stay at the MGM Grand Casino in Las Vegas, Nevada. Wanna guess when it was you stayed there?"

For the first time this interview, the color drained from the general's face.

"General, we know you were at the casino the same night one of the kidnappers, Jonathan Sullivan, first met a group called the Fearless Four. We already know the identities of three of the Fearless Four group members: your son Mike was Cliff; the former Niceville police chief, Chief Billings, went by Bill; and a former FBI agent, Agent James Borman, took on the nickname JB." The chief watched General Clifford's pale face carefully as he handed the word over to his colleague.

"According to Jonathan Sullivan—dubbed Sully by his new, so-called friends—there was, of course, a fourth member to the Fearless Four." Agent Anderson paused for a second. "This fourth member was a guy named Bullet. Sully, though drunk out of his mind, claimed just before his untimely death that he saw this fourth person idling in a cloud of cigarette smoke in the back of a hotel room, watching JB, Bill, Cliff, and Sully play their poker game. The game where Sullivan fell into so much debt with the group that they managed to extort him. He assisted in Maria's kidnapping a few months later."

Both the agent and the chief stared directly at General Clifford. The general cleared his throat. "So? What do *I* have to do with this?"

"Exactly." Agent Anderson smiled. "You were at the right place at the right time. Angry, mad, disappointed that your son Mike hadn't made anything of his life—except for joining up with a strange criminal group and gambling away the money you wired him. Or did you not mind this?"

General Clifford jumped up. "Of course I minded it. I was disappointed and angry with my son. But what does that have to do with the kidnapping?"

The chief grinned. "Well, General, anger can make us do the strangest things, can't it?"

"What?"

"You were at the casino the night the group plotted the kidnapping scheme. The same night the Fearless Four pinned their middleman, the guy who would do all their dirty work—the guy who was supposed to get rid of the body of a little toddler. You were there, even though Mike had moved back to Florida and lived close to you. Why did the two of you meet there, in Vegas? Come on, you're telling us this is all a coincidence?" Agent Anderson raised her eyebrows.

"I don't know a thing about this Fearless Four meeting you're describing."

"Really, General? You're saying you weren't unhappy to see Mike in a funk? Still gambling? Still lost in life?"

"Of course I was. It was hard to watch. Yes, I saw him gambling, I saw him with his friends in the casino. Getting drunk, wasting money."

"Aha, so you were there!"

"Yes… but I still don't know what this has to do with the kidnapping! What the heck are you saying? I don't understand."

Agent Anderson grinned. "Let me spell it out for you, General: *You* are Bullet, the mysterious fourth member of the Fearless Four. *You* are the mastermind behind Maria's kidnapping, to take revenge on the man who was responsible for your son getting kicked out of the Academy. The man who was responsible for your son's downfall, for the wasteful life Mike had fallen into. The man who inadvertently ruined your son: Brad Collins."

Both Dorothy's and General Clifford's eyes were wide, their faces pale.

"You lost the son you once knew and cherished, so you decided Brad Collins would suffer the loss of a child just like you had, didn't you?"

General Clifford's mouth dropped open, while Dorothy's face looked even more pale than before, closer now to resembling the whiteness of a ghost.

"You're accusing my client of masterminding the Moana Marie Collins kidnapping?" their lawyer asked.

"Yes." Agent Anderson smiled and glanced over to the chief, who didn't say anything and just stared at the table. *I'm not so sure anymore if I myself believe he is Bullet. All we know is that Clifford talked about 'a father', according to Maria.*

Silence in the room.

Chief Parlot was still lost in thought. *We gotta rule out it wasn't him. Gotta confront him with what Maria has told us.* He looked up and stared at the general. "When your son kidnapped Maria for the second time, he told her he wanted to make his father proud and not let him down again, that he needed to 'finish it.'" Chief Parlot studied the

Cliffords' faces but saw no further reaction. *They're actually speechless? Shocked?*

"His… *father?*" General Clifford mumbled. "He talked about his father? Why would he use 'father'? He always called me Dad. Never Father."

Suddenly, a reddish color returned to Dorothy's face and she jumped up. "This is absurd! Richard would never involve himself with a gang of criminals. And certainly wouldn't give himself a childish nickname like Bullet. We don't know these people you're talking about. Sure, we had met Chief Billings before, but who in this community hasn't? That doesn't make us accomplices to his crimes. We had nothing to do with these kidnappings. God, why torture us like this? Isn't it enough we've lost our only son?" She plopped down on her chair and started sobbing.

General Clifford patted his wife's back, then turned to the chief and agent. "My wife is right. We *are* innocent. We've had nothing to do with this girl. I didn't know a JB and certainly never met Sullivan."

Agent Anderson narrowed her big brown eyes. "Why were you in Las Vegas at the casino?"

"Because of that shared bank account with Mike I told you about. I watched it like a hawk. I knew when he withdrew money. Saw he'd been in Vegas gambling for weeks, drawing down the account, throwing it all away. He'd promised me he'd get his life together, then pulled this stunt. So Dorothy and I decided we'd talk some sense into him. I was in Florida, and my son in Vegas, so I flew to Vegas to catch him red-handed. Gambling, drinking, wasting his life away. I sought him out, tried to talk to him, but he didn't want to hear any of it." General Clifford blinked back tears. "We had a big argument. I left early. Paid for a longer stay but left the night after we had our big fight. Got out of there. And we never saw Mike again. He refused to take our calls or speak to us again. Even after he turned his life around. So yes, the stories are true; we were estranged. We kept the bank account open for years, wired him money, hoping he'd have a change of heart, but one day he just closed it down. Severed all ties with us."

Both Cliffords sighed. Dorothy wiped away her tears. She took her husband's hand and they looked at each other lovingly.

The chief watched them closely. *Maybe they are a nice couple after all?*

"Chief, this is the truth: we are innocent." General Clifford held his head up high, a determined look on his face. "We had nothing to do with the kidnapping or any of our son's other shady dealings. I bet your team can somehow dig deep and confirm what I say. Look for my early checkout from the Vegas hotel and the early flight home to Florida. No more contact with Mike after that."

Agent Anderson and Chief Parlot glanced at each other. The chief was deep in thought. *Maybe he's telling the truth? Maybe he left before Sullivan's poker night with the Fearless Four? Maybe he never saw Mike again. If so, he can't be Bullet. Maria claimed Mike spoke of his father… but maybe not* this *father?*

CHAPTER 21

Father. I'm finally a father again. A daddy. A dad to my little girl. Brad smiled when he opened his eyes and saw Maria by his bedside, smiling down at him. *Well, not so little anymore. All grown up now, my beautiful daughter. Still can't believe I got her back.*

"Hi there, Dad," he heard her say, and an intense warmth flooded through him, touching his heart. *Dad. I love hearing that word.*

"Hi, there." He smiled, and then noticed the others. "Hi, Aaron, Elisabeth, Martina. So glad you've come to visit me."

"Of course, Dad." Maria bent down to give him a kiss on the cheek and a gentle hug.

"Our pleasure." Aaron shook Brad's hand carefully.

"Sí, happy to see you." Martina lifted her hand in a small wave and smiled at Brad. "How are you feeling?"

"Oh, pretty good."

"That's great to hear." Elisabeth sat down on the opposite site of the bed from where Maria, Aaron, and Martina were standing, then gave Brad a quick kiss. She smiled at him. "By the way, I'm here to stay."

"Here to stay?" Brad studied Elisabeth's face. "What do you mean by that?"

"I'm staying the night with you. Already talked to hospital staff; they cleared me staying with you. Still have my bed in here to sleep on that they don't need."

"But they released you. The beds at the hotel are much more comfortable. Everyone else is there."

Elisabeth smiled. "I know. But I'd like to stay with you."

"Are you sure you don't want to stay at the inn?" Brad raised his eyebrows, then his whole face drooped down, worry washing over it. *Who will care for our daughter if she needs help? Who will make sure she's safe?*

As if she'd read his mind, Elisabeth took his hand. "I'd like to stay with you. There's tons of people there to watch over Maria. Not only Aaron, Martina, and Jack but also all of Maria's friends. And our friends Sarah and Drew. So don't worry, hun."

Brad took a deep breath in. "Alright, sounds good. And I do love the company of my private nurse." He grinned at Elisabeth, then winked at Aaron, Maria, and Martina. "So, what did I miss while I was sleeping the day away? Any updates?"

Maria glanced at Elisabeth, whose face was suddenly stern, all smiles washed away. "Well, no, I guess no real news...."

"No 'real' news? What does that mean?" Brad studied Maria's face. *She looks sad. Or embarrassed? Is she hiding something?*

Aaron jumped in to explain. "No news yet on General Richard Clifford. The chief's probably still waiting to talk to him; he's been stalling with his lawyer nearly all day."

Brad grimaced. "Of course. He lawyered up. The bastard."

"I bet they'll talk to him soon," Aaron said.

"Hopefully. We gotta figure out who the brains were behind this whole operation. It has to end," Brad said, his voice loud and clear.

Martina nodded. "Sí, we need closure. And the truth."

"Exactly," Brad whispered. "I still can't believe someone kidnapped our child out of revenge. Just to hurt me and my wife...." Sadness washed over his face, his eyes now more green than ever.

Elisabeth squeezed his hand. A weak squeeze. Brad looked up at her. Her eyes were moist, her bottom lip quivering. Her hand felt clammy in his, cold not warm anymore. Brad let go and tilted her face toward him.

"Elisabeth? What's wrong?"

"Nothing...." she whispered, but a tear rolled down her freckled nose all the same.

"Come on, I know something's bothering you. I know you well. I can still read you like a book." Brad smiled at her.

She returned her own faint smile but she didn't say anything. Brad turned to Maria, Martina, and Aaron, who were all staring off into the distance.

Brad cleared his throat. "What's going on, everyone? What did I miss? Someone needs to fill me in."

Aaron was the first to speak. "Did you catch any of the press conferences today?"

Brad shook his head. "No, slept through them all. Why? What happened?"

"The chief took Elisabeth's tip seriously," Martina said. "At the second one, he asked the press for help."

"For help?" Brad crinkled his forehead. "Help with what?"

"To uncover a scandal from a while ago," Martina continued, "a scandal at... ah... what's it called, um... Hill..."

"Hill Air Force Base in Utah," Aaron finished for her. "Back when you were stationed there, General Collins. Something to do with the H.O.P.E. Club."

"What?" Brad now turned to Elisabeth again. Her head hung low. "The H.O.P.E. Club? What does that have to do with any of what we've been through?"

"That's the million-dollar question," Aaron said. "Maybe nothing. But maybe you weren't the only one who made an enemy when you were younger."

"What?"

"We think maybe Mom pissed someone off because of her H.O.P.E. Club," Maria said.

Brad laughed. "Don't be ridiculous. They all loved her. Everyone *loved* Elisabeth. She helped those women so much. Right, Elisabeth?"

"Well, yeah," Elisabeth whispered, "But I just abandoned it, left the H.O.P.E Club without warning." She abruptly burst into tears and covered her face with her hands.

Brad's eyes were wide. "We moved. Out of state. Far away. You didn't abandon it, you had to move. That's normal with military families."

"But I broke my promise," Elisabeth whispered.

"*What* promise? You didn't break any promises. You founded this club, built it up, found a successor to run it. It was an amazing club. Well-liked and very important—but then you unfortunately had to leave it behind when we moved to Florida."

"I know. But I promised her I would come back."

"What? Who?"

"I don't remember her name," she whispered.

Brad saw tears streaming down her face. *I can't stand seeing her cry. Why is she so upset? We found our daughter. We found each other. We made peace with Martina. We survived a vicious attack. The police are close to finding the mastermind behind the kidnapping. We have a bright future ahead. Why is she upset about the H.O.P.E. Club, of all things? What does that have to do with anything?* "Elisabeth, I don't understand."

Elisabeth wiped her tears away and exhaled deeply. "I remembered something important earlier today. Someone I likely upset to the point of no forgiveness. A poor young lady I totally let down." She was tearing up again but took a deep breath to steady herself. "A long time ago I told you about this one young lady in my club—a young E-1 Airmen Basic, just nineteen years old, fresh out of high school."

Brad thought for a while. "You had a lot of young women in your club. What was so special about this one?"

"The night before we left, she confided in me. Told me she'd been raped. By a senior Air Force guy. I knew something bad must have happened to her, but for months I couldn't get her to open up. I kept trying to get through to her. She finally told me the whole story the night before we had to leave."

Brad thought about it and suddenly remembered. "Oh yeah, you told me there was a young woman in the H.O.P.E. Club who desperately needed your help. We'd planned out you returning to Utah later that summer to help her."

Elisabeth nodded. "Yes, I promised I'd help her report him. She'd finally agreed to do so, had finally summoned her courage."

Brad thought back to that night. "I remember our last night in Utah. The club was throwing you a farewell party to celebrate everything you'd done, but instead of being happy about what you achieved, happy about all of the gifts and heartfelt notes and amazing shout-outs, you were so sad. Almost like you were in shock."

Elisabeth nodded. "Remember how I was going to fly back to help her talk to the police? We'd talked about you watching Moana with your parents around the Fourth of July weekend."

Brad nodded. "Now I remember, we were starting to make plans. But then it all fell apart. And you never went back..."

"Exactly, I never went back, I never helped her, I didn't even call her once. Didn't return any of her calls. I *failed* her." Elisabeth was crying again. Brad cupped her face in his hand and wiped away her tears.

The room was silent for a while. Maria, Aaron, and Martina all stared at the floor.

"You lost a child, Elisabeth," Martina suddenly said. "It's understandable you didn't have the time or strength to help this young lady back in Utah. You had your own tragedy once you moved to Florida. It's not your fault."

"But it *is* my fault. I let her down. I broke a promise. I need to find her. I need to apologize. See how she's doing now. But *I just can't remember her name.* Oh no, what's wrong with me? I can't even remember her name. I'm a terrible person." Elisabeth sobbed loudly.

"Mom, please don't be sad! Nicht traurig sein," Maria said, somehow knowing those German words she'd heard many times a long, long time ago. She walked over to where Elisabeth was sitting and rubbed her back in comfort.

A faint smile flashed across Elisabeth's face and she leaned into her daughter. "Oh, Moana... Maria, I mean... you still remember German?"

Maria smiled. "Nah, not much. Just a few things here and there."

Brad grinned. "That's a lot more than I remember."

His comment got a slight giggle from everyone in the room, even Elisabeth.

"Mom, let's not get ahead of ourselves. We still don't know if this has anything to do with my kidnapping. I doubt it. My kidnapping happened just a few days after this young lady confided in you, right? There wouldn't have been enough time for someone who learned of what you planned to do to react, time enough to plan out an intricate kidnapping on base."

Elisabeth and Brad nodded.

"Well, this person might have been afraid for a long time his crime would be discovered," Aaron said. "So maybe there *was* enough time to plan it out? Maybe he was keeping tabs on you, knew about you well before you knew about him?"

They all thought on that for a while. "It's possible," Brad mumbled.

"Well, that's why the chief brought up the H.O.P.E. Club scandal, no? At the press conference," Martina said. "Wants to dig deeper. Encouraged the press and public to look into it, no?"

"I see." Brad nodded. "Always good to investigate every angle. But I think Maria's right—it's very unlikely." He turned to Elisabeth. "Anyway, Elisabeth, I need you to not be sad anymore. I need you to focus on the now, not the then. I bet the girl is fine."

"But we don't know that," Elisabeth yelled, "we can't be sure! And I can't forget. Not anymore. I need assurances she's alright. I know it's much too late, but…"

"Better late than never." Aaron finished Elisabeth's sentence.

She nodded. "Exactly. But I can't. Remember. Her name. Goodness, how could I forget? I talked to her many times. It took her a while to open up. A beautiful young lady with a beautiful Hispanic name."

Martina's head jerked at that. "Hispanic?"

"Yes, a very unique name, but I just cannot remember it. I'm terrible."

"Maybe we can help," Maria said. "What was her first initial?"

"I don't know, I just don't know." Elisabeth sighed. "It was very unique!"

"Unique? Mmm…" Maria just started guessing. "Esmeralda? Juana?"

"No, no, not those. It was way more uncommon. She was proud of her name. She was very religious. Said her name referred to the Virgin Mary. And a church or something."

"A church? Like an actual church somewhere?" Maria asked.

"I think so."

"Where was she from?" Martina wanted to know. "Was she born here in the U.S. or abroad? Where did her family come from?"

Elisabeth thought for a while. Her face lit up at a recollection. "Mexico! Yes, I'm positive she told me her family was from Mexico. Said they crossed the Texas border when she was very little. But I still can't remember her name."

"Maybe she's named after a church in Mexico?" Martina mumbled. "A church that can also be a girl's name? Mmmh… ¡No sé!"

Elisabeth's eyes filled with tears again. "This info still doesn't help us."

Aaron grinned. "Maybe it does." He pulled out his phone. "There's nothing you can't google."

Maria waved Aaron over and he stood in front of everyone, angling his phone so they could see the screen and follow along. He typed *Church in Mexico that is also a girl's name* and hit Search. They all watched the spinning circle on Aaron's phone as it dredged the internet.

There! The results popped up.

"'The Mystery of the Mummy Girl in the Guadalajara Cathedral,'" Aaron read out loud.

Maria turned to Elisabeth. "Guadalajara? Is that her name?"

Elisabeth thought about it, then shook her head.

"Guadalupe," Martina now said.

Elisabeth perked up. "What?"

"It's under 'What People Also Asked.' I just read it on Aaron's phone. 'Guadalupe, the Lady of Guadalupe.'"

Elisabeth jumped up, a bright smile on her face. "Yes, that's it! That's her name: Guadalupe! That's also how she pronounced it, the way you're saying it, Martina. Most Americans couldn't get it right. Ah, but she usually went by a nickname." The smile vanished. "I can't remember that one."

"It's okay, hun," Brad said, "I bet she uses her real name in the Air Force anyway."

"See, Mom, we found her. We know her name now." Maria gave Elisabeth a hug but felt her go limp in it.

"But what good does this do us? I didn't help her back then, and who knows how things turned out for her," Elisabeth said.

"We can look her up in the Air Force database," Brad said.

"Yes, Mom, then you can call her. See how she's doing. Apologize to her and explain why you couldn't help back then. How about that?"

Elisabeth nodded. "Yeah, maybe. Maybe we can find her and I'll give her a call. Still, I failed her. Left her in a vulnerable situation. Goodness. She must really hate me."

"No, I'm sure she'll understand, Mom," Maria said.

"Let's hope so. Yeah, I'd like to speak with her. At least explain my side." Elisabeth sighed. "Hope she understands. I'd love to see her again. Maybe she'll agree to a meeting. Maybe, sometime, we'll meet again."

CHAPTER 22

We'll meet again, Elisabeth, Lu thought while staring out the small window of the plane taking off. Soon Orlando was a sea of lights beneath her that she was leaving behind.

It's beautiful. The night sky, the light of the city. Lu shook her head. *I can't believe I'm traveling back into my past. Back to meet Elisabeth. But how will that do me any good? It'll just bring back painful memories. Need those to stay hidden. Nobody can ever know.*

Lu had no idea how long she sat there, watching the little specks of light fly past beneath her in the darkness, when suddenly a voice said, "Cookies or pretzels, ma'am?"

Feeling jarred, Lu turned and saw nobody in the seat next to her, only a flight attendant standing in the aisle. "Oh, hi there, ma'am."

"Hello. What would you like for a snack? Cookies or pretzels?"

"Cookies, please."

"Here you go, ma'am." The flight attendant smiled, her red lipstick bright in the darkened cabin. "And what would you like to drink?"

"Coffee, please," Lu said. She took the cookies from the attendant and unfolded her tray table.

The smile on the flight attendant's face vanished. "I'm sorry, ma'am, we don't serve coffee on our nighttime flights."

"Oh, I see. Well then, I'll take…" Lu paused to ponder it a bit.

The flight attendant leaned in closer to her. "You know what, ma'am? I'll make you some coffee after I'm done serving everyone. I could go for a cup as well. Seems like both of us have a long night ahead of us, huh?" She winked. "How about water for now, then I'll be back with that coffee later?"

Lu's face lit up. "Sounds great. Thank you."

"No problem. Anything for our military. Thank you for your service, ma'am."

Lu nodded and watched the attendant serve the passenger on the other side of the aisle. She took a sip of ice-cold water and watched the night sky outside. They were high up now, above the clouds.

Eglin AFB, here I come. It's a nice base. Right by the water. She shuddered. *I guess that's where Elisabeth lost her child back then? I had no idea. I was living my own personal hell. Preparing to go to the police. I shut out the world while I was collecting evidence and didn't pay attention to the news back then. I suppose Elisabeth ghosted me for a good reason.* Lu sighed. *Still. She broke her promise. Left me all alone, without any defense against* him. *And then he got to me again. Paid me off.*

She blinked back tears. *I never told anyone what happened ever again. Not even Daniel, my sweet husband. My patient husband. I miss you, Daniel. I'm sorry for lying to you.*

While chewing on her cookies, she pulled out her phone to reread the last text exchange between her and her husband before she'd switched her phone to airplane mode. He'd asked, *Why are they making you go to Eglin now? So last minute?*

Lu let out a deep breath as she read her answer. A complete lie. *Because the F-35 program managers wanted me to come visit. Show me their progress. Wanted that for a while. Good timing now since stuck in Florida. No worries, I'll be back by the weekend. XOX.*

Sucks. I'll miss you, Lu. XOX. Luv ya, Daniel's response read.

She sighed again. *He's such a good guy. Always understanding, always there for me. My Daniel.*

139

"Ma'am, your coffee." The flight attendant ripped her out of her thoughts. "And here's sugar and cream and some more cookies." She smiled at Lu while handing over the coffee and cookies.

Lu put away her phone, stirred the creamer and sugar into her coffee, then sipped it carefully. The hot liquid ran down her throat and soothed her, made her calm, relaxed. She took another bite of her cookie and went back to watching the night sky outside.

I'm not sure what to do next, but one thing's certain: I have to make sure Elisabeth doesn't pursue my story. She can't. Lu shook her head, then took another sip of coffee. *I don't want anyone to know I rose through the ranks thanks to him. Because I made a dark bargain with the enemy. With the master, the one who plays everyone. The one who puts his puppets where he wants them. And I'm one of those. One of his puppets. He holds my strings in his hands. I can't escape.*

Lu spent the rest of her flight deep in thought.

"Hello, ma'am," a young Air Force captain greeted her, "welcome to Eglin AFB. We're honored to have you here. I'm Captain Wilkens. I'll be your driver this evening."

Lu smiled at the captain as she shook his hand. "Nice to meet you, Captain Wilkens. And thank you, sir, for picking me up."

He smiled at her. "My pleasure. Do you have any more luggage?"

"Yes, sir, I do. Came from overseas, so I'm toting more than just a carry-on, I'm afraid."

"So I heard, ma'am. You must be tired. Two TDYs back-to-back. Let me carry that for you." He reached for her carry-on but Lu shook her head.

"No, sir, I got this. How about you handle my suitcase once it shows up on the carousel?"

"Sure, ma'am."

Together they walked to the small baggage-claim area. As always, Lu's mind was sharp, the small talk flowed easily. After her suitcase had arrived, Captain Wilkens drove her to Eglin AFB. Once through security, he took her straight to the Distinguished Visitor's Quarters. He stopped the SUV, walked around, and opened the general's door for her. "Thank you, sir." Lu smiled and got out of the passenger seat. "That's a big house. All for me?"

He laughed. "Yes, ma'am. Our generals deserve the best."

"I suppose so." Lu hoisted her carry-on bag and pushed the car door shut.

The friendly captain got her suitcase out of the trunk and wheeled it over to the front door. "Here are your keys, ma'am. Have a great night. I heard your exec is still coming up with an agenda. I'll be in touch with him and pick you up when he tells me to. Until then, enjoy your stay."

"Thank you, sir, sounds great. I'm sure he'll reach out to the both of us once he's ready. This trip was rather spontaneous, after all, can't be too hard on exec. Good night now."

"Good night, General Thomas." The captain waved to her, then got into the government-issued SUV and drove away.

Lu let herself into the grand house. A smile hushed over her face at the building's opulence. *One of the better perks of being a general.* She walked through the house, inspected every room, and decided on one of the bedrooms facing the back of the house, overlooking the bay. She rummaged through her suitcase for pajamas, then headed to the bathroom to take a nice, hot shower.

Once she was all freshened up, she opened the curtains in her room so the moonlight illuminated the room, then crawled into the big, comfortable bed. She texted her husband a good night note and received a cheerful reply right away.

Aw, my Daniel. Still awake, always responsive. He's so sweet.

Lu turned off the nightstand light. Through the darkness the water outside sparkled in the moonlight, casting a shimmer on the ceiling of her bedroom. She smiled. *I love it when the moon's bright. I hate darkness. Nothing good ever happens in the dark.* She shuddered. *Bullet likes it dark. It's his territory, his domain. Darkness covers his crimes. Do I have to let him know I'm here?* She shook her head. *No, not now, not in the dark. Tomorrow. I'll inform him tomorrow.*

Then she forced herself to think of something else. Her wonderful life, her awesome career, her loving husband. She smiled. *Everything worked out well in the end. I've come far. And while I'm not sure what needs doing next, I do know I can't allow Elisabeth to dig up my past. I have to shut her up. I'll figure it out. Tomorrow.*

CHAPTER 23

"Tomorrow, Mamá, I'll see you tomorrow. Mañana." Maria gave her mamá a big hug.

"Sí, mañana. Buenas noches, mija e Aaron." Martina waved to them from the doorway of her room in the Air Force Inn.

"Good night," Aaron said.

Martina waved one last time, then shut the door. Aaron and Maria strode down the hallway until they reached their own room. Maria let them in. Everything was quiet around them.

"Seems like everyone's asleep already, huh?" Aaron followed Maria inside, then closed the door. Took care to engage every lock available.

"Yeah, no kidding. Guess everyone's tired. How's your shoulder feeling?"

"So-so." Aaron stepped inside the bathroom to get ready for bed and tried to squeeze toothpaste onto his toothbrush. With only one working hand, he was running into trouble.

"Aw, my poor Aaron. Let me help you with that." Maria came over and readied the toothbrush, then handed it to him.

"Thanks." Aaron started brushing.

"You're welcome. My poor patient. No worries, Nurse Maria is here." Her grin faded. "I'm sorry you're in pain because of me."

Aaron spit out his toothpaste and flushed out his mouth. He turned around to hug Maria. "Actually, I'm in pain because of that idiot Mike Clifford, not you. It's not your fault, Maria. You know that, right?"

She nodded as she pressed her head against his strong chest. She heard his heart beating slow and steady in her ear. *My Aaron. I love you so much.* His scratchy chin tickled her forehead. "I'm just glad you're alright. Hmm, I guess you'll have to shave soon, Mr. Airman—your beard is growing in quickly." She smiled at him.

Aaron let go of her and turned around to inspect his chin in the mirror. He gave a little chuckle. "I suppose. At least I'm off this week."

Maria nodded. "That's good. But can you even go back to work next week? With your shoulder hurt?" She started brushing her teeth now.

"I think so. I might need help getting dressed, though." He grinned at her. "And *undressed*, too."

Maria spat her toothpaste into the sink, then looked up and winked at him. "I see."

Aaron walked out of the bathroom and started pretending to undress himself. "Oh no, I sure need help with this sling and all."

"I'll be right there, just wait for me, my poor, helpless patient." Maria grinned, a makeup-remover wipe in her hand. "Lie down on the bed. I'll be there in a moment to *assist* you."

Aaron did as he was told, eager for Maria to join him. He smiled. "Sounds like a plan."

They were cuddled up in the darkness, Maria's head on Aaron's chest, his strong, uninjured arm around her. Maria was wide-awake. She felt the slight breeze of Aaron's snore against her. The warmth of his even breathing on her head, a tuft of her hair moving back and forth with every one of his breaths. It made her happy. His heart was pumping evenly, a dull thud in her ear.

She smiled to herself. *I'm so glad he's okay. I was so worried about him. So worried Mike Clifford would kill him.* She sighed. *But he didn't. Instead, I killed him. Clifford.* She shuddered at the thought. *It was horrible. I didn't mean to.*

Despite the Florida warmth she started shivering. She pulled the covers over her, all the way up to her chin. *That bad guy is gone now. But there's another one out there. The mastermind behind my kidnapping. Mike Clifford's dad, General Richard Clifford? Possibly. The chief hasn't called since he visited the hospital. Wish he had. Is there any news?*

Carefully, she slid out of Aaron's hold and moved over to the side of the bed to pick up her phone off the nightstand. Quietly, she opened the news app. The front headline did nothing for her chills: *Breaking News: General Richard Clifford and His Wife Dorothy Depart for Home.*

Maria's eyes widened. *The chief let them go?* She scanned through the article and sighed. *Apparently, father and son were still estranged. But I know he talked about his father. I'm sure he told me about his father. Why won't anyone believe me?*

She closed her eyes. "Wait, just you wait until Bullet gets you!" she heard Mike Clifford call out, as if she were there again, bobbing in the water on Turkey Creek. Maria tried to calm her quick breaths, tried to breathe evenly. She put away her phone and crawled back to Aaron, settled against him, tried to match his breathing. Slowly, she calmed herself, aided by Aaron's warm breath against her body again.

Everything's alright. I'll be alright. I'm safe here. I just need to let the police do their work.

She closed her eyes and listened to Aaron's even breathing. A strand of her hair danced back and forth on her forehead with every pulse of his breath. She smiled at it, concentrated on the hair moving back and forth, back and forth....

145

Back and forth the floor gently moved beneath her feet. She felt the movement, had felt it for days, weeks. Months? She wasn't sure anymore. But she liked the rocking—it reminded her of home, of her mom holding her.

Miss Mama.

A big tear escaped her eye and rolled down her nose, pooled onto her top lip—the "pronounced part of her kissable lips" her silly daddy always said before giving her a big kiss.

Miss Daddy.

More tears were coming, but she couldn't wipe them away. Her hands were tied. Tied to the cage, to big metal poles covered in darkness.

Don't like it. Can't move. Miss Mama and Daddy.

She tried to hold back her sobs. She knew the two bad guys didn't like that. Didn't like it when she was loud. Not that she was loud anymore— but they didn't like hearing a peep from her at all. She had learned to be quiet.

She focused on the rocking again, the gentle rocking. The whole room she was held in rocked back and forth. Sometimes harder than others. Today the rocking was not nice. More and more.

Her little eyes widened as the box she was in started to shift and slide. Her tears dried up now, so focused was she on her cage.

Screech. Scratch.

Her wooden box wasn't just rocking anymore; no, it was sliding from one end of the room to the other. Taking her for a ride.

Screech. Scratch.

The blanket that usually blocked her view of the room slid down and she saw the clean, shiny tan floor underneath her box. She saw part of the small staircase leading upstairs, then noticed one of the tall, white walls coming closer and closer and closer.

Boom!

Her box hit the white wall. She rattled under the blow, but the sticky stuff that bound her hands and feet to the metal poles of the box—her play quarters—held her little body in place. The next moment the box slid in the other direction.

Boom!

It crashed into the white wall on the other side. She screeched then, her eyes wide, her heart beating fast.

Help! What's going on? Don't like it! Mama? Daddy?

She screeched again, but then she heard them. The bad guys. She stopped whimpering.

Don't let them hear me.

But it was too late. They must have heard her. She heard hasty footsteps banging down the stairs. Through her crate she saw big shoes stop at the bottom of the stairs. Before she could make out more, the box started sliding again across the floor.

Her eyes widened as she noticed the shoes getting closer and closer to her box—no, her box getting closer and closer to the shoes, approaching them fast.

Boom!

"Argh," she heard the bad guy scream as her box slid right into one of his big leather shoes, over the top of it. Her nose was so close to the shoe now she could smell the expensive leather, a sweet, earthy, musky smell.

"You okay?" yelled the other man from further away, from up the stairs.

"No, not okay! This stupid fucking crate smashed my toes. Damn it!"

"Sorry, Cliff," the one up top yelled down.

"Don't you be fucking sorry about my toes, Sully! Be fucking sorry about how badly you're handling the boat. C'mon, don't let it rock back and forth like that." The bad guy next to her pushed her box off his shoe, then sat down on the floor while holding his foot. He rubbed the spot her box had run over. "Ahhh... my toes...."

She watched him, the shoe right next to her eyes, the man's big, tan hands rubbing his big foot through the shoe.

All of a sudden her box slid again in the other direction and crashed into the white wall. To her surprise, the bad guy, the curly-haired bad guy who sat right next to her box rubbing his foot, started sliding with her. His body crashed into her little quarters.

"What the fuck? Sully, get this damn boat under control!" he screamed. The man rubbed at his ribs where the box's metal poles had hit his side.

"I'm trying, boss, I'm trying. But the waves are crazy today. Maybe we should get closer to shore again?" the other one yelled down.

Like him better. The one upstairs. Nicer.

But she was stuck with the bad guy down here, who was now rubbing both his foot and his belly. Her little box started sliding again. With wide eyes, she noticed it getting closer and closer to the curly-haired bad guy.

Oh no. Will crash again. Into him. Mad. Will make him mad.

She closed her eyes to not see it.

Boom!

Her little box, her play quarters, crashed again—but, to her surprise, it hit the wall, not the bad guy.

She opened her eyes and noticed he had retreated to the stairsteps. He held onto the railing and yelled, "Sully, get the fucking boat under control, now!"

"I can't. Don't know how," she heard from a distance.

As her little wooden box started sliding again, she heard the curly-haired blonde guy mumble. "Damn it. He doesn't know a thing without fucking it up ten times first. Gotta do everything around here myself. Drive the boat. Check on this stupid little girl. Why's she still alive? Fuck! Well, don't care if her crate tips over. Whatever. Maybe that'll finally take care of the problem." He laughed a loud, coarse laugh. "Shit! She wasn't supposed to live. Now I'm stuck with her and that stupid pig Sully. Fuck!"

She saw him holding onto the railing of the small staircase as her box slid back and forth on the light-tan wooden floor.

"But I can't ask for help, I can't," she overheard. "I promised him I'd finish this, get it done and over with. I can't fail. Can't let him down. My mentor, my father. My Bullet."

He growled. "I'm coming up, Sully. I'm taking over driving the boat. You obviously can't fucking do it right, so I'll do it."

"Okay, better come quickly."

The man let out a big sigh. "Yeah, sure, 'better come quickly'—stupid fucking Sully!" He took a few steps, held the railing tight so he wouldn't fly over the edge. Whispered to himself, "For you, Bullet. I'll tolerate all this bullshit for you 'cuz you're like a father to me. Like you always say, Bullet: 'Never give up. Fight like a fighter pilot.'"

He disappeared up the stairs, and suddenly her whole box was thrown about so violently it tipped over. Then she felt herself being lifted up into the air; she was floating, flying free, before it all came crashing down....

Boom! She landed on the hard floor.

"Maria! Oh my gosh, Maria, you okay?" came a soft, male voice.

She opened her eyes. *Where am I?*

"Maria? Oh my goodness, you fell out of bed. Are you alright?"

As her eyes adjusted to the darkness, she realized Aaron was out of bed, crouching next to her. She was sprawled across the floor. She shook herself, then sat up.

Aaron reached out with his good hand to steady her. "Did you hurt yourself?"

Maria felt her elbows, her knees, her shoulders. "No, don't think so."

He exhaled loudly. "Phew, okay. Good. Glad you're okay. You scared me. Such a loud bang."

Maria got up with Aaron's help. Her knees were wobbly, but nothing hurt. She crawled back into bed. Aaron scooted next to her. "You sure you're alright?"

"Yeah, I'm fine."

"Okay. Good. What happened?"

She shrugged her shoulders.

"Bad dream? A nightmare?"

Maria thought about it. "Don't know." She closed her eyes. "Maybe. I think I was on a boat. In bad weather."

"A boat? Oh, like when your kidnappers held you captive on that yacht?"

Maria thought back to her memory, then nodded. "Yeah. I guess so."

Aaron leaned over to kiss her on the cheek. "I'm sorry, Maria. Sorry, my love. Guess those nightmares will stay with you for a while. But know you're safe here. Both Sullivan and Clifford are dead. Your *kidnappers* are *dead*. They can't hurt you anymore."

Maria lay back down and cuddled up to Aaron. The warmth of his body made her shivers stop. He held her close. His heartbeat in her ear once more, she nodded. Whispered, "I know. They can't hurt me anymore."

"Exactly. And if there's anyone else out there who would dare harm a hair on your head, well… the police will take care of them."

Maria nodded, but deep down inside she wasn't so sure the police were up to the task. She doubted they were on the right track. A nagging feeling haunted her. Told her the dream she'd woken from had been important, though she couldn't remember why.

Aaron felt her uneasiness. "It's okay. We'll figure it all out. Don't worry. For now, let's sleep. You're safe here with me."

She nodded, ignoring her little arm hairs standing on alert. *Am I?* She focused on Aaron again.

"And the police will do everything in their power to make sure nobody hurts you ever again!"

CHAPTER 24

"**A**gain a wrong lead? Man, we suck." Sally fell into her chair in the police station workroom, a dejected look on her face.

"Aw, come on Sally. We don't suck. This is how the job goes—get a lead, check it out, be proven right or wrong, then move on. Don't give up, youngster." Tonya patted her on the shoulder.

"I know." Sally sighed. "I was just so convinced General Clifford was our guy. But his story lines up—he left Vegas early, too early to have been at poker night with Sullivan and the Fearless Four."

"Well, at least we got some real hard evidence, even if it made our job harder as well," Tom said. "General Clifford's story is true. He tried to rekindle his relationship with his son but failed. They were estranged up until the day Mike died."

Chief Parlot nodded. "Exactly. Which is why we had to let him go."

"So, what now?" Sally spun around in her swivel chair, making then breaking eye contact with each of her colleagues. "How do we find the real Bullet?"

"If there even *is* a Bullet," Tom mumbled.

Tonya eyed him. "What's that, Tom my youngster?"

"I'm just wondering if Maria maybe got confused in the moment. She was in shock, after all. Maybe Clifford didn't mean 'a person' when he talked about a bullet. Maybe he just literally meant a bullet—like a bullet from his gun? He'd just been shot… and we already know he was half out of his mind, kidnapping Maria…. Maybe he was delirious, hallucinating by that point?"

Chief Parlot now stared at Tom. "Well, I guess we can only take Maria's word for it. But Sullivan *did* talk about a Bullet, the possible fourth member of the Fearless Four."

Tonya chewed on the pen she was holding. "True. So, I suggest we reexamine everything we have on the Fearless Four. Look over all the angles again. Shall we?"

Sally jumped out of her chair, leaving it spinning beneath her. "We've only pinned down three identities for sure: Agent James Borman, a.k.a. JB, former Police Chief Billings, a.k.a. Bill, and Senator Mike Clifford, a.k.a. Cliff."

"Exactly. Look over everything we have on them. Maybe we missed something," Tonya said. She paused. "Agent James Borman. Graphic material was found on his FBI computer. He was stationed in Utah. Elisabeth Collins's H.O.P.E. Club was in Utah."

Tom's eyes widened. "You think maybe JB was one of the higher-ups that allegedly abused young Air Force women?"

"But… but…" Sally struggled to find her words. "JB… James Borman, I mean… was an FBI agent. He worked for the FBI, not the Air Force. What business would he have had with an Air Force base in Utah?"

Chief Parlot scratched his chin. "We don't know. Let's find out. Come on, team, let's do some research. Let's focus on James Borman. Find out more about what we already know. The gambling. The graphic material on his computer. The reason he was fired from the FBI. His suicide. There's still a lot of unknowns surrounding him we haven't had time to chase down yet. And yes, the FBI is currently doing an internal investigation on him, but until we receive their report we're on our own."

Tonya snorted. "You won't lay eyes on that report for months. It takes forever to process an internal investigation, I tell ya."

"Well, then, let's get to it," the chief said, and they all got to work.

Chief Parlot paced back and forth in the cramped workroom, looking over some printouts. *Connection.... What's the connection here? I still can't figure it out. Why in the world would Agent Borman kidnap a toddler from Eglin Air Force Base? What did he even have to do with the base?*

"Was James Borman married?" Sally's question drew him from his thoughts and broke the silence in the workroom.

Tonya was the first to respond. "Why?"

"Because he left a suicide note."

Chief Parlot frowned. "Suicide note?"

"So? We all know Borman killed himself. Back in 2009, years after the kidnapping," Tonya said.

Tom nodded. "He killed himself two days after he was fired from the FBI because they found pictures of young girls on his computer. He was immediately suspended, then let go. Lost his pension. Lost it all. He knew there were charges on the way. Major jail time. He didn't see a way out and—boom—shot himself."

"That's right," Tonya said. "Shot himself with his own gun."

"I see," Sally said.

Chief Parlot kept staring at her. *What's she getting at?* Then suddenly he remembered something, something from earlier that day. His eyes widened. *Oh my.... Could it be?*

He cleared his throat. "Sally... you think it wasn't a suicide, don't you? You think Maria was correct when she said everyone involved in her kidnapping ended up dead—murdered. You think Borman was murdered and the FBI called it wrong?"

Sally shook her head. "Um, no, it was definitely suicide. He shot himself in the head. No question there. They even found this note, this suicide note... but the circumstances surrounding it I find strange."

The chief raised his eyebrows. "Like what?"

"First of all, whom do you leave a suicide note for, if not a loved one? He wasn't married. So, was this a note for a friend? His mom?"

Everyone shrugged their shoulders.

"Who is it made out to?" Tonya wondered.

Sally shook her head. "That's exactly my question."

"Let's find out then." Tom's fingers flew across the keyboard. He combed the internet at a blinding pace, jumping between various police and FBI databases, then stopped typing, a grin on his face. "Will this picture of the note do?"

Tonya, Sally, and the chief assembled around his chair to stare at the computer screen. There it was. A handwritten note. They all started reading it.

Bullet. My dearest Bullet. Time to end this, sweet Bullet. End this with me. Can't do it anymore. I have sinned but hope to be forgiven. Join me, Bullet!

The team looked at each other, all eyebrows raised.

"Very cryptic. A note to the bullet that took his life?" Tom shook his head. "Very strange. Well, let's see what the FBI have to say about this."

Before anyone could stop him, he clicked the note down and pulled up the police report, autopsy findings, and more.

"No further mention of the note. Guess they concluded he killed himself over losing his job, over 'having sinned' with all that graphic material they found on his computer. They wrapped up their reports, filed the note as evidence, and shelved the case. Their findings make sense," Tom said.

"Does it make sense? Pull up the suicide note again, please, Tom," Chief Parlot said, a slight grin on his face. "And now, *look* at it. Look closely. I think Borman is using personification."

"*Personification?*" Tom raised his eyebrows. "What do you mean, Chief?"

Tonya laughed. "C'mon, youngster, you know what personification is, don't you?" Tom shook his head. "Guess you didn't pay much attention in literature class, did you? Let me explain it to you then. It's a figure of speech. You take an object and make it into a person."

Sally nodded, her eyes sparkling. "Exactly. Here in this note, Borman is making the bullet into a person. He's talking to the bullet. He even capitalized the word. Why would he have done that if it was just a regular gun bullet?"

Tom scrunched his forehead. "I'm still confused."

Sally rolled her eyes. "Come on, Tom, think about it. Bullet is capitalized. People don't normally capitalize random letters in their writing, only proper nouns, like people's names. See it? 'My dearest Bullet...' Reads as though he's talking to a person."

"A person?" Tom was about to laugh when it dawned on him. "Holy cow, he's talking to a person? A person!" He looked at his colleagues, who were all grinning.

"Exactly. A person. He's talking to a person named Bullet," Chief Parlot said.

Tom almost fell off his chair. "Oh my, you're telling me Borman left a suicide note addressed to our mysterious Bullet? The guy we're looking for?"

Sally and the chief nodded, Tonya patted him on his back. "You finally got it, Tom. Thank goodness. Now, let's follow our new lead."

"Yes, let's do it. Great work, Sally." The chief gave her a high five. "Glad you researched that note. Come on, team, let's find out exactly what happened right before James Borman killed himself. Phone conversations, last-minute emails, anything that might lead us to Bullet."

Tonya walked over to the snack area, opened the fridge, and tossed an energy drink to Tom and Sally. "Let's get to work, team. I have a feeling tonight might be a long night, but at least we're on the right track here."

Chief Parlot nodded. "Agreed. Let's go. And, Tonya, since you're over there… make some coffee, will you please?"

"Sure, Isaac my man. I get you. Us old folk need some good, old-fashioned caffeine to stay awake." Tonya winked at the chief and started brewing a pot of coffee.

☻ ☻ ☻

"Look at this." Tom waved everyone over. Without hesitation, Sally, Tonya, and the chief dropped what they were doing and crowded around Tom's chair. They all stared at his computer screen.

"What am I looking at, Tom?" Chief Parlot wanted to know.

Sally scratched her chin. "Yeah, what's this? A phone number? And a time? Explain."

Tom grinned. "Take a closer look at both."

Tonya leaned over him and intensely studied the computer screen. She squinted, then her face lit up. "Aha. It's the day Agent James Borman took his life. Just a few minutes beforehand. Meaning this must be a number he called right before he shot himself?"

"Wow, good work, Tom," the chief said. "So who did he call?"

With one click, another site popped up on Tom's screen. They all leaned in even closer.

"It's a… prepaid cell phone number," Sally read out.

"Shucks. Prepaid?" Chief Parlot sighed. "Always tough to trace burner phones."

Tom grinned. "Usually, yes, Chief, but we've got a leg up this time. Got a copy of the receipt here. Lucky for us, this store that sold the phone did a good job keeping up their books. Cataloged every single payment. No tax evasion, that's a first! Thanks to them, we know this prepaid phone was bought a few weeks before Borman's suicide. In Texas."

Sally raised her eyebrows. "Texas? Why Texas? Who's in Texas?"

"Good question," the chief mumbled.

Tonya studied the receipt. "What about how the phone was paid for? Do we have a credit card we can trace to a name?"

Tom shook his head. "Nope. Cash payment."

"Shucks again." The chief sighed.

Tonya fingered the screen. "What's that on the receipt there? *There*. That extra line?"

Tom grinned again. "Military discount."

Sally's mouth fell open. "No way. Someone in the military bought and owned this phone? Then Agent James Borman called this person's phone minutes before he shot himself? He had a military friend in Texas?"

"Guess so," Tonya said. "Must have been a good friend. Usually you don't call random people right before you commit suicide, do you?"

"I wouldn't know, I've never tried." Tom chuckled, then stopped when he saw the appalled look on his colleagues' faces. "Sorry, that wasn't funny...."

Chief Parlot shook his head. "Anyway, Tonya is right. This person must have been close to Borman. It's reasonable to think it was Bullet."

"Right. Well then, guys, down your energy drinks and coffee and get back to work. Come on, let's go." Tonya clapped her hands together. "Chop-chop."

Sally yawned, then whispered to Tom, "How can she have so much energy this late at night? I'm much younger than her, and all I can think about is taking a nice nap right now."

Tonya laughed. "I heard that, *Officer* Sally Johnson." Sally's face turned red. "And I assure you, young lady, it's the good, old-fashioned caffeine that's keeping me going and alert. You should try it sometime instead of those strange energy drinks you youngsters chug."

Sally got up from her chair and saluted Tonya. "Yes, ma'am, I will try it again. Sometime. But not now. For now, I'll have another one of these *strange energy drinks* again." She smiled her beautiful, wide smile.

The chief chuckled. "Pound the caffeine one way or another. Either way, we gotta catch this military 'friend'—only then will we take a quick break to rest. How does that sound, team?"

"Fantastic," Tom said, and the ladies agreed.

"Good." The chief pulled out a large paper map from a filing cabinet and sat down at a table with it. "I'll look at military bases in Texas to pinpoint which is closest to the store the phone was bought. Knowing the base where the friend was stationed should help us out."

"Great idea, my man." Tonya gave him a pat on the shoulder. "Alright, alright, alright, my team, let's chug those caffeinated drinks and get a move on! Find that old military friend of JB's in Texas."

CHAPTER 25

I n Texas, the sun was just rising. The bright, orange-yellow ball rose in the clear blue sky, its rays shining through the white blinds of his bedroom window, illuminating his Air Force-blue bedsheets. He tossed and turned, then pulled the cover over his head.

I should get blackout curtains. These ones don't let me sleep in at all. He sighed and turned onto his back. With a long yawn, he opened his eyes and searched his nightstand for the remote control.

He turned on the TV to catch up on the news. While stretching and yawning, he listened closely to the news report. *Nothing new yet. General Clifford was released and seems to be staying put, camping out in his home. He's stuck there. Bad press. Fucker deserves it. He should've taken better care of Mike.*

For a brief moment, sadness washed over his face. His green eyes watered. *Oh, Mike. My son. While your real father scurries and hides, this one won't stand still. Don't worry, son, I'll avenge you. And bury my dark secret at the same time.*

He grinned now. *The news reports carried nothing else on the H.O.P.E. Club—and I'll make sure it stays that way. Hidden and buried in the past. Lulu-girl will take care of it.* His smile vanished, his eyebrows scrunched in. *At least I hope so.*

The phone on his nightstand vibrated. He turned around to pick it up and look at it. Incoming text message. He read it, a big smile back on his face. *Lulu-girl. She's made it to Florida. She'll take care of everything. Nice.*

Good was all he texted back. No reply came from her.

She can do it. She's strong now. She's a somebody now. I raised her up the same way I did with Mike. Made them into somebodies. He smiled. The sunrays shone brighter now onto his dark-blue sheets. The TV was running, but he was no longer listening. Instead, he was lost in thought.

I raised them both. Held onto them with invisible strings. Like puppets. Mike was always willing to do as I say. He was eager to please me. Lulu-girl... not so much. She was always the stubborn one, had her own ideas about right and wrong. He frowned. *Women. Hard to keep them in their place. You never know what's going on in their heads, even when they nod and smile at you. And then those emotions of theirs... yuck.*

He shook himself. *Those female emotions always get in the way. I don't get it at all.*

Abruptly, the color drained from his face. He picked up his phone and reread her text message: *I'll find Elisabeth today and talk to her. No worries.*

His hands got sweaty. *No worries? But what if Lulu-girl suddenly gets emotional? Changes her mind? What if the strings that bind her to me aren't strong enough? What if she becomes convinced it's in her best interests to bring up the past again, to go back to being who she was, to feel the way she felt back when she was Elisabeth's?*

His pale face starkly contrasted with his red hair and the blue bedsheets. His green eyes opened wide. *No, I can't rely solely on Lulu-girl. Too much risk. I need to be there to guide her. I have to. 'Cuz this time, there might be two Collins girls trying to influence my Lulu-girl. And I can't let that happen.*

Quickly, he jumped out of bed and started pacing back and forth, phone still in hand, the TV still running. The news had moved on to the weather. He glanced over at the screen. Sunshine. Clear skies. Beautiful day to go on a trip.

A big smile spread across his face. He stopped pacing. *Beautiful day to go on a trip? Indeed, a beautiful day to fly. Brilliant.*

He unlocked his phone and started dialing. After a few rings, someone picked up. "Tyler, hey, good morning. Sorry to call so early but it's looking like a beautiful day out there and I'd love to take good ol' Cassie out for a spin. Just wanted to catch you before you head to work."

He forced a warm laugh at Tyler's response and continued, "Yeah, you're right, nobody goes to work this early. I'm sorry, Tyler. Sorry I woke you. I just got excited about flying today. Still, please have her ready for me. Looking forward to taking the Cessna out."

Still smiling, he listened as Tyler gabbed on. Responded, "That's right. Always takes a while to make sure everything's ready. And yes, great day for flying for sure. In fact, I'd like to fly all the way to Florida and stay the night. Please have everything ready. Including permission from Eglin AFB to land there. And let them know my plans."

He nodded. "Correct. The Aero Club at Eglin AFB. I'll store my Cessna there and remain on base. I'm sure they won't mind."

CHAPTER 26

"*I'm sure they won't mind. I already told Brad it might get late today and he's taking care of our little one.*" *Elisabeth smiled at the beautiful young Airman with the long, dark hair. "I'm here for you. You can tell me, Lu. I know something's been bothering you, and I'd like to help."*

The young Airman stared at the tabletop, her long, dark hair falling down, hiding her pretty face. Elisabeth put an arm around her. "Lu, you've come to every single meeting we've held since last year. You've listened to all the others complain, listened to them share their stories. But you've never spoken. Why?"

Lu shrugged her shoulders slightly. Elisabeth sighed. I know something is bothering this young lady. Why doesn't she open up to me?

Elisabeth looked up as two women in uniform, the last of the going-away party attendees, approached her and Lu. "We're leaving now," one of them said. "Thanks again for everything, Elisabeth. It was a pleasure working with you. Learning that some things aren't right and worth speaking up for."

The other nodded. "That's right. We learned a lot, and now we'll never forget to speak up if something seems unfair or mean. All thanks to you."

Elisabeth blushed. "Aw, thanks, ladies."

"We'll miss you," the first woman said, and the other nodded.

"Don't worry, you're in good hands. Riley has what it takes to keep the club going strong," Elisabeth said, then got up and gave the two ladies a hug. She waved them off as they left the restaurant.

She sat back down next to Lu. They were the only two left now. Everyone else had left.

Elisabeth glanced over to all of the gifts and tokens she'd been given this evening. Sighed. It's hard to leave. I really don't want to, but a new assignment is a new assignment. Florida it is. Maybe it won't be so bad? And I know Riley is good. She'll take care of these women and continue our good work within the H.O.P.E. Club. And perhaps Eglin needs a club like this, too? I could certainly try to establish a new branch there.

She glanced over at the young woman next to her. She hadn't moved. She hadn't looked up. Her hair was still covering her face, hiding it from Elisabeth. From the world.

Elisabeth studied her. What's up with her? She's been coming to the club meetings for so long yet hasn't said a word. All I know is that her name is Lu.

"Lu?" she said softly. The young woman now looked up at Elisabeth, her dark-brown eyes sad. "I get the feeling you have something you want to share. If so, I'm all yours. I'm all ears. Everyone else is gone, you have my full attention. I assume you didn't come to the H.O.P.E. Club for fun. I figure you had an experience you want to share as well, don't you?"

Lu's big brown eyes, still fixated on Elisabeth, started watering. Lu nodded slightly.

"What is it, Lu? You've heard other women talk about their experiences in the workplace. How they were unfairly treated. How they were often subjected to harassment."

Lu nodded, her eyes wide.

"Do you have a similar story?"

Lu nodded again but didn't say anything. She stared back at the table, her long, straight black hair covering her face once more.

"Lu, was someone unfair to you?"

The young woman nodded so hard her black hair whipped wildly all around her.

"Someone in the workplace?"

Another nod, slighter this time.

"Was this person mean to you?"

Lu nodded again, still not saying a word, still covering her face with her dark hair, hiding behind it.

Elisabeth put an arm around her shoulder. "Lu, this person who was unfair and mean to you… is it a man?"

Lu nodded again. Elisabeth felt the girl's shoulders droop. She had made herself physically smaller. A fear response. Elisabeth's heart started beating fast. She knew something bad must have happened to this frail young lady who tried so hard to hide herself from the world.

"Did this man hurt you?"

A violent nod, black hair flying all around, brushing Elisabeth's face. She smelled the fruity flavor of the shampoo Lu used. An innocent smell, a young girl's smell.

Elisabeth felt a knot form in her throat. She had to take a deep breath in to clear it. "How did this man hurt you? Did he touch you inappropriately?"

No response. With her arm around the young lady, Elisabeth shook her slightly, grounding her. "Please tell me, Lu. I cannot help you if you won't tell me. I assure you, whatever happened, we'll make sure it never happens again. Whoever did this, we'll bring him down."

Lu lifted her head, her brown eyes now piercing through Elisabeth. Finally used her words. "Do you promise to help me bring him down, even after you leave?"

Elisabeth nodded. "Yes, I promise. Whatever needs to be done, will be done. No matter if I'm here or in Florida. I'll help you. I'll be there for you."

Lu turned away from Elisabeth again.

"Lu, do you hear me? I'll be there for you. I'll fight for you like I have the other women in this club. We can fight together. But you have to tell me, please. What happened? What did this guy do to you?"

With a determined look in her dark-brown eyes, Lu turned to Elisabeth. "He raped me." Elisabeth gasped. "Not just once. Often. For months. And he brought his friends along for the ride."

With a scream Elisabeth woke, her heart racing, her forehead wet with sweat.

"Elisabeth? Are you alright?" came Brad's familiar, soft voice in the darkness. Sunrays snuck through the blinds and illuminated the hospital room in a pale sheen.

Elisabeth calmed her breaths before she answered. "Yeah."

"What's going on? Bad dream?"

"Yeah."

"About our daughter?"

"Nope. Not this time." Elisabeth wiped the sweat off her forehead. She kept silent for a time.

"Hun?"

"Yeah? What is it, Brad?"

"I'm worried about you. What's going on? I can see you right now, you know, crouched over on your bed, I hear you breathing fast. What's happening? Talk to me."

Elisabeth took a shallow breath. "I had a dream about the young lady from the H.O.P.E. Club."

"The Guadalupe girl?"

"Yeah. She went by Lu."

"What?"

"Her nickname was Lu. Went by Lu."

"Okay, good. So you remembered her nickname."

165

"Yeah." Elisabeth's eyes followed the sunrays, which left a streaky pattern on the hospital room floor. Suddenly, she felt sick. Sick to her stomach, just aching everywhere. She groaned in pain.

"Goodness, Elisabeth, are you okay?"

"Just my stomach." She rubbed it. She knew where the pain came from. Regret. Sorrow. Shame. She burst into tears.

Brad tried to get up but was held back by the monitor cables still attached to his body. "Elisabeth, please. Come here. Talk to me. Please, hun."

Tears streaming down her face, she slowly rose from her bed and shambled over to him. She sat down, her head leaning on his uninjured shoulder. Helplessly, she cried into his strong chest.

"Oh, Brad. I've made a mistake, a huge mistake. I promised Lu I'd be there for her. But I broke that promise, just forgot about it. Forgot there was someone in this world who needed my help desperately, someone who was counting on me. Just as much as our daughter."

Brad stroked her back as the whole story poured out of her. "But I forgot about Lu, forgot about her pain and her gut-wrenching story, because our daughter disappeared. I was so caught up in my own pain that I forgot hers. Completely forgot hers. Forgot her."

"Hun, it's understandable that—"

"That young woman was just as lost as Moana was! Cast away, never to be seen again. Never to be heard from again. I let her down—just like I let down our little one. I failed them, failed to protect the both of them."

"Oh, hun, it wasn't your fault." Brad stroked her back as she sobbed into his hospital gown. "It's gonna be okay. It's okay, hun."

But Elisabeth barely heard his soothing words. As she sat there, rocking against him, her thoughts were far away. Back in Utah. Back at that restaurant. Back with the young woman crying into *her* shoulder, mascara smearing on Elisabeth's white shirt. She closed her eyes and a scene from long ago played out before her.

Elisabeth's shoulder was wet from the young woman's tears. "Lu, you need to report this. This isn't just intimidation or harassment. This is rape—serious sexual abuse. You need to speak up and report this guy."

Lu shook her head. "No one will believe me. Who am I compared to him? A nobody. He's a somebody—he's so high up the chain of command."

"Lu, rank doesn't matter here. If anything, it makes it worse—*much* worse. It's abuse of power, on top of everything else."

The young woman sat up to wipe away her tears with her bare hands. Elisabeth searched her purse and handed her a tissue. The woman blew her nose. "I can't do it. It'll destroy his career."

Elisabeth nodded. "Yes, it will. But he deserves it. The bastard deserves it."

Lu looked up at Elisabeth, tears still caught in her long, black eyelashes, her dark-brown eyes filled with sadness. She stared down at the table. "Maybe I led him on? Maybe it was my fault."

"No, it wasn't *your* fault. It's definitely *not* your fault," Elisabeth said, her voice sharp. She turned Lu's head to hers. "Lu, look at me, listen to me. *It's not your fault!* You said he called you into his office one day and took advantage of you. You couldn't have possibly led him on. You did nothing wrong. You're the victim here. He had no right to touch you, especially not after you asked him to stop. But he didn't stop. He did it over and over again. Used his power over you, threatened harm if you dared say anything."

Lu nodded. "Yeah, he said he'd end my career in the Air Force if I ever spoke out. And that nobody would ever hire me again."

"Exactly. That's intimidation. Abuse of power. It's so wrong, Lu, so wrong." Elisabeth's lip started quivering and a big tear ran down her straight, freckled nose. "Wait, you said he invited his friends to take advantage of you, too? Oh no.... I'm so, so sorry this happened to you. It's so wrong, so disgusting. It just makes me sick! Lu, who is this bastard?"

"I can't tell you," Lu whispered.

Elisabeth enveloped the young woman in her arms. Both women cried while hugging each other. Elisabeth stroked her back. "You don't have to tell me. But you do need to report him."

The young lady sobbed. "I can't. They won't believe me. Nobody'll believe me."

Elisabeth cupped Lu's face and looked directly at her now. "*I* believe you. And if I do, so will others. Trust me."

Lu sobbed again. Elisabeth hugged her tight. *This poor, young Airman. I know she has a point—it'll be a long, long fight. And not a fair one. But she needs to do this.*

"Lu, you deserve justice, he deserves jail. And just think about it: If we don't report him, he'll continue his games, his crimes. Men like him always do. Think about how your actions can help others, how you have the power to protect other women in the future. Protect them *from him*. You have to protect others from going through what you've been through."

Elisabeth felt Lu stiffen in her hug. The young woman wrested free from the embrace and took hold of Elisabeth's hands. "You're right. I need to do this. No matter what. Regardless of if I lose my job, or others look down on me. He needs to go down. He needs to lose his job. His power. I need to report him."

"That's right, that's right, Lu. You can do this." Elisabeth smiled at the young woman and her newfound courage.

Then the sparkle in the girl's eyes vanished. They were watering again. "I… I can't do this without you."

Elisabeth stared at her. *But I'm moving. Tomorrow.* For the first time that night, Elisabeth turned away from the young woman and focused on something in the distance.

"Elisabeth, please, I need you. I can't do this alone. Will you be there for me? Will you support me?"

Elisabeth sighed. "You know I'm leaving for Florida tomorrow…."

"I know, I know. But can't you come back? Please? Fly back to help me?"

Elisabeth looked at Lu's hopeful, beautiful face, her big brown eyes begging for her help. Her heart hurt.

"Please come back. You're the only one I've told. You're the only one who knows. The only one I trust. I just need you here for one weekend. To hold my hand when I report this guy. Please."

Elisabeth sighed, her mind racing. Then her face lit up. "You know what? Fourth of July weekend is coming up. Still a ways off, I know, but you'll be safe for now because the guy is gone, right?"

Lu nodded. "Yeah, he got stationed somewhere else."

"Okay, good. So we have time, right?" Elisabeth saw Lu nod, her big brown eyes hopeful. "I think I can get away that holiday weekend. I can leave my little one with Brad and his parents, who plan to visit us that weekend. That should work."

She saw the hope in Lu's face. It lit her up. Her tears dried, her face took on a determined expression. "Fourth of July weekend it is, then. The weekend we'll bring him down. You're right, he deserves it. We need to protect other women from him. We just have to. They can't go through what I did. Nobody deserves that."

Elisabeth smiled. "That's right, strong woman. You're right; nobody deserves it. We'll take him down, together. Fourth of July. And wherever he's stationed now, they'll find him and lock him up for what he did to you. And then you will tell your story. It'll help you and others. Yes, you can do this!"

Lu smiled wide, a big, beautiful smile. "I can do this. With you! Promise me you'll be there."

Elisabeth lifted her pinky. "I promise. Pinky promise I'll be there. And I never break my promises. I will be there—with you, for you!"

Elisabeth opened her eyes again and heard Brad's heartbeat in her ear. The dull sound somehow calmed her down. And just like that, she felt determined. She sat up and looked straight at Brad. "We need to find her. The girl. I have to find her and apologize for not being there for her. I have to explain to her why I couldn't be there. I just have to."

Brad nodded. "Sure. That's a good idea. And you'll see. Doubt she's mad at you. Surely she'll understand there were powerful, unbelievable circumstances holding you back from being there for her. By now there's a good chance she's doing just fine."

Elisabeth nodded. "I hope she is." She did her best to ignore the big knot in her stomach.

CHAPTER 27

"**S**tomach, ahhh, my stomach." Nick put both hands over his belly. "I'm so, so hungry. Please, Maria, can we start now?"

"No, my mom isn't here yet." Maria looked out the inn's dining room window. "Drew said it wouldn't take long to pick her up so she could eat breakfast with the rest of us."

Keisha shrugged. "Maybe she decided differently and stayed with your dad for breakfast at the hospital instead?"

Maria shook her head and pulled her phone from her pocket. "Nope, she would've texted me."

"Maybe she forgot," Jim said.

"And somehow, darlin', I doubt she'd be mad if we started without her. You know how it is, we can eat for hours and hours. Especially if there's a waffle maker like they have here." Brandy pointed to the hotel's breakfast area.

"Please, please, *please*, Maria. I'm so hungry. Starving." Nick pouted and threw Maria a puppy-eyed look.

But Maria remained resolute. "Nope, Germans always wait for one another before they begin eating together. Right, Sarah?" Maria turned to her mom's friend, who nodded. "See, I'm right. So we'll wait."

Everyone sighed. Then they saw a car arrive.

"There she is." Jack smiled and pointed out the window.

"Gracias a dios." Martina grinned. "We can all start eating now."

They all watched as Elisabeth and Drew got out of the car and walked inside together. Drew was dressed in a suit and tie, Elisabeth in a nice summer dress. "Good morning," Drew said as the pair joined the group in the dining room. "How's everyone this morning?"

"Starving to death," Nick said, and got elbowed by Brandy.

"Good, sir." Brandy smiled. "We're all good. Ready for breakfast, though."

Maria ran over to give her mom a hug. "Hi, Mom, how's Dad?"

Elisabeth hugged her back and smiled. "He's alright, mein Engel, doing just fine. How are you? And how's Aaron?"

Aaron got up to greet Elisabeth as well. "I'm fair. Shoulder still hurts, but not too badly. Can't complain."

"That's good, Aaron, very good." Elisabeth patted him on his good shoulder, then turned to Jack. "And how are you, Jack?"

"I'm well, Elisabeth. Happy to hear everyone's doing good."

"Sí, and I'm happy you're back, Elisabeth. Everyone's been waiting for you." Martina gave her a warm hug. The two moms smiled at each other. "Especially Maria. Has been waiting for you. Refused to eat without you."

Elisabeth looked at the others in the room. "You haven't started yet?" Everyone shook their heads. "Oh dear."

Sarah winked at Elisabeth and laughed. "Ja, ja, somehow your daughter is very German."

Elisabeth glanced at Maria, who was still standing next to her, then gave her another quick side squeeze. "Meine Süße," she whispered in her ear, then turned to everyone. "I'm here now. So, what are you waiting for?"

Nick and Jim jumped up at the same time and ran toward the waffle maker. Jim just managed to beat Nick there. "Not fair, man." Nick pouted as Jim poured a large spoon of batter on the waffle maker. "I'm the super hungry one."

Jim grinned. "You were too slow, dude."

Keisha rolled her eyes as she walked by. "Knock it off, guys."

"Yeah, don't be silly, y'all won't starve." Brandy batted her long eyelashes. "And if you were super hungry, my darlin' Nick, you'd be smart and get something else to eat first. Like this good Southern cookin'." She showed Nick her steaming plate of biscuits and gravy. "Oh well. See ya at the table."

Nick sniffed the air. "Oh man, that smells good. But there's a line there now, too."

He looked back to where the offered eggs and bacon, biscuit and gravy, oatmeal, bagels, and toast were laid out. Sarah and Elisabeth were occupying the toaster, Aaron and Jack stacking eggs and bacon on their plates. Martina filled her bowl with oatmeal. Back at the table, Drew was already munching on bacon while Keisha and Brandy had started in on their biscuits. Only Maria was in line for waffles, behind Nick.

She grinned at him. "Good things come to those who wait."

Nick shook his head. "Not if everything's been eaten up."

She gave him a pat on the shoulder. "You're funny. C'mon, there's plenty of food for all of us. And look, we're the only large group here, no major competition. I'm sure you'll find something."

Jim put a nicely browned waffle on his plate, then turned to Nick. "Your turn now. Enjoy."

"Oh, good." Nick stepped forward and poured batter into the waffle maker with gusto.

"Nick, if you were a gentleman you'd let me go first. After all, I'm the poor girl who's been through so much and you drove so far to see." Maria batted her eyes at him.

"Hey, Nick," Brandy called over, "you should let Maria go first."

"See?" Maria laughed.

Nick sighed, then stepped aside. "Fine. Ladies first."

Maria grinned. "Thanks, Nick, you're a real gentleman. Appreciate it." She turned the waffle maker over, popped it open, and a nicely browned waffle fell onto her plate. "Perfect. Your turn now."

She walked over to get some syrup and a side of oatmeal. Plate in hand, she turned to look around the room, listened to all the friendly conversation. She smiled. *I love having my friends and family here. It's good. I feel happy and safe now.*

She sat between Aaron and Keisha, across from Elisabeth and Sarah, and started eating her waffle, a smile on her face. Once she was finished, she watched as her friends and loved ones made the trip back and forth to get seconds and thirds. She listened to the conversations around her and smiled. *It's good to see them all together, getting along so well. It'll only get better from here. Life's gonna be just fine.* She caught herself clenching her hands in her lap. *Well, at least that's what I'm hoping. I don't want anything else bad to happen. I have everyone I need. I have my parents, I have my mamá, I have Aaron, I have my friends. They're enough for me.*

She frowned. *But I killed someone. Oh my gosh, I killed someone!* She closed her eyes. *But he deserved it. He attacked me. It was self-defense.*

Keisha elbowed her. "You alright, girl?"

Maria opened her eyes and nodded. "Yeah, I am. Glad you're all here."

Keisha studied her face. "Are you? Didn't seem too happy there a moment ago."

"I just have a lot on my mind," Maria whispered, then smiled at her friend. "But I *am* glad you're here."

"That's good, girl. So am I. I'm glad we came. Happy to meet your real parents. And of course, you needed us here."

Maria raised her eyebrows. "I needed you?"

"Yeah, girl. Not just for support but to help you two move into the new apartment, right? He sure can't carry much now. Just look at him, his arm in a sling and all."

Maria smiled. "That's right. We did need the help. Otherwise, poor Jack would've had to carry all our heavy things up by himself. Probably thrown out his back in two minutes flat."

Keisha winked at her. "Exactly. So cheer up, girl. We're all here and from now on it's gonna be fine. Try to look forward to the next chapter of your life. With Aaron, with your parents. Right?"

"Right."

Keisha turned back to their friends and was quickly drawn into their banter. Aaron was chatting with Sarah and Martina. Drew and Jack were deep in conversation also. Maria sighed. *All is well.* She watched the little hairs on her arms stand up. *But somehow, I still feel like we're missing something. Something big. But maybe I'm just making it up? Nobody else seems to be worried.*

She looked around and realized Elisabeth was staring at her empty plate, not engaging in conversation with anyone. *Well, maybe I was wrong? Mom seems awfully worried.* "Mom?" Elisabeth didn't react, so Maria reached across the table to lay a comforting hand on her. "Mom? Alles okay?"

Elisabeth sighed. "Yeah, I guess."

"You guess? Not very convincing. What's bothering you?"

Elisabeth let out another deep sigh. "I had a dream. About the girl from the H.O.P.E. Club."

Maria's eyes widened. "Guadalupe?"

Elisabeth nodded.

"What about her?"

Elisabeth squeezed Maria's hand. "Not now, mein Engel. I'll tell you later."

"Why?"

"Because I don't want everyone to overhear us."

"Oh, okay." Maria thought for a bit. "Maybe you and I can take a walk together after breakfast?"

Elisabeth smiled. "Okay. Maybe."

The two women listened to the conversations around them until Drew stood up. "Well, everyone, time to head to my meetings. I'll see you all later."

The group all waved goodbye, then discussed their plans for the day. "Okay, sounds good, everyone. Try to be ready to leave for the apartment in an hour or so," Aaron said.

"Sounds good, man," Nick said, took Brandy's hand, and they both left for their room. The rest soon followed.

Aaron was about to walk upstairs when he realized Maria hadn't moved. "Maria, you coming?"

Martina smiled. "Mija, vamos," she added.

Maria shook her head. "I think Mom and I are headed out for a quick walk. We'll be back in about half an hour, okay?"

"A walk? A walk sounds nice," Martina said. "Can I come?"

Maria glanced at Elisabeth. "Well, Mamá, I'm not sure—"

"Sure," Elisabeth interrupted Maria, "let's take a walk together. Just us girls."

"Are you sure?" Maria asked her mom.

"Yes, Maria, I'm sure. I think it'll be good for your mamá to hear this, too."

"Okay."

Aaron looked from one lady to the next. "Technically, you ladies require a sponsor while outdoors on base. You can't be by yourself on a military installation without—"

Lieutenant Martinez cleared his throat. "I'll keep an eye on them. The chief wants me to keep a close watch over Maria and Martina anyway." They all exchanged glances. "No worries, I'll keep my distance. You won't even notice I'm there. Or did you catch me at breakfast?"

Maria laughed. "No, sir, we didn't. You're very discreet."

The lieutenant smiled. "Exactly."

"Alright, I'll see you ladies later, then." Aaron came over and gave Maria a quick kiss. "Lieutenant Martinez, take good care of them, please."

"Yes, sir." The men saluted each other, then Aaron walked upstairs while Maria, Martina, and Elisabeth stepped out into the humid Florida air, Lieutenant Martinez not far behind.

😀 😀 😀

They'd been walking for a while without saying anything, just admiring the landscape around them. The sandy ground, the cypress, pine, and palm trees, the blue sky.

Martina was the first to break the silence. "Beautiful, no?"

Maria and Elisabeth nodded.

"But so hot and humid. Already sweating." Elisabeth pulled a tissue from her purse and dabbed her forehead with it.

Martina laughed. "Welcome to Florida."

They kept walking. Maria noted Elisabeth's determined steps. "So, Mom, what's bothering you? You told me at breakfast you'd share it with me later. Now seems like a good time."

Elisabeth abruptly came to a halt and sighed. Martina almost bumped into her. "Dios mío, Elisabeth, next time warn me before you just stop."

Maria laughed. "You guys are funny. But anyway, Mom, what's going on?"

Elisabeth turned to look at Maria and Martina. "The girl from the H.O.P.E. Club…."

"Guadalupe?" Maria said. "What about her?"

Elisabeth sighed. "Well, nothing to do with the recent craziness here…."

"But if it's bothering you, Elisabeth, it is worth talking about. Tell us. Please," Martina insisted.

"I realized just recently I let that girl down. Really failed her. I promised I'd meet with her to do something very important twenty years ago, but never did." Elisabeth closed her eyes, her lips quivering.

"Oh, Mom." Maria walked over to give her a hug.

"Nonsense, Elisabeth! This again?" Martina crossed her arms in front of her chest. "I told you before: you had other problems. Suddenly, your daughter was gone. Anyone who doesn't understand how much pain you were in is an idiot. I'm sure that lady would understand."

"Let me ask you this, Martina. You've been through bad times before. You were harassed, abused."

"Sí. So?"

"If you were to finally reach out for help, confide in someone who promised to help you report your abuser, but then that someone failed to show up when it mattered most, just ghosted you, forgot about you... how would you feel?" Elisabeth's blue eyes rested on Martina.

Martina thought about it. "I'd feel betrayed. Upset. Very sad. Then very mad."

Elisabeth sighed, her blue eyes sad. "Exactly."

Maria looked back and forth between her two moms. She saw Martina's eyes widen. "¡Dios mío! Are you saying this young lady got so mad she kidnapped your child?"

Both Maria and Elisabeth raised their eyebrows, then Maria started laughing. "Come on, Mamá. That's ridiculous. First of all, the timeline doesn't add up. Mom was going to help this young woman around the Fourth of July weekend. I disappeared before then, which led to Mom not seeing her, not the other way around. If she was so mad she wanted to hurt my mom and dad, she would've kidnapped me *after* Mom failed to show up. But Mom only failed to show up because I wasn't there."

"Sí, makes sense," Martina mumbled. "But why so upset, Elisabeth?"

Elisabeth stared at the sandy ground now. "Because I've failed them both. I've failed to save that young lady, I've failed Moana— Maria, I mean. They both needed saving, but no help came. They lost their rock, their person who should've been there for them. I've failed.... I'm a bad mom, a bad friend..."

Maria gave Elisabeth a big hug. "That's not true! You're not a bad mom and you're not a bad friend either. All of this wasn't your fault. You know that, right?"

PUPPETS OF THE PAST

Elisabeth nodded. "I know, but I feel so guilty. She went through so much. I had a dream about her last night. I really just want to see her again, make sure she's alright, and apologize."

Elisabeth nodded. "Yes, I need to find her. She went through so much. I really hope she's doing alright now."

"Let's do that then. Let's find her so you can apologize. I bet that'll make you feel better." Maria's eyes lit up. "Who can we ask about finding her? Maybe Dad? Didn't he say she might be in the Air Force Network System since she was Air Force herself? Or maybe Aaron could help? He has access, right? Or Nick and Jim? Anyone in the Air Force could technically look her up, right?"

"I guess so." Elisabeth nodded. "That would be a good start to track her down."

"Let's do it, if it makes you feel better, Elisabeth." Martina checked her watch. "We better head back to the inn soon." She turned around to walk back, her eyes still on Elisabeth. "But I still don't understand why this girl is so important *now*. Thought the H.O.P.E. Club was only important because you thought you made some enemies there?"

Elisabeth sighed. "I don't know. I figured at least one of the men on base got pissed off after we found out about them, enough to possibly retaliate. That was my first thought, even before I remembered Lu's story."

"¿Quién? Lu?"

"Lu is the name Guadalupe used to go by. Her real name was just too long and too hard for most people to pronounce right."

"I see. She might use the shortened version in the Air Force," Maria said. "Glad you remembered that, Mom."

Martina nodded. "Sí. But still not sure what this Lu has to do with enemies? I understand she might be upset with you. But no enemy, no?"

Elisabeth shook her head. "No, she would never be my enemy. And the other guys we reprimanded in the H.O.P.E. Club were for minor things. Inappropriate language, gender discrimination, the occasional inappropriate touch. All minor offenses. Until Lu came along. When she told me she was raped by a higher-up."

Maria thought for a while. "Who did this to poor Lu? Do you think *that* guy became your enemy?"

Elisabeth buried her head in her hands. "I don't know, just don't know. I don't think so. He wasn't even stationed at the same base anymore when Lu told me. He'd moved on. And you disappeared just a few days after Lu confided in me. The timeline doesn't make sense. Would have been way too fast for him to react even if he found out."

Martina nodded. "Sí. The kidnapping was planned. For a long time. So no, doesn't make sense, a few days after this girl exposed her rapist."

Maria's arm hairs stood up. *They're right. It doesn't make sense.* She ignored her body's reaction and focused again on her two moms. "Lu never told you who did it?"

Elisabeth shook her head. "No, she was going to tell me the weekend we were supposed to report him. Which didn't happen...." Elisabeth started crying. "I let her down. I *so* let her down."

Both Maria and Martina comforted her. For a while, they just stood there in a group hug. Then they heard footsteps in the distance. Maria looked up. A jogger was running toward them, her long ponytail bobbing with every stride.

"I have to find her and apologize. She was such a beautiful young Hispanic lady. Long, black hair, beautiful skin complexion, skinny."

Maria watched as the jogger came closer. *A woman. Perfect running form. Her arms supported each long stride, elbows braced in perfect ninety-degree angles. Long black hair in a ponytail. Short, probably Mamá's height. No more than five foot three. Petite.*

"She was probably your height, Martina. A petite young lady. Big brown eyes like yours. But long, black, straight hair, not curly."

Maria listened to her mom's description of Lu as she watched the jogger approach. She stood tall and kept studying the jogger. *An older lady, probably middle-aged. Definitely looks Hispanic. It's almost as if Mom were describing this woman....* Maria gasped. *No way!*

She tapped Elisabeth on the shoulder. "Do you think Lu's still in the Air Force?"

Martina raised her eyebrows. "¿Qué?"

Elisabeth got out of the group hug to better address her daughter. "What?"

The jogger drew close now, and Maria could see the smile on her beautiful face, but then it abruptly vanished. Before Maria could raise a hand in greeting, the jogger turned and sprinted away in the opposite direction she'd been headed. Away from the three women.

Maria tilted her head as she watched the bobbing ponytail fading into the distance. *Odd. Very odd.*

She turned to her mom. "Mom, did Lu like to work out?"

Elisabeth smiled. "Oh yes, she loved jogging. Always had perfect form. She always made a point of showing others how to hold their arms while jogging to make their stride more efficient." Elisabeth giggled. "She corrected me. And others, too. She was often used as an example on base of how to run. Something to do with the posture of her arms."

Maria watched the jogger's figure get smaller and smaller as she receded. "Did she hold her arms like this, elbows at a perfect ninety-degree angle?"

Elisabeth laughed. "That's right. She was dubbed the 'ninety-degree runner.'" Her smile vanished. "But how would you know that?"

"And you're sure she's not mad at you and doesn't want to hurt you?"

"What?" Elisabeth shook her head. "No, she wouldn't dare. She has every right to be mad at me, but she's not a violent person. She's a victim. Had a hard time standing up for herself and—"

"Why, Maria?" Martina interrupted, her eyebrows scrunched. "Why do you ask?"

"Because I just saw a jogger who totally fit your description of Lu, Mom." Maria pointed at the figure who had nearly disappeared into the distance.

Elisabeth stared in that direction but couldn't make out anything. "Are you saying you saw Lu? Someone who looks like her?"

"There was a lady who was jogging toward us and suddenly turned around right before she passed by. Sure looked like an older version of the young Guadalupe you were describing."

Elisabeth's mouth dropped open. "You think she might be here?"

Martina spotted the woman's figure in the distance and studied her. "Sí, could be a Hispanic middle-aged woman. Maybe really her? Maybe she's still working for the Air Force and is stationed here—or here on business? Like Brad. Possible, no?"

Elisabeth's eyes lit up. "That would be awesome. That would make it really easy to talk to her in person. Explain what happened. Come on, ladies, we better head back. I need to call Brad. I'll have him look her up. We'll find out if she's still in the Air Force and here at this moment. And if she is—my goodness, what a coincidence."

Elisabeth turned and briskly walked back in the direction of the hotel, Martina in tow. Both of them determined, both of them smiling. "This should be great for you, Elisabeth." She squeezed Elisabeth's hand as they walked side by side. Elisabeth nodded.

Maria followed her two moms. *Great?* She turned to look over her shoulder, but the jogger was gone now. *Just a coincidence, huh? Nobody else finds this very strange?*

CHAPTER 28

Strange. I feel so strange. Lu's thoughts raced as she picked up her pace on her jog back to the Distinguished Visitor's Quarters. She ran even faster, almost sprinting now. *I chickened out. But I didn't expect to see her so soon. Elisabeth.*

Despite being in excellent shape, Lu was breathing hard with every stride she took. Sweat ran down her forehead, pooled around her chin, then dripped onto her shirt. *I'm sure it was Elisabeth. I already know she chopped off her hair. And the other ladies? One of them looked like her daughter. She has the same hair Elisabeth used to have, the same slender, tall figure. Her long-lost daughter. All grown up now.*

The stately Distinguished Visitor's Quarters appeared in the distance. Lu sprinted toward it. As she drew closer to the front doorsteps, she threw her head forward, as if running a race crossing the finish line, then finally let up. She slowed to a walk, her hands above her head. Her breathing came fast, her heartbeat loud in her ears. She checked her smartwatch. *Got a good one in. Quite a lot of miles.* She smiled. *A good pace today. I'll ace the Air Force fitness test again, I bet.*

She walked around a bit in front of the house she currently called home, cooling down, then sat down on the front steps. Her smartwatch blinked and informed her of an incoming text message. She checked it, then smiled. Her husband, Daniel, had wished her a great day. She quickly texted back, then went inside.

Lu gulped down a whole glass of water, then jumped into the shower. The warm water ran down her sweaty body, the aroma of lavender bodywash filling her nostrils. She felt good, healthy, strong.

After my shower I'll find Elisabeth. She must be staying on base somewhere. Probably in one of the TLFs or the Air Force Inn. I'll find out. And then I'll talk to her. Make sure she won't say anything else to anyone about the H.O.P.E. Club. What happened to me needs to stay a secret. Her face took on a determined look. *Definitely. Nobody can find out.*

She finished her shower, dressed, then went to the kitchen to find some food. There were cereal bars and Keurig cups in the pantry. *Not much, but it'll do for now.*

She sat down at the round kitchen table by the window and overlooked the bay. *It's so beautiful here. Very pretty. I wouldn't mind getting stationed here. I bet Daniel wouldn't mind either. Pretty beaches, shallow water. Safe even for little kids.*

Lu sighed. *Kids.* She took another sip of her coffee. *I know Daniel would love to have kids. I'm glad he's okay with never being a daddy, though. 'Cuz he sure can't have kids with me.* Sadness washed over her face. *He's so understanding, but I lied to him. Couldn't tell him why I can't have kids. I just lied. Couldn't stand to tell him I'm damaged goods because other guys—a bunch of mean bastards, especially* him—*took that away from me while they had their fun.*

Her hands started shaking as she lifted the coffee mug to her lips. Her lips had almost touched the rim of the mug when hot, black liquid spilled over the top, splattering onto the round kitchen tabletop.

Damn it. She smashed the mug down onto the table. *Look at me. Can't even drink my coffee in peace. But when have I ever been at peace?* She sighed, then got up to find a paper towel to wipe away the spill.

What a mess. Lu sighed as she wiped the table clean. *Basically my whole life is a mess.* She sighed again.

Then her face took on a determined look, and she shook her head. *Stop thinking like that. Instead of kids, I was gifted with a wonderful career. An amazing career. So many opportunities. I grabbed every one of them by the horns and ran with them. To become a successful Airman, a young general. A respected leader in the Air Force.*

Thanks to him.

Lu gasped for air. Just thinking of him made her short-breathed. Whenever she thought of him, her throat tightened, as if someone was trying to squeeze the air out of her lungs. The same way he had done to her on a few occasions during his sick games.

She scrunched up the dirty paper towel and threw it away in the trash can. For a while, she just stood there. She closed her eyes to steady her breathing, to slow her pounding heart. *Elisabeth only knew the smallest part of it. She was the only one I told anything. But I was prepared to tell the world about it. About how sick he really is. How brutal, how condescending, how heartless. How he treats other human beings like they're not even human. As if they're puppets and he's the puppet master. Playing his games.*

She grunted. *Bullet. Yeah, he came on strong as a bullet. Piercing not only my body, but my heart. So sick. How can anyone be like that?*

Lu started breathing hard as painful, hidden-away memories flooded her brain. She tried to suppress them, as she'd done for years, tried to keep those experiences from coming back to haunt her. She was mostly successful, but couldn't block the noise. She heard herself screaming—then realized she actually *was* screaming.

She quickly stopped, then walked over to the window to dose herself with the serene view. Slowly, she was able to calm herself, but still couldn't quite tame her thoughts. *I had forced myself to write it all down so I could report every last detail of every time he abused me. I was ready. Ready to report him. Had pages and pages of evidence. But I couldn't do it alone. And Riley, her replacement, just wasn't her.*

Lu shook her head. *No, I needed her. I needed her to hold my hand. And she promised she'd be there for me. But she didn't show... Elisabeth just didn't show. Didn't respond to any of my calls or texts. I didn't know why. Why would she hurt me like that? I took sick leave and barricaded myself inside my apartment. Just shut out the world. Was ready to starve myself to death in my tiny little dorm room on base.*

A tear escaped her big brown eyes. *And then the phone call. I thought it was finally her. But no, it was* him. *Bullet. I almost died when I heard his voice again.* Lu felt her heart skip a beat as if reliving the moment. She heard his dark, calm, but determined voice in her ear, as if he were standing right there beside her. And just like she'd done twenty years ago, she closed her eyes.

🎭 🎭 🎭

"Lulu-girl, so nice to hear your voice. Always loved your voice. I miss you."

Lu couldn't say anything. She was standing in her darkened bedroom inside her dorm. Her breathing was fast, out of control.

"Listen, Lulu-girl, I understand you tried to be courageous. Heard you even told someone about us. But remember what I said?"

Silence. She couldn't speak. But he was waiting for her to respond. "Lulu-girl, answer me," said the rage-filled voice on the line. "Remember what I told you?"

"Yeah," she whispered. "'Don't tell anyone or Bullet will get you.'"

He laughed a loud, coarse laugh. "That's right, Lulu-girl, that's right. You're lucky this Bullet has decided not to punish you yet."

Silence.

"You hear me, Lulu-girl? You were a bad little girl. And I don't like bad little girls who share secrets. Do you understand?"

"Yes."

"Good, good. Well, it's time for me to do something about this, Lulu-girl."

Her eyes widened in horror. He's going to destroy my career. Or kill me. Oddly, she suddenly felt at peace. Maybe it's for the best. Not living anymore.

"I've been watching you. Ever since I left a year ago. You knew I have eyes everywhere, didn't you? Should've known I have my puppets lined up. I know of your plans. I know you were planning on going to the police. But guess what, Lulu-girl?"

"What?" she croaked, her eyes closed, the phone pressed to her ear with such force it was as though an invisible hand gripped it. She couldn't put it down, even though she really, really wanted to. All she wanted was to hang up.

"Your friend, the one who encouraged you to tell the world about us, won't be there. She'll never be there for you again. You see, she's already forgotten about you, because you were never anything to her. She'll never, ever call you again. Will never, ever help you again. She has her own family. Her own things to worry about. Important things. But not you. You're not important to her. She doesn't want anything to do with you."

Lu started crying, sobbing inconsolably. That's not true!

"Or has she returned any of your calls? Your texts?"

While sobbing, Lu shook her head.

"No? Didn't think so. She left you for dead. Don't think she'll ever come back to help you. She's gone. Out of sight, out of mind. Gone from your life. For no reason besides her own selfishness."

Lu sank to her knees, the phone still to her ear.

"But listen, I have a proposition for you. 'Cuz you know, Lulu-girl, I actually do care about you. You know that, right?"

Lu didn't react. She couldn't. She was heartbroken. I thought Elisabeth was my friend. I thought she was honest. Someone I could trust. I was wrong—again.

"Lulu-girl, here's my offer. Listen real close, got it?"

But Lu couldn't say anything. Her silence angered him.

"Lulu-girl, come on, get it together. Suck it up and be a good little airwoman. Come on! I know you have talent in spades. I know you can make it far. I know you're a natural-born leader. I know that deep down inside that broken little girl sobbing over the phone is a fierce fighter. A real leader. You know that, Lu, don't you?"

Lu? He called me Lu? He's never called me that before. Suddenly he shows respect? What's going on? *She stopped sobbing and listened more closely.*

"Lu, you there still? Are you ready to make a deal?"

A deal? *She was so overwhelmed that her tears had all dried up.* *"Yeah," she whispered.*

"Okay, great then. Here's what I propose: you can never, ever tell anyone what happened between you and me. If you promise to do so, and make good on your promise, I'll make sure you enjoy a good life. A happy life. An awesome Air Force career. You can start this fall. I'll send you to college—hear that, a college career—that way you can become officer material, not a run-of-the-mill enlistee. You'll find you jump the ranks quickly. Sooner than later, you'll be a high-ranking officer. If you work for it, of course. If you really want it. All it takes is me making a few phone calls to get the ball rolling."

Her eyes widened. She stared into the dark bedroom.

"All I need from you is to promise you'll never mention what happened between us. Never ever. To anyone. *But if you do, if you disobey me again, you* will *go down. If you ever confide in anyone again, you know I have my ways of finding out. So, burn the evidence, all the notes you've made, and we'll turn your life around* today. *Seal the deal with me."*

Lu didn't know what to say. Her head was spinning. He knows about the notes I wrote down? How? He's watching me, even now? He must have people, eyes everywhere.... *Lu took a deep breath in.* And now he wants me to make a deal with him?

She was so dizzy, she plopped down on the floor again. She didn't know what to do. Elisabeth's gone forever? She's abandoned me? That's... How dare she leave me? How dare she break her promise? *Lu's face turned bright red.* But she got a few things right: I am strong. And I do want to live. I am someone. I deserve justice. I deserve a good life.

She rose from the floor, and before she could really second-guess herself, she heard herself say, "Yes, fine then. Bullet, we have a deal."

Take that, Elisabeth! I'm taking charge of my own life. I'll be someone. Yes, I will be. I'll show you how strong I am. And I hate you. Hate you for abandoning me.

Lu flung her head back and forth as if trying to shake the memories out of it. She opened her eyes again and stared at the emerald-green water outside the window. The big kitchen window overlooking the bay.

I am someone now. Someone important, living in the Distinguished Visitor's Quarters. And I like my life. It's too late now for Elisabeth to turn it all upside down, to bring back long-forgotten things. I need to stop her. She picked up her coffee mug again and downed the last bit of coffee. She was ready for her mission: stop Elisabeth!

CHAPTER 29

Elisabeth was determined, forceful. Brad noticed it in her tone from the moment he picked up her call. "Brad, I need you to tell your exec to find Guadalupe. There can't be too many Airmen out there with such a unique name."

"No, probably not." He put his phone on loudspeaker and set it in his lap so he could free up his hand to scratch his chin. "And you really think you saw her on base just now?"

"Maria saw her. And I have a feeling she's not wrong. It must have been her. You believe me, right, Brad?"

Brad suppressed the sigh that was about to escape his throat. *Glad it's only a voice call.* "Sure."

He immediately heard suspicion in her tone, anger as she said, "You don't believe me, do you?"

He briefly closed his eyes. *Sometimes it sucks knowing each other so well. Hard to hide anything from her.* "Elisabeth, I'm just saying, it would be a crazy coincidence if she ended up at Eglin after all these years."

Brad heard Elisabeth chuckle on the other end of the line. "That's what Maria said. You guys seem to think alike. Anyway, I need you to find out. You know I need to get this off my chest, need to talk to her. Apologize for not being there for her."

"I know, hun. I know how important this is to you. Don't worry, I'll call Major Starke, my exec, right now, and he'll start working on it. I'll call you back once I've heard from him. Okay?"

"Okay. Thanks, hun."

"You're welcome. I know this means a lot to you. And I hope you'll come to accept that it wasn't your fault. Especially considering if this Guadalupe of yours is still in the Air Force, she must've had an amazing run. An amazing career. So you don't need to feel guilty about letting her down. And it's not like you just didn't call her—you lost your daughter. Everyone will understand you were preoccupied."

He heard Elisabeth sigh on the other end. "I guess so."

"Let me call my exec then, and I'll get back to you. Until then, enjoy spending time with our daughter and her friends. Okay?"

"Okay. Brad? I love you."

His heart skipped a beat. A warm, fuzzy feeling came over him, a big smile that lit up his face. His unique eyes sparkled, the golden flecks in it shining in happiness. "I love you, too, Elisabeth."

"After we hang up, I want you to get some more rest. Get better so you can get out of that hospital, you hear me?"

He grinned. "Yes, ma'am. Talk to you soon then. Love you."

"Love you, too. Can't wait to talk later. Bye."

"Bye, Elisabeth." Brad hung up, the big smile still on his face. He dialed Major Starke's number next and gave him instructions. Once done, he closed his eyes and did what his love had asked of him.

The ringing of his cell phone tore him from his sleep. He opened his eyes, only half-awake, but within seconds knew exactly where he was and what was happening. He picked up his phone right away. "Hello, this is General Collins."

"Hi, General, this is Major Starke. I have news for you."

Brad smiled. *I knew I could count on my exec. He's fast, efficient, a hard worker. A smart guy.* "Hit me. What did you find out?"

"Believe it or not, there's only one lady in the Air Force with the first name Guadalupe. She enlisted in the military right after her high school graduation. She was stationed at Hill Air Force Base in Utah as a Squadron Aviation Resource Manager in the SARM program."

"I see, the SARM program. Then she was responsible for tracking pilot and aircrew medical and operational training certification out in Utah, right?"

"Correct, sir. There's a good chance you may have even worked with her at the time."

Brad thought about it. "Probably, if she did all the pilot certification at Hill. But I certainly didn't work closely with her."

"No, sir, probably not."

"So she was enlisted. Then what happened to her? Did she do her time then get out of the Air Force?"

Brad heard his exec laugh out loud. "No, sir, that's not quite the case. And you certainly *have* crossed paths with her since."

Brad raised his eyebrows. "I have? I don't recall anyone with the name Guadalupe."

"You wouldn't, because she goes by Lu. As in, General Lu Thomas."

Brad almost choked on his own spit. "General Thomas? *The* General Thomas? Fast-burning Brigadier General at Joint Base San Antonio-Lackland?"

"Correct, sir. The commander of the Air Force Civil Engineer Center."

"Wow," was all Brad could say.

"Yeah. She's had an impressive career. After working at Hill, she went to the University of Utah to study at the John & Marcia Price College of Engineering."

"She cross-trained? Went from enlisted to a career officer? Man, she made it big. She's pretty young for making general."

"Yes, sir."

"Wow, no way…. General Thomas… I recall talking jets with her a few times at Lackland. Very smart lady, great leader. Only heard good things about her."

"Yes, sir. Great career, impressive résumé, a well-respected leader. Soon to pick up another star, I would think."

"Thanks, Major Starke. That's fantastic. Glad to hear her career has been so successful. Never did put it together—General Lu Thomas is Guadalupe." Brad shook his head in disbelief, a smile on his face.

"Yes, sir. Though I'm still not sure why you asked me to look into her…"

"Because my wife—um, ex-wife—knew Guadalupe back when she was that young enlistee doing certifications at Hill AFB. Elisabeth just wanted to…"—Brad thought for a moment to find the right words—"…to catch up with her, as they fell out of touch with each other over the years."

"I see, sir. Happy to report Lu Thomas is doing great. And, sir?"

"Yes, Major Starke?"

"I'm even happier to hear *you're* alright, sir. And that you found your ex-wife and your daughter. It's wonderful. Very happy for you."

Brad grinned. "Thank you, Major. Appreciate it." He could almost hear his exec's smile through the phone. *He's a good guy. I like Major Starke. I'll do my best to make sure he has a nice career of his own.*

"Yes, sir. Please stay safe."

"I will, I will." Then Brad remembered, "Oh, Major Starke, where is General Lu Thomas now?"

"In Texas, sir… at Joint Base San Antonio-Lackland," he heard the major say, faint irritation creeping into his voice. "I thought I already mentioned that in my report—"

"Oh, you did, Major," Brad interrupted him, "I know that's her current duty station. But any idea if she's on TDY at the moment? Let's say, here at Eglin?"

"Not sure, sir. Let me find out. Hold, please." Brad heard his exec hammering the keys of his computer in the background.

For a while Brad listened to him type, but then his thoughts drifted off. *At least Elisabeth should feel reassured to learn Guadalupe did very well for herself. She's doing just fine—meaning Elisabeth has nothing to be sorry about. Even if Guadalupe was raped when she was young, like Elisabeth said, she clearly got over it quickly.* Brad sighed. *If anyone can truly get over such a thing. Is that condescending thinking? A smug guy's perspective?*

"Sir?" Brad almost jumped when his exec's loud voice came on the line again. "General Thomas was just in London, England. But while en route to Texas, she stopped at another base for the rest of this week. Seems a bit unplanned, but she has a few meetings set up, starting tomorrow. Your hunch was correct: she's at Eglin AFB at this very moment."

Brad gasped. *At Eglin? Right now? Here? Elisabeth and Maria were right! They must have seen her this morning.*

"Sir? Did you hear me?"

"Oh, yes, Major Starke, yes. Thank you."

"No problem, sir. Anything else?"

"No, Major, nothing else. Thank you for your time. I will tell my wife—err, ex-wife—that her former friend is doing well. She'll be excited to catch up with her."

"I'm sure, sir. Well, have a great day. Get well soon. And know that everything is under control here."

Brad smiled. "No doubt, Major Starke. You're doing an excellent job."

"Thank you, sir."

"You're welcome. And thank you. Have a great day. I'll be in touch."

"Okay, sir. Have a good day also."

Brad hung up. *General Thomas. Wow. Quite the big name in the Air Force. Lu Thomas is Guadalupe. Impressive career. Elisabeth will be thrilled to hear about it. A true success story for the H.O.P.E. Club.*

He smiled and was about to dial Elisabeth's number when his finger froze above the phone lying in his lap. Words his exec had spoken took on new meaning. *Unplanned trip to Eglin AFB.... Unplanned? Why on earth would she stop by Eglin after returning from an overseas TDY?*

Suddenly, he felt sick to his stomach, words spiraling around in his head.

"A crazy coincidence she's suddenly here..."

"She hates Elisabeth..."

"An enemy of the H.O.P.E. Club..."

He shook himself out of it. *I need to find out exactly why General Thomas is here and not back at her home base in Texas.*

CHAPTER 30

"In Texas, there's a whole bunch of military bases. We've pinpointed the cell tower that routed the call from Agent James Borman right before he killed himself. The base closest to it is Joint Base San Antonio-Lackland," Chief Parlot said, summing up the team's overnight research.

Tonya, Sally, and Tom all nodded along wearily.

"Agent James Borman's military friend must have been stationed there then. What else did we find out, team? Let's recap, to make sense of it all."

"Yes, Chief," Sally said. She yawned, then started recalling their research. "We know that Agent James Borman was stationed at the Salt Lake City FBI field office in Utah, close to Hill AFB. He also liked to vacation in Destin, Florida, close to Eglin AFB. We've identified a few important individuals who were also stationed at both Hill AFB and Eglin AFB the same time James Borman was working for the FBI—namely, his friend, former Niceville Police Chief Jim Billings, and our dear Senator Mike Clifford hung out with him in both places. Neither of them was ever in Texas, though."

Tonya scratched her head, then took another sip of her coffee. "Well, team, not much new here, huh?"

Tom shook his head. "Nope. I personally combed through the list of everyone who were stationed at Lackland AFB in Texas back in 2009—the year Agent Borman killed himself—and came up empty-handed. We really don't know who Borman called right before he shot himself. And I really don't know how to find out. Honestly, that spooks me. They left no trace. There's nobody in Texas that Borman seems to have known."

Chief Parlot started pacing back and forth. "Regardless, we know he exists. We need to find out who this guy is. He's important, I just know it. He very well could be our mysterious Bullet."

Tonya took another sip of coffee but failed to suppress the yawn that followed. "We know, we know, my man Isaac. But right now, I'm all out of ideas, I have to admit."

"Me, too." Sally plopped down on a chair, her eyes glassy. "Unless we figure out who James Borman had contact with in the military, this might just be another dead end."

Tom nodded and yawned. "Sally's right, unfortunately. My research didn't show anything either. Unless we unexpectedly figure out which military guys Borman used to hang out and party with, it's no use."

Chief Parlot stopped pacing. "'Party with'? The guys who Borman partied with.... Of course, Tom, of course! Gosh, we're so silly. It's been right there all along—well, maybe."

Sally tried to focus on her boss. "What are you going on about, Chief?"

"The party! The party on base," he said. "Whose party was it again?"

Tonya raised her eyebrows. "Which party you talking about? I'm lost here, too. My man Isaac, you're being very cryptic. And we're all very sleepy."

"Come on, team, the *promotion party* everyone was at the night of little Moana's disappearance." The chief grabbed a stack of papers off a nearby desk and began riffling through them.

Tom, who had leaned his chair back, closed his eyes, and nearly dozed off, jumped when he suddenly heard the chief slam his hand flat on the table, right onto a piece of paper. "What?" Tom yelped.

"Here it is," Chief Parlot said, "the guest list. Remember the guest list?"

Sally's eyes were watering now. "Guest list? *What* guest list?"

Tonya came alert. Her eyes lit up, and she smiled now. "The guest list to the promotion party! Of course, Isaac. Smart, smart." She smirked and gave him a pat on the shoulder. "Remember, team, we called some of those guests? That's how we found out James Borman, Chief Billings, and Mike Clifford were all friends, with access to Eglin AFB. That's how JB managed to drag a little toddler out of her bed, through the water, and onto the boat with Jonathan Sullivan. Remember, youngsters?"

Sally jumped up. "Oh, that party! Yeah, yeah of course I remember. It was a promotion party for someone."

"Precisely." The chief smiled. "A promotion party *for a general in the Air Force.* He got his second star at that party and invited his friends. Agent James Borman must have been a friend of this particular general."

Sally's eyes widened. "A military friend…. Wow. Of course. You're thinking he's the one Borman called before he killed himself?"

"Maybe," Tonya grinned. "We just have to find out if he was stationed in Texas around 2009."

Sally jumped up. "That should be easy enough. Come on, everybody!" She walked over to Tom's chair, just to realize he'd fallen asleep. "Oh no, Tom's out. But we need him to work his magic on the computer. He's the fastest."

Chief Parlot nodded, then sighed. *I kept everyone up way too long again. We kept at it all night and didn't sleep a wink.* Through Sally's excitement he saw her glossy eyes, the dark circles underneath. *And those energy drinks don't seem to be helping our youngsters at all.*

Tonya bumped elbows with him. "I know what you're thinking, my man. You're ready to switch our young colleagues to coffee because those energy drinks are fake as a preacher's smile on a hot Sunday morning, huh?" Tonya took another sip of her steaming coffee. "Look at us old ones. We're still raring to go, aren't we?"

The chief winked at her. "Sure are, old partner." He then turned to Sally. "Well then. Sally, how about we let Tom sleep? You get some shut-eye, too. It's been a long day. Everything is under control at the moment, Maria and family are safe on base. We can afford the luxury of sleep and research this guy later."

Sally pouted. "But I'm wide-awake now, Chief. The adrenaline kicked in because I'm excited to find out more and—"

"Fine, how about we research the general, find his résumé? That shouldn't take too long and will give us a useful starting point. Then we can rest, take a nice, long morning nap, and resume after. How does that sound?"

"Good with me," Tonya said.

Sally nodded and sat down in front of her computer. "Okay then, let's get the scoop on this guy. It was General Jones's party, right?"

"Correct," Tonya and the chief both said at the same time, then walked over to Sally and took a seat on either side of her.

Tom started snoring in his chair. They all giggled at that, then refocused on the research. Within a few minutes, Sally had the general's résumé up on the screen. They all leaned forward to read it.

"Will ya look at that." Tonya grinned, while pointing at three entries. "Stationed at Hill AFB in Utah. Then at Eglin AFB. Then retired after his time stationed at Lackland AFB. Folks, I think we just found JB's military friend."

Chief Parlot nodded. "The timeline fits. General Robert Jones was at Hill while Borman was stationed in Salt Lake City. We know they met here at Eglin and—"

"But Jones was stationed at Lackland in Texas way before 2009," Sally interjected. "It doesn't line up at all!" She sighed.

"Nah, not so fast, my young one." Tonya pointed at the last entry. "Says here he retired from the Air Force in 2006 at Lackland. General Jones likely settled down in Texas and continued to peddle influence on base, so maybe in 2009 he was still there. Possibly is still there now."

Sally's eyes lit up. "True, true. We need to find out what General Jones is up to nowadays." She hit a few more sites. "Looks like he did stay in Texas. Still has a Texas address."

"Good job, Sally." Tonya patted her on the shoulder. "Now we just need to find out if he knows our other friends. Perhaps he was into gambling, maybe?" Tonya winked at Chief Parlot and Sally.

A loud snore interrupted them. Sally laughed, but her laughter quickly turned into a big yawn.

"Okay, guys, let's take a break," the chief said. "Obviously, when we resume, we'll look into General Robert Jones in far greater detail. Tom can help us research him later—sadly, he's currently unavailable." The chief grinned and gestured at Tom sleeping in his chair. "Thanks to Sally, we know the general's still in Texas, so even if he's the guy we're looking for, he's far away from here. No need to worry about him yet. Maria and her family are safe here."

Even though his colleagues nodded, the chief's stomach dropped as soon as his last words left his mouth. He shook it off. *Probably just hungry. Maria's safe right here.*

CHAPTER 31

"**R**ight here." Aaron pointed at the building and their car rolled to a stop before it. "The Distinguished Visitor's Quarters, house number three. Guadalupe's house—well, General Thomas's house, I should say."

Maria, Martina, and Elisabeth tilted their heads up to take in the house. Martina whistled. "Wow. Pretty, no? And so big."

Maria, sitting next to her mamá in the backseat, nodded. "Very majestic."

"Only the best for our generals," Aaron said, then turned to the three ladies in the car. "What's the plan now? We're here—even though I shouldn't be here, as I'm definitely not a general…."

Elisabeth, who sat in the front seat, gave him a pat on his uninjured shoulder. "Don't worry, Aaron. We won't tell your commander you were here. Or that you were driving with an injured shoulder while on pain meds."

"Hey, this was your idea," he protested.

Elisabeth grinned. "I know, don't worry, Aaron. It's all fine and perfectly legal. Don't worry so much all the time. I'm just teasing. You know that Lieutenant Martinez is behind us, right? Escorting us as usual. If he thinks it's okay to be here, it's okay."

"I guess so." Aaron stared at the steering wheel.

Maria laughed and Elisabeth chuckled. Martina realized Aaron was uncomfortable. *Poor Aaron. They shouldn't tease him. He's been through a lot lately. If he feels uncomfortable, there's something to it.*

"What now, Mom?" Maria asked, interrupting Martina's thoughts.

She looked at her daughter, then realized she was speaking to Elisabeth. *Her other mom. I'm still getting used to that.* She sighed, then focused on the big house in front of them. "Sí, what's the plan, Elisabeth? Go in and talk to her?"

Elisabeth turned around in her seat to look at both Maria and Martina. "I don't know. Do you think I'm allowed to do that?"

"Of course you can. It's what you want, right, Mom? That's why we came here." Maria smiled at Elisabeth.

She sighed. "I suppose so."

Martina studied the big house again through the car window. "And you're sure this is the right house?"

Elisabeth nodded. "Yep, this is the address Brad gave me. The one he got from his exec regarding General Thomas's TDY here at Eglin."

Martina nodded. "Good. ¡Vamos, Elisabeth! Go on then. It'll be fine."

"Really? You really think so?" Rather than jumping out, Elisabeth slid down in her seat as if she were about to hide.

"Sí, it'll be fine." Martina gave Elisabeth's shoulder a squeeze. "This lady is a general now. High-up, no?" Everyone nodded. "She obviously had a good life, even without your help, Elisabeth. She's fine. You'll be fine. Maybe she'll quickly say thank you for the apology and let you be on your way, or maybe you will be great friends again. Either way, it'll be fine."

Elisabeth let out a sigh.

"I agree with Mamá," Maria said. "It'll be fine. Probably even a happy reunion."

"Sí. ¡Vamos, Elisabeth! Come on, you can do it. Just get out and ring the doorbell. See what happens. We'll be right here, watching and supporting you. You can just jump in the car if it turns out bad or uncomfortable."

"Exactly. We're like your getaway car, Mom." Maria laughed.

Aaron shifted in his seat. "Great. A getaway car. That sounds *very* legal."

Martina had to grin. *Poor Aaron. He likes to follow the rules. I secretly love that about him. He'll keep our adventurous Maria in line.*

"Okay, I'm getting out. I'm ringing the doorbell. Now." Elisabeth opened the passenger door and set one foot on the driveway.

"Good luck, Mom, you can do it," Maria encouraged her.

"Good luck," Aaron mumbled.

"Sí, you got this. Good luck," Martina said.

Elisabeth let out one last big sigh, then got out of the car, closed the door, walked the few steps leading to the house's front door, and rang the doorbell. Aaron, Maria, and Martina all held their breath from inside the car.

Nothing happened.

Elisabeth rang the doorbell once more.

"Oh no, she's not there?" Maria's shoulders drooped. "I know Mom really wanted to talk to her, to apologize. It's very important to her. And I think she needs to do this to move on and understand it wasn't her fault."

Martina nodded. "Sí, it's not her fault. She could not help this girl because her own little one disappeared. Everyone will understand that."

Aaron snorted. "At least everyone should."

Elisabeth turned back to them and shrugged. They gestured for her to try one more time. She rang the doorbell again, then knocked on the front door.

"Maybe she's in meetings?" Aaron checked his watch. "It's late morning already. Usually work time for everyone."

"Usually." Martina sighed. *Hope my store is okay. My sisters said it was, but I hate leaving it unattended for so long. And I miss my sewing.*

It makes me calm—and that's what I feel like I need right now. As she thought about it, Martina realized just how nervous she was. She felt her stomach aching but knew she wasn't hungry. *Just nervous. No need to be, though. Right?*

She refocused on Elisabeth in time to see the front door suddenly open. A beautiful, middle-aged lady in uniform appeared in the doorway. Her smooth, dark-black hair in a low bun, her pretty face accentuated with subtle makeup that brought out her high cheekbones and made her dark-brown eyes shine. Martina saw surprise on her face, then her tan complexion flushed, her cheeks rosy in embarrassment.

Aaron, Maria, and Martina watched the scene from the car. Maria leaned over her mamá to see better. "Too bad we can't hear anything."

"Mija, give them some privacy." Martina pushed Maria back into her own seat. "Elisabeth will tell us all about it later."

Maria sighed. "Fine, I just wanted to see. What do you think? Does it look like it's going well?"

The three of them stared in Elisabeth's direction. They saw her talking, talking fast, gesturing with her hands while the lady in uniform just stared at her, her whole body rigid in the doorway. Then Elisabeth hunched over and her whole body shook.

Aaron's blue eyes widened. "Is she okay?"

Maria shrugged. "Don't know."

Martina smiled. "Sí, she's okay. She's just emotional. See, she's crying."

"Oh no," Aaron said, but then all three of them saw the uniformed lady in the doorway move for the first time. She let go of the doorframe with one hand, took the other off the doorknob, and took a step toward Elisabeth to envelop her in a big hug. She had to reach up to find Elisabeth shoulders, but then they were both standing there, embracing each other, swaying back and forth.

"Aw." Maria wiped a tear away from her eye. "They made up. Look at them, they made up."

Martina smiled, her own eyes watering. "Sí, they did."

Aaron turned to Maria and Martina in the backseat. "Good. Now Elisabeth can move on. That's all she wanted, right?"

Maria and Martina nodded. The warm embrace continued on the doorstep. Maria put her head on Martina's shoulder. "So glad Mom got the forgiveness she was looking for. Right, Mamá? It's all good now."

Martina nodded and tried to ignore the little hairs on her arm standing on end. *It's all good*, she tried to convince herself. But the bad feeling she had persisted without her knowing why. *We're okay. Everyone's okay.* She closed her eyes and inhaled. The fruity smell of Maria's shampoo made her smile.

"I think she's waving us over," Martina heard Aaron say. Quickly, she opened her eyes and looked out the window again.

"Sure looks like she wants us to come over," Maria agreed, and before anyone could say anything else, she opened the door and got out. Aaron sighed, then unbuckled himself and got out as well. Both him and Maria were now walking to the front door—hand in hand—to meet General Guadalupe Thomas.

Martina sighed. She saw the group shake hands, smile, talk. Then Maria and Elisabeth gestured her to come over.

I guess I better go. Not sure why, but I really don't want to meet her. Have a bad feeling about this. With a big sigh, she pushed the car door open, stepped out, and closed it behind her. She glanced at the police car parked behind their own. Lieutenant Martinez gave her a nod.

Guess he's okay with all of this. She nodded back, then walked toward the little group by the front door. She put a smile on her face. *Hopefully not too fake.* They all saw her coming. She waved and walked up the steps to stand next to Elisabeth.

"Lu, this is Martina Sullivan, the woman who raised my daughter after the kidnapping. She's Maria's other mom," Elisabeth said with a big smile on her face, then turned to Martina. "Martina, this is Lu, also known as General Thomas."

Martina stared at the Hispanic lady in uniform, who reached out to grab her hand. "Hi, Martina. It's so nice to meet you. Mucho gusto."

Martina shook her hand, surprised by her strong grip. "Sí, mucho gusto. Nice to meet you, Lu. I mean, ma'am."

Lu laughed. "Please don't call me ma'am. Already told Aaron and Maria the same. Call me Lu. Simply Lu."

"But you're a general, no?"

"Yes, Martina, I am. But this is personal, not work-related. Elisabeth and I used to be friends long before I became a general. Lu is fine, please." She winked at Martina.

She seems nice, no? Martina eyeballed the general. *She's very pretty. And aged well. Must be close to my age. A bit younger, I suppose, going off Elisabeth's stories.*

With a big smile on her face, Lu gestured for them to step inside. "Please, come on in. All of you."

Aaron glanced from one person to the next. "Oh, I don't know...." He then glanced back at Lieutenant Martinez's car. "Not sure if we should...."

"Nonsense, of course you should. I don't have any meetings scheduled till tomorrow and I'd love to catch up with Elisabeth. And get to know you all." Lu smiled, her white, pearly teeth shining.

"Well, ma'am, I—"

"Oh, Aaron, *please* call me Lu. We've been over this already, right, Lieutenant Heikinnen?" Lu winked at him.

Aaron blushed. "Yes, Lu. Thank you."

"So, coming in?" She smiled at Aaron and Maria, and stepped aside to make room in the doorway.

"I... I can't," Aaron said. "I don't know if our escort is okay with this and..."

"Call him over," Lu said. She was already waving to Lieutenant Martinez.

He saw her and got out of his car. Came over, his steps short, a bit timid and uncertain. He stopped and saluted her.

She smiled and saluted back. "Hello, Lieutenant."

"Hello, General. Ma'am, it seems you wish to speak with me?"

"Yes, Lieutenant. First of all, nice to meet you." She now shook his hand. "Second, I'd like to have coffee with these fine folks. Which means inviting them inside. Is that okay with you and your protocol?"

"I-I... yes, ma'am, I-I think so," Lieutenant Martinez stuttered, clearly starstruck. "I do need to keep an eye on them, especially Maria, but it should be okay."

Lu smiled. "Excellent. Come on in then—all of you."

Aaron shook his head. "I'm really sorry, ma'am—Lu, I mean—but I can't. My friends are all here to help me unload my moving truck and move me into my new apartment. We had plans to do so after breakfast and—"

"Can't you change your plans?" Maria interrupted Aaron.

He shook his head. "Maria, you know I have to return that truck after five days. The deadline's getting close. Besides, I thought you were excited for us to move in, especially now that we have strong guys to help us carry things and—"

"You're right, Aaron," Maria said, then gave him a kiss on the cheek. "Fair enough. We better get this guy moved into his new apartment."

"Okay, understandable," Lu said, then turned to Martina and Elisabeth. "What about the two of you? Are you helping with the move, or can you stay for a coffee?"

"¿No sé?" Martina shrugged and looked at Elisabeth.

"I came here to see you, Lu," Elisabeth said. "So I would like to stay for sure. Martina, care to join us? You and I can't carry those heavy boxes anyway—let the young ones handle that. What do you say?"

Martina stared at Elisabeth. *I don't know. Don't really want to stay.* She realized Elisabeth had an interesting expression on her face, almost as if she were begging her to stay. *Maybe she's seeking support while spending time with Lu? Maybe she needs someone to be here with her? I know it's hard on her. I know she feels bad about having abandoned this young lady, even though she shouldn't. Lu looks great, is a general now.*

"Please, Martina," Elisabeth whispered to her.

Guess she does need me. Martina sighed, then took a deep breath in. "Yes, I'll stay, if that's okay with Lu. And with Lieutenant Martinez?"

"Well, I don't know..." Lieutenant Martinez started, but Lu interrupted him again.

"Lieutenant, see to Aaron and Maria. As you mentioned, you need to keep an eye on them. I in turn will keep close watch over Martina and Elisabeth. I'm a general, I think that's something I can handle on my own. I'll return them to the Air Force Inn later. Trust me."

Lieutenant Martinez looked unsure, but then nodded and saluted. "Yes, ma'am. Sounds good. Will do. And I'll let the chief know."

Lu smiled at everyone. "Alright, sounds like a plan then?"

Maria gave Martina and Elisabeth a big hug, then left with Aaron. This time, Maria took the wheel. Lieutenant Martinez followed them. Maria honked as they drove away while Lu, Elisabeth, and Martina waved them off from the front steps.

"Okay, they're gone," Lu said. "Ready to come in?"

Elisabeth smiled and nodded, stepped inside without hesitation. Martina followed her, unsure of herself, the knot in her stomach tightening the moment she stepped inside.

CHAPTER 32

Inside the police workroom, the phone rang. Tom, asleep in his chair, jumped up abruptly while Chief Parlot stirred on the couch in the break area. He opened his eyes and searched all over for his loudly ringing cell phone. *Where is it? It must be here somewhere. I never put it out of reach, even when I'm sleeping.* He found it on the floor in front of the couch and picked it up.

It was Lieutenant Martinez. The chief listened closely, nodding his head a few times, then raised his eyebrows. "Elisabeth and Martina are *where?*" he said, his eyebrows still raised as he listened to the lieutenant on the other end of the line. Phone to his ear, he walked over to his desk, took out a sticky note, and wrote something down. "Okay, Lieutenant Martinez. Thanks for the heads-up. Appreciate it."

He listened again to the somewhat nervous-sounding lieutenant on the other end of the line. "No worries, Lieutenant, you did the right thing." He paused. "You're welcome. But I definitely need you to stick close to Maria and Aaron. Especially when they go off base. And, yes, we'll send one of our guys to the apartment complex as well to meet you there for support and to help out." He paused to listen. "Sure. No problem." Paused again. "Okay, thanks. Talk to you later. Bye." He hung up and let out a sigh, then stared at the sticky note.

Tom cleared his throat. "Everything alright, Chief?"

Chief Parlot just stared at the sticky note containing only one name: "General Lu Thomas." He was deep in thought. *Who is this person? Another Air Force General? And why are Martina and Elisabeth with her? What do they have to do with this general? An old friend, according to Lieutenant Martinez.... Who exactly is she to them?*

The touch on his shoulder made him jump. Only then did he notice Tom standing right next to him. "Goodness, Tom, you scared me. Where did you come from?"

"My chair," Tom said, eyeing both the chief and the sticky note. "Right over there." He pointed to his swivel chair.

"Oh yes, that's right." The chief grinned sheepishly at him. "Did you have a good nap in that?"

Tom moved his head around in a circle. Several bones cracked. "It was a bit uncomfortable."

"I imagine. But there was no waking you—trust me, we tried." Chief Parlot patted him on the back.

Tom looked around. "Speaking of 'we'—where is everyone?"

"The ladies took a break. Decided to lie down in the official break room. You know, nice couches there." Chief Parlot winked at Tom.

Tom massaged one side of his neck. "Lucky." Then he checked his watch. "Chief, it's already noon? How long was I asleep?"

"Oh, three hours, I'd say." He winked at Tom again, then patted his shoulder. "Remember, we didn't sleep all night, broke around nine this morning. You just got a head start. But no worries, you didn't miss much. And besides, you earned that sleep."

"I suppose."

"But we do need you for something, Tom. Need you to look into something."

"Yes, Chief, what is it? This Air Force General?" Tom pointed at the name on the sticky note.

The chief sighed. "Well, no. I need you to focus on General Robert Jones."

"But it says 'General Lu Thomas' right here." Tom pointed at the note again. "I'm confused, Chief."

"So am I," the chief replied. "While you slept, we figured out General Jones is likely the military friend Agent James Borman knew. The one who had his promotion party a few blocks down from Moana Collins the night she disappeared."

Tom nodded. "I remember the name."

"Sally found out he was stationed separately at Hill and Eglin, then Lackland. Way before James Borman committed suicide, though. But nevertheless, he might have been Borman's friend even after he retired in Texas. We just don't know. So I need you to find out whether this guy was somehow connected to Borman. Say, whether they went on the same trips together, liked the same things."

Tom's eyes widened. "You mean, find out if this guy was also in Vegas?"

The chief smiled and nodded.

Tom bolted for his computer, his eyes sparkling. "Yes, Chief, I'll find out." He sat down and within seconds was hammering away on his keyboard. He suddenly stopped. Turned to look back over his shoulder. "But who's General Thomas?"

The chief shrugged. "Lieutenant Martinez said she's here at Eglin...."

"*She?*"

"Yes. She. General Lu Thomas, apparently a former friend of Elisabeth's she met through the H.O.P.E. Club. Both Elisabeth and Martina are with her right now at Eglin's Distinguished Visitor's Quarters."

"No way," Tom said. "You think she's involved in the H.O.P.E. Club scandal Elisabeth was telling you about yesterday?"

"I don't know, Tom. I'm equally confused." The chief scratched his chin, then used his index finger to point at his colleague. "But I need *you* to focus on researching General Robert Jones for now. Find out where he liked to hang out and if he was in Vegas with his friend James Borman."

"Yes, Chief, will do." Tom turned to his computer screen and his hands flew across the keyboard again.

The chief yawned. "I'll get the ladies in here to start researching Elisabeth's friend now. Do you need anything before I step out, Tom?"

"Yeah, another energy drink, please," Tom yelled without taking his eyes off his computer screen.

The chief shook his head. *These young people and their energy drinks. What's even in those things?* He walked over to the rest area with the couch, coffee machine, and mini fridge, and grabbed an energy drink off the fridge door shelf.

"Here you go, Tom. Catch!"

Tom swiveled in his chair absentmindedly. His face turned pale then bright red when he saw the can flying toward him. He raised his hands quickly and caught the energy drink a split second before it was about to hit him in the face. The can safe in hand, he scrunched up his eyebrows. "Nice one, Chief. Good thinking, testing my reaction time this early in the morning. *Before* I've had my energy drink."

The chief grinned. "Remember, Tom, it's already noon." He turned around and walked out the door. Called from the hallway, "Good catch, by the way. Impressive."

The chief returned a little while later, Tonya and Sally in tow, rubbing at their eyes. Tom was still focused on his computer. The chief got busy brewing some coffee while Tonya stretched her limbs in the corner. Sally searched the mini fridge for a suitable source of caffeine. "Oh, I like this one." She grabbed an energy drink off the shelf.

Pop!

The loud sound that came from Sally opening her can made Tom jump in his chair. "What the heck?" He turned around and saw Sally, the chief, and Tonya all standing around the workroom rest area. "Oh hey, didn't see you all come in." He pointed at Sally. "You, young miss, scared the crap out of me."

"Excuse me?" Sally crossed her arms in front of her chest. "You're telling me that popping the lid on my drink is too loud, while Chief is over here brewing coffee using this loud sputtering machine that could be mistaken for a lawnmower? The coffee machine doesn't disturb you?"

Everyone giggled. Tom grinned. "No, it doesn't. Only you and your can."

"Well, that's ridic—"

"Ridiculous, yes, Sally?" Tom interrupted her, a big grin on his face.

Sally nodded, arms still crossed in front of her chest. Tom waved his own canned energy drink in her general direction, laughed, then said, "Well, ladies and gentlemen, what's really ridiculous is that I found out our friend General Robert, better known as Bob Jones, was in fact in Vegas the very same weekend the Fearless Four played poker with Jonathan Sullivan."

Sally uncrossed her arms. Her mouth dropped open. "You're kidding me."

"Nope, not kidding at all. Found receipts made out to one Bob Jones dated that weekend. And a room booked in his name. A big penthouse suite."

Chief Parlot grinned. *Bingo! He must be our missing guy. Bullet.*

Tonya and Sally walked over to look at Tom's screen, the chief close behind. "Wow, good work, Tom my boy." Tonya patted him on the back. "Anything else?"

Tom nodded. "He was stationed at Hill, Eglin, and Lackland. He retired in Texas and still lives there now."

Sally closed her mouth again and found her words. "We knew that already. What I really want to know is, did you find out whether James Borman called him before he shot himself?"

"Not one hundred percent sure he's the one JB called, but the cell tower that picked up his call was, in fact, close to Bob Jones's address. Given he lives so close to Lackland."

"Wow, you're a genius, Tom." Tonya grinned. "A real asset to this team."

"Aw shucks, I know, thanks." Tom leaned back in his chair, his cheeks smoldering.

"General Bob Jones...." the chief mumbled. "What's his motive?" *Does Bob Jones even know Brad Collins? What beef do they have with each other? And is he the one Mike Clifford referred to as his father? Why? How would they even know each other?*

Tonya elbowed him. "What's up, my man Isaac? Can't hear you. You're mumbling to yourself."

Chief Parlot focused on his team again. "Oh, ahem, I was just wondering what this guy's motive is. And how he ended up joining the Fearless Four—or if he was a part of it at all."

"Chief, what's going on?" Sally crossed her arms again, her face flushed. "We've got a new lead here, a strong lead, and you're being all negative about it. Why?"

Tonya raised her eyebrows. "Yeah, I'm wondering the same."

"Because we lack a strong connection tying Jones to Clifford. How do they know each other? And does Brad Collins know Jones? It's all so unclear. Very unclear. And then there's General Thomas. What about her?"

"General... who?" Tonya raised her eyebrows even higher.

Tom got out of his chair and picked up the sticky note from the table to show it to Tonya and Sally. "This general here. A lady general who's Elisabeth Collins's friend from the H.O.P.E. Club."

"What?" Both Tonya and Sally were still confused.

"She randomly showed up here on base just yesterday. And Elisabeth and Martina are with her, last I heard. Lieutenant Martinez called a little bit ago. Not sure if they're still with General Thomas or not, but they met her on base," the chief explained.

"This lady general is here on base... you mean, like, Eglin AFB?" Sally looked confused. "And she's usually not stationed here?"

"Don't think so." The chief sighed.

Tonya started pacing back and forth. "Strange. Very strange so many people are suddenly showing up at Eglin AFB the past few days."

The chief sighed again. "Exactly."

"Let's do some more research, then." Tonya stopped pacing and pointed at Tom. "You. Focus on Bob Jones, see if there's a connection with Senator Mike Clifford."

"Yes, ma'am." He put the sticky note back on the table, walked over to his chair, and got to work.

Tonya now pointed at Sally. "My girl, I need you to process General Thomas's résumé. Where was she stationed? What's she doing now? And most importantly: who is she?"

"Yes, Agent Anderson." Sally nodded and sat down in front of her computer.

The chief stared down at the bright-yellow sticky note with the general's name scribbled on it. *General Lu Thomas. Who the heck are you? Why are you here? Why are you with Elisabeth Collins? Something's not right. We're missing something here. A connection?*

CHAPTER 33

"**A** connection is everything. Important connections are made throughout your career, but it's up to you to decide who you keep in touch with, who you know that will help you gain that extra edge, that better rating, that better assignment." Lu smiled at Elisabeth and Martina, who sat across from her on the couch, each holding a steaming cup of Keurig-brewed coffee.

Lu saw Martina stir her coffee again, mixing the cheap creamer from the packs Lu had found next to the coffee machine. *Like me, she takes lots of creamer. And she's very quiet. Kinda like me, too. But likable. Like me. I have more in common with this lady than with Elisabeth, that's for sure.*

"Fascinating, Lu, very fascinating," Elisabeth said. "I'm just so glad to hear you're doing so well. What a career, wow! And to say nothing of the smarts you've shown in climbing the ladder. I always knew you were a tough cookie, a strong woman. Just look at you now. You got to the top all by yourself. You gotta know that. Hard work and determination." Elisabeth smiled a genuine smile that warmed Lu's heart.

Lu tried hard to keep the smile on her face. *That's what I need her to think. It's all me, my doing. My hard work and determination. Keep thinking that, Elisabeth. That's exactly why I came here.*

"I'm very proud of you, Lu, so very proud." Elisabeth was practically gloating now, as though she were talking about her own daughter. Yet Lu recognized her honesty, the candid pride in her voice. She didn't dare look Elisabeth in the eye and instead stared down at her coffee. "Thank you, Elisabeth, thanks. That means a lot, coming from you."

"I'm glad." Elisabeth smiled, then took a sip of her black coffee. When she put down her cup, her smile vanished and her forehead wrinkled. "And you're... sure you forgive me?"

Both Lu and Martina looked at Elisabeth. They saw her lip was quivering. Her hands folded in her lap started shaking.

Lu didn't know what to do. *I thought telling her at the front door I forgive her would be enough. Now she brings it up again?* She watched Martina lean over to gently rub Elisabeth's shoulder, worry on her face. Lu recognized the genuine respect and love shared between the two ladies. Her heart melted. *The two moms. One gave birth to the child, the other raised her. Poor Elisabeth, I can't imagine having and then losing a child. What a nightmare.* She saw a tear drip out of Elisabeth's eyes.

"Lu, I'm really, *really* sorry. I absolutely hate that I wasn't there for you, I hate it so much, I really wanted to be there—but my world was turned upside down. I'm so sorry." Elisabeth broke down in sobs.

Lu felt a sharp pain in her chest. *I feel so bad for her. She really does care about me. She did back then, she does even now. She looks so frail now, so different from the strong woman I got to know in Utah.*

"It's okay, Elisabeth." Martina was still rubbing Elisabeth's back. "You're here to ask forgiveness, and Lu already said she forgives you. It's understandable, Elisabeth. You lost a child. That was all your mind could think of at the time."

Elisabeth lifted her head and looked directly at Lu. "Did you understand? Back then? Now? Please... I need to know, Lu...."

Lu shifted in her seat. "Well, I... I..."

Martina's face flushed and suddenly the sweet, round woman stood up. "Don't you tell me you don't understand. ¡Dios mío! You *must* understand. Losing a child is the worst thing that can happen to you and—"

Lu's face hardened. She barked, "I don't have any children."

"What?" Martina stared at her, face bright red. "Well, that's too bad, but if you have a heart, you could imagine what it feels like—"

"I *do* imagine. Almost every day. I wish I had a child. But I can't." Lu jumped up and stared directly at Martina from across the coffee table. "I can't *have* any children. Not after… you know, after…"

Lu found she couldn't go on. She sat down and buried her hands in her face, then started crying. She shook her head. *I didn't even want to talk about it, I can't show weakness. But here I am, the lost little weak girl again.* She sobbed even harder now into her hands.

She felt a gentle touch on either side. Two warm, gentle hands on either shoulder, one slender and slim, one thicker with callouses on the fingertips, a worker's hand. "I'm so sorry. I didn't mean to hurt you or your feelings. Perdóname," Lu heard Martina's gentle voice whisper.

She felt that same strong, thick hand with the callouses on the fingertips now touch her knee. Between the fingers in front of her face, she watched as Martina kneeled down next to her. "I understand, Lu, I understand. I had bad experiences, too. Mala experiencia con un hombre."

She had a bad experience with a man. This woman is an abuse survivor, too?

"I married the guy. Bad idea. It got worse every time. Eventually, I just had to stand up to him. Call the police. I had nobody to turn to. But I really wish I had."

"Me, too," Lu whispered. "I had Elisabeth, but then she was gone. And I had nobody."

"But you did it, right? You did stand up. On your own. You made something out of your life. You were strong, you got free."

Lu didn't say anything else. *That's false.* He *made something out of my life. He still has power over me. Look at me. I'm here 'cuz he wants me to be.*

She kept listening to Martina's soft, kind voice. "Even though we wish someone was there to hold our hand and we feel like we need them, we don't always have them, no? I wished my sisters were there for me, but I didn't even tell them anything. They were far away. Still in Venezuela. I even got mad at them. Imagine that."

Lu nodded. *Don't have to imagine. And I did get mad. Mad at someone who was supposed to be there to help me.*

"But I knew that my sisters wanted to help me and would try everything to do so if they could, but they couldn't. They had a lot to deal with back at home. Their own issues, their own lives. And I had to respect that. Just like you have to respect that Elisabeth couldn't help you. Because Elisabeth suddenly had her own issues, her own demons. Her child gone."

"I know," Lu whispered.

"So you forgive her? You understand, no?"

Lu took a deep breath in, then laid her hands in her lap. She shook slightly but her voice came out strong, her big brown eyes fixated on Martina. "Yes, I understand. I didn't at first. I was waiting and waiting and waiting for a call from Elisabeth. A text, a sign, like she had sent me every day before she disappeared. I was mad. I was sad. I was all kinds of things. All kinds of feelings. I called in sick to work, locked myself in my home, ready to let my pain take over, let the life run out of me. I had no idea Elisabeth had lost her child, I didn't watch TV. I just laid in bed, covers over my head. Waiting."

Lu felt the slender hand on her other shoulder tremble, then heard a loud sob. "Oh, Lu. I'm so, so sorry!"

Lu now turned to Elisabeth. She took Elisabeth's other hand into hers. "You know what? Don't be. Don't be sorry. I was miserable, I was ready to not live anymore, but then I pulled myself together. Somehow, I pulled myself together and just focused on my career."

Elisabeth looked at her, her blue eyes in turmoil, filled with tears. "That's good, really good. Did you ever report him?"

Lu shook her head. "No, I didn't. Didn't have the strength. Needed all my strength to focus on my career and put my broken life back together."

"Sí, makes sense, Lu. And wow, you really did do it. You should be proud of yourself." A wide smile crossed Martina's face, her big, brown eyes sparkling. Lu couldn't help but smile as well.

Elisabeth nodded, her tears dried up. "What made you change your mind, Lu?"

"Change my mind?"

"You know… how did you come to the decision of putting your life back together?" Elisabeth squeezed her hand.

"Oh, that." Lu stared at the floor. "Well, I… you know…" She took a deep breath in and closed her eyes briefly. *Obviously can't tell them it was* his *idea. That's dangerous. Needs to stay a secret. Nobody can know I'm his puppet. Have to come up with a good reason.*

"My mom," Lu finally said. "It was my mom. Like you both said, the mother–daughter bond is strong. And even though my mom died before I grew up, I knew she gave me this life and would be heartbroken if I just threw it away."

"Exactamente." Martina clapped her hands together. "But now she's smiling down on you from heaven, proud, so proud of her daughter."

Lu could barely force a smile. *Doubt it. Proud of a loser? A weakling like me? No. I'm despicable. Still listening to him. I despise myself for it. But can't help it. Can't cut the strings he holds in his hands.*

Elisabeth's squeeze took Lu out of her thoughts. "That's beautiful, Lu. What a beautiful story."

Yeah, a story. That's all it is. A story. She forced her teeth together again, then returned the squeeze. "Anyway, please know, I forgive you, Elisabeth. Now that I know what happened, I completely understand. I really do. Now, please, I don't wanna talk about this anymore. It's in the past."

"I agree, Lu. Let the past be the past." Martina smiled at her, then got up and walked over to the coffee table in front of the couch and lifted her coffee. "Salud and cheers to that. Let the past be the past, and let this be a new beginning."

Elisabeth squeezed Lu's hand one last time. The two women embraced one another, then Elisabeth joined Martina and lifted her coffee cup as well. "To a new beginning. And to both of you leaving the past behind. Cheers to two wonderful, strong women."

"*Three*," Martina corrected.

"Yes, to three wonderful, strong women." Lu smiled, but her thoughts wouldn't let her pain go. *Let's hope we're strong enough.*

CHAPTER 34

"Let's hope we're strong enough." Nick wiped the sweat from his brow and bent down to lift another box. "I mean, how much stuff can a single guy own? Heck, these boxes are so heavy. And there's so many of them."

Aaron was standing next to the almost-empty Penske rental truck and grinned. "C'mon, Nick, they're not *that* heavy. And there's not that much stuff. You own way more than I do—those different hair gels you use could probably fill up a few boxes all on their own."

Nick winked at Aaron and ran his fingers through his hair. "These precious locks deserve only the best."

Jim laughed as he lifted another box and walked down the ramp of the moving truck. "Afraid to tell you, man, your precious locks are looking pretty rough right about now. All that sweat's ruined them."

"What? You serious? Oh no, I better check it out. Need a mirror, stat." Nick scanned the parking lot, then sprinted around the truck to check himself out in one of the big side mirrors. He adjusted a few strands of hair, then rejoined Aaron and Jim. "Better now, all fixed."

"Not to worry, you're always good-looking, Nick. And you already have a girl anyways." Aaron winked at him.

"I sure do." Nick grinned. "Brandy is awesome."

"Exactly." Aaron gave him a pat on the shoulder. "Brandy won't mind your future messy hair."

Nick raised his eyebrows. "What makes you think my hair will be messy in the future?"

"Just saying, you should expect to have helmet hair a lot." Aaron -laughed. "So better get used to not having perfect hair."

"Helmet... hair?"

Jim giggled. "Yeah, future navigator pilot. You'll be wearing helmets a lot. Better get a buzz cut like mine. Then you won't have to worry how it looks after getting off the job."

Nick frowned. "Oh, man. Helmet hair.... Didn't think of that. Sucks, man."

Aaron laughed. "You'll be fine. Besides, pilots are cool no matter what."

"Exactly. Even navigators." Jim grinned, then his grin faded as he shifted the box in his hands. "Nick's right, these boxes *are* crazy heavy. I better bring it up." He took a deep breath, then walked toward the stairs.

"What's happening down there? Aren't you guys coming? We're waiting for more boxes," they heard Maria yell down from the apartment front door.

"Jim is coming up right now," Aaron yelled back. "Then Nick with the second-to-last box."

"Good. What took you so long?"

"We were just discussing our new jobs," Aaron yelled up to her.

By now, Jim had climbed the stairs and reached the front door. He was breathing heavily. "Yeah, we were discussing the virtues of being a pilot and having helmet hair." He set down the box at Maria's feet.

"What? Helmet hair?"

Jim laughed. "Don't worry about it, Maria. It's an inside joke. Where do you want this?"

Maria bent down beside the box and pointed to "KITCHEN" written in big, bold Sharpie. She stepped aside to let Jim in, then saw

Nick coming up with another one. She briefly checked the label and sent him to the kitchen as well. She looked over the railing down to where Aaron was standing.

"Just one more, then we're done," he called up, and gave her a thumbs-up.

Maria walked inside, where Brandy and Keisha were already unpacking plates and mugs. Jim and Nick were just standing in the middle of the living room, bent over, hands on their thighs, heads hung low, breathing heavily. "Come on, guys, just one more box. Almost done. Let's go. Vamos." She started pushing them out the apartment's door. "One of you can bring up the box—or both of you together, don't care, but it needs to get done. Then you guys can return the rental."

Jim looked at Maria. "Don't we have to weigh it first? Get the empty weight ticket so Aaron can hand it in to finalize his moving expenses?"

Maria shook her head. "Nope, already done. Aaron and his dad did that when they first picked up the truck back in Daytona."

"Got it." Jim nodded, then searched the apartment. "Where is Jack hiding anyway?"

Nick looked up now, too. "No kidding, where is he? We hauled most of these heavy boxes while he only helped carry a few furniture items in."

"Yes, and then I told him he could start building the furniture while you guys took care of the rest." Maria smiled. "Thought you two strong, young guys could handle it."

"Oh, no worries. We can and we did," Jim said, and Nick nodded. "Was just wondering if Jack bailed on us."

Jack appeared in the doorway to Aaron's bedroom, screwdriver in hand. "Who you talkin' 'bout?"

Jim's and Nick's faces flushed. Maria laughed and pushed them out of the front door, sent them both downstairs, back to Aaron and the moving truck. She waved down at them, then shut the door behind her.

"Alright, girl, we got these boxes unpacked. Do you want to wait for Aaron to organize the glasses, mugs, plates, and bowls, or—"

Maria's laughter cut Keisha off. "Definitely no need to wait for him. If Aaron had it his way, he'd just leave everything out on the counter and call it a day."

"No kidding, y'all. Remember when Nick and Aaron moved into their apartment their senior year and didn't organize a thing for months, until Maria and I swooped in to help?" Brandy shook her head. "Those boys. So lost without us, right, darlin's?"

They heard a giggle from the other room. "Indeed," Jack yelled through the open bedroom door. "Glad you're all here to help out, girls. Aaron would be lost without the three of you."

"Thanks. And thanks for building the bed and dresser, Jack," Maria shouted back.

"You're welcome. I'm glad none of the guys are here for this. I'd rather work on it by myself—they get too hasty and start screwing things in before it's time."

"Enjoy your solitude, then, Mr. Heikinnen," Keisha yelled, and smiled.

"It's *Jack*. Remember, just Jack. No need to address me as Mr. Heikinnen, girls."

"Okay, Jack," all three of them yelled back, and giggled together.

There came a knock at the front door. They all exchanged glances and shrugged their shoulders, then Maria walked over to open it. Jim was standing right there. "I'm back." He stepped inside. "What should I help out with now?"

Keisha came over. "What are you doing here, boyfriend? I thought you were gonna help return the truck?"

Jim shook his head. "Nope, there's only two seats in front, and I can't sit in the car loaded on the trailer. And I don't feel like riding in that escort's police car. So, here I am."

"Oh, I see." Keisha gave him a hug. "I'm sure we can find some use for you."

Jim gave her a kiss. "Glad *you* have some use for me." He grinned. Keisha laughed. They kissed. Didn't let up.

"Oh no, darlin's. That's just wrong, y'all." Brandy turned around and focused on setting glasses inside the cabinet Maria had chosen for them.

Maria giggled. *I just love having my friends with me here. They're not only great helpers, they make the ordeal fun. Make me forget the terrible things that have happened lately.* She picked up a glass to put in the cabinet and found her hand was shaking terribly.

"C'mon, girl, let me help you with that." Keisha plucked the glass out of Maria's hand.

Keisha and Jim crowded into the small kitchen area. "I can help as well," Jim offered, but Maria shook her head.

"No, too crowded in here. How about you help me put books on the bookshelf in the living room?"

Jim saluted her. "Yes, ma'am."

Maria gave Brandy and Keisha more instructions, then walked into the living room with Jim. They started unloading the boxes of books by the window overlooking the water. Everyone worked on their assignments for a while, chatting away.

Finally, Jack came out of the bedroom. "Bed and dresser are built. What's next, Maria?"

She stood up and thought about it. "Do you want to wire the TV into the wall and get it and the TV stand in the right position?"

"Sure." Jack got to work right away. He hummed to himself for a bit, then glanced over his shoulder. "So, Jim, you're gonna be a fighter pilot?"

"Yes, sir," Jim replied as he transferred more books onto the shelf.

"Congrats. That'll be exciting. Tell me, what's the journey like becoming one? Aaron said you'll start in Texas for pilot training, then move to Tampa?"

The two guys found themselves in a deep conversation about pilot training. Maria got lost in thought and only half-listened to what they were saying. She heard Keisha and Brandy chatting in the kitchen, but instead of engaging with any of them, she checked her phone. *Nothing yet from Aaron. Or Mom and Mamá. Are they still with Lu? Guess it's going well then? How's Dad feeling? Hope he gets released soon.*

She set her phone down and continued unpacking. *My poor dad in the hospital. Hurt and injured. Can't believe Mike Clifford shot him. Then I shot* him. *I shot Mike Clifford.*

She closed her eyes and tried to calm her breathing. *I shot a person. Oh my gosh, I shot him.* It was happening again. She opened her eyes and tried to concentrate on the book she was holding, but all she could focus on were her hands trembling, the book shaking back and forth as she squeezed it.

Maria read the title. *The Air Force Manual.* She put it on the shelf. *Nice to have a manual, but life in the Air Force is definitely not cookie-cutter—it's different for everyone. Different experiences. Pilots. Maintenance. Engineering. All different. Some fit in, some don't. It's all different, yet all the same. The same bases, same training protocols, same—*

"Any ideas, Maria, darlin'?" Brandy said.

Maria looked over to the kitchen island breezeway that connected the kitchen to the living room and focused on Brandy. "What?"

"Any ideas for Jim, honey?" Brandy smiled at her.

Maria wrinkled her forehead. "Ideas? Ideas for what?"

Keisha started laughing. "You don't listen, girl. You have no idea what we've been talking about the past five minutes, do you?"

Maria blushed. "No, not really."

Jim rolled his eyes. "Very nice, Maria, very nice. We all drive out here to help you and be there for you, and you just block us out."

"I'm sorry, guys, I didn't mean…"

Keisha gave Jim the evil eye. "Jim! C'mon, don't be mean. Maria has a lot on her plate right now—"

Jim lifted his hands up in the air. "Goodness, guys, I was joking, you know. It's called *sarcasm.*"

Jack laughed. "Well, son, we'll have to work on your delivery. But anyway, back to the point…"

"Yeah, let's get to the point." Brandy smiled. "Maria, darlin', we were wondering if you had any good ideas for Jim's call sign?"

"Jim's call sign? What do you mean?"

"His fighter pilot name, girl," Keisha said. "All pilots have a call sign, right?"

Jim grinned. "Yep, sure do. And I want something good. Something cool. Like Maverick in *Top Gun*, for example."

"Or Iceman. I always thought that one was very cool." Brandy smiled. "Right, y'all?"

"I think Goose isn't a good one, though," Keisha said. "Not so cool to be named after a bird that honks and constantly poops on you."

They all laughed.

Jim winked at her. "Got it, Keisha, bird names are out."

"You better not associate with any birds, then, Jim." Maria laughed. "'Cuz as far as I know, you don't just *choose* your call sign, you *earn* it."

"Earn it?" Brandy scratched her chin. "Whatcha mean, darlin'?"

"There's always a story behind every call sign. It fits your personality. The way you fly or behave on the ground. At least, from what I understand," Maria said.

Jim sighed. "She's right. I better behave and go out there full force so I don't get labeled with some stupid call sign."

Keisha laughed. "Good luck with that, Jim."

"Your dad has a call sign, right, Maria?" Jack asked. "What is it again?"

Jim was all ears. "Yeah, what's his call sign? How did he earn it?"

Maria thought about it. "It's Cave Man, I think."

Jim laughed. "Cave Man? Funny. Does he speak like one or what?"

Maria had to think about it for a while. "I think it's because he likes to contemplate his decisions. Takes a while to make one. Like going into a cave to think rather than rushing into a situation just to confront it. And it helped that his initials are 'B.C.' Like 'Before Christ.' Caveman times."

Jack laughed. "Very interesting. And I think Drew Markas's call sign is Screw, isn't it?"

Maria shook her head. "I have no idea."

"Anyway, fun to think about," Jim said. "So, ladies, which of my character traits stands out to you? What should I emphasize to get a good call sign?"

"You're hot." Keisha grinned. "And kind, and a good kisser, and—"

"Keisha, that's really sweet," Jim interrupted her, "but those definitely aren't qualities that make for a good call sign."

Maria laughed. "Is that so? I think Jim 'Hottie' O'Brien sounds kinda cool."

"Y'all, let's welcome Jim 'Pucker-Up' O'Brien," Brandy joked.

The girls giggled and threw out all kinds of ideas, to which Jim kept shaking his head. "C'mon, you girls are just being silly now. I need a name that's really cool. Manly. Strong."

"Jim 'The Beast' O'Brien, y'all?" Brandy giggled.

"'The Beast'? You think I'm a beast, Brandy? Well, that's nice...." Jim pouted.

Jack laughed. "Watch that sarcasm, Jim. And don't think about it too much. It's definitely considered bad form to choose your own. Just focus on being the best pilot you can. That way you'll get your call sign based on memorable moments or inside jokes—like Maria mentioned. Don't worry about it."

Jim nodded, his smile fading. "I know. I'm just so nervous I'll mess up. Nervous about pilot training and all."

"Aw, boyfriend, you'll be fine." Keisha came over and gave him a big hug. "I know you'll do great. I'll always be there for you."

"She's right," Maria said, "you'll be fine. You got this."

"Definitely, Jim, you got this, darlin'," Brandy agreed.

A slight smile came over Jim's face. "Thanks, guys. Appreciate your support."

"It's tough, starting a new career, your first job," Jack said. "But I have no doubt you'll do just fine. All of you will do just fine. You're all such wonderful young men and women. You make your parents proud."

"Thanks, Jack," they all said, and smiled at him.

Jim took a deep breath in. "Guess I just have to see what happens, right? Even if I get a silly call sign like Carrots—'cuz, man, do I like to eat carrots—then that's the way it goes."

"Exactly, Jim 'Carrots' O'Brien." Maria laughed, then picked up the last of the books to place them on the bookshelf.

Keisha was still standing arm in arm with Jim. "It's not a bad idea to show off your strengths. We all know you're a good shot and hit bull's-eyes on the range all the time, so maybe they'll call you Jim 'Bull's-eye' O'Brien."

Brandy nodded. "Or fire your plane's rotary cannons superfast, so you're just Jim 'Bullet' O'Brien, right, ya'll?"

Bullet? The books Maria was holding slipped out of her hands and crashed to the floor.

"Goodness, Maria, you must really be worn out from moving." Keisha laughed, but her laugh faded when she looked at Maria more closely. Maria's hands were shaking, her skin pale like paper, sweat forming on her forehead. The golden-greenish flecks in her unique hazel eyes had turned bright green.

"You okay, Maria?" Keisha asked, but Maria didn't hear her. Even though she was kneeling right there on the floor of Aaron's new apartment, her mind was far, far away, her thoughts whisking her along as they swirled around in her head.

Bullet. "Just you wait until Bullet gets you."

Maria closed her eyes. She felt the ground beneath her swaying. As if she was back on that rocking boat, that big yacht, locked inside her small, little crate. Her mind transported her back to the day of the big storm.

😈 😈 😈

Her eyes still closed, she listened to the mean blonde, curly-haired guy named Cliff talking to himself again. She was doing her best to be quiet so as not to upset him even further. She listened to him rant. "Bullet is a big shot, a somebody. He helps me. I can't let him down now. My mentor, my father. My Bullet." He growled. "I'm coming up, Sully. I'll take over driving the boat. You can't fucking do it right, so I'll do it."

She didn't dare open her eyes, but heard Cliff take a few steps away from her, toward the staircase he had come down earlier. His shoes made squeaky noises on the floor; his hands thumped into something as they grabbed on. Her ears picked up that he was trying to climb stairs, his hands slapping against the railing, grabbing the railing wildly with every step so he wouldn't be tossed back down by the rocking boat.

The man was muttering to himself. Over the creaking of the ship, she heard, "For you, Bullet. I'll tolerate all this bullshit for you, my mentor, my guide. Like you said, Bullet: 'Never give up. Fight like a fighter pilot.'"

😈 😈 😈

A warm hand's touch on her shoulder made Maria jump. *Who is that? Bad guy?*

She opened her eyes and stared right into Keisha's face. "Maria, are you okay? What's going on, girl?" Keisha took her hand off Maria's shoulder and took a step back when she saw Maria's freakishly green eyes.

"Bullet," Maria whispered. "A fighter pilot. A fighter pilot's call sign."

"What's that, girl?"

Maria's head was pounding. A bad headache was already spreading from her forehead to the back of her head, ricocheting down every slope of her brain. She touched her head, held it tight, kneeled there in front of the bookcase.

"Darlin'? You alright?" came Brandy's voice.

"Maria? What's going on?" she recognized Jim saying.

"Are you okay, Maria?" she heard Jack ask in the distance.

"Bullet. He's a fighter pilot," she whispered again, tried to make eye contact with the others, but couldn't. Everything went black around her. Pitch-black.

CHAPTER 35

"**B**lack hair is so pretty." Martina smiled and touched Lu's hair. "And so shiny. How do you get it so shiny?"

Lu's long hair was falling down her shoulders, covered the whole back of her Air Force camo uniform. It swung back and forth slightly with every movement of the porch swing the three ladies were sitting on, Lu in the middle, Martina and Elisabeth to either side of her. The swing overlooked the bay, granting a beautiful panoramic view from the back porch of the Distinguished Visitor's Quarters.

Elisabeth studied Lu's hair now. "You always did have fantastic hair, Lu, but it looks even better now. Not a single strand of grey in it. So shiny and healthy. You should wear it down more often."

Lu laughed. "Thanks. I do on the weekends. My husband, Daniel, really likes it down as well. But it's Air Force protocol to wear it in a tight bun."

"Like the bun you had earlier today?"

Lu nodded. "Correct, Martina. Like when you arrived. See, I always feel weird wearing my uniform without my hair in a bun, even in the privacy of my own home."

Martina felt at Lu's hair. "But so pretty. And so straight."

"I'd rather have curls like you, Martina." Lu winked at her. "Don't we all want what we don't have?"

Elisabeth laughed. "So true. So true."

Lu got up. "Is there anything else you'd like, ladies? More water? Another slice of pizza?"

Elisabeth touched her belly and shook her head. "No, thank you. Pizza was wonderful, Lu, but I'm full."

"Sí, me, too. Full." Martina patted her belly but then lifted her empty glass. "Más aqua por favor. Gracias."

"Ciertamente." Lu took Martina's empty glass and walked inside to get more water for her. As she was filling up the glass from the fridge, she watched the two ladies outside on the swing porch share a laugh together.

Lu smiled. *It's been wonderful seeing Elisabeth again and meeting Martina. Such kind ladies. And I understand now that Elisabeth still cares. So much that all she wanted was to apologize for not showing up back then, for not keeping her promise.*

She filled up a glass for herself and walked back outside with the waters in hand. *But I know she'll keep her promise this time. She won't talk about the H.O.P.E. Club anymore. She won't bring up my past anymore. I know she won't. Because she promised me—and she won't break her promise again.*

"Here we are." Lu gave Martina her water glass, then sat back down between them. "Are you sure you don't need any more water, Elisabeth? Pizza always makes me thirsty."

Elisabeth laughed. "Me, too. But really, I'm fine. I'm just glad we got to share these precious moments with you, Lu. It's been fantastic seeing you. What a coincidence you're here at Eglin."

"Yeah, big coincidence." Lu blushed a little and cleared her throat. *They can never find out I came here to quiet Elisabeth. But at least it worked out. I'm sure of it. Now I can assure him it's all under control.*

She felt something buzz next to her. They all heard a buzzing sound.

"What's that sound?" Martina looked around. "Bees?"

Elisabeth laughed, then searched her purse. "No, it's my phone buzzing. Vibrating from a call or text. Now, which pocket did I put it in…." She found her phone the instant after it stopped vibrating. Just as she pulled it out of one of her purse's pockets, a loud ringing came from Martina's purse, which was sitting on the porch floor.

Martina jumped up. "That's *my* phone." It stopped ringing before she could get to it. Martina looked at the screen. "Oh. It's Maria. Just missed a call from her."

"Me, too," Elisabeth said, studying her phone. "Oh dear, there's a bunch of text messages. From her. From Brad. From Sarah. Oh no, poor Sarah is all alone at the inn now. Apparently finished her book and is hungry now."

Lu checked her watch. "No wonder, it's well past lunchtime. I kept you ladies way too long. I'm sorry."

"Nonsense. Not your fault, Lu." Martina laughed. "We should've kept better track of time, no?"

Elisabeth nodded. "We should've. What's the plan now?"

Lu got up again. "How about I drive you two back to the inn? We can bring your friend Sarah some leftover pizza—I'd love to meet her, too. I'll have some emails to catch up with this afternoon, but maybe we could meet again for dinner afterward?"

"Really?" Elisabeth's face lit up. "That would be awesome."

"Sí, fantástico." Martina smiled at the ladies. "Vamos, sounds like we have a good plan now. We can touch base with Maria once we're at the inn and see how the move went. Maybe they want to come back and meet us somewhere?"

"Great idea. Let's go then." Elisabeth took her empty glass and the pizza box with her and walked inside. She put the glass in the sink. "Can we help with cleanup?"

Lu shook her head. "You already did. Just leave the glasses in the sink. Let's hold onto the pizza and off we go."

Martina put her glass in the sink as well, then turned to Lu. "Dónde está el baño?"

Lu pointed her in the direction of the nearest bathroom, then walked over to Elisabeth and gave her a hug. "I'm so glad you're here, Elisabeth. Glad we get to be friends again."

Elisabeth smiled. "Me, too."

Another humming sound. "Wow, everyone seems to be worried about you," Lu laughed, and let go of Elisabeth.

Elisabeth checked her phone, then shook her head. "Not mine this time. Yours?"

Lu walked over to the kitchen table where she'd put her phone. She picked it up. "Yep. Just a text message."

"Probably your husband, Daniel, worrying about you." Elisabeth winked at her. "He has every right to worry about you. You're so beautiful and smart, Lu."

Lu blushed. "Aw, thanks." She checked the text message. All color left her face as she stared at it. It wasn't from Daniel.

I hope everything's under control, Lulu-girl, it read.

Lu closed her eyes, then did some breathing exercises.

"Everything okay?" Elisabeth asked.

Lu nodded. *I can't let her know. Can't tell her he still has this weird power over me. I need to be strong.* She let out a deep sigh. "Everything's okay. Just work. A few fires I need to extinguish when I get back." She smiled, hoping it was a convincing smile.

"Oh, I see." Elisabeth nodded. "Just like Brad. Always something to take care of, even if you're technically not available and have passed the reins to someone else, huh?"

"Exactly. Would you excuse me for a second?" Lu turned around so that there was no chance Elisabeth could see her phone screen and started texting back. *Yes, it's all under control.*

Immediate response. *I trust you, but in this case I'd like to make sure of it myself. Be there soon.*

Lu stared at her phone. Her hand started shaking. *Be here soon? What the heck? He's coming here?* Her whole body started trembling.

It took everything she had to control herself, to not wince. *I can't let Elisabeth know.*

"Are you sure you're alright, Lu?" came Elisabeth's concerned voice.

Damn it! She always could see right through me. What now? Lu nodded, took a deep breath in, blinked back the tears from her eyes, and turned around. "One of my colleagues just lost her mom. I'm grieving for her loss."

"Oh, I'm so sorry to hear that. You're so sweet, Lu. Sweet and caring. Always looking out for others, making sure they're okay." Elisabeth came over and gave her a big hug.

Lu felt the warmth of her hug, but the warmth couldn't reach her inside. She felt cold, so cold. She shuddered. *I do care, but I can't promise everything will turn out okay if he comes here. Why in the world is he coming here? I had it all under control.* She sighed. *But that isn't enough for him. He needs to feel in control no matter what. I have to protect Elisabeth and her family. But how?* A sob escaped her throat.

"Lu, that colleague of yours will be fine." Elisabeth gave her another big squeeze.

Lu nodded. "Yeah, I know." She tried to smile, even as her thoughts were racing. *But maybe you won't be fine....*

CHAPTER 36

"Fine, really, I'm fine." Maria sat on the couch in Aaron's new apartment, surrounded by Jim, Keisha, Brandy, and Jack.

Keisha eyed her. "But, girl, you fainted. That was real scary."

Brandy nodded. "Keisha's right, darlin'."

Maria sighed. "I know it was, but I'm fine now. I don't know what happened, but I'm okay now. I'm telling you, I'm fine."

"Maybe we all need to eat something soon. It's way after lunchtime." Jack pointed at his watch. "And we've all been hard at work."

Jim rubbed his belly. "I'm hungry. We only had breakfast."

"Maybe we can order something?" Keisha suggested, but then the front door to the apartment opened. In walked Aaron.

"Hey, we're back."

Nick was right behind him, carrying four big pizza boxes. "And we brought pizza for all of you!" His grin faded. "I know we just had pizza last night, but it was right there, and we thought you must be hungry after the move."

Brandy jumped up, walked over to Nick, and gave him a big kiss. "Pizza is always a crowd-pleaser. You've read our minds, darlin's. We're super hungry. Maria even fainted out of hunger."

Aaron stopped immediately and stared at Maria. "What?"

She waved him off. "Oh, it's nothing. Really, I'm fine." She jumped up, gave Aaron a quick kiss, then walked into the kitchen to gather plates and glasses for everyone. "We only have filtered water from the fridge to offer, I'm afraid."

"That's alright. Water is the healthiest choice anyway, right, boys?" Keisha filled up a glass for everyone.

The friends sat down at Aaron's small kitchen table. Jack sat on the couch while Aaron and Maria stood next to the small kitchen island that perfectly fit two. They all dug into their pizza. The room fell quiet, apart from the chewing and slurping sounds from their eating and drinking.

"Wow, nobody's saying a thing. Y'all know what that means, right?" Brandy grinned. "We all were super-duper hungry."

"For sure." Jim grabbed his third piece of pizza.

Keisha rolled her eyes. "Slow down, boyfriend, or you'll make yourself sick. It's not like we're starving to death."

"Maybe some of us were," Jim mumbled in between big bites of pizza. "Take Maria, for example. Seems like she fainted from starvation."

Maria rolled her eyes. *Does he have to bring that up again?*

"Yeah, what was that all about?" Aaron glanced at Maria.

She shrugged. "Don't know. But I'm fine." She turned to him. Said in a low voice, "Really, I'm fine."

"Sure," he replied, and kept chewing, one eyebrow raised as only he could.

Maria sighed. *He doesn't believe me. I knew it.* She focused again on her food and ate while her friends at the kitchen table joked and laughed. Jack interjected a few times, but Aaron and Maria ate their remaining pizza in silence.

"Alright, I'm done," Nick finally announced. "Where do I put all this?" He held up his empty glass, greasy plate, and three cleaned-out pizza cartons.

"Plates and glasses in the sink for now. I'll put them in the dishwasher later," Maria said. "Trash in the trash can, please."

Nick brought his glass and plate over to the sink, then looked around. "And where is the trash can?"

Maria rolled her eyes. "Oh no, we forgot to get a trash can, Aaron. That sucks."

"No worries," Keisha said. "I unpacked the trash bags earlier. We can just use those for now. Here, I'll show you where I put them. Under the sink." She got up to help Nick find them.

"We can go to Target or wherever to get a trash can and maybe some food to fill your empty fridge. You also need a toaster. I kept the one we had in our apartment," Nick said. "Or do you need us for anything else?"

Aaron thought for a bit. "No, looks like everyone did a great job unpacking. Just need to sort out all my clothes, but it's not like I need any of you going through my underwear."

Jim laughed. "No kidding. I'd rather not touch all your boxer shorts or whatever else you like to wear under your pants. Probably radioactive."

Laughter filled the room as they discussed what jobs needed to be done next. Keisha, Jim, Nick, and Brandy left to get the needed supplies, while Maria, Jack, and Aaron stayed behind at the apartment. Jack stowed away towels and bedding in the linen closet; Aaron and Maria sorted Aaron's clothes inside the walk-in closet.

Maria neatly folded and put away a T-shirt. "Hand me your other undershirts, please."

Aaron bent down to get them out of his suitcase, careful not to tweak his collarbone, but before he could hand the shirts to Maria, they all fell to the floor.

"Oh, Aaron. Now I have to refold them."

"Sorry, I just can't do it one-handed." He pouted and batted his long eyelashes over his bright-blue eyes. "Still injured. Can't do much yet."

She rolled her eyes as she picked up articles of clothing off the ground. "Poor injured Aaron. Too weak to pick up a few shirts," she teased.

He nodded. "Poor me. I feel so useless. I think I need a kiss to feel better."

"Really?" She leaned over and gave him a nice, long kiss. She felt his soft lips brush hers and smiled. "Oh, turns out you're not so useless after all."

Aaron laughed. "Not entirely. And I'm also not forgetful."

Maria paused. "What do you mean?"

"Your fainting spell. We both know it's not because you got hungry. Lately you've been fainting whenever an old memory comes to you, right?"

Maria shrugged her shoulders.

"C'mon, Maria. What was it? Anything new I need to know?"

She paused. "Mom and Mamá had a great time with Lu, sounds like. They texted me about it after I tried to call them both. They're back at the inn now. Seems Mom and Lu made up and hung out all morning and early afternoon. Even Mamá likes this Lu lady a lot. They seem to have become friends."

Aaron raised his one eyebrow again. "Um, that's great to hear... but not really what I was asking about, is it?"

Maria sighed. *He knows me too well. He knows I'm stalling.*

"C'mon, Maria. What happened right before you fainted? What were you talking about?"

"I don't remember." She turned around and started placing shirts on the shelves again. Aaron touched her arm. *He doesn't believe me. I really don't want to think back on it. It was scary—that's all I know.* She felt her arm hairs stand up.

"Maria, *what happened*? Think back to the moment right before you fainted. Please."

Maria side-eyed him, and he saw it: the blue ring around her hazel eyes with the golden-and-green flecks in the dark-brown center was shining one moment, then the green flecks surged and washed everything else out, making her eyes shine bright green. Aaron touched her arm gently. "What did you guys talk about? Please, it might be important."

She closed her eyes and thought back. "Fighter pilot names, I think. Yes, Jim was trying to think up a good call sign."

Aaron laughed. "He does know he can't just choose his own call sign, right? That's totally cringe, so uncool."

Maria nodded. "That's what we told him."

"Okay. Good. But what about that set you off? You already know your dad's a fighter pilot. Nothing inherently scary about fighter pilots, right?"

At that, Maria felt cold. A shudder ran down her spine. *Nothing scary about fighter pilots?* Her head started hurting; a headache came on so quickly she felt the pounding spread from her temples all around her head. She closed her eyes.

"Maria, what is it about fighter pilots?" came Aaron's gentle, dark voice. "You don't have to be afraid. I'm right here, you're safe. But we need to know."

Her breathing got faster as her memories took her to that rocking boat, that small crate, she was taped to it, overhearing Mike Clifford. *I can't let him down now. My mentor, my father. My Bullet.* Maria gasped for air. *Think like a fighter pilot.* Her head spun, then she was suddenly at Turkey Creek, standing in the river, pistol in her hand. Mike Clifford, blood gushing out of him, stumbling toward her. *Just you wait until Bullet gets you.*

She screamed. Next thing she knew, big arms wrapped around her, a thumping sound in her ear. That thumping calmed her down, those arms' warmth gave her strength. She realized it was Aaron's heart pounding, his arms protecting. Her head was pressed against his chest.

"Bullet. It's a call sign. A fighter pilot's call sign. Clifford's father. Bullet," she whispered, just loud enough for Aaron to hear.

He stroked her hair, then lifted her face closer to his, so that they met eyes. "Maria, you're saying Mike Clifford's father was a fighter pilot called Bullet? That's his call sign?"

Maria wavered. "Bullet is a fighter pilot's call sign. But maybe not his dad's."

Aaron thought for a while. "I can't remember what Cliff's dad's call sign was. But I thought his dad had nothing to do with your kidnapping? The police let General Clifford go."

Maria nodded, her eyes still green. "Another guy. Another pilot. One that Mike Clifford saw as a mentor, a second dad. That's Bullet."

Aaron's blue eyes widened. "Oh my gosh. So you think we need to find another fighter pilot? A fighter pilot whose call sign was Bullet?"

Maria nodded. "I think so. And we need to do it fast, because Bullet will come for me." She burst into tears, and Aaron gave her another big hug, started rocking her back and forth in his arms like a baby.

"Don't worry, Maria. We'll find him. We'll find Bullet—should be easy if he's a fighter pilot."

CHAPTER 37

"A fighter pilot sure seems like the ideal setup for a long, successful career in the Air Force. Most generals have a pilot's background. Interesting," Sally said.

Tom nodded. "Yeah, but General Lu Thomas defies the convention. She isn't a fighter pilot yet still made it to the rank of general."

"True. She's an unusual fast-burner," Chief Parlot said. "What else do we know about her? About Elisabeth's old friend?"

Sally studied her notes, then briefed everyone on what she had found out. "Lu is short for Guadalupe. Thomas is her married name. Maiden name Rodriguez. Married another AF officer in 2010, who's since retired. Lu is still active duty and very successful. She enlisted right after high school. First job was the Air Force job back in Utah—that's where she met Elisabeth, I suppose. Then she went to college, studied engineering, and cross-trained into a commissioning path. Had a great career since. Lots of praise for her. Got promoted quickly, often BTZ—"

"BT what?" Tom interrupted Sally.

"BTZ stands for 'Below The Zone.' In Air Force parlance, there are certain zones, certain spans of years where your year group is up for promotion. Usually about three years long. The best Airmen promote in the first year, then the second, and so on. But if you're really good, you can promote ahead of time—below the zone."

"Got it," Tom said.

The chief nodded. "Good stuff. Had no idea. Thanks, Sally. Please continue."

Sally nodded. "They don't do the BTZ thing anymore for some reason. But it was still around during Lu Thomas's early years in the Air Force, and that's how she rose to the top so quickly. Only because she did really well, of course. She's like a poster child for the Air Force: a fast-burner, a woman, Hispanic background, now a brigadier general leading the Air Force Civil Engineer Center at Lackland in Texas."

Tonya whistled through her teeth. "Impressive."

"Agreed," Chief Parlot said. "But what exactly does she have to do with our case? With Maria's kidnappings?"

Sally shrugged. "Not sure if she has anything to do with it at all. All we know is that she's an old friend of Elisabeth's dating back to the H.O.P.E. Club, according to what Lieutenant Martinez told me. Guess we'll have to talk to Elisabeth directly to find out exactly how they met back in Utah."

Tonya started pacing. "This was Lu's early years, right? Her first job was in Utah back when she first enlisted, you said?"

Sally checked her notes. "Correct."

"So Lu Thomas was a young, impressionable girl back then…. Question is, why did she join the H.O.P.E. Club? Could that have anything to do with the original kidnapping?"

The chief scratched his chin. "I'm not sure the H.O.P.E. Club is of any importance here."

"Except, Elisabeth Collins thought she might have made some enemies back then, some high-ranking enemies," Sally said.

Chief Parlot nodded. "True. But couldn't be Lu Thomas, right? She was practically a little girl back then, a freshly enlisted Airman at the time."

Tonya was still pacing. "Correct. Still, I think we need to focus on higher-ups back then. Generals. Mike Clifford's dad, General Clifford, didn't have anything to do with it, we learned that much. But what about General Jones? Did he know our corrupt senator? What did you find out, Tom?"

Tom cleared his throat as if getting ready for a big speech. "General Robert Jones, a.k.a. Bob Jones, was a guest speaker at the Air Force Academy's graduation ceremony in 1997."

Tonya stopped pacing abruptly. "You mean the year Brad Collins graduated?"

Tom grinned. "Bingo."

Sally lifted up her hands. "Wait, wait, wait. That means Brad Collins would have seen him on stage, but had nothing else to do with him. And Mike Clifford, the main guy behind the kidnapping, wasn't even around because he got kicked out of the Air Force Academy after Brad told on him. He wasn't at the graduation ceremony, right?"

Tom nodded again. "Right. But he hadn't moved away yet, he was hanging out nearby. And guess who else was?" The rest of the team collectively shrugged their shoulders. "Seems General Bob Jones enjoyed frequenting certain taverns there in Colorado Springs."

The chief raised his eyebrows. "So?"

"Our friend Mike Clifford also enjoyed his taverns, especially after he got kicked out. Hung out there most days. I found all kinds of bar receipts from him eating and drinking following his expulsion, leading up to the end of term. He burned through his cash. And yes, he saw his dad after graduation, and they cut off his allowance. Mike was pretty broke—until he met someone who took him in."

Sally's eyes were wide. "Who?"

"Can't say I'm one hundred percent sure, but it's likely he met General Jones somehow, and the general decided to take him under his wing. General Jones was stationed in Utah then. And somehow, Mike Clifford ended up there, hanging around Hill AFB's bowling alley, not long after the Academy's graduation he didn't take part in.

He somehow ended up in a small apartment in Ogden, Utah, got a job at Target in Riverdale, Utah, but also had access to Hill Air Force Base after joining the bowling club there. And guess who his sponsor was for being on base?" Tom grinned. "General Robert Jones."

"I'll be damned," Chief Parlot mumbled, then stared at Tom. "How long was Mike in Utah? Still there when Collins got stationed there?"

Tom clicked on his touchpad to check something. "Yes, but they only overlapped a few months. Mike moved back to this area summer of 2002."

Tonya started pacing again. "Interesting, interesting. What about the general? General Jones? I assume Mike didn't move back down here to Florida to see his parents?"

"No, he sure didn't. He lived pretty close to Niceville, and therefore his parents, but we know they didn't speak much, if we can trust what Mike's dad told us. Mike had a small place in Valparaiso and continued to work a job at Target. Did well enough for himself working retail."

"I read his bio when he became senator. 'From Rags to Riches— The True Story of the Awesome American Wonder Boy.' Better vote for him," Chief Parlot snorted.

Sally laughed. "Rather, from rich to poor to rich again. Not exactly the American Dream, was it?"

"Not the usual route, nope," Tonya said, and stopped pacing. "Tom, did Mike have access to Eglin as well?"

Tom nodded. "Member of the Bowling Club again. Same sponsor on base."

"Wow, so General Jones really took a shining to him, huh?" Sally shook her head. "Can't believe it."

Me neither. Chief Parlot was lost in thought. *Mike Clifford and General Bob Jones become best buds. The general takes the black sheep in. Why? Out of the goodness of his heart? Treats him like a prodigal son come home.* The chief turned pale. *Son?* "Tom, does General Bob Jones have a family?"

Tom turned back to his computer; his fingers flew across the keyboard. He rapidly pulled up a bunch of databases and scanned through them. "Married. Later got divorced. Had one son." Tom read on. "Teenage son died in a car accident."

"Oh no, that's really sad." Sally swallowed hard to not let her emotions show.

Tom nodded. "It is. Especially since he got divorced *before* the accident happened. No wife there to comfort him."

"He didn't remarry?" the chief wanted to know. Tom shook his head. Chief Parlot scratched his forehead. "Interesting. Can you find out anything about the ex-wife?"

"I suppose." While Tom hammered on his keyboard, the chief started pacing. *He lost his son, so he adopts Mike as a new one? Is this the so-called father we're looking for? The one Mike told Maria about when he kidnapped her?*

"Hey, Isaac my man, what's going on?" Tonya ripped him out of his thoughts. "I have to say, watching everyone pace all the time makes me nervous."

The chief stopped and winked at her. "Then you know how we feel when you do it."

They all laughed together before Tom interrupted. "Hey, team, look at this. Found an email to General Jones from his ex-wife. Very interesting."

They all huddled around Tom, who summarized the most important parts. "Says she can't stand his behavior anymore. Apparently he accused her of adultery, even though she sought out intimacy while he was spending all his free time visiting strip clubs, hanging out with young girls, gambling."

"Gambling? Young girls?" The chief gasped. "Did he get divorced before he was stationed at Hill?"

Tom nodded. "Years before."

Chief Parlot took a step back. "Get Elisabeth on the line. Now. And Brad Collins, too."

The team looked up at the chief. "What?"

"I think General Bob Jones was involved in Elisabeth's scandal involving the H.O.P.E. Club. He liked gambling and young girls. Can't be a coincidence."

"Good point." Tonya patted him on his back. "Okay, let's do it. Who calls whom?"

"You ladies take Elisabeth. Ask her about Lu Thomas, please," Chief Parlot said. "Tom, you and I will call Brad. Find out if he knows General Jones personally."

When Tom and the chief walked back into the workroom, they found Tonya and Sally sitting on the couch talking casually, Tonya sipping a coffee and Sally her energy drink. Chief Parlot raised an eyebrow. "What's happening, ladies? Seems like you're having a good old time relaxing on the job."

"Relax, Isaac. We've already done our work. Just waiting for you slowpokes." Tonya winked at him, then pointed at the little snack table nearby. "Want a coffee? Freshly brewed. Or some donuts?"

"Donuts? Yummy." Tom pushed past Chief Parlot and grabbed a chocolate-covered donut. He then rummaged through the mini fridge for an energy drink. Both in hand, he plopped down on the couch next to Sally and took a big bite out of the donut. "So, what's new?"

Sally side-eyed him. "How about you mind your manners and don't talk with your mouth full? It's disgusting. And you're getting crumbs all over the floor."

"Nonsense." Tom shook his head, dusting the floor with crumbs, and took another big bite. "Besides, that's why I asked you to report to us first. Gives me time to chew."

Tonya laughed. "Okay then, Tom. Well, we talked to Elisabeth. She doesn't know a General Jones. At all. Thought she'd never heard of him before but then recognized his name as Eglin's base general when her daughter disappeared. Said she met him during the investigation. He seemed polite and concerned but wasn't helpful. She recalled the general moved soon after the disappearance."

"True enough," the chief said. "Brad Collins said General Jones left Eglin spring of 2004. A little less than a year after the kidnapping."

"You're saying Brad Collins knew General Jones, then? Or still knows him?" Sally's eyes were wide, her eyebrows raised.

"Neither. At least that's what he told Tom and me. Brad remembered he was the guest speaker at his graduation. Jones wasn't a general back then, just a colonel. Brad remembers their time overlapping in Utah for a year or so, then again at Eglin for another short period of time. But they never really worked together."

Tonya raised her eyebrows. "But aren't they both fighter pilots?"

Chief Parlot nodded. "Yes. But they were pretty far off in rank. Brad Collins never worked for Jones directly."

"I see. Neither Brad nor Elisabeth knows him." Sally pouted. "Too bad. Wrong guy. Why would he want to hurt them by orchestrating the kidnapping of their only child if he didn't know them at all? Why would he want anything to do with it?"

Tom shrugged, then licked the chocolate off his fingers.

"But here's the rub—he's the one guy who knows *everyone*." The chief started pacing again. "Think about it; he knew Agent Borman so very well, to the point that Borman likely called him right before he killed himself. He knew Mike Clifford, treated him like a son. He must have known Chief Billings, not only from being Eglin's AFB commander and working with local police during Moana's kidnapping investigation but also as a friend because Billings was invited to Jones's private promotion party. We gotta dig deeper, team. There must be a clear motive because I really do think he's our guy. He must be our Bullet."

CHAPTER 38

"**B**ullet sure is an awesome call sign," Aaron said. "And you're sure Mike Clifford said a fighter pilot was involved in your kidnapping?"

Maria rolled her eyes. "No, I don't know *for sure*. But I have a feeling that's the case. Look, we need to find out *if* there's a fighter pilot named Bullet, that's all I'm saying."

"Okay, fine. Let's call the police and tell them to look into—"

"No, definitely not." Maria got up off the floor they'd been sitting on. "The team's busy right now doing their own research. And I want to know *now*. *Need* to know *now*. *Right now*."

Aaron stood as well and took her hands. "Maria, I really think it's best we talk to the police and wait for—"

"No, Aaron." Maria shook him off. "I don't want to tell them. I'll just google it."

Aaron shook his head. "Maria, come on, don't be like that. Let's talk to the police. I don't think googling is gonna…" But Maria had already pulled out her phone and started googling. Aaron sighed and ran a hand over his face. "I'll go help my dad then."

He walked out of the bedroom over to the living room TV stand where Jack was trying to set up cable and internet. He sat down and helped his father sort out the cables.

Maria heard them talking quietly. *Aaron's probably complaining about me. About me being stubborn.* She sighed. *But I really want to find this out for myself. It's my life. I like the police team, but I don't trust them anymore. It was* their *idea to go see the guy who kidnapped me as a toddler, and then they failed to prevent him kidnapping me* again. *Their plan went all wrong....*

She sighed and joined the others in the living room. Walked over to the couch and sat down, focused on her search. She tried combining all types of terms like "fighter pilot" and "Bullet," but got no meaningful hits. *Nothing. It just shows me generic pilots and all kinds of weird bullets for guns. Damn it.* She threw her phone on the ground, right into the fluffy carpet. Her face turned red. She buried it in her hands. *I know there's something to it, I didn't just make it up. I know Clifford mentioned a fighter pilot back then, twenty years ago. It must be Bullet. But how can I confirm it?*

"You alright, Maria?" Jack asked.

She lifted her head. "Oh yeah, I'm okay... just a bit frustrated."

Aaron tilted his head. "No luck, huh?" She shook her head. "Told ya. You should reconsider my earlier suggestion." He eyed her. "And be less stubborn. Let others help."

Maria shook her head, then picked up her phone off the floor, crossed her arms in front of her chest, and walked back into the bedroom's walk-in closet. *I don't want to argue right now. He doesn't seem to understand I've lost trust in the police.*

"Hey, what are you up to, Maria? You okay?" Aaron called after her.

"Yeah, fine," she grunted. "Just need some alone time right now. I'll be organizing the empty bins in here."

"Okay?" he said, but she closed the door to the walk-in closet and started moving the empty bins around, stacking them on the far side of the wall. As she worked, she thought more about Bullet. *A fighter pilot. A call sign. Most famous pilots are known by their call signs. Wait... famous?*

Her face lit up with an idea. She quickly googled "famous fighter pilots." She held her breath as the little loading ring spun, indicating it was searching for answers.

"Erich 'Bubi' Hartmann, the 'Red Baron' Manfred von Richthofen," she read aloud. She sighed. *The heck, these guys are all old. Long dead by now.* "Chuck Yeager, Jimmy Doolittle." *Getting closer to our time now.*

She kept scrolling down and clicked the button "Famous Fighter Pilots Today." She almost dropped her phone the moment the entry popped up. The text practically seared her vision: "Bob 'The Bullet' Jones." There it was, black on white. *Oh my gosh. Is that him? Bullet?*

With shaking hands, she scanned the article. *"Young Bob 'The Bullet' Jones is famous for flying the F-15 Strike Eagle during Operation Desert Storm in 1991. He was commended for destroying a tremendous amount of mobile Scud missile launchers in the western deserts of Iraq. During combat missions, he discovered new, innovative ways of flying the F-15."*

Squeak.

The door opened unexpectedly, and Maria jumped to the side involuntarily. She crashed into one of the open bins, lost her footing, and tumbled backward, right into the bin, bottom-first. Her phone flew out of her hands and crashed into the bin next to her.

Loud laughter erupted from outside the closet. "Girl, what you doing?" Keisha grinned.

"Y'all, you've gotta see this; Maria is sitting in a bin," Brandy called over her shoulder to the others.

Within moments, Nick, Jim, Jack, and Aaron had joined Keisha and Brandy in the doorway, laughing at the sight of Maria's predicament. Maria was stuck in a bin, her legs dangling over the sides, arms splayed out at odd angles.

Her face turned red. "You guys scared me! I didn't know you were back from your errand already. And you all could've at least asked if I'm okay."

"Sorry, girl," Keisha gasped through tears. She held her breath, tried to stop herself from laughing. Failed. "Are you okay?"

"I'm fine," Maria said. "But I'm stuck."

More laughter.

"Nice big hips, eh?" Jim joked. "Good for some things, but not when you're trying to fit inside a bin." Keisha elbowed him, and he stopped laughing immediately. "Sorry. Insensitive." Keisha nodded, her arms crossed in front of her chest.

"Can someone please help me out?"

"Of course, we're coming, darlin'." Brandy was first to her side, followed by Keisha. They each grabbed hold of one of Maria's arms and pulled. Maria rolled forward onto her feet—but the bin remained stuck to her bottom.

The boys slapped their thighs in laughter. "She looks ridiculous," Nick spit out between a laughing spree. "Like a turtle wearing its shell on its butt!"

Maria rolled her eyes and tried to wiggle the bin off her, but its rim seemed stuck on one of her jeans' buttons.

"C'mon, keep wiggling," Keisha encouraged her. "Shake it, girl!"

That finally did it. Even Maria began to laugh, recognizing the comedy of the situation. At the same time, the bin fell off and plopped onto the floor.

Everybody clapped. Nick threw his hands up into the air. "She's free! Yay!"

Aaron came over. "You okay, Maria?"

She nodded. "I'm fine."

"Good." He gave her a kiss on the cheek. "And we're good?"

She sighed, and eyed him closely. His blue eyes were begging her like a puppy dog's. "Yeah, we're good. You're forgiven for acting so smug earlier." Then the color drained from her face as she remembered what she'd just found, but before she could say anything, Aaron leaned in to kiss her on the lips and her brain went blank.

They were interrupted by a cell phone's loud ringing. Maria pulled away from Aaron. "That's mine. Where'd it go?"

Jack pointed. "Over there. On the floor."

Maria retrieved the phone. Her face lit up. "It's my mom."

"Which one?" Nick joked, but Brandy gave him the evil eye.

Maria picked up, then walked past the others into Aaron's bedroom. "Hi, Mom, what you up to?" She listened for a while and glanced over occasionally at the group crowded around the walk-in closet. They were chatting with each other while stacking the last of the bins.

Maria listened to everything her mom had to tell her. "Okay, Mom. Good to know. Hey, don't worry, we'll take care of Mamá and Sarah. I think we're about finished with moving in. Say hi to Dad for me." She smiled at her mom's reply. "Okay, talk to you later then. And yes, we'll make sure those two are comfortable at the inn. Thanks." She listened again. "Okay, yes. Sounds like a great plan. I'd love to meet her tonight." Maria smiled, then blushed. "Love ya, too, Mom. Bye."

She hung up, then peeked inside the walk-in closet. She smiled at everyone. "My mom's going to see my dad at the hospital with Drew. Mamá and Sarah are at the inn and were wondering if we could meet them there. We're pretty much done here, right?"

Aaron nodded. He walked past Maria into the living room and looked around. "I think so."

The others followed. "You're definitely more moved in than we were at our place last year, remember?" Nick grinned. "We were living out of boxes for about a month."

"No kidding." Brandy rolled her eyes. "If it wasn't for Maria and me, y'all would've lived out of boxes your whole senior year."

Aaron laughed out loud. "Probably. Good progress here." He smiled at his friends. "And thanks to you guys, we even have a trash can."

"Yeah, man!" Jim said, and high-fived Aaron.

"So, boss, what's the plan then?" Nick winked at Aaron.

Aaron grinned. "I think it's about time for a break."

"Yes, please. I'm dying to see the beaches around here," Keisha said. "How about we go swimming this afternoon?"

Brandy jumped up in the air and clapped her hands together. "Yes, please, please, please y'all. I think we deserve it. And Maria can get her mind off all the crazy things that happened lately."

"Hmm, the reporters will definitely find us if we go to a public beach," Jack mumbled. He turned to Aaron. "Doesn't the base have its own beach?"

"It does. A small one. Postal Point. By the Fam Camp, right next to the..." He glanced at Maria and frowned. "The TLFs."

It got quiet in the apartment, all eyes on Maria.

She exhaled deeply, then smiled. "It's okay, guys. I already know I got kidnapped there. It's not a surprise anymore. Besides, I'd rather take my chances with my own memories than deal with reporters off base."

"Okay then. Let's head back to the inn. Grab our swimming stuff, pick up the ladies—your mamá and Sarah, that is—then head out. Sounds good?" Keisha waited for everyone to either nod or give her a thumbs-up.

"I'll let Lieutenant Martinez and his colleagues know." Aaron got up to walk outside. It didn't take him long. "All set," he said when he came back in.

"Awesome, guys." Jim smiled. "Let's go then."

Nick, Jim, Keisha, and Brandy headed for their car. Jack asked Maria and Aaron for a moment to make sure the cable and internet were good to go, then the three of them locked up the apartment.

"Oh, I forgot to tell you, we have dinner plans," Maria told Aaron as they headed downstairs.

Aaron raised his one eyebrow. "Dinner plans? *We?* As in, just you and me?"

Maria laughed. "No, silly, not just you and me. We were invited. I assume the invitation's only for us—probably not your dad or our friends."

His one eyebrow went even higher than before. "Who invited us to dinner?"

"Lu," Maria said. "Mom told me she'd really like to meet us. Get to know us over dinner, not just a casual hello. She'll host us at the house we visited this morning. Mamá and Mom will be there, too."

"Really? Things worked out that well? They became so close in such a short time."

"No, silly, they already knew each other, were close from before, remember?"

Aaron's eyebrow was still raised. "But not for the past twenty years. Before yesterday, your mom didn't even remember her name. I don't call that 'being close' at all."

"Oh, Aaron, just be happy they made up and still like each other. Mamá seems to have hit it off with Lu as well. Be excited for them. And let's meet her tonight."

They got to the car. Jack hopped into the driver's seat. The police escort, along with their friends, were ready to go. Aaron walked Maria to the driver's side and opened the rear door for her. "Fine, we'll see Lu tonight. But I feel strange going there."

"Why? Don't worry, it'll be fun." Maria gave him a quick kiss, then got into the car. They waited for Aaron to get into the front passenger seat.

As she watched him buckle up, she thought about Lu. *It'll be fun going there, right? I mean, she's an old friend of my mom's. Mamá likes her, too. It'll be fine. She's a nice lady, isn't she?*

CHAPTER 39

"**I**sn't she here on business?" Brad raised his eyebrows as he studied Elisabeth's face from his hospital bed. "I mean, how can she just hang out on base with barely anything to do all day when she's on a TDY? She's a general—*General* Lu Thomas. She must have a lot to do and no time to host a dinner party. Especially a home-cooked meal she's preparing personally. Don't you find this all a little strange?"

Elisabeth laughed. "Come on, Brad. It's not strange. This TDY was a last-minute addition to her overseas trip. She doesn't really have any serious meetings till tomorrow."

Brad scrunched up his eyebrows. "Last minute. That's strange also."

"Not necessarily, Brad. You've had this type of stuff happen to you plenty of times. Don't forget that," Drew said.

Brad shrugged. "I suppose." *I still feel like it's more than strange. Lu, here, at this moment in time. Right after Elisabeth got hung up on her. Can it be a coincidence?*

The warmth of Elisabeth's hand holding his drew him back to the present. He smiled and listened as Elisabeth told him about their morning with Lu. "We got along so well. Martina, too. We had a lot of fun just hanging out together, catching up. And Martina likes Lu. They had an immediate connection." Elisabeth smiled. "And guess what? She forgave me, Brad. Lu even said she understands how losing a child would be the worst experience ever." At those words, Elisabeth's smile vanished, and Brad saw tears forming in her blue eyes.

Brad stroked her hand. "What's going on, Elisabeth? Why so sad all of a sudden? We found our daughter. And you got Lu's forgiveness."

Elisabeth blinked back tears. "I'm just sad for Lu. You know, she told me she can't bear children. Not after what her rapist did to her." Elisabeth's lip quivered.

Brad's eyes widened and turned slightly greener. "The abuse was that bad? Oh my.... Did she ever report the guy?" Out of the corner of his eye, Brad saw his friend Drew swallow hard.

Elisabeth shook her head. "No. She said she couldn't find the strength. She ended up locking herself in her home and was ready to starve herself to death. She never found out our child went missing. She didn't have anything to do with the outside world for a while—took a leave of absence from the Air Force and was lost, totally lost." One big tear escaped Elisabeth's eyes.

"Oh, hun, I know it's a terrible story. But look at her now." Brad squeezed Elisabeth's hand. "She's doing very well."

Elisabeth wiped away her tears. "I know." A slight smile spread across her face. "She had an amazing career, looks amazing, even forgave me without any hesitation. She said she just started fighting for her well-being and success, found her strength after all. Said she had me in the back of her mind, as if I were there telling her to stand up and fight."

Brad smiled. "That's wonderful, hun."

"And goodness, Lu Thomas is definitely a hotshot. Not just with her own career," Drew said. "She's opened doors for other females to rise in the ranks. A real trailblazer."

Elisabeth nodded. "It's impressive. And she's married to this nice guy. Daniel. He was an officer also, but since retired."

"Sounds like she's come far in life," Brad said.

"She has. I wish you could come to dinner. I'd love for you to meet her and be there with me and Maria."

"I wish that, too. But they won't let me leave yet." Brad sighed. *I really wish I could go. Despite all the positive sentiment, for some reason I don't have a good feeling about this.*

"I'll take pictures and send them to you, okay, hun?"

Brad nodded. "Yes please. Who all's going?"

"Martina and me. And she wants to meet Maria. Then—"

"Bring Aaron along, will you?" Brad interrupted Elisabeth.

She raised her eyebrows. "That was the plan. Of course I was going to introduce my future son-in-law to her. But why did you ask?"

"Oh, no reason." Brad cleared his throat. *I need him to be there to keep an eye on the ladies. That boy is good at sensing danger, has the guts to defend my daughter. He's proven that. He's a good protector. Need him there.*

"Hun, you're alright? You seem absent-minded." Elisabeth squeezed his hand, and he focused on her again.

"I'm okay."

Elisabeth tilted her head and looked at him. "Something bothering you?"

Drew laughed. "Yeah, Cave Man, I'm wondering that also."

Brad frowned. *They can read me like an open book.* He cleared his throat, then turned to Elisabeth. "Nothing bothering me. Just thinking about Sarah and Jack. What about them? What will they be doing for dinner?"

"You're so sweet, Brad." Elisabeth gave him a kiss on his cheek. "Don't worry. They're taken care of."

"They'll hang with me," Drew said. "I'll take them to Wings and Grill on base. No worries, Cave Man, I got them."

Brad nodded. "And Maria's friends? What about them?"

"They'll figure it out. They're kids. And safe from the press, unlike us, meaning they can go wherever they want." Elisabeth smiled at him.

"Don't worry about any of us. We're all fine. You need to worry about yourself, get healthy so you can get out of here."

"I know. I'm working on it. Shoulder feels better already."

"That's good, hun. Very good. So, get healthy and don't worry about us. Dinner at Lu's will be fun." She winked at him.

He smiled back at her, a weak smile. *Yeah, dinner at Lu's will be fine. Just fine.*

CHAPTER 40

"Just fine, doing just fine, thank you," he said as he climbed out of his Cessna to the guy who had helped him park his plane at Eglin's Aero Club. He shook the young man's hand. "Very nice to meet you, Captain…"

"Martin," the young guy said. "I'm Captain Martin, and part of Eglin's Aero Club. We're happy to have you here, General."

He grinned, his green eyes smiling, his greyish-red hair shining in the sun. "It's good to be here, indeed, Captain Martin. Thank you for letting me park my baby here." He patted the airplane's side. "Really appreciate it."

"Anytime, General Jones, anytime." Captain Martin smiled at him. "We'll take good care of her. Fuel her up and have her ready to go for whenever you decide to fly back."

"It'll just be a quick visit. Probably fly back tomorrow," General Jones replied.

"Very well, sir. Please follow me inside for some paperwork, then you can be on your way."

"Wonderful, thank you." He smiled and followed the captain inside the little hut near the flight line, his small black bag in his hands. *Yeah, wonderful to be here. Wonderful that I'll be visiting Lulu-girl soon.*

Always good to check up on my puppets. Make sure everything's going according to plan.

😈 😈 😈

Captain Martin drove him to the Distinguished Visitor's Quarters, to the second house in the roundabout. "This one's yours, General. That one next door is occupied by a last-minute visitor as well. Another general. General Thomas. Do you know her?"

He grinned. "Oh yes, we've crossed paths. Wonderful woman."

"Yes, she is." The captain parked the car in front of the steps. "Here we are. Let me get the door for you, General."

General Jones smiled. *What a sweet guy. Won't go far in life. Gotta be cutthroat to do so.* The captain opened his door, and he stepped out. "Thank you, Captain Martin. Very kind of you."

"You're welcome, General. Do you need a hand with your bag? Or anything else?"

"No, I got it. Got just the one for this short trip. Thanks again."

"You're welcome, sir. It's an honor to meet you. You were quite the fighter pilot in your time."

General Jones laughed. "I suppose so. Well, can't do the roll so well with my Cessna, but it sure was fun in the Strike Eagle back then."

"I bet, sir. Enjoy your short vacation—and the beach. It's right over there." The captain pointed to the left.

"I know, son. I've been here before."

"Oh yes, of course, sir. It's just so exciting to have you. So many visiting generals here at the same time. Very exciting times."

Jones smiled. "Yes, you mentioned my neighbor already."

"And then General Collins is here, too. But you know, he's in the hospital right now. Unbelievable story, that, just unbelievable, he—"

"*Yes*, Captain Martin, I've heard it. Unbelievable indeed. But I'd like to go inside now. I'm very tired from the long flight. Not used to flying long hauls anymore."

The captain blushed. "Of course, sir, I'm sorry for keeping you so long. Here are your keys. Enjoy your stay."

"Thank you, Captain Martin." He saluted, then turned around and walked inside. *It's a big house just for me. Guess I'm still respected around here. A somebody. Famous.* He frowned. *And I can't let my name be tarnished.*

He stowed his bag in one of the bedrooms, then walked over to the kitchen to get a glass of water. He gulped it down, looking out the window overlooking the bay, emerald-green water sparkling. *Beautiful place here. I remember it well. Was great living by the water. And convenient for my little stunt. It all worked out well enough. If only Cliff hadn't messed up and kept the girl alive....*

He filled up another glass of water and took a sip. *And now she's back. And so is Elisabeth. They're both a threat to me. Not sure how much Elisabeth knows, but I have to assume it's too much. And the girl? She took my son away from me. Another son dead.*

He bit his lip. *Man, I loved him. My dear Mike. Loved him like my own son. Built him up from scratch, that lost young man I met at the tavern in Colorado Springs. He became my son, willing to do anything for me. I miss you, Mike. I miss you.*

He gulped down the rest of the water. *I'll avenge you, Mike. I will. And I'll also make sure nobody ever finds out what I did. Nobody.*

He put down the glass of water and walked over to the living room side window that overlooked the other Distinguished Visitor's house. He peeked through the window to see if he could detect any movement. Saw nothing. He walked around to acquaint himself with the rest of the building, and just as he looped back into the kitchen again to scrounge up some coffee, he saw a black SUV arrive in front of the other house.

Jones stood near the window, made sure he couldn't be seen. He grinned when he saw who got out of the car. *Lulu-girl. Still beautiful. Always has been. Even in that unflattering uniform, she looks stunning. I can see her curves.*

He let out a deep breath to avoid getting too excited just seeing her. *It's been too long, Lulu-girl. Guess we have tonight to discuss plans—and pick up where we left off, maybe?*

A big grin spread across his face as he watched her unloading a bunch of shopping bags. "COMMISSARY," they read. *Commissary? She went grocery shopping here on base? What do you need all those groceries for, Lulu-girl? Dinner plans? With whom?*

He watched her every move and realized he was also able to see her once she went inside, through her kitchen window. He brewed himself a cup of coffee, then positioned a chair at such an angle that he could watch her without her seeing him. He just sat there, enjoying watching her cook in the kitchen.

He grinned and sipped his coffee. *Beautiful day. Just love watching her.*

CHAPTER 41

*J*ust *love watching her, Maria and her friends. It's a beautiful day and they're having so much fun.* Martina smiled and adjusted her sunglasses as she lay on the towel by the little beach strip on base, alongside Sarah. Sarah was sun-tanning and almost looked as if she'd fallen asleep right there on her beach towel.

Martina grinned. *It's a nice, sunny afternoon. The warmth makes for good napping, I suppose.* She focused on Maria and her friends again, floating in the shallow water. They were at least half a mile out yet still seemed to be only waist deep. Because of the shallows, Aaron was able to be in the water as well. He carefully held his arm in a sling above the surface, taking care to make sure no rogue waves splashed his injured shoulder. Maria kept an eye on him as well as she watched the youngsters play their games.

Martina wasn't sure what it was they were playing. Brandy and Nick were floating on their backs, trying not to sink. Keisha and Jim would try to push them underwater whenever they came close to them. The laughter of their little group carried across the slight breeze and warmed Martina's heart.

Almost like a normal day. She glanced over her shoulder to the police car. *If it wasn't for constantly having to be escorted, you could mistake it for a normal day.* She sighed. *But nothing is normal. My daughter has two moms now. She's survived several attacks and been injured. She's killed someone.* Martina shook her head at that, her brown curls bouncing. *Unbelievable. She'll need help. Therapy. I should get her to see someone. Maybe that guy with the police—Dr. Davies?*

"Beautiful day, ne?" Sarah ripped her out of her thoughts.

Martina turned to her and nodded. "Sí, beautiful day." *Not napping after all.*

Sarah sat up. "I just love the beaches here. The beautiful, soft sand, the warm water. And it's—how do you say?—not deep."

"Shallow?"

"Yes, that's what I mean. Shallow. Shallow water." Sarah pointed to Maria and her group of friends. "Look. They are far away and still can stand. Wow."

Martina nodded. "It's nice. And not too wavy, here on the bay."

"Right. No waves. Look there." Sarah now pointed at a family with two little kids. One about three or four years old, the other barely walking. "The little kids can even play in the water. No waves to push them over."

Martina grinned. "Right. No waves to topple the toddlers."

Sarah turned to Martina. "Is it the same in Miami?"

Martina shook her head. "No. Very wavy there at the Atlantic Ocean. Often big waves. Good for surfing, though."

"Is it deep there?"

"You mean, the water?" Martina looked at Sarah, who nodded. "Yes, the water is deep there. Not shallow. Drops off quickly, not like here."

Sarah watched the little family again. "Ja. I remember Elisabeth talking about that when they moved here. Such—how do you say again?—*shallow* water. Good for little Moana—Maria, I mean."

Martina's heart dropped. *Elisabeth was robbed of experiencing what that family over there is experiencing right now.*

"She told me her little one loved playing at the beach. I think this beach here. Right by the TLFs where they stayed after the move.

Elisabeth was so happy; their daughter loved splashing in the shallow water and building sandcastles with Brad." Sarah laughed. "She did tell me it was annoying that her little one often got sand in her eyes, or tried to eat it."

Martina was staring ahead, tears in her big brown eyes. Like she was the one who'd gotten sand in them. *A perfect family. Torn apart by a kidnapping. And a stupid woman who didn't go to the police when a little toddler appeared on her doorstep. I was that stupid woman. I should've gone to the police—then Elisabeth would've gotten her daughter back, her family. And then Maria wouldn't have been attacked multiple times twenty years later.*

Martina threw her hands over her face and started sobbing.

"Oh nein. Are you okay, Martina?" she heard Sarah ask, then felt a warm hand on her shoulder.

"It's all my fault," Martina whispered, "all my fault. I should've gone to the police. I robbed that precious time from Elisabeth. Twenty years of time."

Sarah scooted onto her towel and gave her a side hug. "Nein, Martina, nein, nein. Elisabeth already forgave you. Please, don't think this way. It's okay. Look how happy Maria is now. And Elisabeth is happy now, too. I, too. We're all happy. All is good."

Martina wiped away her tears. "I still feel guilty."

"Nein, nein. All is good." Sarah gave her another squeeze.

Laughter reached their ears. They looked up and saw Jim and Nick splashing through the water awkwardly, Brandy and Keisha chasing them. Maria and Aaron were standing next to each other, waist-deep in the water, watching their friends, laughing. Maria put her head on Aaron's uninjured shoulder; he wrapped his good arm around her.

"See. Beautiful couple, those two." Sarah smiled. "Elisabeth is happy her daughter found such a nice young man to be with."

A smile crossed Martina's face again, the salty tears on her cheeks dried up in the warm breeze. "Sí, Aaron is a very loyal, caring young man. And nice family also."

"Ja, Jack is nice." Sarah nodded. "Intelligent, too. He's a lawyer, ne?"

"Correct. A lawyer. Aaron's mom, Grace, is a teacher."

"Oh, like Elisabeth?"

Martina nodded. "Sí, like Elisabeth. Grace and her would get along very well. And she'd like Aaron's younger sister Emma, too. I've met them only once, but we had a blast."

Sarah raised her eyebrows. "Blast?"

Martina laughed. "Fun, a lot of fun. Having a blast means 'having a lot of fun.'"

"Oh, I see. So not 'boom.'"

Martina shook her head, grinning. "No, no booms today." *Fun, having another second-language learner here. Guess my Maria is right: I should be proud of what I've accomplished. Learning English, coming here, starting a new life for my sisters and myself, running my store.*

"What about the wedding?" Sarah asked.

"Aaron and Maria's wedding?"

"Ja. When? Where?"

Martina shrugged. "I don't know. Not sure yet. Maria said she might want a spring wedding."

"Spring?" Sarah looked confused.

"Spring like the season. When all the flowers come out and bloom. A wedding in April or May," Martina explained.

"Oh, I see. Fun."

Martina and Sarah watched the youngsters again for a while. They were playing tag now, they noticed. Maria had joined the fun, while Aaron just watched. He played referee and helped out whenever it was unclear who got tagged.

Maria was chasing Nick when he suddenly plunged into the water and swam away as best he could in the shallows.

"I clearly got him!" they heard Maria yell.

"No, you didn't," Nick shouted back when he finally stood up again. "I got away."

Aaron shook his head. "No, you didn't, Nick. I saw Maria tag you. You're *it* now."

"Oh man, that's not fair." Nick pouted. "You're only saying that because she's your fiancée."

Aaron laughed. "Either way, you're *it* now, Nick."

"In that case, I'm coming for revenge," Nick yelled, and the water erupted all around as he took off in a half run, half swim toward where the others were standing. The girls all screamed. Martina and Sarah laughed watching them.

"Will they all be at the wedding?" Sarah asked.

Martina nodded. "Sí, Maria wants all of them there. They're best friends."

"Nice. What about the dress?"

Martina now turned to Sarah. "Dress?"

"The wedding dress. Does Maria know what she wants?"

"Ah, wedding dress." Martina smiled. "No, she hasn't had time to think about it. But she played wedding a lot when she was little. Always had this specific design in mind."

"Oh, ja?"

"When she was older, she even drew it for me. She's very good at drawing, our Maria." Martina's face lit up as she talked about it. "And guess what?"

"What?"

"Maria doesn't know, but I already designed her dress. This beautiful halterneck dress with pearls on the top and the bottom. Mermaid style, open back."

Sarah raised her eyebrows. "Mermaid?"

"It's a style of dress. Tight even over the bottom. You know, to show off your figure. Your butt." Martina winked at Sarah.

"Oh, I see. Nice."

Martina nodded. "Sí, she'll look stunning in it. I made it to her specifications, but she'll have to try it on. Might need adjusting."

"You think she'll like the dress you made?"

"Sí, she will. It's her dream dress, I just know it. And she always loved what I made for her when she was little." Martina smiled.

"You know her well, ja?"

"Sí, I do." Martina bit her lip. *Better than Elisabeth.*

"Elisabeth will have to get to know her better," Sarah said, as if she had read Martina's mind. "She's looking forward to it. I would not be surprised if she moved back to the United States now."

"Really?"

"Ja. She now has Brad and her daughter back again. I'm sure she wants to be close to them."

Martina nodded. "That makes sense. And would be good. For Maria. Maybe Elisabeth can move close to her."

"Ja, hopefully." Sarah watched the friends again.

Martina got lost in thought. *It's Elisabeth's turn to take care of Maria. I owe her that. She deserves it. And so does Maria. She deserves to be with her birth mom, her real family. Mija. I love you so.*

An ear-splitting scream cut through the air that made both Martina and Sarah jump up. The little kids nearby stopped playing. Everyone on the beach stared across the water at Maria, who was neck-deep in water, screaming.

Nick plunged into her. "Got you!" Then he took a few steps back in confusion. "Maria? You okay? Stop screaming, please. You're hurting my ears." Then Aaron rushed over and lifted Maria out of the water as best as he could. Those on the beach saw him hug and comfort her.

Sarah raised both her eyebrows. "What's happening? That was a big scream. Scary."

Martina had a knot in her throat, tears forming in her eyes. "She's afraid. She hates water. Flashback. Bad flashback—either to when she was little or to the recent attacks. Poor mija. Oh dear, poor mija."

Martina ran to the edge of the beach and warm water surrounded her feet, but the warmth didn't spread. Instead, a shudder ran down her spine. *It's not over yet. Somehow, it's not over. Maria is not merely disturbed, she's in danger. Can't say why. But I know her well. She's afraid of something. Someone bad still out there. I know it. I just know it.*

CHAPTER 42

I just know it. There's someone next door. Lu tried to peek through the window of her house without making herself visible, peering through the blinds to see whether there was someone in the house next door to her. *Another guest maybe? Who?*

She didn't spot anything and, with a shrug, finally returned to the stove to prepare the rest of dinner. *I'm looking forward to having them over. I really want to get to know Elisabeth's daughter. I think we can all be friends. Bet nobody asks about the rape again, hah.* She shook her head, her black hair flying around her. *No, Elisabeth won't. She's accepted I don't want to talk about it, bought into the story I'm a self-made woman. And that's all she'll ever need to know.*

As she was putting the chicken dish in the oven, she heard an unfamiliar sound. *What was that? A squeak of a door?* She looked around, then closed the oven door. *I must be imagining things. Maybe it was just me working the oven door?*

She slipped off her kitchen mitts and walked into the living room. She peeked toward the front door. *Closed and bolted. All good. I'm on a secure military installation anyway. I'm just being silly.*

She turned around and there he was. Inside her house. Just sitting there on the bottom step of her staircase, grinning. "Hello, Lulu-girl. Good to see you again."

She screamed and stumbled backward, right into the living room couch. She lost her footing, toppled over the armrest of the couch, slid down the armrest, and ended up on her back on the couch.

She saw him stand up and walk over to where she was, grinning, his green eyes shining in delight. "I see, Lulu-girl.... You're inviting me to lie there with you on the couch? How forward of you. What a wonderful greeting after such a long time."

Oh no. No, no, no. Her mind was racing, her breathing fast, her heart thundering. She tried to sit up but her elbows gave out from under her, and she slumped back down, her legs still dangling over the armrest. *No, please... don't hurt me....*

She couldn't form any words. She wanted to scream at him, fight him off, but she was paralyzed. Paralyzed just seeing him there. Right there in her current residence at the Distinguished Visitor's Quarters at Eglin AFB.

He leered over her, a big grin on his face. His perfectly straight white teeth almost blinding her. He still looked strong—older, but strong. His red hair showed streaks of white in it, was much thinner than it used to be, but still didn't give away his age. "I missed you, Lulu-girl. Or should I say... *General* Lulu?" He laughed as he stood at the end of the couch, looking down on her. "Don't you want to at least say hi, Lulu-girl?"

She stared at him. *Stop calling me that*, she wanted to scream, but her throat was tight. Not a word left her mouth.

"I see, you're stunned to see me again, aren't you? Still looking good, huh?" He turned around as if he were a model in a fashion show twirling on a runway. "Don't I look good, Lulu-girl?" All she could do was nod. He laughed again. "Yes, thank you, I know. I know I'm still a good-looking guy. Irresistible, right?"

She nodded again.

"As are you, Lulu-girl. Irresistible, as always. You aged well. And made it high up there. Just like I promised. Told ya you would." He winked at her. "Thanks to me. Sweet little deal, huh?"

Another nod from Lu. She tried to sit up again and made it onto her elbows, but by now he was holding her feet, which were still dangling over the armrest of the couch. And before she knew it, he threw himself onto her.

Her elbows buckled under his heavy weight that threatened to crush her. He started kissing her, planted hot, slimy kisses all over her neck, her cheeks, her mouth. Lu struggled to breathe, tried to push him away, but her arms were pinned to her sides under his weight.

Tears started forming in her eyes, her mind racing. *No, no, no. Please don't. Please stop. Leave me alone. I'm a general now, just like you. I'm a hotshot now, just like you. Strong, just like you.*

At that, her reality shifted. *Yes, I'm strong now. Maybe stronger than you. You won't hurt me anymore. Because General Lu Thomas won't allow it. Daniel won't allow it. Elisabeth won't allow it.*

With all her might, she wiggled her hands out from under her while rocking back and forth on the soft couch. She pushed against the couch's back with both a hand and foot and managed to push him off of her. He fell to the wooden floor with a loud crash.

"Uff," he grunted, surprised, and stared up at her from between the coffee table and the couch.

She jumped off the couch, straightened out her uniform, and growled at him, "You can't get to me anymore, Bullet. You can't. I'm General Lu Thomas now, and you can't push me around anymore."

He stared at her wordlessly as he started getting back on his feet.

"Get away from me! Just leave!" Lu screamed, and took another step back.

He started laughing then, stood up and clapped his hands together as if giving her a round of applause. Irritated, Lu watched him applaud her. "Very good, Lulu-girl. Very good. Feisty. I like it." He stopped clapping. "But you know I'm here for your own good, don't you?"

"What the heck are you talking about?" She crossed her arms in front of her chest. "What are you doing here?"

"Lulu-girl, you damn well know the answer: The same thing you are. Protecting my reputation. In fact, protecting *your* reputation, too." He grinned at her. "You don't want anyone to find out how you got to be a general, do you? You don't want to tell the Air Force that their poster child for women's rights was actually arranged by a man, do you?"

Lu's heart skipped a beat, she turned pale. She shook her head. *No. Nobody can find out. Nobody can find out how weak I am. Not Daniel. Not Elisabeth. Nobody.*

"See, Lulu-girl? We need to make sure they stop digging into the past. Both the police and the Collinses. That's why I'm here."

She tilted her head, her eyebrows scrunched. "But... but... that's why *I'm* here. *You* told me to take care of it."

He laughed now. "Correct. I did. And I'm very pleased you listened to me. In fact, it was your idea to come here. Very good thinking." He gave her a thumbs-up.

"And I told you it's all under control, I told you."

"Oh, I know, Lulu-girl. But you know me. Always having to check on things myself. Make sure everything's okay. You know that about me, Lulu-girl."

Lu nodded. "I do. But the situation *is* under control." She uncrossed her arms and stood taller now. "And now I need you to leave. Go! I've got this. You gotta trust me. Remember? Just like you told *me* to trust *you*."

He laughed again. "You surprise me, Lulu. But I *can't* trust you. Not unless you tell me exactly how you handled it."

Lu eyed him. *Is he serious? If I tell him what I did, how I made sure nobody will dig deeper, he'll just leave?*

"Here's a deal, Lulu-girl: if you tell me exactly how you handled it, and I agree the situation is under control, I'll leave you alone." He lifted his hand and held up his pinky. "Pinky swear."

Lu wasn't sure what to think. *I guess it's proper to inform him about Elisabeth? Because he did keep his promise to leave me alone all these years*

275

while helping me climb the ranks, so long as I didn't tell anyone about what happened between us. So, he'll keep his promise again, right?

And then Lu decided to tell him. She told him everything about the meeting with Elisabeth and Martina. Told him she was sure Elisabeth wouldn't talk about it anymore.

Bullet raised his eyebrows. "Are you positive all Elisabeth wanted was to apologize to you? She wanted to be forgiven, not help you hunt me down?"

Lu nodded. "Yes. She wants to be friends again. And I would like that. And I certainly don't want her knowing how I got to where I am now. I need her to see me as the strong woman everyone else sees."

"You promise to be good, Lulu-girl?"

Her face red and hot, she nodded. "I promise. I promise, so long as you leave me alone. Don't you ever do what you tried to do earlier again."

He frowned. "But you're beautiful, Lulu-girl. A beautiful woman, just gorgeous. Hot. It'll be hard to keep away from you." He sighed, then put his hand on his heart. "But I promise I will behave myself. I don't want to create any more evidence. It was a close call last time. Glad you got rid of it."

All color left Lu's face. *"Evidence?" "It?" That's what he calls our child? Our child that wasn't allowed to live.* She swallowed hard, holding back tears. *Because he decided a child would be evidence of all his evil. Yet getting rid of our child just made him more cruel.* She closed her eyes, trying to shake off the memory of the dirty needle in his hands that destroyed "the evidence" and made sure she could never conceive again.

A sob escaped her throat.

"Lulu-girl, don't be sad. It was for the best. Look where you are now. Wouldn't have been able to get here without sacrifice, right? A child is binding, holds thousands of women back from opportunity. Come on, Lulu. Do we have a deal? I restrain myself, and you make sure they don't dig deeper."

"Deal," she whispered.

A wonderful smell was wafting in from the kitchen. He sniffed the air. "Are you cooking? I smell garlic, onion, and… chicken?" Lu nodded, still numb from the awful memories. "Who are you cooking for? I saw you carrying in tons of groceries earlier. Can't all be for you?"

She looked up at him. *Knew I was being watched earlier by someone. Now I know who. It was him. Bullet.*

"Lulu-girl. I'll ask you again: who are you cooking for?" His stern face told her he was getting angry.

"Friends," she whispered.

"Friends? Who did you make friends with in a day? You only just got in yesterday, saw Elisabeth and that other lady earlier today." A big grin wiped the sternness off his face, he let out a laugh. "No way. You're cooking for them, aren't you?"

Lu stared at him, unsure what to do or say.

He came closer to her, stood face to face with her. "Lulu-girl, this deal only works if you're honest with me. Did you invite Elisabeth and the other lady here? For dinner?"

Lu couldn't say anything. She didn't want him to know.

"I'll ask politely one last time: did you invite them to dinner here?" His face turned red, his hands started shaking in a rage. "Lulu, I *do not like* being lied to. Talk to me. Now!"

She just stared at him, as he grew angrier by the second. Suddenly, he wrapped his hands around her neck and squeezed, squeezed so tight she struggled to breathe. Her eyes started watering, almost bulging out.

"Tell me! Now!" he roared while squeezing and squeezing her elegant neck.

A slight nod was all she could manage. He let go. She stumbled backward, wheezing while holding her neck, tears streaming down her face. The smell of chicken cooking in the oven almost made her vomit.

"So, what do you have to say for yourself, Lulu-girl?"

"Elisabeth and… the other lady… Martina…" she whispered, struggling to get air inside her burning lungs. "They are… coming."

He grinned. "I see. Anyone else?"

She didn't say anything further, just rubbed her neck.

"*Lulu*, anyone else?"

She nodded. "Yeah. Elisabeth's daughter. And the daughter's fiancé."

His grin took on a wicked quality. "What a nice dinner party you've put together. And such nice food. Smells delicious. Dinner sounds grand. Just wonderful, Lulu-girl. Make sure to set a plate for me. What time will I see you all?"

Lu's eyes grew wide. She didn't say anything.

"Lulu-girl. You wouldn't leave an old friend and supporter like me out to dry, would you?" He looked at her, but Lu just stood there. "Would you?" She shook her head. "Good, I'm looking forward to it. What time should I come over?"

"At six. Six o'clock," she whispered.

"Grand. Wonderful. I'll see you then." With a chuckle, he turned around, walked down the hallway, and exited the house.

Click.

Once Lu heard the door shut, she found she could breathe freely again. She quickly went to the window and watched him walk over to the house next door. She closed her eyes. *I narrowly escaped another attack. Another attack by Bullet.* She started shaking, her whole body shaking. *I can't believe he's here. I shouldn't have told him I was at Eglin. But I had no choice. Thought he'd let me take care of everything. But I was wrong.*

Her nostrils caught the smell from the kitchen. *The chicken. I need to check on it.* She opened her eyes, let out a deep breath, and walked over to the oven to tend to dinner.

Food for six now. Six people at six o'clock. Six and six. Sixty-six. Add one more six and you get the number of the beast. She laughed nervously to herself, her hands still shaking as she turned down the oven heat. *Bullet will be here. But why? What could he possibly want?*

CHAPTER 43

"What could he possibly want?" the chief asked Sally as she handed over the phone to him. "We're quite busy at the moment."

Sally shrugged. "I'm not sure, Chief. But Brad Collins was very insistent about wanting to talk with you."

The chief sighed. *We're in the middle of something important here. We're close. He better have some crucial info we can throw on the pile.* He took the phone from Sally. "Hello, General Collins, this is Chief Parlot." He listened for a while, only nodded or interjected a few little "ahas" and "okays." "Thanks for letting us know, General," he finally said, "and don't worry, we'll send Lieutenant Martinez to keep an eye on them. He'll idle outside the home while they're having dinner."

The whole team looked at the chief now, impatient for him to get off the phone so they could get back to work.

"Okay, General Collins. Get some rest, feel better, and don't worry about your family. We have everything under control. Remember, we've already established General Thomas is not a threat." The chief listened again. "Yes, sir, we will. Thanks again for letting us know." A pause. "Yes, thank you. Goodbye, General." He hung up.

He looked up and found everyone staring at him and had to grin. "Interested in hearing what Brad Collins had to say?" They all nodded.

"He told me Elisabeth, Martina, Maria, and Aaron are having dinner over at General Lu Thomas's house tonight."

Tonya scratched her chin. "Interesting. Dinner with an old friend from the H.O.P.E. Club. I guess they're just catching up?"

The chief nodded. "Yes, Brad Collins said his wife and Martina had a great time with General Lu Thomas this morning. Reestablished their friendship."

"Guess that's good, right?" Sally looked at everyone. "General Lu Thomas doesn't seem to be a threat, now does she?"

"I don't think so," Chief Parlot said. "But according to Brad, she was in the H.O.P.E. Club because she had been abused. She confided in Elisabeth right before the Collinses had to move. Apparently, Elisabeth wanted to help her, but then lost contact with her because, you know, she lost her only child and moved back to Germany to grieve. Brad said she felt bad about never contacting Lu again, never knew what happened to Lu. She had a guilty conscience. But when they met this morning, Lu told Elisabeth she understood and assured her she turned out fine, is doing well."

Tom let out a grunt. "Well? *Very* well, I'd say. Being a general in the Air Force and having an amazing career is much more than just *doing well.*"

They all nodded.

"Anyway, I assured Collins their escort will be there this evening. Would have been regardless. But it shouldn't be an issue. Lu Thomas isn't Elisabeth's enemy, she's a friend."

"Indeed," Tonya said. "Let's refocus on General Jones. Anyone have any updates to share? Now that we've been interrupted, might as well brief each other quickly."

Sally yawned, then nodded. "I didn't find much more, unfortunately. Just that the car accident his son died in was caused by underaged drinking. His son drove his sports car right into a tree. Sped around a curve, lost control, and boom. He died at the scene. Sad."

The chief bit his lip. *Very sad. But hardly an excuse to hurt others.* "Thanks, Sally." Chief Parlot turned to Tom. "Got anything for us?"

"Hold on." Tom turned back to his computer and his fingers flew across the keyboard. With one loud click, a website appeared on-screen. "Aha, yup, I knew it. Got him!" He leaned back in his swivel chair and spun himself around to look at his colleagues.

Tonya's face lit up. "Alright, alright, alright, Tom, what did you find? C'mon, don't leave us in suspense here."

"Remember how I found out that General Robert Jones uses the shortened version of his first name a lot—even on credit cards?"

The chief nodded. "I remember. He goes by Bob. However, that's not very unusual if your given name is Robert."

"True, true," Tom said. "But Bob has the same first letter as Bullet. *B.*"

Sally raised her eyebrows. "So? What does that have to do with anything?"

"General Jones is a fighter pilot—"

"Yes, Tom, we know that," Tonya interrupted.

Tom laughed. "Patience, patience, team. Anyway, we didn't look at call signs."

"Call signs?" The chief scratched his chin now.

"Yes, all fighter pilots have a call sign. They earn it due to something extraordinary they did or because of something silly. Our guy here, General Jones, was an amazing fighter pilot back in the Gulf War."

"Operation Desert Storm?" Tonya clarified.

"Correct." Tom nodded. "He became famous for scoring tons of kills on Scud mobile missile launchers in the western Iraqi desert. Big deal back then. That's how he earned his call sign."

"Destroyer?" Sally guessed.

"Nope. He scored hits. Bull's-eye hits. As precise as a bullet." Tom grinned. The others stared at him. "His name is General Bob 'The Bullet' Jones."

Chief Parlot's eyes widened. "I'll be damned. Bob 'The Bullet' Jones? Of course, a fighter pilot's call sign! Shoot. Why didn't we think of that earlier?"

Sally shrugged and yawned again. "Sleep deprivation?"

"Because we usually don't work with the Air Force, my man Isaac. It's a very typical Air Force thing, those nicknames—well, call signs." Tonya patted the chief on the back. "But now we know. Now we got him. Great job, Tom." She walked over to give Tom a high five.

"Yes, great job, Tom." Chief Parlot high-fived him also. "Wouldn't know what to do without you. So General Jones is Bullet. Pretty straightforward evidence here. But still, a few questions remain: What does he have to do with the Collinses? Why did he organize the kidnapping of their only daughter? What's his motive?"

"Indeed, that's the million-dollar question, Isaac my man." Tonya sighed. "There's got to be something. They didn't know each other personally. It must have something to do with Jones's career. Typical motive—perp's career gets threatened, they respond by lashing out, try to defend it with all their might."

The chief nodded. "Very true, but we can't be guessing here, not after our recent failures. We need to be diligent, by the book. Let's bring him in for questioning."

Tom laughed. "If *you* want to fly all the way to Texas to take him in, be my guest, Chief."

Sally yawned again. "Oh man, I'm so tired. We've barely slept. Yet made such good progress. Can we get some sleep for once and come back rested? If this guy is all the way in Texas, he's of no threat to anyone here."

"Sally has a point," Tonya said.

The chief started pacing back and forth. "Team, let's not forget we thought the same of Clifford, that he was nowhere near here, but then he ended up right on our doorstep. We can't make that same mistake again, lulling ourselves into a sense of complacency."

They all nodded. "What are you suggesting, Chief?" Tom said.

"I agree that we need to establish motive before questioning him—but the most important thing is to pinpoint exactly where General Jones is at this very moment." Chief Parlot stopped pacing and looked every one of them in the eye.

"Okay, back to work, gang, chop-chop." Tonya turned to Sally now. "And, Sally, try some real coffee for once. It'll help you stay awake. Those energy drinks fade too quickly."

Sally yawned. "But I *hate* coffee...."

"Come on, get to work, please," Chief Parlot said. "Tom, find out where he's at. Check credit cards, cell phone location, and so on. Work your magic."

"Yes, sir." Tom saluted, then turned to his computer.

"Sally, help Tonya and me figure out what his motive is. I know we've dug deep already, but clearly we've missed things. Gotta link him to the Collinses."

Sally nodded. She walked over to the coffee machine, eyed it suspiciously, then poured herself a cup and tried a sip. She shivered a little. "Throw some milk or creamer in, girl," Tonya called out. "Takes away the bitterness. And then get going, Sally. Come on, move it. Let's go."

CHAPTER 44

"Let's go," Elisabeth said once their car was parked in front of Lu's place. "She's waiting for us. We're already fifteen minutes late."

"That's Maria's fault," Aaron said. "Took her forever to get ready."

Maria gave him the evil eye as she pulled her key from the ignition. "I just wanted to look good meeting my mom's friend."

Aaron gave her a kiss on the cheek. "You *always* look good, my love."

They all piled out of the car. Martina waved to Lieutenant Martinez, who had pulled up and parked behind them.

Maria shut the driver's door and locked the car. She straightened out her summer dress and exhaled deeply. *I'm super nervous for some reason.* She walked around the car to Aaron and took his hand.

"Ready, Maria?" He squeezed her hand, noting it was somewhat clammy.

She nodded. "Yeah. Sure."

He winked at her. "Good, because your mom already rang the doorbell."

The door opened and a lady in uniform appeared at the front door, her long hair pulled back into a low bun. She wore a smile on her face. "Hi there. Come on in, everyone, thanks for coming."

Maria watched Elisabeth give Lu a big hug, then Martina embraced her as well. They both stepped past her inside.

Aaron was standing in front of her now. "Hello, ma'am, nice to see you again."

Lu smiled at him. "Hi there. Aaron, right?"

He nodded. "Yes, that's me, ma'am. Maria's fiancé and Elisabeth's soon-to-be son-in-law."

Lu laughed, her dark-brown eyes twinkling. "Yes, I've heard. So nice to see you again—this time, hopefully, for longer than a few minutes. And please remember, Lieutenant, you can call me Lu. We're not at a work dinner here, now are we?"

Aaron blushed and shook his head. "No, ma'am."

Lu laughed again. "And please, don't call me 'ma'am' either. Just Lu. Okay?"

"I'll try."

"Good, good. I know it's trained into you to adhere to courtesy, especially since I'm in uniform, but I really do want us to keep this dinner casual. I promise if I had brought civilian clothes, I would be wearing them right now. Please, come in." She winked at Aaron as he stepped inside.

Maria was facing her now. "Hello again."

Lu's face lit up. "Maria. Such a pleasure to see you again and have you over tonight. Oh my, you're the splitting image of your mother. I notice it now even more than I did earlier today. You're like a young Elisabeth—just different eyes, maybe a slightly different mouth."

Maria nodded. "Yeah, I get those from my dad."

"I bet you do." Lu shook her hand. Maria was surprised to find Lu's hand was as cold and clammy as her own. "Come on in, please." Maria turned around and waved at Lieutenant Martinez in his police car, then walked inside. Lu shut the door behind her.

Maria was greeted by a delicious smell of garlic-roasted chicken and steamed vegetables. She walked through the hallway to the living room and stopped abruptly when she found an older man sitting on the couch.

Who the heck is that? She eyed him. He was partially bald, with thin, greyish-red hair, but she could tell it used to be thick and red in his prime. His eyes were small, very green. He had a strong build, especially for a guy his age. *Guess he's in his late sixties, maybe early seventies. Who the heck is he?* He waved at her, the big smile on his face showing off his pearly white teeth. *Those must be fake.* She waved back.

"Everybody," Lu said, "I'd like you to meet Robert. Former General—"

"We've already met," he interrupted.

Maria blinked at him. *How rude.*

"I've met Elisabeth, Martina, and Aaron already. Just not this young lady here." He rose from the couch and walked over to shake Maria's hand. "You must be Maria. The missing daughter who's just been found."

Maria nodded and almost winced under his strong handshake. *He's squeezing way too hard. What the heck?* She ripped her hand out of his. "That's me. Who are you?"

He laughed. "I'm Robert, but you can call me Bob, young lady. I'm a friend and supporter of our hotshot general here." He winked at Lu.

Lu smiled back.

A fake smile, Maria thought as she watched them. *What's going on?* She turned to the unexpected dinner guest again. "So, Bob… why are you here?"

Lu laughed out loud. *A nervous laugh?* Maria was confused.

"Wow, young lady, you're not afraid to speak your mind, are you? I'm sorry to crash the dinner party here, but Lu and I go way back, and she was kind enough to invite me over once she realized I was here at Eglin. Right next door to her, as luck would have it."

Lu's smile stretched wider.

Maria eyed her. *Fake, fake, fake! Even more fake now. What's going on? She doesn't want him here, does she?*

"I see," she finally said, and smiled at Bob. "Are you on business here as well?"

Bob laughed out loud. "What an inquisitive young lady. Impressive. Well, no, I'm here for fun. A little vacation on the beautiful emerald coast."

"Ah. And it's just you? No family?"

"No family. Just me."

"Why?"

"Maria, mija! ¡Basta!" Martina interrupted Maria's interrogation. "Be polite. Come and sit here with us." She waved at the spot next to her on the couch where she and Elisabeth were sitting. Aaron was in the armchair across from them.

Maria nodded and came over to squeeze between her two moms. Lu and Bob followed. He took his place in the other armchair he'd been in when they arrived. Lu kept standing. "What would you all like to drink? I have soda, water, beer, wine...."

"We need something to toast with," Elisabeth said. "How about a glass of wine for all?"

"Sí." Martina nodded.

"Just a little bit for me. I'm still on pain medication for my shoulder, but I can have a tiny bit to toast with. And I'd love a Coke, if you have one, ma'am." Aaron blushed. "Lu, I mean."

She laughed. "Sounds good, Aaron. Yes, I have regular Coke. Is red wine good for everyone?"

Elisabeth and Martina nodded.

"Yes, red wine sounds fantastic." Bob smiled, his eyes sparkling. "It finally doesn't clash with my hair anymore now that I'm slowly balding." He burst out into a deep laughter at his own joke. Everyone but Maria joined in.

She stared at him. *He's not funny at all. Trying too hard. Something's going on here.*

"Red wine okay for you, Maria?" Lu asked.

"No, I'll just have water, please." Maria didn't even turn around to answer Lu, just kept staring at Bob as she spoke. *What is it about him?*

"Oh, okay." Lu left for the kitchen.

Maria almost jumped at her mamá's touch. Martina squeezed Maria's clammy hand that was lying in her lap. "¿Mija, qué pasa? No wine to toast? Not even a little, like Aaron?"

"No."

Elisabeth now took her other hand. "Mein Engel, what's going on? Are you okay? You're acting a bit strange. I thought you were excited to meet my friend Lu, but now I feel like you don't even want to be here."

Maria finally took her eyes off Bob. "I am happy to be here."

Martina raised her eyebrows. "Huh, I agree with Elisabeth. You seem almost... hostile? Very strange, mija."

"No, I'm just..." Maria searched for the right words. In a whisper, she said, "Irritated about having an unexpected guest."

"So are we," Elisabeth whispered back. "But it is what it is, and we should all enjoy our time with Lu while we can. She's super nice."

"Sí," Martina agreed.

Maria sighed. *I don't want to disappoint either one of my moms.* "Lu?" she called over. Lu stepped back into the living room, eyebrows raised. "I'll have a bit of wine to toast also. Not too much. I'm our designated driver, and usually don't drink much as it is."

"Okay," Lu said. "Very responsible, Maria. I'll pour you the tiniest sip. How does that sound?"

"Fantastic." Maria felt both her moms squeeze her hands, then they let go. She noticed Aaron and Bob had started up a conversation and turned her attention to them.

"Yes, Aaron, I was a fighter pilot back in my day. Been a while, you know."

"What did you fly?"

"F-15Es. Back in the nineties," Bob explained.

Aaron's eyes lit up. "The Strike Eagle? Wow, nice plane."

Bob laughed. "For sure. Very nice plane. But not as nice as the fighter jets nowadays. All that technology, packed into such a small space—phew, impressive."

Aaron nodded. "Yeah, sure is. I'll be working with the F-35s soon."

Bob whistled through his teeth. "The Lightning. Very nice. Are you in pilot training then?"

Aaron shook his head. "No, maintenance."

"Ah, I see. Well, maintenance is a very important job. Us pilots couldn't even fly without our maintenance crews." Bob winked at him.

Lu returned with a tray of drinks. She set the tray on the coffee table and handed out drinks to the ladies first, then Aaron, lastly Bob. *Her hand is shaking*, Maria noticed as Lu handed him his glass of wine. *Why? Is she… afraid of him?*

Lu took the last glass of wine off the tray and lifted it in the air. "Cheers! To old friends reunited, to new ones made, and to a wonderful evening together."

"Prost." Elisabeth raised her glass.

"Salud," Martina said before taking a sip.

"Cheers." Both Aaron and Bob raised their glasses and downed their wine.

Maria was the last to try hers. She swallowed and shook a little. *Bitter, very bitter.* She watched as Bob took big gulps.

"Good, strong wine," Martina said. "Merlot?"

Lu nodded. "Yes. My favorite."

"Mine, too." Elisabeth smiled, and clanged glasses with Lu. "You should sit, Lu. Let's get you a chair from the kitchen table."

"Okay."

The two ladies set their wine glasses on the coffee table, left for the kitchen, and returned with a chair for Lu. Aaron and Bob resumed their conversation about fighter jets, while Lu and Elisabeth talked about the men in their lives. Martina listened and kept sipping her wine. Maria took the last sip of hers, then switched to the water Lu had brought for her.

She took a big gulp of water. Felt the coldness run down her esophagus, all the way to her belly. She realized then she was feeling hot, almost sweating, as though the heater had been turned on inside the house despite the warm weather. Her clammy hands left big sweat prints on the cold glass of water. The conversations around her started to blur, her breathing came faster. *Gosh, I've no idea what's going on. I guess I feel… afraid? Anxious? Panicked? Why?*

She put her glass of water on the tray again, then leaned back against the couch and closed her eyes. A touch on her shoulder made her open them again. Martina was gently rubbing it. "¿Mija, estás bien?"

Maria nodded. "Sí. I'm okay, Mamá." She managed a weak smile.

"Sure? You look pale," Martina whispered. "That time of the month?"

"What? No, I don't think so…." Maria shook her head, but then thought about it. *Maybe I should excuse myself. So I can get a grip on these weird feelings.* "Guess I should check," she whispered to her mamá, "just to be safe." She turned to Lu. "Where's the bathroom?"

"Right around the corner there." Lu pointed down the hallway.

"Thanks." Maria got up and walked down the hallway to the bathroom. She closed the door behind her and turned on the faucet. She splashed a little water onto her flushed face and stared into the mirror. Her unique hazel eyes were bright green. *What's going on?*

A knock on the door. "Maria? Are you alright?" came a dark male voice full of concern.

A smile lit up her face. *Aaron, my Aaron. He's so sweet. And knows me well.* "Yeah, I'm okay." She took one last look in the mirror, then opened the door. "Hi there."

"Hi, my love," he said, and took her cold hand. "Your hands are very wet. Couldn't find a towel?"

Maria laughed. "It's hanging right there. I just didn't use it."

Aaron raised his now-damp hands. "So I see. Why not? Hey, what's going on? You're acting kinda strange. You seem… agitated?"

Maria sighed. "I don't know, Aaron. I didn't expect there to be another stranger here. Thought it would be just Lu and us."

"C'mon now, if he's Lu's old friend and happens to be here, why not…."

"See, that's the thing. I think Lu doesn't want him here either."

"What? Why would she invite someone she doesn't want to have over?"

"I don't know, Aaron. I just have a feeling…."

He frowned. "Maria, c'mon. That's crazy. Lu is a general in the Air Force. She can decide for herself who she wants or doesn't want inside her home. She's a grown woman who makes her own decisions. She invited him, no need to second-guess her decision."

Maria shrugged. "I guess."

"Besides, he's an interesting guy. Was quite the fighter pilot back in his day. Flew F-15s in Operation Desert Storm. Has some very cool stories to tell." Aaron's gaze grew dreamy just thinking about them, then took Maria by the hand and led her back to the group.

"Ah, good, just in time," Lu said upon Aaron and Maria's return. "We're ready for the first course. Find a seat at the dinner table, everyone."

"First course?" Elisabeth raised her eyebrows. "How many courses are there, Lu?"

"No worries, just three," she said with a wink. "Appetizer, main course, then dessert. Nothing too fancy."

"Excelente." Martina got up and followed Lu into the dining area. Her eyes lit up, and she turned around to catch Maria's attention. "Tamales! Maria, mija, Lu made tamales."

"Sí." Lu smiled. "I figured you'd like that."

"But you must have cooked all afternoon?" Elisabeth asked. "Don't tamales take a lot of time?"

Martina nodded. "Sí, it does. Lu, looks great, just wonderful."

"Thank you. Hope everyone enjoys them."

Bob came over and grabbed the chair at the head of the table, opposite Lu at the other end. "I've never tried them before. Very ethnic."

Maria stared at him. *"Ethnic?" Is he serious? What a rude thing to say.* Martina and Elisabeth held their tongues and sat down opposite Maria and Aaron. Somehow, Maria and Martina ended up closest to Bob.

Maria had to hold back the urge to roll her eyes. *Oh great. Right next to the rude guy, the strange guy.* Still, she sat down, and Aaron pushed in her chair for her.

Lu served everyone tamales and the table erupted in chitter-chatter as they all started eating. Only Maria was quiet, kept eyeing the unknown man sitting near her. *I have to find out more.*

She turned to him. "Bob, Aaron told me you were in Iraq during the nineties?"

He blew on his food and steam billowed into the air. "That I was. Flew in Operation Desert Storm."

"I see. What exactly was your mission?"

He laughed. "Well, I can't tell you about *my mission*, young lady, but let me assure you, I did well. Received a bunch of medals."

"Good for you, sir. Good for you," Maria mumbled. "What for?"

He winked at her. "Well, let's just say, I had a special affinity for taking out Iraqi missile launchers. Important to the mission."

Maria nodded. *Missile launchers. Iraq? Desert Storm?*

"In fact, I got kinda famous for that." He grinned at her, then took a bite of tamale.

Maria stared at him. *Famous? A famous fighter pilot? From Operation Desert Storm? Flying F-15s?*

"How are the tamales?" she heard Lu ask.

Martina clapped her hands together. "Fantástico."

"Agreed. They're delicious," Elisabeth said.

"Absolutely." Aaron smiled, then turned to Maria. "Right, my love? Very similar to your mamá's."

But Maria didn't react. She was deep in thought. *Oh my gosh, is he...*

Aaron elbowed her. "*Right*, Maria?" She looked up at him, her face pale. "Aren't the tamales excellent, Maria?"

She realized everyone was staring at her. "Oh, I haven't tried mine yet. Sorry." She smiled, then stabbed a piece with her fork and pushed it into her mouth. Chewed mechanically, not really tasting. "Mmmmm.... Yes, very good. Thank you, Lu."

Lu smiled, and the dinner table conversation resumed.

Maria side-eyed Bob. *I gotta find out. I just need to know his full name.* "So, Bob... what's your last name? You're General who, exactly?"

Aaron looked at her, one eyebrow raised. Maria knew he didn't approve. She knew her question was rude. *But I need to know.* She took another bite of her tamale and tried to project an air of casualness.

Bob laughed. "Not sure why it's of importance to you, young lady, but I'm General Jones. General Bob Jones."

The bite of tamale got stuck in Maria's throat. *Jones? Oh my gosh, General Bob Jones?* She started coughing loudly, her now-green eyes wide. *Bob "The Bullet" Jones? Famous fighter pilot in Operation Desert Storm. Bullet! The Bullet who'll get me?* She almost choked on her tamale, coughed and coughed, finally spat it out onto her plate.

Everyone stared at her in wide-eyed concern. "Sorry," she mumbled, "kinda choked there. Excuse me a second." She rose and quickly left the table, retreated to the bathroom.

She locked the door behind her and stared into the mirror. *General Bob "The Bullet" Jones is here? Dining with us? Why the heck is he here? He's the mastermind behind my kidnapping. Nobody else has realized who he is?*

Then, it dawned on her. *I told Aaron I thought Bullet was a fighter pilot's call sign, but never told him any more about what I found out. It was too painful to think about at the time, so I didn't tell him. Or Mom. Or Mamá. Or Dad. Or the police. I didn't tell anyone I figured out*

General Jones is Bullet. Mike Clifford's mentor. Nobody here knows who he is. Oh no, what should I do?

She splashed cold water in her face again. The coldness cooled her thoughts. She looked in the mirror again and this time saw a determined look on her face. *I'll find out why he's here. Why he masterminded my kidnapping. I'll find out the truth. Yes I can, and I will.*

She stood tall and stared at herself in the mirror. *He doesn't know I'm onto him. Nobody does. But just you wait, Bullet. 'Cuz this time, I'm coming for you. Right here, right now.*

CHAPTER 45

"**R**ight now! We need to figure out where he is this very instant." The chief slammed his fist on the table. "Why don't we know where General Jones is at? I don't understand what the holdup is. We're the police, for goodness' sake! Tracking him down should be easy."

"I'm sorry, Chief," Tom whispered, "but his phone is off. Last signal came out of Texas, then nothing. It's been off ever since this morning."

Tonya raised her eyebrows. "Very strange. Who these days has their cell phone off for that long? It's nighttime now."

Sally hopped one leg to the other. "Maybe he's on a plane or something like that?"

"On a plane?" The chief turned pale. *Like when Clifford jumped on a plane to come here and attack Maria. "Bullet will get you." Oh my.*

A touch on his shoulder made him jump. "Goodness, my man Isaac, what's going on?" Tonya took her hand off his shoulder. "What are you thinking?"

"We need to find him. What if he's here, after Maria? Mike Clifford said Bullet will get her. What if Bullet makes good on that promise? We gotta make sure he didn't already leave Texas," Chief Parlot mumbled.

Sally was still hopping about, unable to stay still. Tonya eyed her. "Well, well, Sally, seems you're full of energy now."

Sally grinned. "Yeah... who knew coffee and energy drinks make for an awesome combination? I'm not tired at all anymore."

Tonya and Chief Parlot looked at each other, and despite his anxiety he had to grin. "Sally, why don't you use your caffeine high to research flights out of Texas to VPS? See what you can find. See if there are any Jones on the passenger list."

Sally saluted. "Yes, Chief."

"And then make sure you don't drink any more caffeine. Too much is dangerous, girl," Tonya told her.

Sally saluted her. "Yes, Agent Anderson." She then hopped over to her chair and started researching flights on her computer.

Tonya elbowed the chief. "Hey, if you really want to find out if he's still in Texas, call our colleagues there to check on him. See if he's there. Maybe his phone died. Or he's out for the day and forgot his charger. You might be panicking for nothing."

Chief Parlot nodded. "Great idea, Tonya. I'll call right away to see if they can locate him. Guess they can let him know as well we've got questions for him."

"Sounds great, Isaac." Tonya smiled at him. "In the meantime, Tom can keep searching for Jones's phone. If it's working, he'll turn it back on eventually."

The chief's face lit up. "Maybe then Tom'll uncover some implicating text messages? Something that will shed light on his motive for kidnapping Maria?"

Tonya nodded. "I like the way you think." She called over to Tom, "Hey, Tom, keep researching Jones's cell phone. He can't keep it off forever. If you find it, see if he's been texting with anyone interesting lately. Or ever."

Tom turned around in his swivel chair, a grin on his face. "So... I have permission to hack General Jones's phone?"

Tonya and Chief Parlot looked at each other, grinned, then nodded.

"Awesome." Tom spun back around and his hands flew across the keyboard.

The chief pulled out his work cell phone and started texting. Tonya looked over his shoulder. "What are you up to? Thought you're calling your contacts in Texas?"

"I will, but first I gotta text Martinez. Need to know if Maria and the others are okay."

Tonya gave him another pat on the shoulder. "Alright, my man Isaac. You do that. I'll look up the number to the closest police station where Jones lives." She sat down at the worktable and got busy while Chief Parlot kept texting.

His phone blinked with a response from Lieutenant Martinez. *Yes, they just sat down for dinner. Everything looks good and calm. I can sorta see them through the dining room window.*

The chief exhaled. *That's good, that's real good. I need him to keep an eye on them. Especially Maria.*

Don't let them out of your sight, Lieutenant Martinez, the chief texted back. *And let me know if you see or hear anything unusual.*

Martinez's response came quick. *Yes, sir, will do.*

Chief Parlot put his work phone in his pocket and joined Tonya at the table. She had already dialed the number to the police station closest to General Jones's residence in Texas and was making her way through the automated menu. She got an officer on the line. The chief listened for a while as she made introductions and gave them instructions.

He sat down in his chair, and leaned back, deep in thought. *Hope they'll find Jones at his house. Back in Texas.* He sighed. *And we better find a motive. Why the heck would a fighter pilot like him want to kidnap a captain's child? What does he have to do with the Collinses?*

Tonya hung up the phone. "They're on it. Going over to Jones's house right now."

"Wonderful," the chief said. "Thanks, Tonya."

She grinned. "You're welcome. And don't worry. We'll find him. But more importantly, we'll keep Maria safe this time."

Chief Parlot snorted. *Yeah, this time. Can't make any mistakes this time. We need to keep her safe and away from Jones. That's our priority.*

CHAPTER 46

"That's our priority," Elisabeth said. "Maria's happiness and safety. All that counts right now, Bob. Hope that answers your question."

Bob nodded. "Yes, after all the madness she's been through, makes sense to focus on the young lady's well-being."

Maria side-eyed him and didn't say anything. Martina noticed her daughter's abnormal behavior. *What's going on with mija? She's been quiet and in a bad mood ever since she came back from the bathroom.*

"Absolutely, Maria's happiness is our top priority right now," Aaron agreed, and wiped his mouth with a napkin. "Hey, Lu, my compliments to the chef. The tamales were excellent."

"Yes indeed, Lu, excellently cooked *ethnic* food." Bob smiled right at her.

Martina saw Maria roll her eyes, then noticed Lu was avoiding all eye contact with the other general. Martina tilted her head and focused her attention on Lu instead of her daughter. *Lu seems intimidated. Why? She's a strong woman, a hotshot general herself. She seemed completely confident this morning. Why the change?*

Lu got up to clear the plates. She started at the opposite side of the table, with Bob's plate. Martina noticed her hand shake when she grabbed the plate in front of him. "Thanks, Lu," Bob said, and gently touched her arm in thanks—but Lu jumped to the side, almost losing her grip on the plate.

Martina saw the exchange. *Very strange. She seems afraid. Afraid of him?*

Lu walked around the table and gathered up Maria's plate, then Aaron's, then her own. She now came over to Elisabeth and Martina's side.

Martina jumped up. "Let me help you, Lu." She had already grabbed Elisabeth's and her own plate before Lu could even react. "I'll help you carry these to the kitchen."

"Oh, okay, thank you, Martina." Lu smiled and turned around, then walked into the open kitchen.

Martina followed and put the two plates she was carrying next to the sink beside the others. "Anything else I can help with?"

Lu shook her head. "You're my guest, Martina. You shouldn't be helping at all."

"But I'd love to. Please, let me help."

Lu glanced over at the table, closed her eyes a second, then exhaled deeply. "Okay, Martina. Gracias. We need fresh plates for the main course. They're in the cabinet to your right." She pointed.

Martina walked over and opened the cabinet. The dinner plates were up on the top shelf. She tried standing on her tippy-toes but couldn't reach them. "Ack, I'm too short."

Lu laughed. "Oh, here, let me try." She walked over, stood on her own tippy-toes, but couldn't reach them either. She laughed again. "Oh no, the small plates were a shelf lower and I had no issues with them—I didn't foresee we'd encounter such a predicament." She winked at Martina.

Martina laughed. "Guess us Latinas are not the tallest, no?"

Lu grinned and shook her head. "Definitely not. Too bad my Daniel isn't here. He always handles the top shelves for me."

Martina winked back at her. "Sí, gotta need those men sometimes, no? Well, let's call the men over. Bob is tall. Let's ask him."

Quickly, Lu shook her head. "No, we don't need him, I can do it." She tried to reach the plates again, but no matter how tall she made herself, she wasn't able to reach them. She sighed.

"Why not ask your dinner guest? He's a tall guy."

Lu stared at Martina, her dark-brown eyes sparkling in anger. "No! ¡Basta!" Then she started looking around. "I bet there's a stepstool around here somewhere."

Martina watched as Lu began to frantically search the kitchen for something to step on in order to reach the top shelf. *She's avoiding all contact with her dinner guest, Bob. An old friend? Doubt it. She's afraid of him. Uncomfortable when he's close, jumpy when he touches her, even gently. She reminds me of how I used to act around Jonathan. I have to find out more.*

"Lu, Aaron is tall, maybe—"

"Perfect idea, Martina," Lu interrupted her.

She was about to call Aaron over when Martina finished her thought. "Except his shoulder is injured and he probably can't lift the plates even if he can reach them."

Lu sighed. "Oh dear."

"Bob is probably the best choice for this…."

"No, *definitely* not," Lu said in a raised voice at Martina, her eyebrows scrunched in.

Martina raised her eyebrows. *This is not normal. Not normal behavior. What's going on? If she's afraid of him, why did she invite him? I need to find out. Talk to her in private and find out.*

Lu resumed her search. "There must be something…."

Martina had an idea then. "Maybe there's a stepstool in the bathroom? You know, for little ones to use."

Lu looked up. "Sí, maybe?"

Martina took her by the hand and they rushed past the dinner table. Elisabeth, Aaron, and Bob were talking, Maria just staring at the linen placemat in front of her. *She's also acting strange*, Martina thought, but ignored it for now and pulled Lu along to the bathroom down the hallway. She opened the door and gently pushed her inside.

Lu immediately started searching under the sink. "Nada." She sighed. "Nothing here. No stepstool." She was about to turn around and leave when Martina came in as well and closed the door behind her.

Lu raised her eyebrows, her mouth half-open. "What are you doing, Martina?"

"You and me, we need to talk," Martina said.

Lu laughed. "But not here in the bathroom. That's kinda weird, Martina."

"Maybe weird. But it's a safe space away from *him*."

All color drained from Lu's face. Martina took Lu's hands in hers. "You didn't actually invite him, did you? And he's not a friend and supporter of yours, is he? He's the opposite, isn't he?"

Lu's lip was quivering. She said nothing.

"Lu, what did he do to you?" Martina firmly held Lu's hands, even as the general was trying to wiggle out of her grasp. Finally, Martina let go.

Lu now crossed her arms in front of her chest. "I have no idea what you're talking about, Martina. This is ridiculous."

"I know what it feels like, Lu. Remember?"

Lu just stared at her.

"Remember, I told you my ex-husband was abusive. He hit me. He belittled me. He made me feel so small. I hated him for hurting me, and hated myself for being so weak, so despicably weak, for not leaving him. But I put on a brave face. I smiled, laughed, held dinner parties when he was there, even though I wanted to throw him out, scream at him, tell him to stop. I put up with it—for years. And even after I stood up to him and got divorced, he had this power over me. The power to make me a weakling."

Lu's eyes watered. Her arms remained crossed in front of her, but her muscles had gone limp. Her shoulders drooped down. "How did you find the strength to completely get away from him?"

Martina shrugged and sighed. "I guess I never did get away from him completely. I only found the strength to stand up to him when Maria came to me. To protect this other little human being from him, I stood against him. And, you know, he kept his promise to leave me alone."

Lu uncrossed her arms. "Did he?"

Martina nodded. "Yeah, for many years. But when he returned, he had the same power. I was completely intimidated. So weak, so terribly weak. And ashamed for it."

"I understand that," Lu whispered. "But now you're free of his power?"

Martina nodded and stared at the floor. "Sí, free now."

"How?"

"Because he's dead now." Martina sighed.

"Dead?"

Martina dared to look up at Lu. "Yeah, he attacked Maria, and she fought him off. Then, someone else finished him off in the hospital. I think the police concluded it was the former police chief, Billings. Did it because he was pressured by Mike Clifford. You've heard the story...."

Lu nodded. There was silence in the bathroom for a while.

Martina took Lu's hands again. "Lu, I was never strong enough to get completely free of him until he died. And I despise myself for that. But you, you still have the chance. Because I know that guy out there, the unexpected guest, is someone who's intimidating you. No?"

A slight nod from Lu.

Martina squeezed her hands. "Lu, tell me. What did he do?"

Lu's lip started quivering. Martina gave her a hug, and all of a sudden, Lu silently sobbed into her shoulder. Martina stroked her back. "What happened, Lu? What did he do?"

Lu's silent sobs shook her whole body. Martina held her tight. "It's alright, Lu. It's alright. We're all here for you. We can help you. Me, Elisabeth, Maria. Even Aaron, if you want. So, what did he do to you?"

Lu started holding back her sobs and took a few deep breaths in. She lifted her head. "You already know what he did," she whispered. "Twenty years ago. And I haven't seen him since. Until tonight."

Martina stared at Lu. "¿Qué? I already know? Twenty years..." She threw her hands over her mouth. "No! He's the one..."

Lu nodded.

"The... the general who... who... raped... you? The... one you told Elisabeth about?"

Another slight nod from Lu.

"¡Dios mío!" Martina grabbed hold of the bathroom sink to steady herself. "Why in the world is he here now?"

Lu grimaced. "Because of this." She pointed to Martina, then herself. "Because he didn't want me to tell anyone. Wants to make sure I comply with his demands. To make sure I never tell anyone what happened."

Martina was as pale as the white bathroom sink keeping her upright. "¡Dios mío! Lu, this is terrible. But it's good you told me, because now I can help you and protect you. Just tell me how. How can I help?"

Lu smiled a weak smile. "We have to make sure he doesn't find out I told you about him. Can you act as if nothing has happened?"

Martina shrugged. "Sí. I think so. I was used to acting with my ex-husband. Not let my true feelings show."

Lu nodded. "Good."

"But what about justice, Lu? Justice for you?"

Lu shrugged. "That won't come tonight. Maybe later. I still need to find more strength for that. 'Cuz I'm so ashamed." She closed her eyes.

Martina let go of the sink and hugged her again. "Don't be, Lu. It's not your fault. Never your fault. And everyone who learns of this will know who is to blame: him. Just him. Trust me, I learned the hard way. But I know now. And I want you to know that also."

Lu nodded, then smiled at Martina. "I'll try to remember that. Eventually, yes, I want justice. But let's worry about that later. We just need to get through tonight. Tonight is all about survival."

CHAPTER 47

"**S**urvival in the desert is intense." Bob took another sip of his merlot. "You'll learn that if you ever deploy to the Middle East, Aaron."

"Hopefully he won't," Maria snapped, her eyes sparkling emerald green. "We need more peace in the world."

Bob laughed. "Oh, I see. A little diplomat in the room with us tonight, huh?"

"Whatever, *Bob*." Maria rolled her eyes and took another sip of her water. She almost choked on it when Aaron elbowed her.

"Show some respect, Maria," he whispered through gritted teeth. "What's gotten into you?"

She shrugged, even as her thoughts raced. *Maybe I need to tell Aaron now? Take him aside and tell him that guy over there is Bob "The Bullet" Jones? No, not yet. I need Bullet to confess first. Somehow. By the time dinner is done, my kidnapping will be solved. Once and for all.*

"Alright, everyone, here's Lu's amazing chicken dish," Martina announced, and trundled out of the kitchen carrying a huge platter in both hands. She set it in the middle of the table between the guests. It had a whole chicken on it, with onion slices, garlic, small potatoes, and vegetables nestled around it. Cabbage leaves formed a nest underneath the big bird.

"Looks delicious." Elisabeth licked her lips. "And smells so good. Wow, Lu, you've outdone yourself. Fantastic."

"Thank you," Lu said, and came over to the table with a big knife. "Who will do the honors?"

Bob jumped up. "I will."

"No, Elisabeth should. It's thanks to her we have these plates on the table that neither of us short Latinas could reach." Martina winked at Lu, who smiled back then handed the knife to Elisabeth.

"Thank you, ladies," Elisabeth said, "But maybe we should let Bob—"

"No." Lu shook her head. "I'd like you, my good friend, to do the honors. Please. Us women can handle ourselves, right?"

Bob sat back down and frowned. Maria had to suppress her giggles. *Serves you right, asshole.* She glanced at him. He was staring across the table right at Lu, his lips pressed together. Lu ignored him.

That's interesting. Ever since Lu and Mamá were gone for a bit, she seems different. More like the woman Mom and Mamá talked about when they came back from spending time with her this morning. A strong, independent woman. A general in the Air Force. What changed? She seemed so timid earlier.

Maria kept watching the scene quietly while sipping her water. Elisabeth served everyone a slice of chicken and some of the surrounding potatoes and vegetables. "Dig in, everyone." Lu smiled and raised her glass. "Cheers."

"Cheers," they all said, and raised their own glasses. Except for Bob. He didn't say anything. Maria watched him out of the corner of her eye and noticed he was just sipping his wine, still staring across the table at Lu.

She glanced at her two moms. Elisabeth easily made conversation with everyone, seemed very happy to be here, and continued to shower Lu with praise for her cooking. Martina seemed more quiet now. She talked to Elisabeth and Lu, smiled at Aaron, but avoided all eye contact or interaction with Bob.

Maria knew something was up. *And I need to find out what. When the moment's right, I'll excuse myself and Mamá so I can talk to her.* She patiently waited for that moment to come.

Once everyone was done with their first serving, the women passed on seconds, but both men took a second serving. "There you go, mijo." Martina smiled at Aaron as she served him. "Enjoy."

Bob then handed his plate over to Martina as well. She took it but didn't so much as look at him, just plopped some chicken onto his plate, smashed some potatoes and veggies next to it, then handed it back over without saying a word.

"Thank you, Martina." Bob smiled, looking up at her, but she didn't respond, just sat back down and nodded at the others.

Maria watched. *That's very unlike Mamá. She's being as rude to him as I am. Wonder why? I know my reason, but surely she didn't figure it out on her own? But what does she know, then? Something I don't? I just gotta talk to her. How? When?*

Then Maria had an idea. "Oh no… I forgot something in the car."

Aaron looked up from his plate and swallowed. "You did? What?"

"Just… something," Maria said. "Mamá, can you come with me, please?"

"Me?" Martina raised her eyebrows. "Why me?"

"Come, please. It'll be quick."

"Oh, mija, no sé…"

"Can we please be excused for a bit?" Maria asked the others.

"Sure?" Lu said.

Elisabeth had her eyebrows raised. "Okay, I guess. Make it quick."

"Will do." Maria got up. "Vamos, Mamá."

Martina got up slowly. All of them watched as Maria and Martina headed down the hallway to go outside.

Beep!

With a click of her key fob, Maria unlocked the car as she walked toward it, Martina in tow. Maria waved to Lieutenant Martinez, who was still parked behind Maria's car. She then opened the passenger seat door and pretended to search for something inside.

"Mija? What are you looking for?"

"Gum," Maria said, her back now turned toward her mamá.

"Gum? Why do you need gum now?" Martina sighed when she realized Maria wasn't going to answer. So, she opened the door to the backseat, kneeled against the seat cushion, and helped search. It didn't take her long. "I see gum right there. In the middle console, in front of the cupholders."

Maria nodded. "Yes, I see it." But instead of reaching for it, she sat down in the passenger seat and turned to face Martina. "Sit down, Mamá."

Martina raised her eyebrows. "What? Why? *There's* the gum. Just grab it and let's head back inside."

"No, Mamá, please sit."

The urgency in Maria's voice made Martina comply. "Mija, I'm not sure what's going on here…."

"I need to know what you know."

"¿Qué?"

"I know there's something weird going on. You suddenly don't want to look at our unexpected dinner guest anymore. You're rude to him. That's not you, Mamá. That much I know. So, what made you dislike him? Something Lu said?"

Maria watched all the color rush out of her mamá's face. But she didn't reply.

"Mamá, come on. No more secrets, right? No more lies, right? Please, I know something is up, and I need you to tell me."

Martina closed her eyes. "I can't, mija. I'm sorry."

"You can't be serious. Mamá, come on. We lived twenty years of lies—you promised you'd never keep anything from me again." Maria's face flushed red, her freckles contrasting with the ruby color.

Martina looked into Maria's emerald-green eyes. "I know you're upset with me, but I promised Lu not to say anything."

"But you promised *me* to never keep anything from me anymore. Please, Mamá, tell me. This is important."

Martina shook her head. "I promised Lu this will stay between her and me. Nobody else. I must honor her wishes. You need to understand that, mija."

"But, Mamá, you need to understand—"

"*No*, Maria. ¡Basta! I won't tell. I'll keep my promise." Martina crossed her arms in front of her.

Maria sighed. *But I need to know. I need to know more about this guy. He's the key to understanding my kidnapping. I really need her to talk. How do I make her?*

"Let's go, Maria. Grab your gum, then vamos." Martina's hand was already on the doorhandle.

No, I need to stop her! I need her to tell me. And then Maria had an idea. "Mamá, Bob is my kidnapper," she blurted out.

Martina's hand slipped off the doorhandle. All remaining color left her face. "¿Qué?"

Maria leaned further through the console space toward the backseat. She whispered, "I figured it out. Bob is General Robert Jones. Jones is a fighter pilot who goes by Bob."

Martina just stared at her.

"But in the Air Force he was known as Bob 'The Bullet' Jones."

Maria watched her mom's mouth drop open.

"His call sign is Bullet. I know because I researched it online and—"

"Why didn't you *say anything*? Maria! Mija! You needed to tell us. Need to tell the police. If he's Bullet, the guy they're looking for, the one from the Fearless Four, the one Jonathan met, the one Mike Clifford worked for, the one—"

"Behind my kidnapping," Maria interrupted. "Exactly. I just can't quite piece together the story yet, so before we go to the police I need to—"

"Call the police," Martina said. "Call them now." She turned and looked out the rear window. "Or just tell Lieutenant Martinez. ¡Dios mío! We need to tell *someone*. Now!" Martina's hand was at the door handle again. "He's dangerous, so dangerous."

"Stop, Mamá. Wait. We only have a theory right now, there's still more to learn. We can't risk him worming his way out of this. I'd like to go back in there and get him to confess before we tell anyone."

"You loco?" Martina shook her head. "No, no, no. Too dangerous. He's dangerous. Goodness, even Lu's so afraid of him. He's terrible…."

Maria raised her eyebrows. "Lu is afraid of him? Ha, I knew it. And that's what she told you?" Martina bit her lip as if wanting to keep herself from saying anything more. "Mamá, please, I need to learn more about this guy. If he is who we think he is, we need to understand why he came here. I assume Lu didn't really invite him, did she?"

Martina shook her head.

"So why is he here? Do you know, Mamá?"

Silence.

"Please, tell me. It's important we learn everything we can about him. We can use what we learn to get him to confess."

Maria could see her mom thinking. *I just know she's contemplating everything she's heard tonight from me and Lu. That's why her eyes are closed.* Maria was eager to move on with the conversation and get back inside, but she also knew she had to give her mamá time to think. She clenched her jaw to keep herself from saying anything else.

Finally, Martina opened her eyes and moved closer to Maria, stuck her head between the two fronts seats so that she was now nose to nose with her. "Mija, the guy in there is the one who raped Lu when she was young."

What? Maria couldn't believe her ears. Her mouth dropped open.

"Sí, he's the asshole Lu wanted to bring to justice with your mom's help, before your mom…"

"Abandoned her. Because I got kidnapped."

Martina nodded. "Sí." She squeezed Maria's suddenly cold, clammy hand.

"This is unbelievable," Maria whispered. "So why is he here?"

"Lu thinks he wants to make sure she doesn't tell anyone. If he finds out how much I know… and now you… ¡Dios mío! I don't know…." Martina's hands started trembling.

This time, Maria squeezed hers in comfort. Her mind was racing. *No, he can't find out we know. Too dangerous. But something still doesn't feel right. Like we still don't know the whole story yet. There must be something more. But what?*

She sighed. *It was certainly convenient that after Mom lost me, she was too distracted to help Lu bring Bob "The Bullet" Jones to justice.*

And then it dawned on her. Her body went rigid. *That's it. That's the motive for my kidnapping! Oh my gosh.* Her head was spinning. *But how did he know where my parents were? How did he pull off such a stunt with so little time to prepare?*

"Mija." Her mamá's voice startled her. "You alright? Please, we have to act normal. Have to make sure he's not suspicious. Or make him mad at Lu. He'll take it out on her. She doesn't deserve that. Doesn't deserve his wrath."

Maria shook her head. "No, she doesn't." She let go of Martina's hands.

"Mija, you really think this guy is Bullet, though?"

Maria nodded.

"I mean… shouldn't we tell the police then? Lieutenant Martinez is *right here*." Martina jerked her head at his vehicle.

"If we tell the police about my suspicion, Lu's story might come out. Do you think she wants the police to know about it?"

Right away, Martina shook her head. "No, no, no, definitely not. She's not ready to face him like that yet."

Maria nodded. *That's what I thought. And maybe we don't know the whole story yet. How exactly does Lu play into this? Maybe she's not just the victim here, is she?*

The warm touch of Martina's hand brought Maria back to the present. "What do we do now?"

Maria sighed. "I guess we better pretend nothing happened, that we don't know anything. Right?"

"Right." Martina exhaled, squeezed Maria's hand one more time, then let go and opened the door. "Bring your gum. We can pretend we looked for it all this time. You and me will discuss this further tonight. Please be careful around this guy. He's bad. A bad guy."

"I know," Maria said, and grabbed the pack of gum.

Both mother and daughter got out at the same time, shut their doors, gave Lieutenant Martinez a wave, linked arms, then walked back inside. As they went, Maria used her fob to lock the car again.

Beep!

The loud chirp almost made her jump, even though she was expecting it. *Am I nervous? Oh yeah, I'm definitely nervous. But I can do this.* She grinned and caught her footing again.

"Alright, mija?"

She looked at her mamá. "Yeah, I'm fine."

"You promise to be careful in there? No stunts, Maria. You hear me?"

"Yes, I hear you," Maria whispered, and blushed a little. She doubted she would be able to keep that promise.

CHAPTER 48

"**P**romise," the man on the other end of the line said. "Yes, Chief, again—I *promise* we've looked high and low for this guy. So far, no trace of the general. He's not at home."

Tonya, Sally, Tom, and Chief Parlot all glanced at each other. The chief raised his eyebrows, then focused again on the voice booming from the loudspeaker of his work cell phone.

"We're checking on base now," the police man on the phone said.

Tonya took over. "Hi, this is Agent Tonya Anderson. We spoke earlier. Just wondering, have you traced his car yet? Might be the easiest way to locate the general."

"Oh yes, we're working on it. How about we call you back once we know more?"

Chief Parlot nodded. "Okay, sounds good. Thanks. Talk to you soon then." He ended the call, then slumped back in his chair and sighed. *Wish they had found him at home. This isn't looking good.*

Sally voiced what the chief had been thinking. "Sucks we don't know where General Jones is at the moment, doesn't it?" They all nodded. "But I didn't find him on any flight manifests." Sally sighed. "Any other way out of Texas?"

"Horseback," Tonya joked.

Sally laughed. "A real cowboy. It'd take weeks."

"Come on, team, let's be serious." Chief Parlot started pacing. "What other ways?"

"Steel horse." Tom grinned. "You know, nice motorcycle? Or by car?"

"They're tracing his car right now. Or any vehicle he owns. We should know soon if he drove out of Texas." Tonya scratched her chin. "Long road trip, though. It'll take hours."

"More like days," Sally said. They all nodded.

Tom's eyes lit up. "How about by bus? Or train? That might be faster?"

Chief Parlot stopped pacing. "Yes, a passenger train would be faster. Amtrak? Let's check on that."

Sally sat back down in front of her computer. "Okay, I'll contact Amtrak to see if there's a ticket in his name."

"I'll work the bus lines." Tom plopped back into his chair, ready to go.

Chief Parlot shook his head. "No, Tom, I need you to continue tracing Jones's phone. Tonya and I will check the buses."

"Sure, Chief, as you wish." Tom's hands were already flying across the keyboard. "Had no luck so far, but maybe that luck will change soon."

"Alright, alright, alright, team, back to work," Tonya announced, and sat back down at the worktable. Chief Parlot joined her.

Ring, ring!

The loud ringing of Chief Parlot's work phone cut through the room's concentration. Everyone looked up from their computers. The chief picked up. "Hello, Chief Parlot speaking. How may I help you?" He put the phone on loudspeaker so that everyone else could hear the Texas police officer on the other end of the phone line.

"Chief Parlot, we located General Jones's primary-use vehicle," the officer said. "It's presently parked at the Aero Club on Lackland AFB."

"The what?" Tom asked loudly enough for the officer to hear.

"The Aero Club. It's a pilot's club on base. Many military officers keep private planes there—mostly Cessnas, Beechcrafts, Dorniers, and so on," the officer explained.

The chief's eyes widened. "You're saying General Jones's car is parked there... but he's gone?"

"Correct, Chief."

"Why would he park it at the Aero Club?" Sally stared at the phone as if the policeman on the other end could see her. "Does Jones own a private plane?"

"Yes, he does. A Cessna 172 Skyhawk. Blue, four-seater, single-engine," the police officer told them.

Oh my gosh. The chief paled. "And the Cessna is gone, isn't it?"

"Yes, Chief."

The chief slammed his fist on the table. The phone jumped briefly into the air. *I knew it! I freaking knew it! He's after Maria.*

Tonya held Chief Parlot's arm, then took over. "And where did General Jones fly off to?"

"Well, ma'am, we don't know."

"Why not?" the chief yelled. "You gotta know. There must be a flight log or something."

"I'm sure there is," the police man said. "But the club is closed."

Tonya raised her eyebrows. "Already? It's awfully early still. Aren't you on central time over there?"

"We are, ma'am, but the club here closes at six p.m. You know, it's run by volunteers, and they—"

"I don't care," Chief Parlot yelled, "we gotta access that logbook. We need to find out where General Jones flew to. Right now!"

"I assure you, Chief, my team and I are working on it. We just tracked down a volunteer who said he can come here and open up for us. Same guy who told us about the general's plane."

"Can't you just break in?" Sally said.

Laughter on the other end. "No, we can't."

"But you're the police and this is important, so—"

"I'm not sure how your police department does things over there in Florida, ma'am, but we play by the rules here, *especially* when it comes to military installations," the officer said, his voice stern. "I'll be in touch."

Beep, beep.

He hung up the phone. Chief Parlot sighed and pressed the End Call button.

Sally bit her lip. "I'm sorry, Chief, I didn't mean to offend him, I just thought—"

"No, you and I were thinking the same thing," Chief Parlot said, and grinned. "Don't worry, Sally, it's all good. While we wait to hear back from him, we have a new task: find out if Eglin AFB has its own Aero Club."

"On it," Sally called over her shoulder as she sat back down in front of her computer. "Let's find our little pilot and his Cessna."

CHAPTER 49

"Cessna? You fly a Cessna now? That's so cool," Aaron said.

Bob laughed and took another sip of his merlot. "It is. I should take you along on a trip sometime. You and your lovely fiancée."

Aaron heard Maria snort and mumble something beside him. *What's wrong with her? She's being so rude tonight. Not herself at all.*

"That'd be great." Aaron smiled at the general and lifted his glass in a silent toast. The last sip of merlot ran down his throat. He shook himself. *The wine is as dry as the atmosphere at this party. Everyone seems determined to ignore Bob, aside from Elisabeth and myself. Guess Maria and Martina don't like uninvited guests....*

Aaron set down his empty wine glass and switched to water. Just as he was taking a sip, Maria asked a direct and unexpected question that caused him to nearly choke.

"Bob, what about your son? Did you ever take him flying?" Maria side-eyed Bob, who seemed visibly shocked.

"My son?" He lowered his wine glass. "Did I mention I had a son?"

"Nope. I just had a feeling you did. Or did you not, Bob?" Maria looked at him directly now.

He cleared his throat. "Well, I... I... ahem... did."

"You did, did you?" Maria pursed her lips.

Bob sighed. "Yes, I did." He hesitated. "He died unexpectedly."

"Oh no, so sorry to hear that," Aaron said.

"Too *bad.*" Maria's sarcastic tone didn't go unnoticed by Aaron. He raised his one eyebrow at her.

"That's awful, Bob, I'm very sorry," Elisabeth chimed in. "Losing a child is the worst—trust me, I know." She sighed.

"Exactly, my mom knows how hard it is." Maria now pointed at Bob. "And *you* should understand, of all people. Or don't you?"

Aaron and the others watched helplessly as Maria fired off one question after the other at the general in rapid succession.

"How did he die?"

"Um, in a car accident. He was young and speeding—"

"Are you *sure*?"

Bob raised his eyebrows. "Excuse me?"

"Are you sure he died in a car accident—or was it, oh, I don't know, more like a shoot-out?"

"What?" Bob seemed confused.

Aaron just stared at Maria. *I don't even know what to say. What's gotten into her?*

"You know what I mean. You were a mentor, too, right? Not just a father?"

"Well, I suppose every father is a mentor to his—"

"But not everyone fails at mentoring their children, do they?" Maria tapped her fingers on the table. "If you're a good parent, you raise your child to be kind, someone who cares for others, someone who would never commit a crime."

"Well, of course you should—"

"*Unless*, of course, the parent is unable to. Say, because they hold different values. In that case, they might raise their child to be like them: cutthroat, egotistical, manipulative—"

"Maria, stop it," Aaron said, and put his hand on hers to stop the tapping. "What's gotten into you?"

She shrugged her shoulders, refused to look at Aaron. Her eyes were still fixated on Bob's. "I just get the feeling there's something about you we all should know, isn't there, Bob?"

Bob now burst into laughter. "I have no idea what you're talking about, young lady, but—"

"Oh yeah, you have no idea, *Bob*?" Maria spat out his name in disgust. "If I were you, I'd think harder about this, *Bob*. Maybe it'll come back to you then, *Bob*. You and your precious so-called son had a lot in common, didn't you?"

Aaron's mouth dropped open. *She's lost it! Talking this way to a person of respect, a general in the Air Force. What the heck is going on here?* He looked at Martina, who was staring at her daughter, her eyes wide. He tilted his head, not sure what to make of Martina's expression. *Is that fear I see?*

Aaron now turned to Elisabeth. She appeared frozen, her glass halfway to her mouth, her mouth hanging open. *She's shocked as well. Just like me. Shocked by Maria's strange behavior.*

He glanced at Lu. She was very pale. Biting her lip. *Can't tell if she's shocked or angry. Or afraid, like Martina?* He saw her glance at Martina, but Martina avoided eye contact with her, just focused on Maria.

Aaron couldn't believe it. *I'm lost here. What's going on?*

Bob was the first to find his words. "Young lady, I have no idea what you're getting at, and I'm feeling kinda attacked here. Please excuse me. I'll be right back." He pushed his chair away from the table, stood up, and left.

"Fine, goodbye, Bob!" Maria taunted him as he walked down the hallway. "Go ahead and think about it. I'll be here, waiting for answers."

They all heard the door to the bathroom shut. Silence at the table.

"We better get these plates cleaned up," Martina finally said. She got up and started gathering the empty plates.

"And the rest of the food needs to go in the fridge," Lu said, and grabbed the large platter piled with leftovers. Both Lu and Martina walked into the kitchen together.

Elisabeth finally noticed she was still holding her glass aloft. She took a sip, then set it down and stared at Maria. Her daughter grinned back at her as she swished the ice cubes in her water glass lazily, rocking the glass this way and that against the table.

Aaron heard whispers coming from the kitchen. He briefly turned around to look over his shoulder and saw both Martina and Lu standing together by the sink. He couldn't understand what they were saying. *They're too far away, and speaking Spanish, I think. But judging by their tone, sure sounds like an argument. Over Maria? Or what?*

He turned back to his fiancée, who was still playing with her water glass. *She looks amused. What's going on with her? I've never seen her this spiteful, this malicious. She's being so disrespectful and unkind. Just nasty.* He shook his head. "Maria, my love. What's going on here?"

She turned to him, the slight smile still on her face. "I have no idea what you're talking about."

Aaron scrunched his eyebrows and felt his face slowly turning red. "Seriously? What a lie! You're not usually like this. You know better."

"I agree with Aaron," Elisabeth said. "You were very rude, interrogating a fellow guest that way. It's not a very kind thing to do."

"*Kind?*" Maria laughed out loud. "No, not kind. But he deserves it."

Both Aaron and Elisabeth stared at her. "How can you say that—" Aaron started, but was interrupted immediately by his fiancée.

"You'll see. I'll explain later. Trust me, I have it all under control."

CHAPTER 50

"I have it all under control," Bob mumbled to himself as he stared into the bathroom mirror, his green eyes sparkling in anger. *That Collins girl needs to be controlled. Like Lulu-girl. At least Lulu-girl is playing along.* He splashed himself with water, then stared back into the mirror. *Or is she?*

He turned off the faucet and leaned on the sink. *Martina and Lulu were gone awhile. Did Lulu dare tell her about me? Martina was much colder toward me the moment they returned. And Elisabeth and Aaron? They seem totally unaware. Charmed by me. As most people are.* He grinned at himself in the mirror and marveled at his perfectly straight, white teeth. *Glad I had them fixed when I was young. A perfect pilot's smile. Fits the image. Sexy smolder. Helped me a lot throughout the years.*

He shook himself. *Focus, Bullet, focus. Focus on the main issue here: Maria. That damned little girl. She shouldn't even be here. She should be dead.* He sighed. *Instead, she shot him. My Mike. The second son I've lost.*

He formed a fist. It took every ounce of willpower to keep himself from hitting something. He felt like smashing the mirror in, or the sink. He wanted to put a hole through the door. *Obviously can't do that. I need to think smart. Think, Bullet! Because if Maria is onto me, if she's somehow figured out who I am or what I've done, I'm in trouble.*

He closed his eyes and thought for a while. Then opened the cabinet doors underneath the sink. *If this house matches my own here in the Distinguished Visitor's Quarters, then this bathroom should have one, too.* He bent down and rummaged through the cabinet drawers. He tossed aside extra rolls of toilet paper, a tissue box, and then he saw it. He grinned. *There it is.*

He pulled out the small bottle of bleach cleaner meant for the toilet and stuffed it inside his pocket. *Glad I'm wearing khaki cargo pants with my nice, fancy shirt. Cargo pants have so many fun pockets where you can hide things.* A vicious smile flitted across his face. *This will do.*

Carefully, he unlocked the door and opened it. Peeked down the hallway. *Nobody here.* He glanced at the front door. *Can't take any chances. I know they have an escort.*

He snuck over to the front door, threw the deadbolt so that it could only be unlocked from the inside, then noticed the wooden bench underneath the coatrack. As quietly as he could, he picked it up and braced it against the old-fashioned door handle. *Good luck getting in now. Or out.* He grinned.

He then returned to the bathroom and took his time peeing with the door cracked open so the others could hear, then loudly flushed the toilet. *Better ruse. Need them to think I've been in here this whole time.* He washed his hands, dried them, and walked back into the living room.

Elisabeth, Aaron, and Maria were still sitting at the table. Martina and Lu were in the middle of setting out crystal bowls on the table in front of each guest.

"For dessert," Martina said, when she noticed him. "Please sit down, Bob. It's almost ready."

He watched her. *Still avoiding eye contact with me, I see.* He glanced at Lu. *So is she. Her face is flushed. Did she just have an argument with someone? Martina? Maria, more likely? Wish I knew. Hate not knowing.*

"How about I go fetch the dessert, ladies?" he asked. "I'm standing already."

"No, it's okay, I've got it," Lu replied.

"Sí, or me. I'm still standing also." Martina stood up tall now.

"I know, ladies, but it seems as though I'm still not welcome at the table...." He nodded toward Maria, who was pointedly ignoring him. "I'd rather have something else to do than pick up a ridiculous conversation again."

He watched everyone exchange embarrassed glances, except for Maria, who burst into laughter. "Well, it's only as ridiculous as—" She got elbowed by Aaron and cut her sentence short.

"Sure, Bob, you can help," Martina said. "Thank you. Lu and I will sit down then. The dessert is cooling in the fridge."

"It's the big glass bowl that looks like yogurt. My homemade yogurt with cherries and brown sugar." Lu smiled. "Hope you'll all like it."

"I'm sure we will, Lu, thank you." Elisabeth rubbed Lu's arm, which was lying next to her empty crystal bowl on the table.

"Okay, ladies, thank you. I'll be back shortly. And I'm sure we'll all enjoy it."

Bob walked past them into the kitchen. He opened the fridge and saw the big bowl filled with a delicious-looking yogurt dessert. *Perfect. White yogurt. It'll be even more white soon. Or should I say,* bleached? He had to suppress his laugh.

He lifted the dessert bowl out of the fridge and carefully carried it over to the kitchen island. The island opened into the dining room but there was a low ornamental barrier ringing it, partially blocking him from view. *Wonderful. They can see me, but they can't see any lower than my chest. Meaning they sure can't see what I'm about to add to the dessert.*

He glanced over to the table. Everyone except Maria was caught up in conversation again. *Good, good.* He smiled. Unnoticed, he pulled the little bottle of bleach out of his pants and poured it over the yogurt dish. He made sure to leave one corner untouched by it. *That'll be mine.*

He grinned, then called out, "Where's the serving spoon?"

Lu turned around. "Not on the island. Underneath the kitchen cabinets along the wall. The drawer to your left."

Bob walked over, opened the drawer, and saw the serving utensils. "Found it, thank you." He picked out a large black spoon, then walked back over to the dessert and stuck the spoon inside. He mixed the yogurt with the bleach, burying the bleach odor underneath a layer of delicious smelling yogurt, quickly rinsed off the serving spoon, and stuck it into the portion of yogurt he had left bleach-free.

He picked up the bowl and brought it over to the table. "It looks fantastic, Lu. And smells amazing. Do you all mind if I take the first serving? My mouth was watering the moment I opened the fridge."

Elisabeth tilted her head. "I guess that's okay?"

"Sure, go ahead, Bob. Help yourself. You deserve it." Aaron smiled at him.

Bob set the bowl down and scooped out the portion the serving spoon was stuck in into his own bowl, then started serving the others one at a time. When he made it around the table to Maria, she covered her bowl with both hands. "No, thanks, I'm full. Have a lot of other things to digest in here, you know?" She looked up at him and patted her taut stomach.

Bob scooped the serving spoon through the dessert so that there was just a little on the end and offered it to Maria. "At least try a little?"

Maria shook her head. "No, thank you."

Lu looked disappointed. "Maybe try just a tiny bit, Maria?"

"Yes, you really should." Bob made to ladle the spoonful into Maria's bowl, but she continued to cover it with both hands.

She shook her head again. "No, and I will not be forced."

Lu frowned. "But it's very good. I worked hard on it...."

Aaron said loudly, "Come on, Maria. Just a tiny little bit. I think it would make Lu happy."

"Okay, fine then. But I'll serve myself." Maria ripped the spoon out of Bob's hand.

He shook his head and sat back down. *What a feisty one. She really doesn't like me. Well, that'll change soon enough. Just wait for it.*

They all waited for Maria to serve herself. When she was done, Bob lifted his spoon. "Thank you for the dessert, and the invitation, Lu. Enjoy your desserts, everyone." He took his first bite. "Mmmmm…. Delicious."

He watched as everyone else took their first bites and had to hide his smirk. *Soon, I'll be in charge of you all. You'll do as I say. You'll look up to me, your master, as you lie at my feet. And I'll be in charge, holding the strings, the ultimate arbiter of your misery. Because I am who I am. The master of manipulation, the master puppeteer. Oh yes!*

CHAPTER 51

"Oh yes, we got him now." Chief Parlot smiled. "There's an Aero Club here at Eglin Air Force Base. No need to wait for Texas to call back and confirm. I'll bet money Jones flew his private plane here. Let's go, team. Gotta see if his Cessna is parked here at Eglin's Aero Club."

Tom turned around in his swivel chair. "You want me to suspend what I'm doing over here, Chief? We still don't have Jones's phone's location, but I've gained access to where his texts are encrypted and I'm close to cracking them. I'm certain whatever we find will be interesting. Got a dedicated FBI supercluster brute-forcing a solution, just need a little more time to churn."

"It's fine, Tom, you can stay here and finish. Call us when you get through." The chief had already grabbed his jacket off the hook.

Sally stood up. "What about me, Chief? Do I go with you and Tonya?"

Tonya and the chief looked at each other and shrugged. "It only takes so many people to check if the plane is there. We might need someone else here who can coordinate a search with base police, don't you think, my man Isaac?" Tonya said.

He nodded. "Good point." He turned to Sally. "You stay here. While Tom cracks those texts, I want you to figure out who's on call tonight for the base police. Get all the contact info lined up for everyone we might need to contact. If we see Jones's plane parked at the Aero Club, we'll call you so you can call base police—maybe even a SWAT team—whatever backup we can get. We'll all need to work together to locate General Jones. Got it?"

"Yes, Chief, got it," Sally said. "Drive safely. And good luck. I'll be on standby here. With Tom."

"Wonderful. Thanks." Chief Parlot and Tonya departed for Eglin AFB.

"Closed," Chief Parlot said with a sigh as they parked the police car in front of the Aero Club. "Of course."

"What did you expect, Isaac? Different hours than Lackland? Remember, it's run by volunteers." Tonya winked at him as they got out of the car. "But don't worry. We can inspect the parked planes from the fence line. There's only a few. Come on, help out with shining a flashlight on them."

The chief fumbled with his flashlight. Tonya was already as close to the fence as she could get. Her beam of light illuminated every plane parked along there. Two white ones, two blue ones, one off-white one. Chief Parlot finally joined her and peered through the fence. "How did the Texas police describe his plane? A Cessna Skyhawk and what else?"

"It's blue." Tonya shone her flashlight at one of two blue planes. "A four-seater Cessna Skyhawk." The beam illuminated the inside of the plane. "Just like this one right here."

Chief Parlot's flashlight slowly sank down in his hands as realization hit him. "Damn it, that must be his plane. That must be Jones's plane."

"Very likely." Tonya sighed. "Come on, my man Isaac, let's give our youngsters back at the station a call, shall we?"

They turned off their flashlights and rushed back to the car, the chief already on his cell phone. While it rang, they piled inside and waited. Chief Parlot put his phone on loudspeaker.

"Hello? Officer Sally Johnson speaking."

"Sally, it's me. We've got news."

"Found General Jones's plane, have you?"

He nodded. "We think so. There's a Cessna parked here that fits the description...."

"Definitely his plane," Sally said. "The Texas police just called to let us know they gained access to the logbooks at Lackland. Shows General Jones flew his plane to Eglin AFB early this morning."

The chief rolled his eyes. "They're a bit slow to the game....Anyway, Sally, go ahead and call base police to find out where General Jones is staying. They must know. Once you do that—"

"We've got other news," Tom yelled in the background, interrupting him. The chief and Tonya looked at each other, eyebrows raised. They heard Sally move closer to Tom to pick up his voice. "You'll want to hear this, I bet."

Tonya tilted her head. "We're all yours, Tom. Make it quick. We have a general to apprehend."

"*Or two*," they heard Tom say.

What? Chief Parlot scratched his chin.

Tom continued, "I got through to some of the general's texts—"

"Did he turn his phone on again?" Tonya asked.

"No, it's still off. But the hack on his texts yielded partial results: I was able to recall a few text messages he sent earlier and then deleted."

"Get to the point, Tom, we don't have much time. Jones is already on base."

"Yes, yes, got it, Chief. So listen, General Jones was texting with one of his contacts. Someone named Lulu-girl."

"*Lulu-girl?* What does that have to do with our case?" the chief said irritably.

Tonya shushed him and pointed at the phone. "Go on, Tom," she said.

"They texted about flying to Florida, to Eglin, to be precise. Now listen to this exchange between Lulu and him. Lulu told him: 'I'll find Elisabeth today and talk to her. No worries.'"

Chief Parlot and Tonya looked at each other, then continued listening to Tom.

"Then there are some texts time-stamped later on. The general says, 'I hope everything's under control, Lulu-girl.' She texts back, 'Yes, it's all under control.' And he replies, 'I trust you, but in this case I'd like to make sure of it myself. I'll be there soon.' That's quite something, huh?"

Tonya nodded. "I'll say. Okay, so who's this 'Lulu' or 'Lulu-girl'? Did you find out?"

"Yep, I traced who her number belongs to." They could almost hear Tom's grin through the speaker. "And guess who it is."

The chief shook his head. *I don't know, I don't have time for these games! Just need him to tell me so we can focus on the most important thing here: locating General Jones.*

"Guadalupe!" Tonya blurted out. "Lulu is General Lu Thomas?"

Chief Parlot stared blankly at his colleague sitting next to him in the car. *What?*

"Bingo, Agent Anderson, you're correct," Tom yelled through the phone.

"Holy moly, that's not good. Maria and company are at Lu's house for dinner tonight. They're in danger," Tonya said. "Sally, *call the base police right now* and locate General Jones's whereabouts. The chief and I are headed straight to Lu's. Send backup. We'll keep you posted. Talk to you later, team."

"Alright, be safe," Sally said, then hung up.

Chief Parlot stared at his phone. *General Lu was texting with General Jones? What do they have to do with each other? What's her motive? Does she want revenge? For what? Something to do with Elisabeth?*

330

A slight jab against his ribcage made him jump. It was Tonya. She turned to him. "Isaac? Come on, my man, keep it together. Let's go. We gotta make sure Maria and the others are okay. General Lu Thomas.... Who could have seen this coming?"

He stared at her. "But why? What's her motive?"

Tonya shrugged. "Buckle up, and let's go find out."

The chief did as he was told. "Where's Lu staying on base?"

"Distinguished Visitor's Quarters, right? Isn't that what Lieutenant Martinez said?"

Chief Parlot nodded. "Think so." He turned on the car and revved the engine. "Let's call the lieutenant and make sure they're okay. He should still be there."

Tonya grinned. "Great idea, my man Isaac. I'll call him, you drive."

While the chief plugged the address into the vehicle's navigation system, Tonya called Lieutenant Martinez. He picked up after a few rings as the car took off. "Hi, Lieutenant Martinez, this is Agent Anderson. The chief is here, too. You're on loudspeaker."

"Okay. What can I do for you both?"

"Are Maria, Aaron, Elisabeth, and Martina still there?"

"Yes, they're all sitting around the dinner table. Eating dessert, it looks like."

"Good. And you can actually see the four of them along with General Thomas? Do they look—"

"Six, actually."

The chief swerved a little. "*Six?*"

"Yes, six. There's another person there. A man. Older, it looks like. Hard to tell, though," the lieutenant said.

"What? Who is that guy?" Tonya wanted to know.

"Don't know. He was already inside when we all arrived."

"Why the heck didn't you tell us?" Chief Parlot barked at him.

"Well, Chief, I didn't think it was important—"

"*We* decide what's important, Lieutenant," Tonya interrupted him. "And right now, we need to know: what are they doing, and are they okay?"

"Yes, ma'am, they're fine. Just eating dinner."

"Keep watching," the chief said. "We'll be right there. See you soon." He hung up and sped through the base.

"Thinking what I'm thinking?" Tonya said. She side-eyed him. "Jones is there, isn't he?"

Chief Parlot nodded. "Damn it." He hit the steering wheel. "We were supposed to keep them safe. But now they've somehow ended up in the same room as two potential enemies." He drove even faster now. "That's not good, not good at all."

CHAPTER 52

That's not good, not good at all. Maria suppressed a shiver as she licked a tiny little bit of dessert off her spoon. *How can everyone else eat this stuff? It tastes weird. Strange. Disgusting.*

She looked around and saw everyone eating the fruit-yogurt dessert. Aaron was already on his second helping. They'd fallen quiet ever since they started eating.

Guess they're still embarrassed by the way I treated Bob, huh? But he's an asshole, a bad guy, like Mamá said. And I still need him to confess. How? She glanced at Bob Jones and noticed he had only eaten his small serving of dessert, then stopped. *Even though he was apparently so hungry for it....*

Maria watched Bob out of the corner of her eye. Saw him lean back in his chair and watch them eat. *He looks smug. Almost amused. Why?*

Maria glanced at Lu. Her forehead wrinkled. Lu inspected the dessert on her spoon, then put the spoon back down into her bowl, which still had a bunch of dessert in it. "I'm so sorry, guys. This doesn't taste quite right. Not sure what I did differently this time. Maybe one of the fruits wasn't fresh anymore? Anyway, don't feel like you need to finish eating this. I'm so sorry."

Martina put down her spoon as well. "It's okay, Lu. No worries."

Elisabeth still took another mouthful and tried to hide her disgust. "It's not too bad, Lu."

Only Aaron kept eating. Maria glanced back at Bob, who seemed to suppress laughter. *What's going on here? He's acting so strange. And I just can't take this anymore. I need to say something. And make sure it's all recorded.* Maria reached into the purse hanging off her chair, which caught Aaron's attention.

He swallowed a mouthful of dessert, then said, "Looking for something?"

"I thought I just heard my phone go off. Maybe it's Keisha or one of our other friends." She put the purse in her lap and pulled out her phone.

Martina now looked up at her. "Mija, no phones at the table. You know the rule. It's rude."

"I agree with your mamá, Maria." Elisabeth nodded. "You can check your phone later."

Maria sighed, stopped herself from rolling her eyes. *If they only knew what I'm about to do, they'd certainly approve.* She looked back and forth at her two moms sitting across from her.

Bob burst into laughter. "Well, well, young lady, it must be tough having not only one but two moms to harp on you, huh?"

Even Aaron giggled. "Yeah, no kidding."

Maria slipped her phone under her thigh and hung the purse back on her chair. She ignored Bob's comment. "Fine, I'll check later, then."

"Thanks, Maria," Elisabeth said.

Martina nodded. "Sí, good girl, mija."

Aaron glanced at Maria out of the corner of his eye. *Of course, he noticed.* She leaned back in her chair and put her hand on his thigh, slightly rubbing it. Smiled at him. *Don't rat me out, my love.* She saw him nod. *Thank goodness we have this great understanding of each other without having to speak.*

As Maria pushed her bowl with the dessert further back onto the table, she felt Bob's stare and turned to him, looked him in the eye.

He grinned at her. "You don't want any more dessert, Maria? Lu worked very hard to make it. And even if she thinks it tastes different today, *I* think it's very good."

"Do you, Bob? I can't help but notice you haven't had much yourself. Perhaps *I* should serve *you* more?"

Bob shook his head, then touched his belly. "No thanks. I'm stuffed with Lu's wonderful cooking. That chicken dish was excellent." He let out a chuckle. "You're very observant, young lady."

Maria nodded. *That's my cue. A perfect cue.* She took a deep breath, exhaled, and rubbed at her thighs. Only Aaron noticed when she pressed the Record button on her phone's camera and left it running underneath her thigh. She saw Aaron raise one of his eyebrows but quickly took his hand under the table and squeezed it, telling him to play along. He understood her silent hint and obeyed, lowered his eyebrow.

She turned to Bob. "Yes, I *am* very observant, Bob. And I also can't help but notice you weren't actually invited here tonight, were you?"

Bob laughed. "What? Well, I mean… Lu didn't plan on me being here, but—"

"And she doesn't *want* you here, does she?" Maria interrupted.

Cling. Lu's spoon dropped out of her hand and hit the glass bowl. Her mouth dropped open.

"Maria," Elisabeth scolded her, "please, don't be rude and make assumptions you might not know anything about."

"Oh, I know a lot more than you'd think." Maria smiled. "Be warned, Bob."

He now stared at her, his naturally green eyes meeting her feisty hazel ones with the emerald-green flecks taking over.

"You just came here to intimidate Lu, didn't you?"

"Excuse me?"

"Maria, no, no lo hagas!" Martina shook her head.

Don't do it? Maria raised her eyebrows. *Guess Mamá knows what I'm about to do. She knows me well.*

"Do what?" Lu's shrill voice cut through the air.

Maria turned to Lu now, a smile on her face. "Oh, Mamá means I shouldn't expose him right now—but I think it's time."

"What?" Elisabeth and Aaron said at the same time. All eyes on Maria now.

"Bob, I'm afraid your little game is over." She turned to him and noticed that he looked shocked. *He either knows what's coming or is a good actor. Guess we'll find out.*

"*Game?* I'm not playing any games, young lady," Bob said, both eyebrows raised. "I have no idea what you're talking about."

"No? You don't? Should we ask Lu how, exactly, you know each other?" Maria glanced back at Lu, whose face was almost white, starkly contrasting her dark hair and big brown eyes.

"You met years ago in Utah, on that Air Force base there, didn't you?"

"Utah?" Elisabeth said. "At Hill AFB?"

"Yes, Mom. Lu was stationed there as a young Airman, as you know. And so was our big shot pilot here." Maria pointed at Bob. "She worked under you in some capacity, didn't she?"

"No, I didn't work *for* him. I just made sure his pilot certifications were in order," Lu said. "I didn't even work *for* him."

"I see," Maria said, and continued, "But you, Bob, you noticed her, didn't you? 'Cuz she was—still is—very pretty, isn't she?"

She waited for him to say something, but he just stared at her, his green eyes piercing through her, as if he wanted to kill her with his look.

"And somehow, Bob, you got to her, didn't you? Not quite sure how—maybe you can enlighten us later? I bet when you met her, you just couldn't help but notice how pretty she was, huh? And you weren't satisfied with just 'looking,' you wanted more, didn't you? But she didn't. But who says no to a hotshot pilot, a famous superior, right? Who would dare?"

Bob stared at Maria, his lips pressed together, just looked at her without saying a word.

Then Maria noticed the color leaving Elisabeth's face. Her mom's eyes were darting back and forth between Lu and Bob. Martina was looking down, staring at her half-empty bowl. Aaron shifted in his seat next to her. Maria glanced at him briefly. He was scratching his throat and seemed a bit absent-minded, surprising considering the circumstances. But Maria couldn't worry about that right now. She turned back to Bob, her lips pursed.

"And then, Bob, you did the unthinkable, didn't you? You just *needed* to have her, so you forced yourself on her, more than once, I bet, used your rank to—"

Elisabeth interrupted her, "Maria, you can't just accuse someone of… of…" She stopped talking when she saw Aaron shift in his seat while scratching his throat, grasping his belly. Sweat bubbled on his forehead.

He jumped up. "I feel like I'm gonna be sick. Excuse me." They all watched as he ran down the hallway and disappeared into the bathroom.

Is he okay? Aaron's strange behavior distracted Maria momentarily from her mission.

Elisabeth found her words again. "Maria, you can't just accuse an innocent man of—"

"*Innocent*? Are you serious? This guy over here…" She pointed at Bob. "He is *not* innocent at all. He's Lu's abuser."

They all stared at him.

Bob jumped up. "This is absurd. How *dare* you accuse me of such nonsense. Such a crime. I'm appalled. I'm an old friend of Lu's. An old friend and supporter. Just like I said. Come on, tell them, Lulu-girl."

"'Lulu-girl'? Oh my gosh…" Elisabeth threw her hands over her mouth and glanced at Lu. "Maria is right, isn't she? I remember you

told me that high-ranking guy always called you Lulu-girl when he…"
Her voice broke in horror, and a single tear ran down her face.

Lu bit her lower lip, but everyone could tell the lip was quivering;
her nostrils flared as she tried to breathe normally. She was still as white
as a sheet, clearly unsure what to do.

Maria could tell Lu's mind was racing. She saw her look down
at her half-empty glass dessert bowl, her shoulders sunken in. Maria
glanced at Bob. He was still standing at the end of the table, just staring,
staring straight at Lu now, and Maria sensed then he had some sort of
power over Lu. *He's intimidating her with his stare, his stature, his clout.
Maybe if I stand up to face him, she will, too? Maybe that'll help give her
confidence to finally stand up to her abuser—literally stand up.*

Determined, Maria hopped up quickly and abruptly. In her haste
her chair fell over, and her phone slipped out from underneath her and
crashed onto the floor. Everyone saw it.

"Are you fucking recording this?" Bob pointed at the phone, which
lay face up, the red recording button obvious even from a distance.

Oh no. What have I done?

"Are you fucking out of your mind? That's *so* illegal, young lady.
You'll definitely be hearing from my lawyers, not only for recording a
conversation without consent but also for accusing me of committing
a heinous crime that—"

"You actually did it, didn't you?" Elisabeth now stood up and
pointed at Bob. "Of course you did. That whole cutesy name-calling
gave you away. You messed up. Lu already confirmed you met at Hill,
where the crime took place. She confided in me a year later, after the
predator had left. After *you* left."

Bob stared at Elisabeth now, his face red. Elisabeth was still pointing
at him, her finger shaking a little. "And now I finally remember: you
were stationed there around the time we got there but then left for
a new assignment. Our time on base only overlapped a little, didn't
it, General Jones? I knew that last name sounded familiar when you
introduced yourself to me and Martina. You were at Hill, then at Eglin,

weren't you? Of course, Eglin's base commander. Now I see it. We even talked to you once or twice—"

"Elisabeth, that's nonsense; me being stationed at the same bases as you doesn't prove anything—"

"No, she's right." Lu jumped up. "You messed up. Calling me Lulu-girl in front of them fucked it all up. I did share that detail with Elisabeth back then. Not your name, just what you did and what you called me while you did it."

Bob burst into laughter. "So, what now, Lulu-girl? What now?"

"We'll send you to jail, you asshole," Elisabeth yelled at him. "She'll finally get the justice she deserves." Still pointing, standing tall, she suddenly buckled over and held her belly. "Oh… I feel so sick…." She glanced back up at him. "*You* make me sick, you asshole. Abuser. You deserve to rot in jail…." She sat back down and held her stomach tight.

"Mom, you okay?" Maria watched as Elisabeth rocked back and forth in her chair, holding her belly, stricken with pain. *And Aaron is sick, too? What's going on?*

The moment Maria's attention lapsed, Bob bent down, picked up her phone, and ended the recording. "No, don't—" Maria reached for her phone, but he stepped out of reach, holding the phone above his head.

"I'm just helping you get out of doing something illegal, young lady," he told her, and grinned. "Much better this way. Now, let's hear from Lu. She's the only one who really knows the whole truth, isn't she? And I'm telling you, you're all wrong."

Maria didn't know what to do. *He has my phone. Aaron is gone, Mom is in pain, and Mamá?* She glanced over to Martina and noticed her fumbling with her purse. She tightly pressed it against her belly. *Does she have a bellyache, too? She always presses something against her belly when it's hurting her.*

"Mamá?" Maria said, but Martina seemed not to hear her, just stared at the table in front of her.

Maria turned to Bob. "Give me back my phone. Right now."

He grinned and held it high. *He knows I can't reach it. I'm tall, but he's much taller. Over six feet for sure.*

"I'll hand you back your precious phone in a minute, but first I think we need to hear from Lu." He pointed at her. "She *could* identify me right now in front of you all and get her revenge. Take me to court, somehow convince a jury that I was the one who attacked her, assaulted her over twenty years ago—oh, good luck with that pesky statute of limitations, by the way." He grinned. "Even if they agree to prosecute such an old case, the courts will look at *everything*, and I mean *everything*. Uncover *every* detail, no secrets."

Maria raised her eyebrows. *Why did he put such an emphasis on everything? Twice?* She looked at Lu. Her lip was still quivering.

"Excuse me for a second, I need water." Lu picked up her empty water glass, turned around, and strode into the kitchen. She filled up her glass at the sink.

Maria watched her through the pass-through above the island. *Why is she filling up her water at the sink, not the fridge?* She thought she heard cutlery clattering faintly. *Is she fumbling with something in there? Can't see over the kitchen island's ornamental wall.*

Before Maria could ponder it any further, Lu burst into the dining room and ran over to where Elisabeth was sitting in her chair, still holding her belly, rocking back and forth. Lu stood behind Elisabeth's chair, a tall kitchen knife in her hand. The same knife Elisabeth had used to carve the chicken with.

"Lu, what the heck are you—" Maria froze midsentence when Lu grabbed Elisabeth by her short hair to lift her head and held the knife to her throat.

"¡Dios mío! Lu!" Martina yelled, then clutched her purse again, leaning over it while sitting.

Maria's thoughts raced. *I have to do something!*

Carefully, she took a step closer to the other side of the table to get to her mom, but Lu noticed and pushed the knife further into

Elisabeth's neck. "Don't you dare, Maria, or you'll lose your precious mom *again*," Lu growled, her voice suddenly so dark, so unfamiliar.

Maria stopped in her tracks. She glanced at her mom. Elisabeth's eyes were wide, her face pale, sweat coating her forehead. Tiny bubbles coated the corners of her mouth. *She's in shock. And sick? Bellyache, like Aaron? But that looks much worse than a bellyache....* She glanced over her shoulder down the hallway. *Where the heck is he? I need him. We really need him.*

"Nobody move!" Lu yelled. "Nobody."

What the heck is going on here? Who the heck is Lu? Not a friend but an enemy? I can't believe it. I did this, by calling out Bob? Oh no. It's all my fault. Oh my gosh, it's all my fault.

A tear ran down Maria's face, right over the freckles on her nose, the same freckles and nose Elisabeth had. The tear dripped onto the seat of Aaron's chair.

Someone needs to do something. This situation has gotten out of hand. We need help!

CHAPTER 53

We need help. Martina glanced at Lu, who was standing one seat over from her, her knife to Elisabeth's throat. *This situation has gotten out of hand. And it's all my fault. I should have never told Maria what Lu told me. She confided in me, and I immediately blurted out her secret to my daughter. Now look what's happened, Lu's out of her mind. I should never have told Maria.*

Martina glanced over at Maria, who was standing there behind the table, her back unbowed. *She looks strong, but I know she's helpless. I know she's trying not to cry.* Martina saw a tear roll off her nose and drip onto Aaron's chair. *And what's going on with Aaron? We need him.* Martina felt her own belly growl, felt the piercing pain that had been building, bubbling up into her esophagus. *Elisabeth seems to have a bellyache, too. Strange.*

"Nobody move," Lu yelled again. "That includes you, Bob!"

He laughed out loud. "Me? Guess what, Lulu-girl, I don't care if Elisabeth lives or dies. Do what you want. I love seeing you like this, Lulu-girl. A strong woman. It's very sexy."

Sexy? Martina scrunched her eyebrows. *What the heck?*

And then she understood. She understood what was going on, knew what she had to do.

She glanced at Bob, then at Maria, saw that her daughter was about to yell something, but Martina knew she had to beat Maria to the punch. She turned to face Lu and said, "Lu, please. Listen. Listen to him."

"What?" Lu's hand was shaking, the knife skittering along Elisabeth's neck, scoring small nicks that bled.

"Look at what he's *doing*, Lu," Martina said. "He called you *sexy*. That's all he sees in you, no matter what you do. Is it sexy to take your friend hostage? The one who was going to help you? No, it is not. It is not sexy to anyone. That word doesn't even describe it correctly. This situation is best described as scary. Do you feel like you're taking hold of the situation, being powerful, dominant? Maybe. But to him, it's just sexy. That's all this is to him. To him, you'll always be an object. An object of lust. Someone to play with."

Lu's lip quivered even more, her hand freely shaking. Her grip around the knife slackened. She let up on Elisabeth's throat.

"You're more than that, Lu. You're a strong woman *and* you can do what I couldn't until it was too late: You can get rid of your abuser. You can cut the ties to him."

Lu's big brown eyes started watering. Martina saw it. *She's listening to me. I can do this. I know she's afraid, she feels ashamed, but I need to let her know we're here for her. And we'll get him this time.*

Martina glanced into her purse and was assured her cell phone was recording. She looked up. "Lu, I know what he did to you. Elisabeth knows. This man abused his power, he used his rank to intimidate you. He still is."

"What the fuck you talking about, woman?" Bob yelled, his eyebrows bunched, his hands in fists now, one firmly grasping Maria's phone.

"He bribed you," Martina continued, focused on Lu alone. "He bribed you with your degree, helped you go high in the Air Force. Was that a crime? Yes—but not yours. You shouldn't be ashamed of it. You were abused. Taken advantage of. *You're the victim* here, *he* committed the crime. And should you be ashamed?"

A tear escaped Lu's eye and dripped onto Elisabeth's head. Martina shook her head. "No, you shouldn't be ashamed at all. He's the bad one here, he used you—and yes, he gave you opportunities, but *you yourself* are the one who made something out of them. You yourself got to the rank you are now. You yourself are the one who worked for what you have accomplished and achieved. *Just you—not him.*"

"Shut the fuck up, woman! It's none of your business," Bob yelled.

But Martina kept going. Out of the corner of her eye, she saw Maria smile. "You, Lu, are the strong one. You deserve what you've done with your life. You are strong. And you don't need to listen to him now. Don't be his puppet any longer. Let Elisabeth go and know who your real enemy is. That guy over there."

Lu lowered the knife. It hung limp at her side. Elisabeth dared to take a breath again.

"And you know what, Lu?" Martina looked deep into her eyes. "Elisabeth only forgot about you *because of him*. Because of Bob."

Lu stared at Martina. "What?"

"What the fuck, woman? Stop talking, right now!" Bob lurched toward Martina, arms outstretched, when they all heard a toilet flush. He stopped still. Everyone couldn't help but glance down the hallway.

Martina took the opportunity and pointed at Bob. "Maria figured it out. This guy is Bullet. He's the one who orchestrated her kidnapping twenty years ago so that Elisabeth wouldn't—"

"Shut the fuck up," Bob yelled. He climbed over the table to get at Martina, fists clenched.

Martina winced and closed her eyes. *Guess I knew this was going to happen. He's gonna get me.* She waited for the blows to come.

"No," Maria yelled. Martina heard a scrambling of feet moving fast, followed by a high-pitched scream to her left, a darker scream to her right, and suddenly, something hot and sticky dripped onto her shoulder.

What the heck? She opened her eyes and found Maria standing opposite her, staring wide-eyed, her mouth open in horror. Martina glanced at Elisabeth sitting next to her, still crumbled over in her chair. Lu wasn't there.

And then there came a low groan and a moan next to her ear, so close, the red stickiness still dripping onto her shoulder. Martina realized it was blood. Bob's blood. He was standing over her, moaning in pain, grasping his upper arm. Martina glanced over her shoulder and found Lu directly behind her, her warm breath against her neck. The bloody knife raised, ready to take another slice at Bob.

"You? It was *you*? You took Elisabeth's child away from her to make sure she forgot about me? What the fuck? I knew you were evil, I knew you were cruel, but taking it out on my friend and her little daughter? You are despicable, Bullet. I hate you, I absolutely hate you!" Tears were streaming down her face. "You took another child from another woman. How dare you. Two women lost their children because of you!"

"Shit, what the fuck did you do?" Bob growled at Lu. He was still holding his upper arm, blood dripping through his fingers. "How dare you assault me, Lulu? Are you out of your fucking mind? And talking about children? The fuck! You didn't lose a child, Lulu, it was just a bloody little fleck coming out of you."

"You *monster*!" Lu screamed, and stepped closer to him, knife raised. "I should use this knife on you just like you used that dirty, long needle on me to make me abort. Who said I didn't want a child? Even if it was yours, it was a part of me, and I would've loved it no matter what. But you took my child away from me, took away any chance of ever having children again—all because you needed to *kill the evidence*. You left me broken, heartbroken, my body broken. It's all because of you. You're a monster!" She started sobbing but held tight to the knife pointed at him.

"Come on, Lulu-girl, I always did what was best for you, always had your career in mind. I supported you all these years, put you through

345

college then made sure you were always first in line for promotion. A child would've ruined your career."

Lu shook her head, tears dripping down her face. "No, it wouldn't have ruined my career. It would have ruined yours! Because then I would have had evidence of everything you've done to me."

"Come on, Lulu-girl, it's not about that and I—"

"Shut the fuck up, Bob," Lu yelled over him. "*You* listen to *me* now! It's over, Bullet, it's over. Your reputation will forever be tarnished, your name spat on for generations to come, you will rot in jail for everything you did to Elisabeth and me. How dare you take her child. An innocent little toddler you took away. Wanted to drown. All this to hide your pathetic secret?"

He laughed. "Well, it worked, didn't it?"

Elisabeth gasped, tears running down her cheeks. "Oh my gosh, it *was* you?"

Martina glanced at Maria, who was just standing there. *Poor mija. She's in shock. And so is Elisabeth.* Martina glanced into her purse. *But we got him. It's all recorded. We got him.*

Through Bob's cruel laughter, Martina heard an angry, loud growl. It was Lu. "You incredible monster—ruining the lives of those around you just to make yours better? You deserve to go to hell for this," Lu screamed.

Martina heard a loud crash, turned in time to see Lu jump Bob and start swinging her arm, stabbing him wildly, plunging the knife into whatever body part she could reach. "I will fucking kill you like you killed my child," Lu growled. "I will hurt you for all the times you've hurt me. I will—"

"Stop, Lu, stop!" yelled a man's voice, and Martina saw Aaron come running from down the hallway, directly at Lu, who continued to stab at Bob relentlessly. They had fallen to the floor and he was on his back, trying to shield himself from her knife attack.

"Aaron," Maria screamed, "Aaron, make her stop. Please, make her stop."

Despite looking sickly and weak, Aaron skillfully avoided Lu's frantic stabbing, somehow managed to grab her hand with his uninjured hand and overpower her. His whole body shaking, he held her hand gripping the knife over her head, held it tight to keep it from swinging. He looked deep into her dark-brown eyes. "Lu, please. You don't want this. Please don't kill him. He deserves it, but *you* don't. You don't deserve to go to jail for killing him. You deserve justice, not jail yourself."

"Lu, Aaron's right," Elisabeth said. "You need to stop. We'll get justice, the police will come, so please, stop this."

A big sob escaped Lu's throat and she suddenly dropped the knife. Martina watched it fall to the ground. *CLANG.* It hit the wooden floor, blood splattering on impact.

¡Dios mío! I don't know what to say. Didn't see that coming.

Maria ran around to their side of the table. She kneeled beside Aaron, who was holding Lu, while Bob writhed on the ground. "Here, Maria, take care of Lu," Aaron instructed. "I need to assess his injuries."

Maria nodded and dragged Lu away, until they were nestled between Martina and Elisabeth. "Come on, Lu. It's okay. We're okay now."

Lu hugged Maria tight, her hand leaving a bloody handprint on Maria's yellow summer dress. She was sobbing, her body jerking up with every deep sob she took. Maria rocked her back and forth like a little baby. "Ssshhh… it's alright, it's alright. Está bien, Lu, está bien."

A slight smile crossed Martina's face. *Mija. She comforts Lu just like I used to comfort Maria when she was little.* She glanced up at Elisabeth. She looked so pale and was rocking back and forth in her chair, holding her stomach. Martina felt the pain in her own belly. *It hurts. Elisabeth is in pain. Something is not right.*

"Will… will he really go… really… go… to jail?" Lu asked between sobs. "We still… don't… you know… have evidence… of his crimes…."

"But we do." Martina sat up tall, despite wanting to keep pressing the purse against her belly. "We do have evidence." Maria, Lu, and Elisabeth all looked at her. With shaky hands, Martina pulled her phone out of her purse. In front of their eyes, clicked the little red button to stop recording.

Maria forgot her shock for a minute and beamed at Martina. "No way, Mamá! You got him, you made a recording of him confessing. So clever. You're amazing."

With a tired look on her face, Martina winked at her daughter. "Learned from the best."

Lu suddenly sat up on the floor and looked at Bob from underneath the table. "Aaron, is he... is he... okay?" Lu turned back to the three ladies, her lip quivering. "I've ruined everything. I shouldn't have attacked him. It was stupid." Tears back in her eyes.

Elisabeth touched Lu's shoulder. "It's okay, Lu, it'll be okay."

"I think he'll be fine," Aaron said loudly. "Looks like minor injuries. It's a miracle you didn't hit any major organs. Just muscle, mostly on his arms, I think."

Elisabeth slightly smiled at Lu. "See. He'll be fine and go to jail. We got him, Lu, we finally got him."

Martina studied Elisabeth's face. *Behind the smile, she's hiding pain. I can see it. She feels sick.*

Without warning, Elisabeth leaned over to the side and threw up.

"Oh no, are you okay, Elisabeth?" Martina jumped up but had to sit back down. Her own stomach was hurting terribly. She felt dizzy and suddenly bent over and threw up herself.

Maria let go of Lu and jumped up. "Mom, Mamá? What's going on? Are you okay?"

Before Martina could answer, they heard grunting and groaning coming from across the room. Aaron's voice carried to their ears. "He's fighting me. Help. I need help. I'm weak. Help me, Maria. Come on, get my belt off."

His belt off? Martina was confused and tried not to vomit again, tried to ignore the spasm in her stomach. She could see Maria's confusion as well.

"Help me, quick. He's fighting me. I'm too weak to hold him down. I need to tie him up. Get my belt," Aaron yelled over his shoulder. Martina could see he was struggling to keep Bob down on the floor.

Maria rushed over, unbuckled Aaron's belt, and slipped it out of his jean shorts. "Good, Maria. Now, loop the end of the belt back through the buckle to create a figure eight. It'll create two loops we can use as makeshift handcuffs."

Martina watched as Maria fumbled with the belt. After a few tries she succeeded, and handed Aaron the homemade handcuffs. Aaron managed to force Bob's hands through the loops, tightened them, then dragged him over to the table and looped the belt around one of the table's legs. Bob fought and struggled, but then gave up, and just looked at everyone.

Aaron dropped to the ground as soon as Bob was tied up. "Oh man, my belly is cramping so bad."

Martina perked up. *Something is not right! This is strange.* "You said your belly is hurting, Aaron?"

He nodded. "Yeah, really bad cramps. I threw up a few times. That's why I rushed to the bathroom."

Martina raised her eyebrows. "Mine is hurting, too. I just threw up a little. So did Elisabeth."

"What?" Maria looked back and forth between her loved ones.

Elisabeth nodded. "Yes, bad cramps. And sweating. Profuse sweating. My throat is so itchy, too."

"Mine, too." Aaron doubled over in pain. "And these cramps, argh!"

"What's going on?" Maria asked, her voice shrill. "Lu?"

Lu was holding her stomach as well, rocking back and forth on the ground Elisabeth's and Martina's chairs. "It hurts. Bad cramps."

Martina's eyes darted back and forth across the room. She felt dizzy, so very dizzy. The room started spinning. *Oh no, this is not good. Not good. I feel like I'm about to pass out.* She glanced at Elisabeth, who was so pale. Her pretty blue eyes opened wide. Martina saw them cross, then Elisabeth fell sideways out of her chair.

"Oh my gosh, she passed out," Maria yelled, and rushed over to Elisabeth's side.

Oh no. Martina's thoughts were spinning along with the room. *Mija. Watch out. Something is not right!*

CHAPTER 54

"**S**omething's not right, sir," Lieutenant Martinez yelled through the phone. "They were having dessert, then there was a commotion, and now I don't see anyone sitting at the table anymore. As if they all fell to the floor or something."

Oh no. Oh no, no, no. Chief Parlot drove as quickly as he could. *Maria is in danger again, and we allowed it to happen....*

"Martinez!" Tonya yelled. "Get eyes on them again. If they're in distress, get in there ASAP. Got it? Keep us posted. We'll be there shortly."

Tonya hung up the phone and sighed. "Come on, my man Isaac, step on the gas."

Chief Parlot obliged. He not only drove faster but also turned on the sirens full blast. They were rushing past the big buildings on base now, screaming through the dark night. "Call for more backup, Tonya."

"What do you mean? Sally already alerted the base police, and we're not sure if—"

"We are *not* taking any chances anymore. We can't mess up again. Goodness, Maria is in danger again. Under *our* supervision. With not only one, but two lethal enemies that mean to do her harm."

Tonya patted him on the shoulder. "Don't worry, Isaac, we'll be there very soon. But you're right, I'll call for more backup."

Within minutes, everything was set. The chief listened to Tonya give instructions to everyone. "Yes, meet us at the Distinguished Visitor's Quarters. Roll in lights off, no sirens, please." He heard her laugh. "Oh yes, I'll tell him, of course. Thanks. See you there."

The chief glanced at Tonya. "What's so funny?"

"I just told everyone to roll in quietly—yet here we are, waking the whole base up single-handedly." She smirked.

"What?"

"Come on, my man Isaac. You gotta turn off the sirens. Otherwise, they'll hear us coming from a mile away."

"Oh, got it." The chief pushed a button and the sirens cut out. "Better now?"

Tonya nodded. "Much better."

"Good, then we're all set?"

"I think so." Tonya smiled at him, then frowned. "Relax, Isaac, relax. We'll make it. It'll be fine."

"Let's hope so," he mumbled. "Lieutenant Martinez's report was less than encouraging. Any updates from him?"

She checked her phone, then shook her head, avoiding the chief's intense stare. She sighed. "Would it help you feel better if we called him again?"

Chief Parlot couldn't help but grin. *She knows me so well already, after a short time together. She's been a great partner, I have to say. Wish she worked here all the time.* He sighed now. *But if she did, it would mean we'd be dealing with other big FBI cases all the time. And I kinda want it to go back to the way it was. My quiet little precinct.*

Tonya speed-dialed Lieutenant Martinez's number, and he picked up the phone immediately. Tonya put him on loudspeaker. "Lieutenant, what's happening? Any other news?"

"No, I tried to get closer to the house to see what was going on and the floodlights came on."

Chief Parlot couldn't believe his ears. "You set off the perimeter lights? Very subtle, Lieutenant."

"I'm sorry," Lieutenant Martinez said. "I thought I could sneak a peek through the window to see what's going on. I didn't know the house is equipped with perimeter lights, apparently not only by every corner but every other foot."

"Oh, man. Sucks. Anyway, what did you see?" Tonya asked.

"Nothing. The lights are so bright it's impossible to see inside with them right now. Since the lights were on already and surely gave my position away to any bogeys inside, I tried the front door. But it's locked. I couldn't get in and just went back to my car."

Chief Parlot shook his head and pushed the gas pedal down to the max. *Idiot! Setting off those floodlights. Jeez!*

"What should I do now?"

"Nothing," the chief barked. "You've done enough already. Just stay in your car and out of the way."

Tonya glanced at the chief. "Yes, Lieutenant, just stay in your car. We'll be rolling in with backup any minute now."

"Okay, got it," the lieutenant said, and hung up.

Tonya shook her head. "Can you believe it, my man Isaac? Giving himself away like that…. Unreal."

"That's what we get for assigning a base police officer to the job." Chief Parlot started grinding his teeth. "We should've used one of our own guys."

Tonya raised her eyebrows. "Maybe, but to be fair, he was originally assigned to keep an eye on Martina here on base, and he did great with that. Reassigning him afterward was a matter of convenience. Who could have seen any of this coming?"

Chief Parlot nodded. *She's right. We couldn't have foreseen it. This whole crazy situation. We thought it was over. We were wrong. Have to get there soon. Have to make sure they're okay.*

CHAPTER 55

*H*ave to make sure they're okay. I have to. Maria looked all around her. Everyone was passed out on the floor: her two moms, Lu, even Aaron. Only Bob was wide-awake, struggling with the belt that bound him.

Maria went from person to person, making sure they were still breathing okay and lying in the rescue position. The bright floodlights outside blinded her as she leaned over Elisabeth. *It's so bright. Guess an animal scurrying by set it off?*

Her mom's eyelids fluttered. Maria smiled. "Mom, you're awake! You're okay. How are you feeling?"

Elisabeth looked around. She seemed disoriented. "Dizzy. My stomach hurts."

Maria sighed. "I figured that much. Everyone is sick. Not me, though."

"Gut, mein Engel, good." Elisabeth lifted her hand and stroked Maria's cheek. "Why is it so bright in here?"

Maria shrugged. "I guess the outdoor lights came on."

"Oh, good, police are here…." Elisabeth whispered, then closed her eyes again.

Police? Maria jumped up. *Of course! Lieutenant Martinez is outside. I'll go get him. Right now.*

She turned to head down the hallway, then stopped when she heard her mamá call out, her voice weak. "Mija, come back."

Without hesitation, Maria doubled back and went to her mamá's side. She kneeled down next to her and also glanced at Lu. She was lying on the floor, breathing steadily, but appeared comatose. Martina pointed at Aaron. "Mija, check Aaron. Looks like something is coming from his mouth."

What? Maria pivoted on her knees to check on Aaron again. *She's right. There's something coming out of his mouth. Looks like... like... foam?* She screamed. "Oh my gosh, Mamá, Aaron's mouth is foaming. It's like he's..."

"Poisoned?"

Maria's mouth was all dry. She nodded. "I need to call Poison Control. Where's my phone?"

"Bullet had it," Martina reminded her. "But mine should be on the table, or in my purse. Use that. Think we all got poisoned."

Maria shook her head, tears welling in her eyes. "How did this happen?"

Loud, evil laughter filled the room. A dark male voice full of hate.

"Bullet," Martina whispered. "He must have done something. In the food maybe?"

"But I had the food also. I'm not sick."

The laughter turned into an evil chuckle interspersed with grunts. The dining room table began to rattle.

"Think, mija, you'll figure this out. You always figure things out. You're smart. Te amo." Martina stroked her daughter's cheek the same way Elisabeth had earlier.

"I love you, too, Mamá. But don't tell me that now. It almost seems like you're saying goodbye to me...."

"Go... call Poison Control... police... anyone...." Martina's eyelids fluttered. "Take care of Aaron...."

Maria took her mamá's hand off her cheek and squeezed it tightly. "I'll take care of it, I will. Hang in there. All of you."

With that said, she got up and looked for her mamá's phone. *Should be close by. Don't even know where he threw mine.* She found Martina's phone on the table next to her half-eaten dessert bowl.

That terrible dessert… disgusting. Maria shook herself. *Wait a minute. Didn't Bob serve the dessert? Did he put something in it that made everyone sick?* Her eyes turned bright green as the realization sunk in. *He must have. He barely touched his, and I didn't eat much myself. Just one spoonful. But Aaron had seconds.*

Oh no, Aaron.

Quickly, Martina's phone in her hand, she dropped to the floor to check on Aaron again. He was breathing, but a slight foam was still pooling at the corners of his mouth and dribbling down to the floor. *What did Bullet put in the dessert?*

She tried to block out Bullet's chuckles. *He's enjoying this? How can someone enjoy watching other human beings get sick like this? Only someone who's already sick himself. A sick person like him.* Her face turned completely red. *I'll make him tell me.*

She crawled around Aaron over to where Bullet was tied to the table. He was laughing weakly, his arms bleeding from multiple stab wounds. She eyed him. *Superficial wounds. Only the arms seem to be bleeding, nothing else. That's weird. Lu stabbed him so many times. She must have at least sliced into muscle all along his torso? Very strange.* She sighed. *Seems Aaron was right. It's nothing too serious. But it must be painful. This asshole deserves pain.*

She stared at him, directly into his green eyes, his crow's-feet clearly visible as he chuckled. "Stop with the *sick laughing*, asshole, and tell me what you used in the dessert. Now!" She crossed her arms in front of her, Martina's phone still in her hand.

He stopped laughing, but smirked now, gave her an approving nod. "Well, well, clever young lady. You figured it out, huh? Impressive."

Maria scrunched in her eyebrows. "This was your master plan? Poison us all? And then what? How could you possibly explain that away?" She set her mamá's phone on the table and started recording, careful to keep it out of his line of sight.

"Simple. I would've told everyone Lu was behind it. It was her food anyway, her cooking. And she didn't want you guys to find out her career was a fake."

"There was nothing fake about it. She worked her way up through the ranks."

"Sure, sure, sure, you can believe whatever you wanna believe. Fine. But the police wouldn't have. I would've told them about my support after she was raped."

"Yeah, *by you*," Maria screamed. "There's no way you would have talked your way out of that. Or my kidnapping."

"No?" He laughed again. "You're wrong. I would've told them I only gave her money to help my son."

Maria raised her eyebrows. "'Help your son'? What are you talking about?"

He laughed again. "Thought you were the smart one here."

Maria thought for a bit. "You mean Mike Clifford?"

"Of course, he's not my real son, he replaced my firstborn. But I loved him just the same, like my own flesh and blood. I took him in, built him up again."

Now it was Maria's turn to chuckle. "Yeah, nice going there, Bullet. You built him up so he could become a criminal. Like you. Great parenting job there."

"Shut the fuck up!" he yelled. "You have no idea. I gave him everything he needed to find success in politics, to go as far as he did."

"But that has nothing to do with you assaulting Lu, does it? Or my kidnapping. We all know Mike Clifford just worked for you."

"So what? What if it was the other way round? What if *Mike* had assaulted Lu and not me? What if I bribed her to keep her mouth shut and save *his* ass? What if he planned it all by himself?"

"What?" Maria was confused. She closed her eyes for a second and took a deep breath in. *He's messing with me. Think, just think. You got him on the recording.*

She opened her eyes again. He had moved his legs closer to his belly and was lying in a fetal position now, his hands still tied to the table leg. "You're lying. You can't play your twisted mind games with me. You're the mastermind behind all this, I know it. Everything else is just a lie."

He chuckled again. "A good lie anyone would believe."

"Too bad I'm not *just anyone*, Bullet," Maria yelled.

He smirked. "No, you're not. You're feisty, a fighter. You were supposed to die that night. I planned it all so carefully. So perfectly. As soon as I found out Lulu-girl was going to that stupid H.O.P.E. Club, I knew she'd break down eventually and tell on me. She's weak like that, you know. Not strong like you."

Maria stared at him as he went on. "And as soon as I found out the lady who ran that club would be moving to Eglin, where I was already stationed at the time, I started planning. I knew the only way to make Elisabeth stop digging into Lulu-girl's case was to distract her. And not a minor distraction. Something that would preoccupy her mind completely. Destroying her meant destroying any chance of her ratting me out."

Maria started shaking, her face red. "You asshole."

He laughed. "Whatever, young lady. Guess what? Mike was so excited to be a part of it. He could finally get revenge on Brad Collins. He knew losing his child would break him. And boy was he right."

Maria tried to hold back her tears. "Bastards. The both of you. Assholes. Jerks. Unbelievable bastards."

"We were smart though. And, you know you were supposed to die, right?"

Maria nodded. Tried to hold back her tears, then screamed, "But I didn't, you asshole! I didn't die, I didn't give up. And I won't tonight either. You'll go to jail for everything you did. Just watch."

Maria jumped up, braced herself against the table with one hand and stopped the recording with the other. She stood up and began to dial the police when a foot kicked her legs so hard her knees buckled. She crashed to the floor. Martina's phone flew out of her hand. Maria landed underneath the table right next to Bullet, who grinned at her.

"No, mija...." croaked Martina's weak voice.

Maria scrambled to her hands and knees. Her legs burned. *Oh no. Where did the phone go?* She scanned the room and saw it in the corner on the floor, underneath the window, next to the plant.

"Oh, so clumsy, that's too bad. Guess you can't call the cops now," Bullet said. "But don't worry, I think they're outside already. At least the one you brought. I saw the lights come on earlier. Bet they were checking on you."

Maria turned to look out of the window. *That's right, Lieutenant Martinez. I just need to get to him. He can put a stop to this.* Maria pushed herself to her feet, then turned to glance at Bullet, and couldn't believe her eyes. He was sitting up, the belt dangling from one of his wrists. He held a tiny little revolver in his other hand.

"How did you…"

"Get free?"

She nodded and swallowed hard.

He grinned. "You forget, young lady, I was in the Air Force for a long time. Learned a few tricks along the way. More than your young Airman here." He pointed at Aaron with the gun. "And as for this—don't need a concealed carry license in Texas nor here in Florida. People store their guns in bags, around their waist, in their cowboy boots all the time." He pointed to his boots, then held up the gun again. "This baby goes with me wherever I go." He patted the tiny revolver. "That darned Second Amendment, right? God bless the US of A."

Maria stared at him. "But how can you stand to hold it? How'd you have the strength to get out of the cuffs? I thought you were very—"

"Hurt?" Bob interrupted her again. "Oh, yes, yes. Lu got some good stabs in and really did slice my poor arms up, but I can handle a little pain. Luckily, that was all she could get away with. Everything else is protected." He unbuttoned a button on his shirt and revealed a thick, black inner layer. "Body armor. Military-issue. Still fits. Sure comes in handy sometimes." He grinned.

"Mija, gun," Maria heard her mamá whisper.

"Maria, watch out," Elisabeth's weak voice carried over to them.

Bob laughed out loud. "Oh, your two moms are worried about you. And regaining a bit of strength, huh? Yeah, they might make it, especially if they drink a lot of water. Guess they didn't have as much yummy dessert as this young man here." He kicked Aaron.

Aaron moaned.

"Stop it," Maria yelled, tears in her eyes. "Leave him alone." She dropped down to her knees to take care of Aaron.

"Get up," Bob demanded, and pointed the gun at her. "I need you to go to the window to tell your police friend everything's okay in here. Go! Now!"

"What? You can't make me."

Laughter. Loud, evil laughter. "I can't, huh?"

Maria shook her head. "No, you can't." She turned around and sat face to face with him. "I don't care if I walk out of here alive anymore."

"No, mija."

"Nein, mein Engel."

But Maria ignored her moms. *I need to be strong and play his game for now.*

She lifted her chin and looked deep into his eyes. "Fine, then. Go ahead, Bullet. Shoot me. Get me out of this nightmare, just end it all. Go ahead. Have fun explaining that to the police. Maybe crazy Lu did it? Or Aaron turned on me because he's had enough? Or will you have to think up another good story to tell when I'm dead?" Her green eyes bore through him.

He grinned. "Nice try, young lady. Hey, you're pretty good. Not bad ideas, actually. It really has been a pleasure meeting you. You amuse me." His grin vanished. "But you're wrong. You can't mess with me—

only *I* get to play with everyone else. 'Cuz I'm the puppet master. And I know your deepest fears."

Maria stared at him. *What the heck is he talking about?*

He lowered the gun. Rested the muzzle against Aaron's head. Aaron moaned. "Now, do as I say, or he's dead."

No. Aaron. Tears rushed into Maria's eyes, turning her vision blurry. *Don't hurt Aaron.* "What do you want me to do?" she whispered.

"Like I said: go to the window, wave hello to your police friend, give him a thumbs-up, and make sure they stay away. Then close the blinds."

Maria nodded but didn't move. Her mind was racing. *I need to make him believe I'm doing what he says but give the lieutenant a different sign. But what? What can I do that Bullet won't recognize?*

"Move it," Bullet barked, then she heard him cock the gun. A shudder ran down her spine. She got up and walked to the window. The floodlights had gone dark. She glanced outside. Saw her own car and the one behind it. Lieutenant Martinez's car. "No tricks," she heard. "Or he's dead."

Her eyes wide, she waved into the darkness. Then she used both hands to gesture thumbs-up. At the same time, she mouthed the word *help*, but wasn't sure whether the lieutenant would be able to make out what she was saying, or if he was even watching.

"Good job," she heard Bullet say. There followed a shuffling sound, as if he were dragging something behind him. "Now, put your hands down and come back over here."

Maria's mind was racing. *There's a hand signal for help. An SOS. What was it again?* She thought about it for a few seconds, then remembered. As she lowered her hands, she moved them in front of her belly and tucked her thumbs into her palms. She held the gesture a few seconds, then closed the blinds and turned around to walk back as she was told.

She saw Bullet had dragged Aaron over to where the three ladies were. He had propped Aaron up in a chair. Aaron sat slumped over.

Now Bullet was busy moving the ladies about, trying to prop them up in their respective chairs.

Maria watched him. *Maybe I can attack him now?* She discarded that plan in the same breath; Bullet held the gun to each person's head whenever he moved them.

"Don't you dare try anything," he growled at her, "or I'll shoot whoever's closest at hand. Got it?"

Maria nodded.

"Good, glad we understand each other. Now, go sit over there." He pointed at a chair. "Right there, across from Aaron."

She slowly inched over to the chair he had pointed at. She knew all she could do now was wait. *What's his plan? He's absolutely crazy. I just hope someone saw my sign.… And I hope it was the right sign for help.*

CHAPTER 56

"**S**ign for help?" The chief stared at Tonya. They had just arrived, rolled up slowly behind Lieutenant Martinez's car and parked when they saw Maria at the window. Waving in their direction, giving them two thumbs-up... then holding her fist in a strange manner before closing the blinds.

"Yes, I'm telling you, Isaac, you gotta believe me," Tonya said, her face stern. "A thumb tucked into your palm, fingers folded around it? That's the universal sign for 'Help!' And Maria just did that. She gave us that sign. A sign for help."

Chief Parlot leaned across Tonya and tried to see what was happening inside the Distinguished Visitor's Quarters house. With the blinds drawn, he could only make out the outlines of people sitting at a big dinner table. "Looks like Maria sat back down at the table."

"Looks like it." Tonya pressed her nose against the car window but had no better luck telling what was happening. "We need to get closer."

Chief Parlot nodded. "Agreed. Time to storm the house. Now."

"Whoa, hold on, Chief, not so fast. We need to assess the situation first. We can't just line up around the house without having the floodlights giving all of us away. Who knows what might happen in there if they feel cornered?"

The chief sighed. "You're right. We need the element of surprise. But how do we move in without setting off those floodlights? Any ideas? Or should we set them off on purpose by sending Lieutenant Martinez to check on the guests inside? Both generals already know he's posted here."

Tonya scratched her nose. "We could do that. But if Maria and the rest are in danger, a checkup by Lieutenant Martinez might still freak those rotten generals out. We don't know yet if there's guns or other weapons involved. We don't know if we're dealing with a hostage situation. We need to assess the situation." She paused. "Hey, let's shoot them out!"

The chief raised both eyebrows. "*Shoot them out?* We can't just go shooting at—"

"The lights, I meant," Tonya quickly said. "Not the people. Shoot out the floodlight bulbs so they don't go off as we surround the house."

Chief Parlot smirked. "Ah, I see. Knew you wouldn't be so bold as to start a shoot-out right off the bat."

Tonya winked at him. "Glad you learned a thing or two about me these last few days."

"Same to you," Chief Parlot said. "Come on, partner, let's plan how best to storm that building. Backup is arriving. SWAT team's almost here. But we need a good plan. And I have to admit, I'm not very experienced in taking buildings. That's more an FBI thing to do. So, please take the lead, Agent Anderson."

"Alright, alright, alright, my man Isaac. Thanks." She gave him a friendly fist bump into the shoulder. "Let's plan this thing." Tonya's casual demeanor immediately turned grave. She took out her notepad and started scribbling on it. Then she opened the glove compartment and took out binoculars. "Here, take these, try to see what's going on inside."

Duh. Of course. We always keep binoculars in the cruiser. Should've thought of that earlier. He grabbed them, calibrated them, then peered through them. "Can't see much at all. The blinds are shut tight."

Tonya focused again on her notes. She set the notepad in her lap, took the police radio off its holder, and began to bark instructions to the others on site.

Minutes passed as the gathered authorities coordinated with one another. Chief Parlot shook his head. "No, can't see anything. No idea what's going on inside. Come on, we gotta do something."

"We will, don't worry, Chief." Tonya patted his shoulder, then spoke into the radio. "Ready. Now, team. Shoot."

Barely a sound followed, but through his binoculars the chief saw glass shards splatter the entrance steps to the house. He grinned. "The floodlights are out, it looks like."

"Told ya, my man Isaac. One step at a time. Now we can go. Come on, you and I are tagging along." She reached into the backseat and threw a police vest his way. "Put this on and let's go. The breach team is moving into position."

Chief Parlot nodded. Tonya gave instructions over the police radio again, then the chief saw a bunch of men in black make their way across the lawn and surround the house.

"You and I will slip around back. Maybe the back of the house has no blinds? Or possibly even a back door to slip into." Tonya grinned at the chief. They both got out of the car and drew their guns. The chief's heart was racing. "Come on, Isaac. We've got this. Just follow my lead and everything will be fine."

CHAPTER 57

"**J**ust follow my lead and everything will be fine," Bob told Maria. He grabbed Lu's water glass off the table and handed it to Maria. "Good job with the blinds and curtains. Now, give Lu this water. She'll feel much better after."

He saw Maria's hand shaking as she took the water from him. He grinned. *Yeah, she's scared. Told her—I'm in charge here. Not her. I decide the way things go from now on. They're my puppets. And I have the perfect puppet show planned for the police I'm certain are surrounding the house at this very moment. It'll be great.*

He watched Maria hold the water up to Lu's lips. She drank the whole glass. "More, please," Lu whispered hoarsely.

Aw, my Lulu-girl. Still so polite. So submissive. Love it. He smiled, but then his smile turned into a frown. *But you attacked me. Tried to kill me. How dare you.*

He was jarred from his thoughts when Maria stood up and walked toward the kitchen. "Where the heck are you going, young lady?"

"Lu needs more water. I was going to get—"

"No," he barked, and pressed the gun harder against Aaron's forehead. "You do as I say, or he's dead."

"But you said to give her water...."

"Stop it, you disobedient bitch," he yelled, his face bright red.

"Mija, please…." Martina whispered.

Bob heard her pleas. "Yes, your mother is right. Well, stepmother, I guess." He smirked. "She didn't do a good job raising you. You don't listen at all."

Maria plopped back into her chair. Bob stood next to Aaron, the little revolver an ever-present threat. Martina was in the chair next to Aaron's, Elisabeth further down. Lu and Maria sat next to each other opposite the others.

"There's a good girl," Bob said condescendingly.

Maria looked at him, her arms crossed. "What did you put in the dessert?"

"Oh, just your run-of-the-mill everyday household bleach. Cleans up everything." He laughed. "Even your insides."

"It's poisonous, you asshole," Maria yelled.

"Watch your tone, young lady," he scolded her. "And it's not *that* bad if you ingest just a little."

Maria pointed at Aaron. "My fiancé had *two helpings*."

Bob laughed out loud. "And look what his gluttony got him. That's why he's the sickest."

"Please just let everyone have some water." Maria folded her hands together as if in prayer. "Please." She batted her long eyelashes at him, a sweet smile on her full lips.

He started getting that tingly feeling. *She's an attractive young lady. Very pretty, very sexy.* He smiled, then silently scolded himself. *Don't let her get to you, Bullet. You're the man. You're in charge.* "No. No more water for anyone."

Maria crossed her arms again. "I hope you're not planning on letting the poison do its work, are you? I have to believe you're smarter than that."

He stared at her. *What the fuck is she talking about?*

"Before anyone can die from it, it'll be too late for you. I'm sure the police are coming. Soon, probably." She smirked.

"Smart mouth on you, young lady. It'll get you in trouble someday."

She snorted. "I'm just saying, you're doomed, Bullet. You're running out of time to play any of your games."

Sweat broke out on his forehead. *She's right, I need to be quick.*

"What's your master plan now, Bullet? Or have you already run out of ideas?"

He stared at her. *She needs to shut the fuck up. What a smug, sassy, crazy little girl. Bullet never runs out of ideas. In fact, you're about to find out, little girl, exactly what I have planned. And I'm sure it'll be a fun little game to play. Should I explain it to you now? No, I'll wait to surprise you.* He grinned back at her.

Bob glanced at Lu. *Is she strong enough to participate? She didn't eat much dessert either. Just Aaron. And the two moms had a good amount of it. Too bad. Let the show begin.*

With a swift, skilled motion, he wrapped Aaron's belt around the tip of his boot and kicked it up into his hand. Maria watched, eyes wide, as he caught it. *Good thing this amateurish attempt at a makeshift binding came loose so easily. Slipped out of it with hardly any effort. It'll come in handy now. The feisty little girl gets a front-row seat to the show.*

He took a step toward Maria and held up the belt. "This was supposed to contain me?" He laughed. "Bad, *bad* idea. Leave the planning to me. You'll see, young lady, I'm the master planner. I have big plans."

"No, please, don't do it, Bullet…." Lu whispered.

He laughed. "Oh, poor Lu. This belt brings back bad memories, doesn't it?" He savored the tears that now ran out of Lu's big brown eyes.

He was at Maria's side in an instant. She was watching his every little move with trepidation. *Yeah, keep your eye on the ball.* He lowered his gun and saw her squirm in her seat, ready to jump up and seize the opportunity, but he had anticipated that, held her down, and with one quick move looped the belt around her waist to tie her against the chair she sat in. She wiggled in place and found she could barely move as her arms were also restrained by the belt.

Bob laughed. "Well, well, little girl. Good thing you're so skinny the belt goes all the way around you and the chair. I knew it. I have a great eye for size."

"Maria," both moms tried to scream at the same time, but only whispers came out.

He laughed. "Don't overexert yourself, ladies. Too bad you're both too weak to do anything. And look at poor Aaron over there, he's still passed out!"

"What do you want, Bullet?" Lu croaked. "Please, just leave them alone."

He shook his head. "No, Lulu-girl. You know it's always fun with more than one, don't you?"

"Don't do it—she's an innocent young lady. Please. I'm right here. Play your sick games with me."

He grinned. "Very tempting, Lulu-girl. But this time, *you* will play the games *for me.*"

She shook her head as much as she was able to. "No, I refuse to do *anything* for you."

Bob left Maria's side and hovered over Lu now. He stood behind her chair and bent over her. Took a deep breath in and could smell the flowery scent in her hair, the sweet smell of a lady. He closed his eyes and smelled her neck, got lost as memory and fantasy mixed together.

Scratch, scratch.

He abruptly opened his eyes when he heard the scratching noise coming from Maria's direction. She was wiggling in her chair, trying to scoot closer to the others. "Stop moving," he yelled at her, and pointed the gun at her. Maria stopped immediately.

Powerful, these guns. He grinned, then shook his head. *I've got to focus on the mission here. Come on, Bullet. Don't give in to temptation. Don't let your weaknesses get the best of you—again.*

He exhaled, then lifted Lu's right arm. She was too weak to resist. All she could do was watch. The same with everyone else as he put the gun in her right hand, curled her fingers around it, forced her pointer finger inside the trigger guard. She tried to fight him but couldn't. She had no choice but to succumb to his game. He moved her about as if she was his puppet.

"No, please," Lu whispered. "I don't want to hold the gun."

Bob laughed. "I know, Lulu-girl. But *I* want you to. So you will! And you'll shoot when I say shoot." He enjoyed seeing the horror on the dinner guests' faces. Only Aaron's eyes were closed, his head hanging low.

"You asshole! No, don't make Lu do this. Don't!" Maria screamed.

He turned to her. "Shut the fuck up, Maria. This show is for you."

Her big, kissable lips quivered for him, tears forming in her eyes. He grinned. "*You* get to decide who lives and who dies. Lu here will carry out the executions. How's that for dinner and a show?" Everyone stared at him as his laughter filled the room. "Hahahaha...."

CHAPTER 58

*H*ahahaha…. She still heard his laughter, his cruel, evil chuckle ringing in her ears. *Oh my gosh, he can't be serious. This can't be real.* Maria tried hard not to cry and swallowed a sob. *I need to be strong. For them. For all of them. But what should I do?*

Bullet stopped laughing and turned to her. "So, Maria, who do you love most?"

Maria stared at him. "What?"

"Or should Lu start by killing the one you love the least?"

He can't be serious. Oh no, no, no. "Please, just let them go. Take me. Do whatever you want with me…."

"No, mija," Martina whispered.

"Mein Engel, don't let him," Elisabeth whispered.

But Maria was determined. In a loud voice, she said, "Take me. Play your games with me. That's all that you want, isn't it? Watching others suffer so you can get off for your own sick satisfaction?"

Bob laughed and shook his head. "Oh, Maria, Maria… you silly little girl. It's not that easy, see. While I'd love to play some fun games with you in the bedroom—on the couch, on the floor, wherever—I find you've committed a grave error. You've misjudged me."

Maria raised her eyebrows. *Misjudged him? Certainly not. He's obviously evil incarnate.*

"All I want is for folks to play by the rules. *My* rules. I want people to love me." He paused. Frowned. Gnashed his teeth.

Maria stared at him. *Love him? How could anyone love someone who acts this way?*

"You see," Bullet continued, "I lost my parents when I was very young. All I remember is that they took me to puppet shows. We had a great time there. When they passed, I was placed into foster care. It was hell on earth. And when I asked for the tiniest reprieve, asked to go see a puppet show, my foster parents refused. Said they didn't believe in such bullshit." He sighed.

Yeah, yeah, save your sob story, asshole. You're sick in the head. But Maria and the others had no choice but to listen to the man rant.

"I was punted from family to family, I didn't have any control over my own life. As soon as my parents died, so did the control over my own wishes, hopes, and dreams. A simple wish—seeing a puppet show—wasn't even granted. Nobody listened to me, everything was shattered, everyone toyed with me, as if I was a little puppet to be put in new plays, new lives, new homes."

He snorted. "I hated being played with, being put places, having to adjust. I was very sad, very mad. Had no control. Until one day, I decided to pretend my whole life was a puppet show—but I wasn't a puppet in it, I was the puppet master."

He grinned. "The people in my life became the puppets in my show. I learned to manipulate my foster siblings, then the whole foster family, and the next, and the next. I created my path in the military, became a leader, told people what to do. Just like a puppeteer, I'd command them. To my liking. They loved me for it. For my advice, my success. And guess what? I'm just enjoying this new-and-improved puppet show ever since."

"You're sick," Maria spat out. "You need to see a psychologist."

He laughed out loud, then started singing, *"All you need is love, love, love is all you need."*

"Then act like you deserve it!" Maria screamed at him. "Let us go and show some love! It'll come back around."

"No, no, no, little girl." Bullet shook his head. "You see, love isn't constant. You might be too young to understand, but I'm telling you, it's not. It's fleeting. And it's fickle. It changes. You can't control it. Nobody can. Once upon a time I found a great woman and married her—but she cheated on me. I had what I thought was unconditional love with my son—but he was spiteful, he would yell at me, then he went and died in that car accident. *Poof,* love gone. Then, I found a stupid boy to replace my son, someone who listened to me, who was eager to please me…." For a moment, his jaw worked but no sound came out. He swallowed hard.

Maria stared at him. *Are those tears in his eyes? But he's a monster… how dare I feel sorry for him!*

Bullet breathed in deep. "And then *you* took him away from me," he screamed at Maria. "You *killed* Mike."

"It was self-defense," Maria yelled back at him. "He *attacked* me. And he got what he deserved. Just like you will."

Bullet laughed out loud again. "You underestimate the puppet master. But I should thank you. You actually helped me."

Maria stared at him. "What?"

"Your 'Crazy Lu' story. I love it. She goes on a rampage and kills everyone, including herself, to protect her secret, her career."

Maria saw Lu close her eyes and shake her head.

"She even attacks me with a knife, since she knows her little gun only has six bullets to fire. One misses me, so she uses a knife to get me. But again, only the one misses. The others? All perfect shots, one for each person present, the last reserved for herself. Only *I* escape, wounded but alive. The police find me and take me to the hospital—yes, I know they're out there but they won't dare come in, I know how those cowards think. They won't arrive until it's too late. And… *curtains.*" He paused. "Well, well… quite the grand little show we have planned for tonight, huh?"

Maria just stared at him. *Oh my gosh, he's completely insane. Crazy, just batshit crazy. We need to stop him from carrying out his sick plan. But what can I do?*

CHAPTER 59

*W*hat can I do? Martina looked back and forth between the crazy Bob guy and her daughter trying to argue with him. She glanced at Lu sitting in her chair, crying, holding the gun he was pressing into her hand. *The gun meant for me. And Elisabeth. And Aaron.*

She sighed. *We need Aaron. He's helped before. He may be sick, but he's strong.* She eyed him. He was still passed out in the chair next to hers, his good arm hanging down, the other one, closest to her, in a sling. *Maybe if I poke him he'll wake up? I can move my arm. I can't move my whole body, but maybe my arm?*

Martina tried wiggling her fingers. She felt only pins and needles but it worked; they moved for her. She found she could move her whole arm again, slightly. *I'm weak, but that's okay. I can do this.* She started elbowing Aaron's side. He didn't react at first, but then moaned.

Bob glanced at them briefly while he was still arguing with Maria. Didn't notice what Martina was up to.

"Shhh…." she whispered while elbowing Aaron's side. "Wake up, Aaron. We need you." Suddenly, Aaron opened his eyes and looked at her. She smiled at him.

"Martina? What's going—"

"Shhh…." she said, but it was too late.

"Oh, Mister Aaron is awake. What a pleasure to have you with us again," Bob said as Aaron looked around, bewilderment on his face. "So nice of you to join us. Your fiancée here is contemplating an important, rather final decision."

Maria forcefully shook her head back and forth.

"I really wonder who you'll pick, Maria. Whose love is constant for you? Your fiancé's, the woman who raised you, or your birth mom's? What do you think?" He grinned and made Lu point the gun at each of Maria's loved ones.

"Aaron, pretend to get sick so you can get some water," Martina whispered to Aaron when Bob refocused his attention on Maria. "Water will dilute the poison in your body. You hear me?"

A slight nod from Aaron. "Okay. I'll try. I just feel so weak."

"You gotta do it. For Maria, Aaron. Come on."

He grimaced. "I don't understand what's going on…."

"Shhh…. No time. Get sick. Now. Pretend. Act. Then drink."

Aaron looked confused, his blue eyes in turmoil, but Martina knew he trusted her. *And I trust him. He's a good guy. A good guy for my mija. He protects her. Always.*

Aaron abruptly bent over, holding his belly. An unpleasant gagging, retching sound followed from underneath the table.

"Oh no, Aaron's getting sicker," Martina cried out. *C'mon, you sicko, look my way.* "Hope he's okay. Hope he can—"

"Shut up," Bob yelled at her, and guided Lu's hand so that the gun was now directly pointed at Martina. Next to her, Aaron weakly sat up in his chair, his vision swimming, his hair a mess. Everyone saw him reach for a glass of water on the table.

"Stop it, Aaron," Bob yelled. "Sit back down and face us. Now."

"But I only want water. I'm so thirsty after throwing up," Aaron said as loud as he could, but his voice was still weak, barely more than a whisper.

"Liar!" Bob yelled. "You didn't even throw up. You were faking it. I don't like your little games."

Martina turned pale. *¡Dios mío! He noticed. That's not good.*

"Fine, then. Maria, I'll make the decision for you. We'll kill the one whose love is not as steadfast as a mom's love. A lover's love can change at any moment. It cannot be trusted. Meaning your fiancé is the first to go bye-bye."

"No!" Maria screamed.

¡Dios mío! Martina stared at Bob, watched as he aimed Lu's hand carefully and squeezed her pointer finger that was pressed against the gun's trigger. *No, no, not Aaron. I gotta do something. Now.*

She saw Bob grinning in triumph, and in that split second she decided. Summoning the last of her strength, she turned sideways and kicked with all her might.

Boom!

Screams. Crying.

The bullet flew over the table and lodged inside the couch in the living room. Aaron's chair tipped and crashed to the ground.

"Ahhh...." Aaron moaned. Maria was crying hysterically, the whole chair she was tied to shaking with her every sob. Lu's face was covered in tears, while Elisabeth looked practically translucent, her lip quivering.

The bullet had missed Aaron. Martina had been just quick enough to knock him over. *Phew. That was close. ¡Dios mío!* Her breathing came rapidly.

"What the fuck, woman?" Bob yelled at her, but she didn't care.

All I need is for Maria to be safe. That means she needs Aaron with her. I know their love is strong. Their love is constant. They will be with each other forever. True love between those two. They can't lose each other. Martina smiled.

"How dare you fuck with my show, woman." Bob spat out in disgust, but then he paused. Grinned. "On second thought... makes the story more believable. One bullet has to miss its target, doesn't it? I'll just say that one was meant for me, then. My bullet. But now it's time to get on with our little execution game here. Let's choose between the moms first. Maria, which mom do you love the least?"

Martina saw the fear in Maria's eyes. Her beautiful, unique eyes, now bright green, shining through the tears pooling in them. *Poor mija. My Maria. Te amo.*

Bob and Lu pointed the gun back and forth between Martina and Elisabeth. "Come on, Maria, we haven't got all night. Who will it be? We gotta hurry. I wouldn't be surprised if the police heard the gunfire already. That was a loud boom."

CHAPTER 60

"That was a loud boom," Chief Parlot whispered to Tonya as they were crouching by the back porch door. "Definitely gunfire. Tonya, we gotta go in. Now."

Tonya put a finger on her mouth to signal the chief to be quiet. She gestured something to the SWAT team.

"Tonya, what are you doing? We gotta go in now. Maria is in danger. All of them are." The chief stood up. *I can't fail again. I need to protect them.*

"Get back down, Isaac," Tonya whispered. "Be patient. Let the team do their thing and—"

Before Tonya could finish her sentence, Chief Parlot took a few steps back, then ran at the wooden porch door, only to bounce off it and fall on his butt. Everyone stared at him, Tonya's mouth wide open. "What the heck, Isaac? What was that?"

Chief Parlot got up from the ground and dusted off his pants. "I'm trying to run down this porch door to get in, obviously. How can that wood not crack with me slamming into it?"

Tonya rolled her eyes. "Because it's steel-reinforced. The Distinguished Visitor's Quarters were well-crafted to protect VIP guests on base. Everyone knows that."

"Oh…" The chief's head dropped down. "I just really need to get to them and—"

"I know," Tonya said. "But please let the team do their work. Trust us. We all want to save the people inside. Let the professionals handle this one."

Chief Parlot nodded and listened as Tonya gave her instructions. "Come on, boys, get it open. Let's go through the mesh covering the patio. Get the wire cutter out. Now."

Quickly and quietly, one of the other officers used the wire cutter to cut a hole big enough for them to climb onto the screened-in back porch. They passed the table and porch swing, then got to the glass sliding door that led inside. The curtains were closed in front of it.

Tonya waved the special forces team over. "Come on, guys, get this sliding door open."

They cleared the area. One of the SWAT members, who had a silencer on his gun, pointed the gun at the glass next to the door's lock and fired, but instead of glass crashing all around them, the bullet got lodged inside the glass without shattering it.

Chief Parlot raised his eyebrows. "And why the heck didn't *that* work? Don't tell me the glass is steel-reinforced, too?"

"No, Isaac, just bulletproof." Tonya giggled, then turned to the SWAT team. "Come on, boys, let's brute-force it. We gotta shoot at it until we can ram it down. Go, go, go."

POP! POP! POP! POP-POP-POP-POP-POP! A hailstorm of silenced gunfire rained down on the glass.

Chief Parlot stood back, sweat forming on his forehead. *We can't be too late. Please don't let us be too late.*

Tonya patted his back. "Come on, Isaac, we're almost there. We can do this. We'll protect her. All of them."

"Let's hope so," he whispered. "Let's hope so." *Will we? I'm just not sure.*

CHAPTER 61

"I'm just not sure," Maria cried. "How can I possibly choose who I love more or less?" She looked at both her moms, tears streaming down her face. "I love them both equally."

"You're lying, Maria," Bullet yelled at her. "There's always a favorite. So, which one is it? This one…" He held Lu's hand tight as he pointed the gun at Martina. "…or this one?" He now pointed the gun at Elisabeth.

"I don't know. I love them both. Really I do."

"Don't make her do this," came a weak voice from underneath the table.

Aaron, oh my gosh, Aaron! Maria crouched and found him, her eyes met his. *He's in agony. Not just from the bleach, he must have reinjured his shoulder.*

"Oh, the smart guy is calling the shots now, huh?" Bullet stared at him. "You can't even get up anymore, can you? Oh, poor Aaron. Don't worry, you'll get your shot." He laughed wildly. "Get it? *Shot?* Funny, huh?"

"Nobody's laughing," Martina said, and stared at him.

"You getting smart with me, woman?"

Martina smirked. "No, I'm just not afraid of guys like you anymore. Abusers. Assholes. Bad guys. You're all the same. You all will go to hell."

Under all her tears, Maria had to smile. *Mamá. She's so strong. She's been amazing, standing up for all of us. Saving Aaron. Mamá, I love you so much. I'm so proud of you.*

Martina caught Maria's gaze and smiled back at her. It didn't go unnoticed by Bullet. "Well, well, looks like Martina is the special one, isn't she? Guess raising a child gives you that special bond, for sure. She's the favorite. How about we get rid of the birth mom then?"

"No, no, don't hurt her," Maria screamed. "I love her. She gave birth to me. That very first love I experienced was with her. Please, don't hurt my mom." She broke down crying, her mind racing. *I can't lose her again. What should I do?*

"Very touching, Maria, very touching. But Elisabeth *didn't raise you.* That first connection? Worthless. Forgotten. Guess you kinda look alike, but is that enough to call 'love'? What do you think?"

Even though her whole body shook with sobs, Maria raised her chin and said, "All I know is that I can't lose her again. I lost all that time with her. I need to make it up, I need her to be my mom again. She didn't abandon me. She didn't choose to give me up. It was *your* fault, you asshole. And *you can't take her away from me again!*"

Bullet now smirked, an amused look on his face. "Really? I can't?"

Maria shook her head.

"Oh, you poor little girl. But I can." He laughed and pressed Lu's finger down on the trigger. Aimed. "*And I will.* Because Elisabeth is the one who got us into this mess in the first place, isn't she? Twenty years ago. If she hadn't started that damned H.O.P.E. Club of hers, we might not even be here." He paused. "Goodbye, Elisabeth."

Maria closed her eyes. *No, no, no, don't shoot my mom. Please....*

Both Elisabeth's and Martina's eyes were wide open, staring at Lu and Bullet. They both wiggled in their chairs as much as they could. Screams filled the room.

BOOM!

Maria opened her eyes again, and the first thing she saw was Lu sobbing next to her, the gun in her hand still smoking. Bullet still firmly pushing the weapon into her hand, holding her arm tightly so that Lu couldn't move. Maria heard crying from underneath the table. Both her moms' chairs had toppled over.

What happened?

Then Maria noticed the blood. It was pooling on the floor where both her moms were lying, Martina in front of Elisabeth. She couldn't see their faces. Maria gasped for air. "Mom? Are you okay?" Then she cried out between deep sobs, "You're bleeding, there's so much blood!"

CHAPTER 62

There's so much blood? Elisabeth felt at her white shirt. It was sticky, turning red from the blood splattered all over it. *Oh no, what happened?* It was all a blur to her. She patted her upper body up and down. *I feel weak, but not hurt. No real pain. Is this what it feels like when you're shot?*

She looked down and found Martina lying right in front of her. Her eyes were staring up at the bottom of the table above them, her breathing jagged, labored.

Oh my, Martina. Elisabeth sat up, tears now streaming down her face. She touched Martina's face. "Martina?"

A slight smile of recognition came across her face, even though she was clearly struggling to breathe.

Oh no. Elisabeth kept stroking Martina's cheek, then looked over to where her daughter was sitting, tied up in the chair, her body racked by sobs. Elisabeth locked eyes with her. "Maria, it's not *my* blood…. It's not mine. It's your mamá's."

"No, *no!*" Maria sobbed even harder. "Is she okay? Mamá, are you okay?"

Elisabeth saw Martina smile. "Mija, Maria, te amo…." Martina whispered, and slowly turned her head sideways to look at Elisabeth. "Tell Maria… I love… her…."

A tear dripped off Elisabeth's nose onto Martina's cheek. "No, Martina, you tell her that yourself. *You* tell her. You'll be okay. You have to be okay."

Martina slowly shook her head, her breathing coming more ragged now. "No, I might... not... make it. But... it's... okay. She... now... has... you."

Elisabeth was sobbing over Martina, looking down at her small body. She was bleeding from her upper belly, close to her heart. The blood just streaming out of her.

"Mamá, Mamá, oh no.... Mamá, please be okay, please, I need you," Maria yelled through her sobs. She wiggled in her chair, more and more, trying to slip out of the belt holding her down.

Lu was sobbing, her hand with the gun still held by Bob, who was staring at Elisabeth and Martina. His face had turned red. "What the fuck did you do, woman? Why did you protect Elisabeth? It was *her* turn to die now, *not yours*," he yelled. "I don't like it when people change my script. It's *my* show. *Mine*."

"What did you do, Bullet? My gosh, what did you do?" Maria cried, and kept wiggling. Elisabeth noticed she was looking at Aaron, who seemed to be giving her instructions on how to get out of her binding.

Bob smiled at Maria. "Me? Nothing. Lu here shot Martina. Lu did, not me."

"You fucking bastard, you made me," Lu screamed. "I hate you; I hate you so much." She now fought with Bob, tried to get out of his hold.

Elisabeth felt a hand on her knee. She looked down. Martina was gripping her knee. "I... I think... I'm... dying...."

"No, no, Martina. Please hold on. Please. Help will be here soon, I'm sure." Elisabeth listened closely, and over all the crying she heard some noise. "I think the police are coming. They're coming, Martina. They'll help you."

She smiled and somehow looked so peaceful. She slightly shook her head again. "No, Elisabeth... you... help... me."

"Me? How?"

"You... take care of... Maria. Your turn." Martina smiled even wider now. "Your... turn...." She started closing her eyes.

Elisabeth stroked Martina's cheek harder and grabbed her hand when it started to slip off Elisabeth's knee. She shook her hand, squeezed it hard. "No, Martina, no. Please. Just *look at me*, please. You can't leave us. You just can't. We need you. Maria needs you. We all need you."

Martina opened her eyes again. "Maria... has... you. And... Brad... and... Aaron. She'll... be... okay."

Elisabeth tried not to drip tears on Martina's face as she sobbed, but she couldn't help it. Her mind was racing. *I have to help her. She can't die. She can't. She's my daughter's mother. Maria can't lose her. I have to stop the bleeding.*

Elisabeth looked around for something to wrap the wound with, but her mind was blank, paralyzed. She heard Maria's sobs, Aaron's voice, Lu's and Bob's yelling as if she were underwater. It all seemed so far away. All she could think of was Martina dying. Then an idea came to her. She let go of Martina's hand and cheek and started taking off her shirt. *I can use the fabric to stem the bleeding.*

But a hand on hers stopped her. It was Martina. "Don't, Elisabeth. Don't try... wound is too... deep." Her breathing was labored, but her grip firm. The smile still on her face. "It's... okay."

Elisabeth broke down sobbing. "But we need you. All of us. Oh my gosh, Martina, Maria needs you. For her wedding. Remember how much she'd love for you to make her dress and—"

"Shhhh...." Martina comforted her. "Her dress... done... already. In... my store. My special... secret. Tell... her."

"No, Martina, you'll be okay, you will tell her. And you'll be there. On her wedding day, you'll be there. Please."

Martina shook her head slowly but firmly. "Won't... make it. I already... know. I'll... be there... in spirit."

Elisabeth stared at her, tears streaming down her face. "Why? Why did you protect me, Martina? Why?"

Martina's smile turned to a wide grin, her brown eyes sparkling. "Because... I got... the last... twenty years... with... Maria." She fought for air. "And now... you get... the next... twenty... years. Or more... hopefully." She lifted her hand to wipe away Elisabeth's tears. Her breathing turned into a whistle.

"Oh no, Martina! Please stay with us...."

Martina shook her head. "No, your turn... with... our... daughter. Take... good... care... of... her. Promise... me...."

Elisabeth nodded. "I promise," she whispered.

Martina's face beamed with joy. Then her eyes closed. Her hand slipped down Elisabeth's face and fell to the ground.

Elisabeth stared at her, then rested her head on Martina's chest. No heartbeat could be heard. *Oh my gosh, she's dead. She died. Martina died. Took a bullet for me.* She lay there sobbing. The noise around her barely registered in her mind. But then the sound of her daughter crying and sobbing made it to her ears. She glanced up at her.

There sat Maria, her pale face covered in tears. "Mamá, please, Mamá. Are you okay? Mom, is she okay?"

Elisabeth looked back down at Martina. Gave her a kiss on her lifeless cheek. "I promise I'll take good care of our daughter. I promise." She folded Martina's hands over her chest, the blood no longer oozing out of it, and looked at Maria now.

She shook her head. "She's gone, Maria. Your mamá's gone."

CHAPTER 63

*M*amá's gone?

Maria's wordless, blood-curdling scream cut through the air, so terrible it even made Lu and Bullet stop fighting. They stared at Maria, who screamed, "Noooooo! Mamaaaaá!"

She thrashed about in her seat. *She can't be gone. She can't be dead. She's my* mamá. *I need her.*

She kept wiggling, looked at Aaron. Saw tears in his blue eyes. He tried to move, but couldn't. "I'm so sorry, Maria. I'm so sorry," he whispered. "But now, focus. Like I motioned earlier... *slowly* wiggle, left, right, left, right, from your hips, until you get a hand loose. You can do it. Go, Maria."

I have to see Mamá. And Mom. She's with Mamá. At least she's with Mamá. But I need to see her, too. She wiggled and wiggled, ever so slightly, following Aaron's instructions, and finally, her right hand was free.

She glanced over to where Lu was sitting, still fighting with Bullet over the gun. *He's busy. Won't notice.* Quickly, she used her right hand to turn the belt around her torso, until the buckle faced her front side. She managed to unbuckle it.

The belt hit the wooden floor with a loud *CLING*.

"What the fuck?" Bullet yelled, and lurched toward her, but Maria was faster.

"You monster, you unbearable, unspeakable *monster*! You killed my mamá," Maria screamed, and jumped at him. He was still holding Lu's hand that was holding the gun, wrestling with her, and Lu jerked him back as Maria came at him.

Lu, Maria, and Bullet all ended up in one big pile. Aaron and Elisabeth watched in horror, both keeping a close eye on the gun. "Watch out for the gun, Maria," Elisabeth screamed.

Maria looked down and saw it. The gun's muzzle was against her belly. Bullet had control over the gun, was pulling on Lu's trigger finger with all his might, but somehow she resisted him.

Nobody else will get hurt tonight. Nobody. I'll make sure. Maria pivoted and tried to wrest the gun out of their hold, but Bullet's grip was so tight, she simply couldn't free Lu's hand.

All three of them were wrestling when suddenly, the sound of shattering glass filled the room. The melee ground to a halt. "What the fuck?" Bullet leaned over Lu to look into the living room where the sound had come from.

This is my chance. If I can't free her hand, maybe I can—

In that split second, Maria took a step back from Bullet and Lu, dropped onto her knees, wrapped one of her arms around Lu's torso, the other under her elbow. With a mighty push, she forced Lu's arm up, right under Bullet's chin, who was still peering into the living room. In the same instant, she slid her arm upward, jammed her fingers down on both Lu's and Bullet's intertwined trigger fingers, and squeezed with all her might.

BOOM!

The gun went off, deafening Maria. Both she and Lu screamed when something red, hot, and sticky splattered all over them. Bullet's grip went limp, his hand slipped off the gun, and he stumbled backward, then crashed to the floor.

Lu's arm dropped into her lap right in front of Maria. It was shaking hard. Maria let go of her hand, and the gun dropped to the ground, still smoking. Both women were crying.

They heard a bunch of footsteps running toward them, crunching over broken glass. "Police!" a gruff man barked. "Nobody move!"

Officers in tactical gear surrounded the dinner table, the long-forgotten yogurt dessert toppled over by Bullet's earlier assault. Six glass bowls sat, one in front of each seat. "Ambulance. No, a handful of ambulances! We need a bunch of 'em," Maria heard a familiar voice yell over the crowd.

She looked up and saw Chief Parlot standing on the far side of the table. He was pointing his gun at Lu. "Hands where I can see them, General Thomas. Step away from Maria. Now!"

Maria was still kneeling next to Lu, her arms in Lu's lap. Shaking all over, Lu lifted her hands, gasping quick breaths, tears streaming down her face. Maria could hear Lu's heart pounding.

Maria looked at her. *Poor Lu. She's so scared. So, so scared. I need to tell them it isn't her fault.*

Before the police could move in on Lu, Maria stood up and shouted, "Stop it. Lu is innocent. She's a victim in all of this. And she needs medical care. Everyone here does. We've been poisoned. With bleach. In the dessert." Maria pointed at the toppled dessert on the table.

Chief Parlot stared at her. "Maria, what about you? Are you okay?"

"I'm okay," she whispered, then dared to look to her left. There he was: Bob "The Bullet" Jones, sprawled on the floor, half his head blown off.

She quickly turned away. "That's Bullet on the ground. General Bob Jones was Bullet, but he's dead now. Aaron is okay. He's over there, under the table. Needs help, he's poisoned and broke some bones."

"Okay, help is on the way, Maria," Agent Anderson said. "What about your moms?"

Maria looked at Agent Anderson, then at Chief Parlot. "Mom is okay, but I think… I think… my mamá… didn't make it." Tears streamed down her face as she dropped to her knees beside her mamá's body.

Elisabeth was still holding Martina's hands that she had neatly folded over Martina's chest. The small woman was very quiet, very still.

Maria sobbed and stroked her mamá's cheek. It felt cold to the touch. *Oh my gosh, Mamá. You left me. You've been there for me ever since I can remember.* "Te amo mucho," she whispered.

She heard Elisabeth sob. "Your mamá, Maria… she saved me. She saved my life by giving hers instead. She saved me."

Maria nodded. "I know. That's what she does. She saves people. Just like she saved me when I was a little toddler." Maria laid a hand over Elisabeth's, so that they were both holding Martina's hands.

Elisabeth nodded. "She saved us all, Maria. Now this nightmare is finally over. We got the bad guy. The mastermind behind everything. It's finally over."

Maria nodded. "That's all Mamá wanted. For the nightmare to end, for me to be safe."

Elisabeth squeezed Maria's hand. "Yes, that's all she wanted. And I promised her I'd take care of you from now on. I'll be there for you, and she'll be with us, in our hearts, wherever we go."

Through her tears, Maria slightly smiled at Elisabeth. "Yes, she'll always be with us."

Time passed. Maria wasn't sure how long they had been sitting there, hadn't noticed the hustle and bustle around her until Chief Parlot pulled her up by the elbow. As if in a trance, she watched the paramedics surround her two moms. Some of them helped Elisabeth up and carried her away on a stretcher. The other one checked on Martina. Maria watched them shake their heads.

Mamá. You look so peaceful. You'll always be with me. In my memories, in my heart. You taught me all I know. You made me who I am. Thank you, Mamá. Te amo mucho.

Maria gave a start when Agent Anderson spoke to her. "Maria, do you want to go with your mom, or Aaron?"

She shrugged and looked over to where the paramedics were taking care of Aaron. They were just lifting him on a stretcher. His ocean-blue eyes locked with hers. She told the agent, "I'll go with Aaron."

"Okay, Maria. Chief Parlot will help walk you over," Agent Anderson said.

Maria nodded and felt the chief take her side, guiding her along. As they went past the table, Maria pointed to the window on the left. "My mamá's phone landed somewhere over there. Next to the plant. There's a recording of what happened here tonight."

"Oh wow, I didn't expect that. Thank you, Maria. It will be very helpful. Thank you," Chief Parlot said, and continued to guide her through the room.

Maria pointed to the right. "And somewhere there, at the end of the table, beneath it, I think, is my phone. Also has recordings taken tonight. A confession from Bullet."

"Okay, Maria. Thank you. That's good. You did good tonight." Chief Parlot gently patted her back. "Thank God you're safe."

"That's all Mamá ever wanted," Maria whispered, silent tears streaming down her cheeks.

The chief guided her down the hallway. Outside, Maria saw sirens illuminating the dark night, voices all around her. In a trance, she followed Aaron's stretcher, blocked out all the noise until she heard a distinct voice calling her.

Keisha?

She looked up and saw Keisha, Brandy, Nick, and Jim standing behind a line of police cordoning off the perimeter. Jack, Drew, and Sarah were there, too. Keisha waved at her. "Maria, we'll meet you and Aaron at the hospital. We're here for you, girl."

A slight smile flitted over her face. *Yeah, my friends will always be there for me. Everyone is here for me. I'm safe now.*

Once Aaron's stretcher was loaded up in the ambulance, Chief Parlot helped Maria step up inside. She sat next to Aaron's stretcher, close to his feet.

"Bye, Maria. Agent Anderson and I will see you at the hospital." The chief waved to her, then the ambulance doors closed. She silently watched the paramedics stabilize Aaron's shoulders—he moaned in pain—then saw them start an IV for him.

"Young lady, is there anything we can do for you?" one of them asked her, but Maria just shook her head.

"We were told to check you over as well, ma'am," the other one said, but Maria just shook her head again.

"Not now, please," she whispered. "I'm okay."

The two paramedics exchanged glances, then left her alone. The ambulance started moving, shrill sirens blaring. Maria stared out the small rear window into the dark Florida night, until she felt a warm hand on hers. She looked down. It was Aaron's hand. She squeezed it. Looked up at him. Bit her lip. His eyes showed pain.

"Are you okay, Aaron?"

He nodded slightly. "I will be. I'll be fine. Just need therapy for my shoulders, I guess. Or surgery. Whatever. I'll be fine. I'm worried about you."

"Me?"

"Yeah. Tonight was…"

"Indescribable?"

Aaron nodded. "Yes. I'm so sorry about—"

"I know," Maria interrupted him. She couldn't stand hearing the words, the sentence. *Dead. Mamá dead.*

"You know she saved me, don't you?" Aaron whispered. "When she kicked my chair, she saved my life. He would've blown me away if it wasn't for her."

"I know. That's what Mamá does. She saves people," Maria whispered, tears running down her face again.

"Yes, that's right. She saved us all: you, me, Elisabeth. Her sisters. She was an amazing woman."

Maria nodded and tried hard not to sob too loudly.

"And you know what she wanted most?"

Maria shook her head.

"She wanted you to be safe. She always protected you. And she wanted you to have a wonderful life. A life full of peace and lots of love. At least she got her final wish. You're safe now."

Maria couldn't help but sob. "Yeah, I'm safe now. And I promise her… I'll live that peaceful, long, wonderful life. With you. With my parents. With all the people I love."

Aaron squeezed her hand. "Good, Maria. That's good. That'll make her happy as she smiles down on us from heaven. A piece of her will always be with you."

Maria put a hand on her heart and felt it beating. *I promise you, Mamá, I'm safe now, I'll be fine. I'll never forget you. For twenty years you've been in my life. Now, you'll live on in my heart. Forever.*

EPILOGUE
FIVE YEARS LATER

"Forever, I'll love you forever, mija." Maria gave her little daughter a kiss on the forehead as they were cuddling on the couch.

"Love you, Mommy." Her little one returned the kiss on her cheek, then turned around. "Love you, Daddy." She smiled widely and crawled up onto Aaron's lap to kiss him on the cheek also.

Aaron laughed. "I love you, too, sweetie." He picked her up, then got up from the couch and lifted her high up into the air.

The little girl giggled as she spun, her reddish-brown pigtails whirling about. "Vroom, vroom. I jet. Jet like Daddy's."

"You're a jet like Daddy's?" He laughed. "Well then, we'll have to put you back down on the ground so I can work on you." He laid her down on the carpet. "Because Daddy doesn't *fly* jets, he *works* on them. Like this."

He started tickling her. Her laughter filled the air. Maria watched, a smirk on her face. "Make sure she doesn't laugh so hard that she gets the hiccups again for hours."

"No, no, stop, Daddy. No more. No jet."

Aaron stopped tickling her and raised his one eyebrow. "You're *not* a jet?"

The little girl sat up and shook her head, the little pigtails flying all around her, her bright-blue eyes with the green ring around them sparkling. She put a hand on her chest now, a very serious look on her face. "No, I'm Martina."

Aaron laughed. "That's right, sweetie. Your name is Martina."

Little Martina nodded, then jumped up and ran over to the bookshelf. She jumped up and down in front of it. Aaron rose from the floor as well and walked over to where she was hopping in place eagerly.

"Do you want to show me something, sweetie?" She nodded. "Do you need me to pick you up?" She nodded again. Aaron bent down to pick her up.

"Be careful with your shoulder, Aaron," Maria said, and got up from the couch to join them.

Little Martina tilted her head. "Daddy boo-boo?"

Aaron shook his head and laughed. "No, sweetie, that was a long time ago. I had shoulder surgery, but it's all better now. See?" He picked her up again and twirled her around in the air.

Maria shook her head. "C'mon, don't show off. Though I am glad you're feeling good today."

"Don't worry about me, Maria. I'm one hundred percent again, the Air Force says so. Still in it to win it." He winked at her.

"I know, Captain Heikinnen." She gave him a kiss on the cheek.

"No, no kiss." Little Martina tried to push them apart. "*My* turn."

Maria laughed. "*Your* turn to get a kiss? I think you already got your kisses earlier, mija. It's Mommy's turn now. I haven't seen Daddy all day. He just came home from work. See, still in his uniform? So, *my* turn."

The little one shook her head. "No, *my* turn. My turn. Show you picture."

"Oh, I see. She's right, Maria. She *was* first and told me she wanted to show me something." Aaron winked at Maria.

"Yes, Daddy. Me show you this picture." The girl pointed at a framed picture standing on top of the living room shelf. A striking close-up of Maria with her mamá at Aaron's Embry-Riddle Aeronautical University graduation ceremony. "I'm Martina. Like abuela. Mommy's mamá."

Tears glistened in Maria's eyes. "That's right, mija. You were named after my mamá."

Little Martina nodded, then pointed at the ceiling. "Abuela Martina in heaven."

"Yes, that's right, mija," Maria whispered.

Aaron gave Maria a side hug, little Martina wedged in the middle. Maria tried hard to hold back her tears but couldn't. One escaped her eye and ran down her cheek.

Her little daughter noticed. "No cry, Mommy. Mascara bye-bye when cry."

Both Aaron and Maria burst out into laughter.

"Aren't you a smart cookie?" Aaron smiled. "But I'll tell you a little secret, Martina. Mommy is *always* pretty—mascara or no mascara, right?"

Little Martina nodded and squirmed in his arms. Aaron let her down. She ran over to the couch, climbed up on it, and pointed to a big photograph printed on canvas of Maria and Aaron on their wedding day. "Mommy *very* pretty here. Best pretty. Pretty like princess."

Maria and Aaron stood arm in arm behind her and studied the wedding picture their daughter was looking at. Aaron was in uniform, standing in front of Maria, leaning in to give her a kiss on the cheek. Maria in her wedding dress, a beautiful halterneck dress with pearls on the top and the bottom, mermaid style and open-backed.

Little Martina pointed to Maria in the picture. "Love Mommy's dress. *So* pretty."

Maria nodded. "Yes, it's very pretty, isn't it? Very elegant. Do you know who made that dress for me?"

"Yes!" the little one screamed, and hopped from one leg to the other on the soft couch. "Abuela Martina. She made dress. Many dress."

"Many dress*es*," Aaron corrected his daughter's grammar. "Just like you make dresses for your dolls."

Little Martina nodded, her eyes sparkling. "Yes. Go, go, Daddy. Play baby with me." She hopped off the couch and ran into her room.

Aaron sighed, then called over to his little one, "Okay, sweetie, Daddy's coming."

Maria followed him into their daughter's bedroom and stopped by the doorframe while Aaron sat on the floor to play. She checked her watch. "Not for too long now. It's almost bedtime. We have a busy day lined up tomorrow."

Little Martina looked up and pouted. "No bed. Play. With Daddy."

"Yes, you can play with Daddy for a little bit, but not too long. Only until dinner. Then dinner, bath, and bedtime. It's a big day tomorrow, remember?"

Little Martina jumped up in joy. "Yes. Big day. My birthday!" She threw her arms up in the air, a big grin on her little face.

"That's right, sweetie," Aaron said. "And how old will you be?"

"Three," she screamed, then looked at her hand and tried to hold up three fingers but wasn't able to hold down the pinky with her thumb yet. She frowned. Aaron and Maria laughed while little Martina pouted.

"Don't worry, sweetie, we'll practice that later," Aaron reassured her.

She nodded, then turned to Maria. "Who coming?"

Maria smiled. *"Everybody."*

"Oma? Grandpapa?"

"Yes, of course. Oma Elisabeth and Grandpapa Brad will be there." Maria smiled. "Remember, they live around the corner? Oma helps the women at each base we move to. You know that, don't you?"

Little Martina nodded. "Yes, Martina knows. You and Oma help women."

Maria smiled. "That's right."

The little girl hopped from one leg to the next. "And who coming? Tell me. Nana? Nana and Grandpa coming?"

Aaron smiled. "Yes, Nana Grace and Grandpa Jack are coming, too. Their plane lands tomorrow morning."

"And then we have lots of my relatives from Miami coming," Maria said. "And also some of our good friends from college, and Oma's friend Lu with her husband Daniel, and—"

"Auntie Emma?" her little one interrupted her.

Aaron laughed. "Yes, Auntie Emma is coming, too. She's on spring break now."

Little Martina grinned. "Yay, Auntie Emma *so* fun."

Aaron rolled his eyes. "Yeah, I guess my little sis is much cooler than me."

Both little Martina and Maria nodded now.

Aaron frowned. "Oh c'mon, I'm not *that* boring, am I?"

Maria came over, bent down, and kissed him on the forehead. "No, not *that* boring. Just boring enough. We already had enough excitement for one lifetime, didn't we? Boring is good."

"Yeah, boring is good." Aaron winked at her, then picked up little Martina off the floor to stand right next to Maria. He cradled his daughter in one arm, held his wife close in the other. "But so long as I have my two favorite girls with me, life isn't boring. Life is just wonderful."

DID YOU KNOW?

Reader reviews are very important to an indie author's success. They validate our work and help others find our stories. If you enjoyed "Puppets of the Past", please leave a review filled with stars. Thank you!

Big thanks for joining me on this author journey. Don't forget your **free gift**, the **eBook** *The Last Day*! **Click here** to tell me where to send it.

Follow me on Facebook: G. P. Schumacher
Follow me on Instagram: author.g.p.schumacher
Find me on Pinterest: G. P. Schumacher

ALSO BY G. P. SCHUMACHER

ACKNOWLEDGEMENTS

Let me start out by thanking my amazing husband Ben, who always believes in me and encourages me to achieve all of my life goals. Thanks to you, I was motivated to finish what I've started: writing this third novel to complete the trilogy. Thank you for giving me the resources, time, and space to do so. Ben, you're the best husband and friend ever!

Huge thanks also to my two kids, Maila and Ayden, who have not only listened to many drafts of all of my books, but have also served as an inspiration. Without both of you, I wouldn't even understand the strength of a mother's love, the worries and the laughs that come with being a mom—a very important knowledge to have for creating the characters of Elisabeth and Martina.

Thanks to all of my former 2Day2s Class students at SSDS! Because of you, I understand the amazing minds of little human beings much better. Thank you to my former colleagues at SSDS for giving me the opportunity to learn more about little children and their development. This experience on top of having my own kids really helped me in writing the parts out of a toddler's perspective.

Danke to my parents, Renate and Horst Preuß, who have often listened to numerous stories I've written for fun as a child. Danke also to my sister Inga and her two kids, Alissa and Marlon, for being interested in my novels. Your interest helped me in writing and finishing this trilogy.

Big thanks also to my in-laws: Nancy and Charles, Will and Heather and family, Marasie and family. Appreciated your interest in the writing process and thank you for following me on my social media accounts.

Danke also to Gisela and Costa for encouraging me to create a real 'author business'. Appreciate your ideas for marketing and hope I can soon translate the books into German, so you can enjoy reading them as well.

Special thanks to all of my editors at Motif Edits. Jeff, thank you for the fantastic line edits. Your comments helped me become a much better writer. Thanks also to Kathy for proof-reading my novel. Both you and Jeff helped me make it the best book possible. Big thanks also to Shavonne for the plot discussion calls that made me realize what I needed to write to genre. Appreciate everyone's professional feedback and amazing edits. I'm looking forward to continuing my work with you!

Thanks also to Self-Publishing School (SPS) for teaching me how to be a self-published author—how to write, edit, publish, and market my novel. Thanks to my coaches Barbara and Joe for the helpful information and thanks to Ramy, Joe, and Brittany, who run the awesome online coaching calls I love to attend.

Last but not least, thank you to Dakota for being my SPS book production team manager, and for everyone else within that team. Thanks to Joice for the beautiful cover art and thank you, Richell, for the wonderful interior design. Really appreciate all of you for helping me with the finishing touches of the book.

SPS offers a wonderful and supportive online community with an immense knowledge. Happy to be a part of it!

WANT TO WRITE A BOOK OF YOUR OWN?

Self-Publishing School helped me, and I know they can help you!

Check them out now at: https://self-publishingschool.com/friend/

MEET THE AUTHOR

Greta Schumacher grew up in Bad Nenndorf, Germany. She immigrated to the United States in 2010 and has since lived in numerous states and cities while following her husband's Air Force career. She currently lives in Ohio with her husband and two children.

Due to moving a lot, she's had the opportunity to meet all kinds of people, encounter different lifestyles, and opinions. She believes each place, person, and experience shapes your life in one way or another.

Psychology and the human mind have been an interest of hers since she was a teenager, and she loves exploring these themes in her writing.

As a teacher and mom, she's especially interested in early childhood development, language acquisition, and young children's memories. She believes that toddlers' understanding of situations and feelings are often underestimated. Early childhood memories play an important part in her novels.

AUTHOR CONTACT

Interested in learning more about the author?

Follow me on Facebook: G. P. Schumacher

Follow me on Instagram: author.g.p.schumacher

Find me on Pinterest: G. P. Schumacher

Reach me via email: author@gpschumacher.com